IT ALL COUNTS TOWARD TWENTY

by
Everett M. Christensen

LCCN 2004102510

ISBN 0-9753481-0-8

CHAPTER 1

Lt. Jerome Glutz sat comfortably in the air terminal at McCloud Air Force Base, Washington. *Alaska,* he thought, and the word ran through his mind, vividly complete with the dripping icicles on the theater marquees in the local newspaper advertising cool air-conditioned viewing in the midst of hot, dry New Mexico summers he knew so well. *I wonder what it's like.*

It was a moment for reflection, for this was Jerry Glutz's farthest sojourn from home since he'd completed flight school just four weeks before. That cold shiver of pride still ran up his spine when he looked down on the shiny pilot's wings he'd won. And then the shattered glass—no matter that he'd never fly an Air force plane again—he'd won them. He'd proved something that 60 percent of the rest of his class couldn't: that he could fly a jet alone, to the satisfaction of teams of skilled and scrutinizing officer-pilots of the world's number one air force. Not even the glass fragment that now partly obstructed the vision of his right eye could change that. What a graduation party it had been. *If only Charlie Dee had known enough to slow down instead of speeding up when he'd been drinking—right down the main street of the base and into the Bachelor Officers' Quarters. Didn't even dim his lights,* Glutz reflected soberly. *Oh well, it was a shorter trip to the sack that night than usual. Didn't even know about the glass in my eye 'til a couple of days later,* his flashback thoughts rambled on.

Glutz felt somewhat like a knight in armor as he looked himself over with a slow deliberation. The gold bars of a second lieutenant, the U.S. lapel pins in silver, the officer's emblem on his service cap, his graduation ring from New Mexico State where he'd received his ROTC commission—all accented the blue background of his natty officer's uniform. He recognized the change

1

in himself in the five years since he'd graduated from Carroll High in Greyrock, New Mexico. *What would I have,* he thought, *without the past five years.* His face turned scarlet at the prospect of sitting in the terminal clad only in a wristwatch; surely not within the confines prescribed for military bearing.

And now I'm going to be a Public Information Officer, his mind went on; *I wonder what that means?* Glutz had listed public relations as his first choice during the interview with the personnel officer at his last base and was assured that his choice would be given "every possible consideration . . . within the currently existing requirements for personnel in the USAF." But even a shave-tail, brow bar second lieutenant knew that PIO couldn't stand for public relations—except maybe in the air force. Glutz nodded a smiling thank-you to the subconscious part of his mind for that last thought. Why had he said public relations, anyway? Glutz sometimes wondered about that himself but he couldn't seem to find the right fit for his B.A. in physical education. He was tall, slender, reasonably acceptable in appearance and pretty generally fit his stereotype of the "hail fellow well met" though the thought of that old hackneyed expression made him figuratively retch. Well, he'd soon find out if that was enough for a PR job.

Just then the public address system boomed him back into the real world. "Lieutenant Glutz, Jerome V., AO9999999," he heard as he stared dumbly at the box from which the voice emanated while a bead of perspiration formed on his lowest lower back. "Report to the flight deck at once."

"Where's that?" he said aloud, but nobody was near enough to hear him. So off he went, his pace quickening as each successive sign failed to answer his query. Ten minutes went by while he stood in a line at the end of which he could just barely make out a sign saying "Information" in bold black letters three-quarters of an inch high. During his wait, he twice more was greeted by the now familiar, "Lieutenant Glutz, Jerome V., AO9 etc." Finally, his turn came and with a flood of emotion built up over the ten-minute wait he spilled out, "My name is Lieutenant Glutz, Jerome V., AO9—."

"It's across the street in building 249, soldier," said the citizen behind the counter, himself resplendent in a blue suit but with a white shirt and brown tie. I wonder what color socks he's got on, thought Glutz as he hurried out the door.

Across the street he was greeted with more frustration. "I'm sorry, sir, but we won't be able to get your car off the ground today," apologized the airman in building 249.

"But I thought my car was being shipped by water freight," blurted back Glutz.

"Oh it is sir. Just a figure of speech you'll be familiar with when you've been in the air force a while longer."

Glutz looked down to notice the airman's slick sleeve (that means no stripes, for those who haven't been in the air force very long).

"What seems to be the problem?" Glutz asked.

"Nothing serious," said the airman, "just couldn't get her on board. Your car, sir, that is," added the airman, choosing his words more carefully now. "I suggest you wire ahead, sir, and tell whomever it is you're to report to that you won't be there until tomorrow."

"Why is that?" asked Glutz, once more displaying his ignorance. "I'm flying up—that is, I thought I was." He too spoke more cautiously now, reflecting the events of the day so far.

"That's right sir, you are, but you've got to drive your car down to the pier or it won't make tomorrow's sailing either."

"But can't someone else do that?" demanded Glutz, remembering the gold bars on his shoulders.

"Sure can't, sir," responded the airman, giving the first hint he'd have been in a Confederate uniform had this been the Civil War.

"Well, then, it's back to the club," mumbled Glutz indifferently as he tripped over the door sill while stepping lightly through the door. There seemed to be something about the soft lips and smooth, cool scotch he remembered from the officers' club the night before which made it especially hard for him to pick up his feet.

"Ah declare, you've got to tell those ninety-day wonders everything," said the airman—still with no stripes on his sleeve—when Glutz was out of earshot.

At the club it was still pretty quiet. *Only twelve plus three—1500 hours,* thought Glutz (that's 3:00 P.M., for those who haven't been in the air force very long). Glutz washed down a few handfuls of peanuts with several scotch and sodas, staring first at the TV and then at himself in the mirror behind the bar. *Not much to choose from,* thought Glutz. The set on the wall was expounding the virtues of a wheat tycoon from Kansas who had bested fevers and the elements to "make it big" in the early 1900s. Glutz's eyes swiveled back to the mirror. *Not much to choose from,* he thought again.

Glutz looked at his watch. *Twelve, four, 1600 hours,* he calculated, but much faster this time. *More than another hour before any of the PCS group shows up.* (PCS refers to those who are permanently assigned to an installation, for those who haven't been in the air force very long).

"How about a round of liar's dice?" offered Glutz to the bartender, sliding his empty glass toward the object of his comment.

"Just the two of us?" came a voice from behind the bar as its owner poised to haul in the empty scotch glass.

"Got any better ideas?"

"Guess not," was the curt reply.

So on their exciting game went until 5:15 (that's 1715 hours for those who haven't been out of the air force very long).

"Gotta go now," gruffed the humpty-dumpty character from inside the bar. "The regulars will start their charge any moment now."

"OK Fred, thanks for the action. Build me another scotch and soda before you get too busy, please," was Glutz's kind reply.

Glutz lifted a toast to himself and his likeness in the mirror and then spread most of it across the bar in response to a thunderous pat on the shoulder.

"Jerry," said a small, lean figure from behind, "I thought you were off for Alaska today."

"So did I, Warren, but it didn't turn out that way. Seems they can't get my car on board until tomorrow so I'm here 'til Sunday because of plane connections."

"They need you here to get your car on board?" 1st Lt. Warren Huenerloth wanted to know, just as his thoughts followed his eyes away to peruse the entrance of several of the finer assembled secretaries on base. *Wow, bodies by Fisher,* he thought, *Would I like to work in that plant.* And then he resumed consciousness just in time to pick up Glutz's response to his last question.

"Seems no one but I can get my car down to the dock," said Glutz, matching his friend's half questioning, half understanding expression. "But it makes no difference to me," he went on. "I like it here and it won't extend my Alaskan tour any; and besides," he paused pensively and then added with a meaningful grin, "IT ALL COUNTS TOWARD TWENTY" (referring to the usual twenty years' service before retirement, for those who haven't been in the air force very long).

"As long as I'm here, Warren, what about tonight? Got any plans?"

"No, nothing definite," emphasized Huenerloth, unwilling to admit he'd be pressed to remember the last time he did have something planned.

"How does this sound then," suggested Glutz enthusiastically, leaning away from his scotch in the direction of the ear of the 1st lieutenant. "You call a couple of those girls you've been dating, we invite them over here to the club for a few drinks, dinner, wine, the whole works and really make it an evening to remember. After dinner we can drive out to a ballroom or someplace where there's dancing and dazzle the girls with a little fancy footwork. Later we might stop back here or downtown for a nightcap or two and maybe even work in a warm lip massage."

"Sounds great, Jerry, any night but tonight, that is."

"Why's that, Warren?"

"Well, as you might imagine, with so many bachelor officers around here and with the two universities so nearby, girls are pretty much in demand; especially the ones I take out." The last comment was an afterthought, added for effect. "I'm sure they're all dated up by this time and even if they aren't, which is highly unlikely, they've got an unwritten law among them which pretty much keeps them from accepting a date at the last minute. Guess they'd rather stay home than have to admit accepting a last-minute date."

"Don't you want to try anyway?" Glutz pleaded. "Isn't it worth the off chance?"

"There is no chance, off or on," Huenerloth resisted. He wondered if Glutz sensed that he hadn't had a date since coming to the base a year and a half before.

"OK then, here's another idea, Warren. I met a couple of honeys in here last night and I think one was sufficiently impressed to go out on short notice if she's not busy, especially since I couldn't forecast my delay."

"If she hasn't got a date by this time, I'll bet she's really a queen," was Huenerloth's optimistic contribution.

"Well, I think she's pretty nice," defended Glutz, "and even if I didn't see what I think I saw last night, I'm no Don Juan myself." Huenerloth wasn't either, but Glutz had spent too much time developing his leadership ability in ROTC at New Mexico State to commit such an obvious faux pas as to mention that. "Besides, she'd be my date," Glutz added with just a touch of acid in his words. "Maybe she's got a good looking girlfriend. You've heard the saying that opposites attract."

"Yeah, I've heard that but I don't see how . . ."

"Never mind, Ace, are you game or aren't you?"

"I've got the feeling 'game' is just what I will be if I agree to this fiasco," harmonized Huenerloth, proud of the fact that if he couldn't get a date on his own, he could at least drive home a pun every now and again. "But OK, it might be better than another night of total annihilation." If Huenerloth hadn't become familiar with dating over the past years, he had learned something about drinking; at least how to do it.

"Helen? Helen, this is Jerry Glutz, I hope you'll remember me from the officer's club last night. Good. Well, the air force has changed its plans for me briefly. Seems I won't be leaving until Sunday, so on the remote chance that this happens to be one of your few free nights, I'm hoping you'd be interested in dining and dancing with me here at the club."

Helen Clarin knew she was being fed a line, but she found it refreshing—like the soft breeze that weaved through her beautiful raven hair that cool fall night when she had been escorted to midfield to accept the high school homecoming queen crown. But why not? What was wrong with an expense-paid evening at the officers' club? And Lieutenant Glutz seemed nice enough to spend an evening with.

"That's swell, Helen," she heard Glutz say to her affirmative response. "I've still got my car so I can stop by for you anytime that's convenient. Say sevenish?" (That means about 7:00 P.M. or 1900 hours, for those who haven't been anywhere very long). "Fine, Helen, see you then. Oh there is just one more thing. A recent acquaintance of mine, Lieutenant Warren Huenerloth, has nothing planned for the evening and I'm wondering if you might have a friend of your caliber (*more snow*, thought Helen) who might be interested in joining us. I thought it might be fun to double-date, especially since you and I don't really know each other very well yet. I know it's late and we can drop the idea if you like, but both Warren and I would surely appreciate it if you can arrange something. I'll vouch for his character," chuckled Glutz, wondering who would vouch for his own.

The next hour really dragged. Stimulated by the thought of his first date in over three months, Glutz didn't need the scotches he had time for. Besides, he didn't want to show up at Helen's house stupid (that's a synonym for drunk, for those who haven't been drinking long—or much). Maybe she lived with her folks. *I wonder if she does,* Glutz thought, and the possibility sent his mind spinning onward, realizing how little he actually did know about Helen. *I wonder where she works, where she's from, how old she is, if she's a virgin, . . .* his thoughts drifted on.

Meanwhile, across town in the pleasant white frame house at 1930 Vintage Street, a 23-year-old divorcee had some thoughts of her own.

Four 7.50, 14-inch blackwalls rolled simultaneously, moving Jerry Glutz's new looking coral and white hardtop away from the curb in front of the BOQ (bachelor officers' quarters, for those who haven't ever been in the service—or those who just care to know) and on down a base street.

What a dummy, Glutz thought about himself and the association with the car he was driving. He was referring to the day he had walked into Jack Berlatch's Pontiac dealership in Merlon, New Mexico, just 18 miles from his folks' home in Greyrock. He had been looking for a good used car. Something attractive to the young honeys he expected to meet while in flight school in Texas, yet a car not so expensive that he wouldn't be able to pay for it if he were to bust out of training and lose the extra dollars per month that went with flying. Greyrock had the usual run of car dealers, most of whom he'd talked to, but now he was here in Merlon to check on Berlatch's reputation for having the "best deals south of Cherry Hill." Less than thirty minutes later he had walked out the door with a new car on order.

"For a few hundred more you might as well avoid somebody else's troubles," reasoned Berlatch and Glutz had bought.

Some deal Glutz thought, as he yanked the powerless steering wheel around the corner. *No power, blackwall tires. Not much different than maneuvering an armorless tank around.*

Glutz's last thoughts about his car brought him to a halt in front of where Warren Huenerloth lived. Glutz jammed the car's hydramatic shift into park, then literally fell out of the door in his usual exiting fashion and ambled up to the dwelling.

Huenerloth's living quarters weren't too bad. He and a couple of friends rented one-half of a long rectangular building that defied any further description. It sort of reminded Glutz of a mess hall in a pre-World War II CCC camp he had seen pictures of. *Must have taken a lot of big birds to do the paint job on this baby,* he thought to himself as he began rapping on the door. No answer. More raps. Still no answer. Glutz stuck his head inside.

"Anybody home?"

"I'm in the head," (that's the john for those who have been in the air force but not the navy) Huenerloth called from a room inside the building. "Come on back."

Glutz found the well-lathered reflection of a face peering back at him through the bathroom mirror. Huenerloth, less than two inches from the glass, was microscopically inspecting his face for whiskers, safety razor in hand and poised for the kill. So far, it seemed, he had realized little success. The enemy was well hidden.

"C'mon, Warren," Glutz urged, "I told Helen seven o'clock. It's six now and I don't even know where she lives for sure."

"Don't worry, Jerry, let the honeys stew for awhile. It'll do them good. Besides, they'll appreciate us more when we get there." The man who had contributed so much to lining up these dates had spoken. Presently Huenerloth was ready. And, Glutz had to admit he didn't look bad against the bright yellow background of his quarters.

"Where's Vintage Street, Warren?"

"How the hell should I know, I live at the air base, not in town."

Strange that Huenerloth didn't know Rainville any better than that with all the fine girls he'd taken out, Glutz thought sarcastically. His thoughts drifted from Huenerloth to Helen. Glutz took a deep breath and blew it out. *Vigor! That was the only way to describe it. I wonder if it's possible to feel this good all your life; if you're really healthy, that is.* Glutz reflected on some of the things that *made* his life. Not the least of these was the striking taste of scotch, cool all the way down his throat and then peremptory in its race to all corners of the body in its effort to turn him into a giant in any endeavor he cared to think about, not to mention making him "Mr. Personality." *Tonight's surely the night for a few of those. But, not too many lest I turn from a knight into a nightmare.*

I've heard that story before, responded his conscience.

The coastal air had an intoxication of its own by its freshness. Glutz was only partially aware of the early evening life around him and even less conscious of the little squirrel aimlessly chirping beside him. The trip to Helen's house was a short one—or so it seemed. Glutz spotted the porch light from the corner and immediately caught the 1930 off to its left. *Nice little house,* he thought to himself. *Certainly nothing pretentious, but a comfortable little place.* It looked pretty obvious that Helen lived with her folks. "I'll be out in a minute," Glutz turned to Huenerloth as he rose from the car, avoiding his usual falling-body motion.

At the door, Glutz was met by a slender, blond-haired young lad wearing rather thick glasses. Glutz guessed his age at five.

"Good evening, sir," was the young man's polite greeting.

"Is Helen here?" asked Glutz, pleasantly warmed by the young fellow's good manners.

"Please come in and have a seat. She'll be ready in a minute." Then he went over to the stairs and hollered up to the second floor. "Mom, there's a man here to see you."

CHAPTER II

Upstairs, Helen was nowhere near ready. She sat at her vanity, a pretty face in the mirror staring back at her, but she didn't see it. Again and again she combed the same strands of her beautiful silky, raven hair. She felt, instead, the cool wind of a Washington fall breeze as she stumbled across the clumpy turf of the football field on her way to the coronation rostrum. She held tightly to the arm of her Jaycee escort. And then she caught her first glimpse of him, holding a gleaming sword that formed part of the arch under which she'd walk to her coronation. He didn't see her. He didn't see anything. He stood perfectly erect, jutting jaw, steeled eyes looking straight ahead. Helen's 17-year-old heart leaped within her. He just had to be the most perfect "man" she'd ever seen. Receiving the homecoming crown was anticlimactic after that.

At the postgame homecoming dance, Helen would've been hard pressed to tell anyone the score of the game. She led the grand march, danced with the football captain, acknowledged the congratulations and envious looks of well-wishers, but most of all she thought about "him."

The next day at school she was busy seeking out information. Who were the two air force men who had formed the arch in front of the queen's stand, especially the one on the right facing the stand? No one at East High seemed to know, not even the coach nor homecoming chairman, except that they had been sent from nearby McCloud Air Force Base in response to a request from the school.

At McCloud Air Force Base, A3/C (that stands for airman third class, and it's a rank that goes to those who haven't been in the service very long—if they're good) Brian Pearson sat with his feet propped against the end of the bed sucking on a bottle of pop.

"Listen, Darrell," he said, "that babe was really giving you the love-eye at that coronation last night."

But Darrell wasn't listening. He was writing a letter to his mother.

Dear Mom,

    Last night at East High in Rainville I was part of the honor guard for the coronation of the homecoming queen ceremony. A friend of mine, Brian Pearson from Minneapolis, and I held crossed sabers forming an arch for the new queen to walk under. It wasn't any big deal, of course, but somebody had to do it.

    I hope things are going well for you and dad and that his legs aren't bothering him too much. You be sure to get him off to bed when he falls asleep in the chair nights watching TV, Mom. Getting up at 4:45 A.M. to see that everybody else gets their milk for breakfast is no easy job, especially after six hours of sleep in that lumpy easy chair of his.

    Things are going along OK and most of the guys I meet seem to be OK. Maybe I can get home for Christmas, and, if so, I'll tell you more about it then. Guess that's about all for now.

Love, Darrell

Darrell Callanan was kind of a funny guy. In a way he was pretty "regular," and in a way, he was not. For instance, he had been out of high school almost two years now and had never in his life had a formal date. To hear him talking about girls with the other fellows, you'd never guess that this was true. He never brought up the subject, but he didn't shy away from it either. Around girls he talked freely and seemed comfortable. Yet, he had never had a date, nor had he ever held a girl in his arms and kissed her.

Athletically his background was just about as screwy. Darrell stood about 6'1" and weighed about 190 lbs. As a freshman he had gone out for football. Being an only child, his folks had had little trouble scraping together the money for as good a pair of football shoes as you'd find in his small hometown of 5,000. The first day of practice his hands were sweaty as he laced up his shoulder pads. He really didn't want this football at all, but how could he back out now. Darrell looked down on the still new shine of his top-dollar-plus football shoes; then he raised his eyes to take in his entire form in a distant locker room mirror. He was 6'1" and

190 lbs. all right, but there ended the resemblance between him and a football player. He'd finish out the season, if he were lucky enough to live through it, and that'd be all. Darrell was true to his word.

Darrell Callanan tried basketball too, but after two weeks he excused himself with the statement that his dad came home early, they had supper at 5:00 and he felt it would be a great disservice to his mother to miss it. Other than that, he had done all right for a freshman in the two weeks he had been on the hardwood. In spring he fell in love with the shot put and by the time he was a senior had become proficient enough to finish third in the state track tournament. Darrell did well in the classroom. He worked moderately hard and did a bit better than he might have in something involving physical contact. He finished fifth in his graduating class.

After high school, Darrell said, even to himself, that he wanted to go to college. Maybe he was really saying that he felt he should go to college. Anyway, he begged off on the rationale that, although he knew his folks would find a way to put him through, it would be more of a financial strain on them than he wanted to cause. Secretly, he was concerned about being away from his mother; not because he couldn't make it without her, but because he was afraid she'd be so lonesome for him. His thoughts drifted to the service. His mother would be proud of him in a uniform. Oh sure, she'd miss him but it would be different. She'd have the picture of him in uniform on the TV in the living room where she could make easy reference to it on the days her 500 club came over. She'd understand, too, that he couldn't come home whenever she might want him to, and that he couldn't drop out for a quarter or semester as he might if he were to go to college.

So on September 15, after the summer on a job with the town engineer his father had obtained for him, Darrell "went to war." He took the usual four weeks of basic training in Texas and had then been shipped off to McCloud where he remained to this day.

"I said that homecoming queen really gave you the once-over from the reviewing stand." Brian Pearson intoned his observation louder this time. Darrell looked up from the letter he had just finished folding and tucking into its envelope.

"Huh? Oh yeah, she seemed nice." It was all the comment he could muster and God knows where his thoughts went from there.

Just then one of the airmen in the same bay stuck his head in and hollered—"Phone for Callanan and it's a g-i-r-l," the airman's voice trailed off.

"Who, me?" Darrell looked up but the airman was gone. Like any young lad his age, he secretly hoped it would be a young lady though he couldn't imagine who; but secretly he knew better.

What in the world could be wrong for my mother to call, he thought as he leaped off the bed and hustled out the door.

"Hi Darrell, this is Helen Clarin. I know you don't know the name, but if I tell you I was the homecoming queen at the football game you went to last night you might remember me."

"Oh, sure, I remember you. East High played quite a game. Brian Pearson, the other guy in the honor guard, and I were both pulling for East. We're sorry you lost." Darrell was just spewing out the nice kinds of words his mother had taught him to use. Mostly he was pretty nervous talking to a girl, but he also wondered how she had found his name and how to reach him.

"Listen, Darrell, we're having a Sadie Hawkins dance Saturday night and I'd like you to be my date."

"Thanks a lot, Helen, I really appreciate your asking, but I don't have any way to come and get you. I mean I don't have a car or anything."

"Oh, don't worry about that. I can use daddy's car, and I *am* supposed to pick you up. It's a Sadie Hawkins Day dance, remember?"

Darrell didn't want to go at all. To use a little homespun phraseology from his hometown, he was "scared to death," but he didn't know how to get out of it.

"Are you sure you want to take me, Helen? After all, you really don't know me at all."

"Sure I do, I saw you last night at the game. Anyway you've got to go, Darrell. It took me all day to find out who you are. I'll pick you up in front of your barracks at 7:30. 'Bye."

Darrell moved the dead phone away from his ear and looked into it, half expecting to find the answer to his problem. It would be Darrell Callanan's first date! But, he didn't even think of that. His mind was totally involved with just one consideration. *How do I get out of it,* he thought, *how do I get out of it?*

Darrell went back and flopped face down in his rack (that's an air force bed—for those who have never slept in one). He wound his pillow around the back of his head and pressed firmly against both ears, so tight that he hardly heard Pearson's voice until he felt his hand on his shoulder.

"Darly! What's the matter, Darly? Something wrong at home? Something I can do?"

Darrell rolled over onto one side, looked up at his buddy and then off into space. He was momentarily amused by comparing his real problem to what Brian Pearson thought.

"No, it's nothing like that, Brian. The call wasn't from home."

"Then, what is it, pal? You came in and flopped on that bed like it was three minutes 'til train time and you had five miles to go."

"Aw, it's nothing really, Brian."

On Saturday nights Darrell usually took in a flick with Brian and a few of his other buddies, went over to the day room to shoot some pool, or, if they had passes, they headed for town. This particular Saturday morning he had problems. Walking back to the barracks across the parade grounds, pass in hand, he was completely absorbed with thoughts of how he'd explain the fact that he would be "bugging out" of his usual night with the boys.

It's simple, he thought. *I'll do the same thing that used to bail me out in grade school. I just won't feel well. Chances are I'll be back before the rest are, and even if I'm not, I can always say I felt better and decided to go out*

So engrossed was Darrell "Darly" Callanan in his newly fabricated alibi that he didn't hear the footsteps fall into cadence with his own.

"Hey that's great, Darly, you got yourself a pass for tonight. Brian and the rest of the guys have been looking all over for you to tell you we're going 'in' tonight" ("in" meaning "into the big city" for anyone who's never lived in barracks 502 on McCloud Air Force Base).

Curse the luck, thought Darrell so emphatically that the level of his exasperation almost sounded. *What a lousy break to run into one of the guys here.* He was speaking of Pudge Pearland, the "beef trust" of barracks 502 who had spotted him and come puffing across the field to join him.

Most guys would have given a week's pay for a date with Darrell's classy young escort. But, for him, it was something to be avoided. First, he knew he'd be uneasy in any girl's company, as a date, to say nothing of a girl as attractive and popular as . . . as . . . oh, whatever her name is. Second, he was positive he'd blow the whole thing and end up the laughingstock of the whole party. *Oh dammit,* he thought, *How do I get myself into these things?*

"Yeah, Pudge, I figured you guys'd be going in tonight, and when I didn't see anyone around after inspection this morning, I decided to go over by myself and pick up a pass."

With that big lie, somehow the pressure was off. Darrell didn't know why he felt better. He didn't even know whether he was really going out with Helen or just taking off with the guys so he wouldn't be there when she showed up. Anyway, he just sort of forgot about it. He loafed through the Saturday afternoon which was always casual, enjoyed an early sitting at "chow" (that's the term generally used to describe food served to pigs—and servicemen), and headed into the shower at 6:05.

At 7:15 Darrell was dressed and ready. He had on a pair of casual slacks and a sport shirt, partly because Helen hadn't said what to wear, but mostly because it was the usual garb worn into town which wouldn't tip the boys off that he was going elsewhere. He had recognized several hours before why his tension had so suddenly eased that morning. His gang usually took off for town around 8:00, which meant they were performing the four s's from 7:15 until then (the four s's stand for spit, shine, shower, and shave, for anyone who hasn't been in the air force and wants to believe that). By being ready himself at 7:15, he could tell the rest he'd wait for them on the steps in front of the barracks. If Helen came for him at 7:30, which he was sure she wouldn't, he could hop in her car and be long gone when they got out there. If she didn't show up, he could make the trip into town with the gang and they'd be none the wiser. He usually was the first one out there anyway.

At just about two minutes before 7:30, a sleek, jet black sport coupe came to a halt (even cars do that on an air force installation) in front of 502. Behind the wheel, there she was, Helen Clarin. With the top down Darrell got a whiff of her cologne which, along with the intoxicating atmosphere of her presence, made him wonder how he could ever have waited from her phone call until now to see her. "Darrell! Hi, Darrell," Helen greeted him. "Somehow I thought you wouldn't be here."

Somehow I almost wasn't, thought Darrell as he stepped into a car for the first time in a long while. Just as they sped off he heard Brian Pearson's voice from the barracks door.

"Hey Darly," he yelled after them, "where are you going?"

"Sorry, can't make it tonight, Bry. Give my best to the rest," he hollered back. Then he turned around, slumped comfortably in the front seat and thought to himself that this might not be so bad after all.

All the way into town Helen was not only delightful but an informative conversationalist. Everything she said fit right into Darrell's pattern. She began with how she had never called a boy for a date before and was scared stiff working up the courage to do so. Everything Helen said made him feel more comfortable. He began to feel very much at home. The wind sailed through his hair as the open-top car sped along, and the continuous blasts of air felt comfortable against his skin. It seemed to be going right on through him and he felt good and clean and restful inside as well as out.

Helen drove up in front of the school administration building where the dance was to be held, and before making a complete stop, the well known young beauty waved to one of her many friends on the steps. Bang! Helen's attention turned back and she slammed on the brakes, but not before kissing the car in front of her. Darrell, who hadn't been paying any attention either, was caught by surprise, the impact wilting him into a ball on the car floor between the dashboard and seat.

"Why you dumb son . . .," came from behind the car door which was gradually opening on the driver's side of the car Helen had tagged. And then when Wiley Cuet saw whom he was addressing, he called his conversation to an abrupt halt. "Oh, hi, Helen," and then, "what in the world are you doing? You women are always driving with your eyes everywhere but on the road in front of you."

Helen was laughing so hard at the sight of Darrell curled up like a trapped amoeba on the floor that she couldn't even answer. Wiley, failing to see the humor or for that matter the odd shaped hulk of Helen's date on her car floor, took a look at his rear bumper and seeing that there was no major damage, turned on his heel and stomped off in the direction of the administration building. He had forgotten to do just one thing, however, but would be reminded of it later in the dance when the public address system brought to his attention the fact that there was a car outside in front of the administration building with the doors locked, the lights on, and the motor running.

When the tears of delightful laughter ceased running down Helen's cheeks, she finally heard Darrell say, "I can't get out of here, Helen; I'm stuck."

She pushed and tugged at her date for a moment, but seeing that it was obviously useless she pleaded, "What should I do?"

"Open the door on my side and then get back in and push," came Darrell's muffled voice from behind his suit coat and leg on the floor.

This she did and with a third great effort Darrell was unceremoniously unloaded onto the sidewalk. There to meet him were peals of laughter from Helen's classmates on the steps of the administration building, who had witnessed the whole thing.

"Gang, I'd like to have you meet my date for the night, Darrell Callanan."

"Pleased to meet you," said Darrell, on all fours, as he unthinkingly raised his hand to shake. Seeing no one in the immediate area he stood up, brushing his hands together to remove the imbedded stones. For the average person, this would have been a most embarrassing way to meet the friends of a girl who might almost be considered a blind date, but for Darrell it was a relief; at least he had met them.

The rest of the evening was a delight, something he would never have anticipated. After all, Darrell was a nice looking guy, and none of his lack of confidence showed in his conversations with the people he met; particularly since they took the initiative to "carry the ball." Darrell was a moderately good dancer, and he simply drifted along in the atmosphere of Helen's enchantment appearing, even to himself, to be handsome and suave, but mostly he was just complimenting the atmosphere which Helen had woven with her charm, grace, and personality. The very fact that he was her date established his image in the eyes of Helen's friends and acquaintances. No one knew him to be just another face from a small town . . . and, back home surely no one would have believed it.

Helen's card was full almost before the dance started. Darrell, with his new-found confidence, proceeded to amble about the dance floor talking to other fellows who went to school with Helen, but always after they talked to him first. With the girls he seemed to have more confidence getting his name on many different dance cards, but, again, all of the girls were Helen's friends; girls whom he had met earlier in the evening.

Darrell presented an interesting personal contrast this first night out with Helen. He was quiet and reserved, yet very fluent in his conversation. He didn't initiate a whole lot of talk, yet he was able to continue a conversation once it had started. Everyone was obviously impressed. First, he was older and his mild, quiet manner made him seem much more mature than the talkative extroverts in Helen's group. But, the dance was too soon over, and it was time to return Darrell back to his shell. However, on the surface, this never really happened.

On the way home, Darrell was floating on a cloud. He may have been sitting on the seat, but he didn't know it. He was driving now and Helen sat cozily alongside of him. He couldn't remember whether he had suggested he drive or if it was Helen's idea. Nonetheless he was behind the wheel and it felt comfortable. She latched her arm inside of his and ran her soft, well manicured fingers down into his hand. It was almost more than Darrell could take. He had never been this happy before in his life, he had never had such an enjoyable night, and he had never felt about anyone the way he now felt about Helen. His eyes shifted from the road to the rearview mirror in which he could see the reflection of Helen's face, hair, and neck. She was absolutely beautiful, he thought. No, she was ravishing. No, she was much more than that. God had given man no word to describe this creature whom He had created.

Helen and Darrell stopped at a malt shop on the way home. They held hands as they sat across from each other in the booth, and it wasn't important whether he was holding her hand or she was holding his. They were just holding each other's. Yet, although Darrell didn't notice it at the time, Helen, again, had initiated it. Back in front of the barracks the car had hardly rolled to a halt. Helen very subtly cocked her chin ever so slightly, but it would have been obvious to anyone that there was only one thing to do—kiss those beautiful, soft lips. He had never kissed a girl before, and perhaps this was part of his appeal to Helen because surely it was obvious to her. Nevertheless, she was so smooth and deferring in her caress that he felt entirely in control of the situation.

"Suppose we could go out again?" he murmured as he looked down on this lovely creature who was now to be "his" girl.

"Love to, Darrell. How about Sunday? We'll take a basket lunch down to the beach. Then we'll roast wieners for supper and have a beer bust at night."

"Beer bust!" Darrell said in a state of shock.

"Sure, haven't you been to one?" she said. "We have them all the time."

"Oh, sure. Sure I've been to beer busts," was Darrell's somewhat dejected response. *She drinks beer,* he thought to himself, *and, she's only 18 years old.* But, he cast off his slight disappointment rapidly. *After all, why not? She's sensible enough to use her head, particularly when she's with me. And how can anyone say that people all of a sudden become responsible just because they turn 21? Helen's obviously been a responsible person for a long time.*

Helen pecked Darrell on the cheek again and then with a giggle gave him a shove, pushing him toward the door. "It's getting late, big boy. You better get in there," motioning her head toward the barracks, "and, I'd better get this car home. See you on Sunday, Darrell. I'll be by at 2:00."

Darrell opened the door and began sliding out from behind the wheel.

"Oh, yes, and one more thing." Darrell looked back. "Thanks for a wonderful evening, Darrell."

"Yeah, yeah, you too, Helen," he said. "Thanks for inviting me."

With that Darrell got out and went around back of the car toward the barracks while Helen drove out very sensibly, looking back just once for an extended wave to her air force hero. *She's a cautious driver,* Darrell thought to himself; *just like she drinks beer, I suppose.* Then he dropped his head and walked through the barracks door.

The beach party was sort of a strange experience for Darrell—At least to begin with. He probably wouldn't have attended a party like this on his own—at least not back home—and he surely wouldn't have been playing the part he was playing here. Helen and her girlfriends sat around a picnic table chattering like squirrels. The beer cans open in front of them were mostly for effect. The guys were just off in the distance somewhere, a couple of them looking at the motor in one of the cars, two more cutting a limb off a tree. Darrell, although no one noticed it at the time, was sitting alone.

"Hey," Helen said all of a sudden, "we haven't got any wood for the fire. Darrell, oh, there you are. Round up the guys and go gather a bunch of wood for the fire, will ya? Once you get it started we'll get the marshmallows, hot dogs, and the rest of the stuff ready."

"Okay," Darrell said, rising to his feet. And, in a flash the rest of the guys were with him, heading off into the woods. Once again, Darrell was the single leader of the gang. Or, was it Darrell? To an onlooker it would have been obvious that the fellows' respect for Darrell as a leader was based on the fact that Helen was his girl. The girls' idolizing probably had something to do with his good looks, but more important was the fact that Helen, whom they all looked up to because of her ability to attract men, had chosen him.

On and on went the whirlwind. First one party and then another, at the beach, at the Saturday night dance hall, the dances after games, the bull sessions between classes, all the talk was about Darrell and Helen. Or, was it Helen and Darrell? And then came the day when Helen showed up at class with that beautiful, though petite, diamond on her you-guessed-which finger.

It had all begun—or had it?—last Saturday when, hand in hand, Helen and Darrell strolled down the main street of Elam, near the Air Force base. They had just happened to walk past a jewelry store when Helen brought Darrell's attention to the sparkling object in the window.

"Just look at those beautiful engagement rings! Oh Darrell, I hope someday I can have a ring like that for my very own. But, I won't want it to come from anyone else but you."

Darrell could feel his chest expanding and he was walking straighter than ever; perhaps a few feet off the ground.

"Honey, you can have any one of those rings anytime you want it," he was surprised to hear himself say.

"Oh, Darrell, I love you," she burst forth, throwing her arms around the tall guy and giving him a big kiss on the spot. He pulled back slightly, but she had made her impact. *How can I justify this girl's having made me the happiest person in the world,* he thought half subconsciously. *Nothing I could do would be too good . . . nothing I could do would be good enough for her*

"Helen," said Darrell with conviction, "you're going to have one of those rings and you're going to have it right now." He had made another strong decision, hadn't he, Helen! "Which one would you like?"

"Oh, Darrell," Helen gasped, "whichever one you want me to have."

"Okay then," he said, "you'll have that one on the end."

"Okay, but look at the one next to it, Darrell. Don't you think that cut would suit me better?"

"Yeah, I guess you're right," he replied, having made another important decision.

Helen beamed as they came out of the jewelry store. Darrell had maneuvered the jeweler into a 20 percent reduction in price, or was it Helen who had done the maneuvering? In any event, he had made a ten dollar downpayment and could cover the balance very nicely the following Monday, from his savings account. After the initial announcement of the engagement, the courtship was a whirlwind. Helen graduated the following June and in July they were married. Darrell's mother made the trip for the wedding ceremony and the church was filled with friends of the happy couple. No one noticed that all of the "friends" were people Darrell had met only since he had met Helen.

In September, Darrell's hitch with the service was over. He and Helen had made plans that he should enter college the following January to pursue a course in either dentistry or medicine. In the meantime, they'd get a nice apartment and he'd pick up some kind of job through which they could save a few dollars toward his education. When he went back to school, Helen would go back to work and between the money she could make along with him working part-time, they'd make it very nicely. Neither had given much thought to what sort of jobs would be available to them with their limited experience. Helen could type but she hadn't taken shorthand, and Darrell had done nothing since high school other than to fulfill his military obligation and he had picked up no particular skill there.

The honeymoon was all either of them could ever have hoped for. They had so many friends and they were so happy. The world was their very own beautiful rose bush with petal after velvety petal wafting down upon them and intoxicating their relationship with the enchanting scent of each. During the first week of their marriage and on their honeymoon, each day was better than the one preceding. *Who can say there is no such thing as perfect happiness,* thought Darrell frequently as he came to know her physically, watched her running on the beach, or even just spreading the jam on his toast at breakfast. This was truly heaven on earth.

But, the first wrench thrown into their early ecstasy was not long in coming. Helen became pregnant almost immediately and when Darrell got out of the service, he had to go right to work. Prior to having met Helen, he had saved about $600, but this had been pretty well eaten up by the engagement and then wedding ring, and by giving Helen the things and treating her the way "he thought she deserved." A job wasn't so easy to come by and after fall quarter started at the colleges and universities in the area, most of Helen's friends were gone. Money became the main topic of consideration and Helen and Darrell began projecting their frustrations at one another. Mother Callanan sent a few dollars from time to time, but it nowhere nearly met the need. All of a sudden there were no shows, no nights on the town, not much else to do but stay at home, stare at the walls, and wonder how they were going to keep the apartment rent paid and buy the food they needed to eat. No one was even talking about the expense of having a baby.

Helen was ill equipped for employment, even if she had not been pregnant. Because she was pregnant, she assumed there was no question but that she could not work, even in the early stages. Her attitude in general, and, particularly about this subject, complicated matters because even Helen didn't know exactly what it meant. Darrell was confused. It was hard to put a finger on it, but things were not going as well as they had at first. *Who can expect the honeymoon to last forever,* Darrell thought, and sloughed it off.

Darrell began what seemed to be his endless search for employment. There was a pretty good job opening as a truck driver, but he had no experience driving a truck and no chauffeur's license; a position as the manager of a drive-in restaurant appealed to him, but they were looking for someone who had at least some college; janitor . . . and on and on. None of the jobs had a starting salary amounting to much and each required an employment agency fee of over 50 percent of the first month's wages. Darrell crushed the paper in his right hand, massaging his forehead with his left thumb and forefinger. For the first time in years, tears were in his eyes. *My God,* he thought, *what am I going to do?* The vision of Helen holding a new baby came to him and he could feel the pang of tears building in his cheeks. Darrell stood up, half dropped and half threw the newspaper on the bench on which he had been sitting, and pulled out the five dollar bill in his pocket. He looked at it briefly and then headed out the door and across the street toward blinking lights. Ray's Bar, the sign said, but Darrell didn't even notice as he pushed his way through the door.

Too many hours later, Darrell fumbled for the key in front of the door to their apartment. He entered quietly . . . as quiet as his shaky legs would allow—and took a brief look into the living room. Helen was asleep, a magazine in her lap, the tear stains outlined by running mascara obvious even from across the room. Darrell snuck off quietly to the bedroom where he crept into bed without any light. He lay there for what seemed to be only a few seconds and then the room began to spin. He made it to the washroom just in time to call for Ralph-Rork.

Helen was startled by the eruption. She came to her senses shortly and adrenaline flowed through her veins. She had recognized the problem immediately.

"So there you are, *hero*," she said, with a sarcastic emphasis on the last word that would have been obvious to a deaf man. "Spending money we haven't got because you aren't big enough to face problems we have! You're really something, you are, Darrell Callanan. And, to think I gave up my life and my friends and my happiness for you. Boy, did I make a mistake."

Darrell said nothing but began merely to slink away, flushing the toilet, ridding the room of the memory of all that had transpired, except the odor.

"Come back here, you," she glared after him. "Don't think you can just walk away from me." Darrell came back and stood meekly before her staring at the floor.

"Thanks," she said, "just thanks a lot. Thanks for the baby, for you, and for this whole rotten situation. You're a real man you are, Darrell Callanan," she said. With that, Helen burst into tears and ran sobbing into the bedroom where she fell face down on the bed and wept into the pillow.

When she awoke it was light outside. She listened for a voice from elsewhere in the apartment, but there was none. Just the rattle of garbage cans outside, the honking horns in the street, and innumerable other indistinguishable noises. Helen got up and looked around the apartment. She was alone. She looked for a note, but there was none. Darrell was gone. At first she began to feel sorry for herself, for the baby, even for Darrell, but then, as if severed by a knife, that thought process was cut off and replaced by an even stronger emotion of hate and disgust. *Good riddance,* she thought. *Oh, how could I ever have let myself be taken in by such . . . such a nothing.* She moped around the apartment for a couple of days and finally called her mother. The conversation started casually enough, but Helen's mother had lived with her for a long time and she knew when something was wrong.

"Is it Darrell, dear?" she asked. "Oh, mother, he's gone. He's been gone for three days."

"I'll be right over," was the response from the other end of the line and Helen heard the receiver click in her ear.

In just a matter of days Helen was at home with her parents. The marriage had lasted less than 6 months. Except for the mental anguish, the memory was like a dimly lit hall. At times she could almost forget it—the courtship, engagement, the marriage, even Darrell himself—until she looked at herself, and, then, the reality of it all came back only too clearly.

"Oh, what a mistake," she shuddered. "What a horrible, horrible mistake. People have second chances; why couldn't I have had a second chance?"

For the next several months Helen went nowhere, and she saw no one. If one of her high school chums, home from college, called or came to see her, she was not at home. As the time for delivery approached, Helen began to feel less sorry for herself and began to think more and more about the baby. She doted on every word the doctor told her. The fetus seemed to be coming along fine. The heartbeat was strong and regular and the baby was positioned as it should be.

Kirby's birth was a magnificent occasion. The pains of birth were hardly over before Helen had forgotten them. As she held her baby in her arms for the first time, tears came again as they had during that last encounter with Darrell. They looked the same, they made the same marks on her well-formed cheeks, but this time they were totally different. All at once it had all been worth it. She wouldn't give up this baby for anything, not to attend college, not to have never been married, not for anything. This was her Kirby, and she would raise him to be the kind of a man she had thought Darrell was.

*   *   *   *

Five years ago, she thought, five long years since Kirby had come into the world. He had been her whole life during that time. Helen never went back to her old high school chums; she still lived at home. Her mother had died in the meantime and she had somewhat taken on the role of housekeeper and cook for her father who was the main provider for their family of three. But, this wasn't enough to occupy her time and she became bored at home. A job was the obvious outlet. Even though Helen had had only typing in high school, with her industry and ability she picked up shorthand through night school. With these skills, her lovely appearance, and her marvelous personality, it wasn't surprising that she had worked her way into the position of a key executive's secretary even though not having quite reached her twenty-fourth birthday.

Helen continued to run the brush through her beautiful jet black hair as if in a trance. She was almost back to reality now, and it was the night before and in the car pool on the way home from work. Betty Gerard had mentioned stopping off at the air force base officers' club for a drink.

"I've got a better idea," said one of the other girls, "let's make a night of it at the club. It's a wonderful, relaxing atmosphere and who knows, there may be a handsome young pilot or two hovering overhead."

The girls laughed pleasantly at the mental image of a young, tow-headed, crew-cut, with a rotating propeller emerging from his head, flailing his arms as he fought vainly to hang in the air over the bar while looking over the lovelies who sat there.

"I've really got to get home," Helen had said, looking at her watch.

"Oh, come on Helen," Betty Jans had said, "it's only 4:30. You've got time for a drink or two and I'll take you home after that."

Helen went in reluctantly. She wasn't a big drinker and hadn't had a drink for a long time, but the thought of a temporary change in her monotonously rotating world—any change—was quite appealing. After two drinks, it was even more appealing and she finally called her dad near dinner time.

"Sure, Helen, have a good time," he said, happy to see her take the chance to get away for an evening. After all, a 24-year old girl doesn't belong at home every night.

When Helen came back to the table the girls were chirping like squirrels, but she didn't notice it and soon had entered right into the mood. One more drink and then they all began to get hungry.

After dinner the girls had retired to an anteroom of the main bar for a cigarette and a couple of cups of coffee. It had been a nice evening, but the glow was definitely worn off and Helen was anxious to get home even if she probably wouldn't make it before Kirby had gone to bed. She was just about to say something to Betty Jans next to her when, as she turned her head, the legs of a pair of gray slacks came into view. She looked up and there he was, smiling, probably half in the bag, but nevertheless a new, young, male face which entered appropriately into what had really been a very nice evening.

"Hi girls," said Lt. Jerry Glutz, talking suavely through the scotch. "Which of you is that superb dancer the bartender's bragging about?" And then, scanning them quickly, his eyes rested on the most beautiful face in the group. "It must be you," he said to Helen and then reaching out his hand added, "may I have this dance?"

"Well I really . . ." Helen stammered.

"Go ahead, Miss Butterfly," encouraged one of the girls in the group. "I had no idea you had such a marvelous reputation," she added, humorously sarcastic. Reputation was still one of the words Helen hadn't become accustomed to.

"There, you see," said Glutz, "even your girlfriends are your boosters."

Helen wasn't the best dancer but she managed to make it around the floor. A few years before she would have been a scintillating conversationalist, but now she didn't have much to say. Glutz found the silence awkward so after one dance he returned her to her seat, thanked her, and then moved off toward the bar with more thoughts about his upcoming trip to Alaska which he anticipated for the next day.

That's how I met him, Helen thought, still staring blankly into the mirror but seeing nothing. *But why did I accept this date with him? Maybe it's because he's going to Alaska tomorrow and I won't ever see him again anyway. Maybe it's because I haven't had a date for so long and no one even thinks to ask me out. Maybe it's because . . . oh, hell,* Helen thought to herself as she threw her coat over her shoulder and walked out the door.

"Hi," she said to Jerry as she came to the last step of the staircase, trying to regenerate that sparkly personality which seemed so long ago. And then turning to Kirby, "Get to bed when Grandpa tells you, honey. Tomorrow is another school day, remember." Kirby nodded and the door closed behind them.

CHAPTER III

The door was probably 30 feet from the car, but to Glutz it was the length of three football fields. He said nothing, but oh the thoughts he had. A twenty-four-year-old divorcee with a five-year-old kid. *Oh what I wouldn't do to get out of this predicament. I haven't had less poise since I faced the base commander in flight school for shot putting the ice from the punch bowl across the room at the weekly officers-wives cocktail party in the officers' club. Mama-mia,* his mind exclaimed; and the pun served in no sense to humor him.

Glutz opened the door to the car on the passenger side and Warren Huenerloth, having fallen asleep waiting all this time, fell half out of the car before the shock awoke him and he caught himself.

"Halloo, halloo, halloo," said Huenerloth to Helen, acting as if he were the crown prince of charm which probably he thought he was. "And, who have we here," he said to, and with reference to, Helen.

Jeez, thought Jerry Glutz to himself, *what a dunce. He greets women like Santa Claus talks to the kids at a Christmas party. This ought to be a marvelous night, all right.*

On the way to pick up his date, Huenerloth was all in a chatter.

"How long have you lived here in Tacoma?" he asked Helen; and then before she could answer, burst back in with, "I've been here almost a year now, PCS you know, and BO-O-O-Y . . . let me tell you, this is quite a place."

He didn't have to tell Helen anything and, as a matter of fact, he probably didn't, but the chatter went on endlessly. On the other side of Helen and behind the wheel, Glutz's mind was wandering. He stared dazedly at the sets of lights moving toward him,

27

growing bigger and then flashing past at the last second like well-ordered fireballs or meteors. *Wouldn't it be interesting,* he thought, *to know where some of those people are going. Some of them probably going home half drunk after a few too many cocktails following work; others must be depressed or dejected, wondering what the boss really meant by the threat he made this afternoon; and there must be a few with a heavy foot on the accelerator who can't wait to get over to pick up the girl of their dreams.*

That brought his thoughts back to Helen sitting next to him. The door side of his face showed a lingering snile (some sort of a cross between a smile and a snarl) at the thought of Helen straddling the two bucket seats in the front of his car with her appealing fanny. *Saddle spread,* he thought. *That's what they call it. It won't be many years and she'll be blossoming out sideways from sitting too many hours on a secretary's chair each day. Oh well, she could use it to her advantage tonight . . . her perch would be more comfortable.* The smile came back to Glutz's face and then vanished. Suddenly, he was driven back to reality by the recognition that he had no idea where he was going. He didn't even know the name of Helen's friend, let alone where she lived. Paying no attention to where Warren Huenerloth might be in his monologue, the shock of Glutz's voice coming back into the atmosphere cut Huenerloth's squirrel chirping short.

"Say, where are we going, anyway, Helen?"

"Oh, I'm sorry," said Helen, "I'm afraid I haven't been paying much attention. Take a right at the next stop light."

"But, be sure to wait until it turns green," said Huenerloth, obviously amused at his self interpreted witticism. Glutz swung around the corner and immediately found himself in a residential neighborhood which, at least at night, looked very similar to that where Helen lived.

Glutz pulled up in front of the house and measured it carefully, trying to make some kind of a prediction as to what sort of girl would come out of it. He might have inferred that it would be a young single gal, at least, except after the shock with Helen he was making no bets; even to himself. Huenerloth was still talking and he was still saying nothing. The car was parked and the three just sat there. Finally, Huenerloth realized that they were in front of his date's house and his chattering stopped. He said nothing. Neither did anyone else.

Helen looked at Warren and then at Glutz and, finally, Glutz broke the silence with, "Maybe you ought to go up to the house with Warren, Helen, since this girl is a friend of yours." And then, with a short reflection and before Helen had a chance to respond, he added, "What is this girl's name anyway?" Helen didn't respond to this directly, but instead replaced it with a comment of her own.

"Let's all three of us go up there. That way we can make the introductions easier, rather than craning our necks once we get back into the car."

"Open the door, Warren, we can't go anyplace until you do," Glutz shot over to his male compatriot.

"Huh? Yeah, okay." Huenerloth opened the door, got out and half slammed the door back shut until it met the resistance of Helen's body. "Oh . . . , I'm sorry, Helen." Huenerloth was obviously unnerved at the thought of meeting his blind date. *Boy, I'm sure glad I brought him along,* thought Glutz to himself as he made his way around the car and up the walkway to the house.

Helen rang the doorbell once. There was no answer. Glutz peered in through the front window to see a rather dimly lit living room quite modestly furnished. The floor was hardwood, badly scratched and there was only a small oval rug on the center of the floor. Glutz rang the doorbell a second time and the light went out in the kitchen. He saw a form moving toward the door but through the translucent glass it was difficult to make out anything more. The door opened and there stood a girl who, they were to find out, was one Gayle Sterum. Glutz stared . . . Warren Huenerloth dropped his jaw to the ground as if it hadn't been attached to his facial framework. This girl, in the dim light of her living room, was absolutely beautiful. Her navy blue knit dress accented a graceful and properly curved framework. Her face was a picture. Her legs . . . the whole thing was too perfect. And, Huenerloth gets this doll, thought Glutz to himself.

"Hi Gayle."

"Hi fellows," said Ms. Sterum. Her voice was as unbelievable as was her appearance. The abrasiveness of her vocal intonations would probably have been enough to sand the finish off a car at ten paces. Helen had the flow of an angel's whisper compared to it.

"So sorry we're late, Gayle. I wasn't ready when the boys came."

"No problem, Helen. 'sa matter of fact if ya'd come any earlier you'd have seen me in a very unlady-like manner. Carl was screwin' around in the kitchen and I had a helluva time getting the little son-of-a-bitch to bed."

Jerry stared again and Huenerloth went back into his trance. *I can't believe it,* thought Glutz. *The appearance of a Galatea and the class of a cobra.* Glutz had an almost insatiable desire to jump in his car, drive to the BOQ, fling himself on his bunk, and assume the fetal position. *My mother never told me there would be nights like this,* he thought to himself, with only a tinkle of amusement.

The door closed behind Gayle Sterum and then Glutz's over-the-shoulder glance caught her locking it with what appeared to be a skeleton key. Hands in pockets, he shuffled down the front stairs and on to the car where he opened the passenger-side door almost as a conditioned reflex.

"You leave the kid home all alone at night?" he asked Gayle as she crawled past him into the back seat of the car.

"Hell, he's almost seven years old," she responded. "If he can't take care of himself by this time, it's just too damm bad. Anyway, he knows the neighbor's number so he can call them if there's any problem."

Glutz looked at the houses on both sides. They were both totally dark and the time was only 8:10 P.M. For the briefest moment, Glutz's mind flashed a statement back to Gayle. *If you can't take care of your own kid, I'll stay here and take care of him for you.* But, he realized it was none of his business and the thought never reached his lips. He tried to wash the thought from his mind as he dropped into position behind the steering wheel and closed the door, but the thought of the boy in that house alone was destined to come back to him several times that evening and several times more in the years to come. *My folks would never have . . .* but, then he realized again, that it was none of his business.

"Okay," said Glutz, "where to?" Nobody said a word.

Finally, Huenerloth offered, "You're the driver, Jerry." That hackneyed comment, coming from Huenerloth whom Glutz had decided was a real aught, just about sent a hateful emotional twinge down Glutz's spine and to the tips of his fingers. He said nothing, but he was really getting fed up with this whole evening.

"Then, it's the officers' club, okay, Helen?" he forced out with as pleasant a tone as he could muster under the circumstances.

"That's fine, Jerry, let's do it," said Helen turning ever so slightly in her seat and placing her hand tenderly and shortly atop his.

All of a sudden, Helen had some class. Maybe it was only in comparison to Huenerloth and Gayle Sterum, but at least it was that much. If Glutz could have looked past the experiences of a child and then a divorce, he would have seen even much more in Helen which would have impressed him.

The trip to the officer's club was like any other to any kind of night spot of a similar nature. This night, sounds of a band rather than the juke box met them at the door. They moved to one of the tables set near the dance floor in the ballroom and sat down.

"I'll hang up the coats," Glutz said. He needed to get away for a minute. Subconsciously, he probably just wanted to look at Helen and Gayle from a distance. What he saw was probably basic quality. There seemed to be a lot in Helen compared to Gayle. There was very little in Gayle compared to Helen. The silence was awkward. Even eye fixation was a problem. Then the waitress saved the day with her usual, "Do you care for anything from the bar?"

At first, Jerry Glutz feigned his frequent ebullient personality. *A scotch or two,* he thought, *and I'll loosen up and we'll make a good night out of this yet in spite of the situation.* Even Glutz himself didn't know exactly what he meant by that last phrase. But, this night the drinks were obviously not going to do their work. After the second, rather than gay and vibrant, he felt bloated and sluggish. At 23, he was not ordinarily given to periods of withdrawal and depression, but now, he could almost envision the world closing in on him. He looked at Helen and then at Gayle and then at Huenerloth, busily chirping away to the two apparently interested girls. *Shit!* thought Glutz to himself. *Here I am in the midst of some of what should be the most enjoyable and carefree years of my life, spending the night before taking off on my big assignment—to Alaska of all places—with two divorcees, one a raspy gutter-mouth, and that dumb ass Huenerloth.* Only the thought of having fallen upon so accurate a description of his male companion finally brought a smile to Glutz's lips.

"Helen, let's dance," he said leaning over in the direction of his date.

On the floor it was more of the same. Leading with the left foot, he'd run into her knee. Forward with the right foot and he stepped on her toe. He felt it would be good therapy to criticize Huenerloth, but he had been the one to bring him into Helen's life and so he couldn't. Helen was pretty, all right. Her hands were much older than they should be for her age; her cheeks were well formed, but not creamy and pink as it seemed they should be. Helen had beautiful hair but from close up, as he surveyed it, the ends were brittle, some split. It already showed the aging processes of having been burned, baked, rolled, teased and sprayed many times too often. Helen was not the young bud of flowering virginity she must have been just a few years ago, Glutz thought. He became so pensive it took a tug on his sleeve from Helen as the dance number ended to bring him back to reality.

"You're supposed to clap," she said, "even if you didn't like it. Everybody else is and it encourages the band to do a better job."

Just for that moment, Helen had a sparkle in her eye and an impish grin which would've delighted anyone. It was an obvious residue from Helen's past. Surely it was as bright and spry as ever, but a constant observer would have noticed that it came less frequently these days. Glutz was no exception to the spell cast by the momentary charm. He eased a smile back to his date and replied airily, "So who wants to encourage?" Glutz had not really noticed the band, though, and for all he knew they may have all sounded like master musicians. Gingerly, with his hand on her waist, he aimed her off the dance floor and directed her back to the table. He felt the muscle tissue, pressed out and lapped over her girdle *and, at 24,* he thought to himself.

Huenerloth's peripheral vision caught the return of Glutz and Helen and he interrupted his incessant patter to an ostensibly interested Gayle long enough to begin his next point. "Hey, let's do something, gang. The pool will get stagnant, if the waters remain still too long," he smiled, obviously proud of his spontaneous rhetoric. "What should we do, Jerry?"

"I don't care, whatever everybody else wants to do," added Glutz.

"I don't care, whatever you all want to do," mimicked Huenerloth. "What about you, Helen?" he added, "What do you think of a pizza?"

"I don't care, whatever the rest of you would like to do," she added thoughtlessly.

Glutz and Huenerloth got up simultaneously, with Warren jarring the table just enough to send Glutz already off balance, backpeddling into his chair. Bang! Down it went. The timing was perfect to trip up a returning dancer and send her reeling into the back of her escort, just a step or two ahead. *Goddammit,* Glutz thought to himself. *We'd better get out of here before that human booby trap, Huenerloth, permanently maims somebody— probably me.* He looked down and Helen was smiling up at him. Just for a moment he could feel a warmth emanating from inside her. Immediately, and just for an instant, there was a slight quiver in both his upper arms. He liked the sensation.

The pizza wasn't good but it fit in well with Huenerloth's insane running monologue, thought Glutz on the way to the girls' homes. Before the evening started, he had thought of ways to arrange to drop Warren and his blind date off so that he could be alone with Helen. Somehow, the complexion of the evening no longer made that thought appealing. He had enough scotches to make him "winging," but they had no effect on him now except to make him sluggish and feel bloated. The pizza lay like a rock in the pit of his stomach with only an occasional pang of regurgitating acid to remind him what it was. Helen and Glutz sat in the front seat of the same car, but their thoughts were miles away. *I wonder what kind of a guy he really is,* Helen was thinking. *It's so hard to distinguish his real personality with that strange friend he's brought along tonight; and Gayle isn't in exactly her best form either.*

Glutz's car turned the last corner and came to an easy stop in front of Gayle's house.

"Well, here we are," said Warren Huenerloth, a comment equal in depth and value to his earlier offerings of the evening.

"Yep, here we are," echoed Glutz, half mockingly.

Huenerloth and Gayle leaned forward simultaneously on the backs of the seats in front of them, making an effort to exit from the back seat of Glutz's two-door hardtop, causing the backs of the seats to bind about half way to their destination.

"You go first," said Huenerloth, accidentally pushing forward suddenly enough to jerk Glutz against the horn.

"Get off my back," screamed Glutz menacingly.

"I can't hear you, the horn's making too damn much noise," shouted Warren Huenerloth with equal volume, if not higher pitch.

Glutz jerked backward sending Huenerloth reeling back into his seat, one arm flailing into Gayle's midsection.

"Ooof," was the only greeting she could muster.

"Here," said Helen, "I'll get out of the car and then you can get out ahead of Warren, Gayle."

Huenerloth walked Gayle to the door and in a few moments he was back, this time in the front seat. *At least he's not sitting behind me,* thought Glutz to himself. On the way to Helen's house, Huenerloth reestablished his monologue, keeping the partial attention of Helen, at least, by requiring an intermittent response from her. Glutz, therefore, was free with his own thoughts.

What a disappointment the evening had been, he thought. He remembered the feeling of effervescence and ebullience on the way over to Helen's, caused by the anticipation of what might be to come. Now, he was just flat. *She does look lithe and beautiful,* Glutz thought to himself as he and Helen approached the door of her house against the moonlight. Having come from a town where it was fashionable among the young men to always try to kiss a girl at the end of a date, he leaned over to find his mark. Helen turned her head and he found himself kissing her clumsily on the neck.

"Good night, Helen," he said, embarrassed at this culmination of the evening.

"Good night, Jerry," said Helen, backing through the door, "and thank you," she added as almost a preconditioned afterthought.

Glutz had a lump in his throat and an embarrassed quiver in his larynx as he returned to the car and, with no anticipation, Huenerloth blurted, "How did it go, Jerry? Did you like her?"

"She's divorced, Warren, that makes it pretty different, doesn't it?"

"So what?" injected Warren. "She's probably a great lay. You know what they say about those divorced broads. They get used to it and once their ex is gone, they can't get along without it."

"She has a five-year-old son, Warren, with glasses about an inch thick."

"Yeah, but . . ."

"Forget it, Warren, subject closed."

By the time the two air force officers drove up in front of Huenerloth's quarters, Glutz was more than glad to be there. He was tired. The bed would feel good tonight and the stale evening would soon be forgotten.

"So long, Jer. Good luck up in Alaska. If I'm still here when you get back, the drinks and dates will be on me.

"Sure they will," reflected Glutz as he drove off toward the BOQ.

CHAPTER IV

Glutz rolled over in bed and took a peek at his watch. It was 0800 hours air force time, but that was still 8:00 to Glutz who hadn't yet accustomed himself to much of the air force jargon. *Gotta get that car down to the dock by 9:30 so it gets on that boat,* he thought to himself. *Don't want to be late in this man's air force or I'll probably get court-martialed and spend 3 weeks down here before I get to Alaska.* Glutz got his things together and, without breakfast, rolled into the military port authority with plenty of time to spare.

"What do I do with my car?" Glutz asked the first serviceman he saw.

"Just leave it right here, sir," came the quick reply.

"Keys in it and all?" Glutz looked for reassurance.

"Keys in it and all," responded the seaman, giving it to him.

And, I was held over a day for this, thought Glutz to himself. "This air force just isn't real," he said, shaking his head as he walked off toward the air terminal.

"Glutz, Jerome V. AO99 . . ."

"Oh no, not again," Glutz was almost despondent. At least this time, he knew where the information desk was. Just as he arrived at the window, the attendant turned away. "My name is . . ."

"Just a moment, lieutenant," said the attendant, throwing a glance at Glutz over his shoulder. "I'll be with you in a minute." Then the attendant picked up the microphone and the PA system boomed his voice through the hollow terminal. "Lieutenant Glutz, Jerome V. AO9999999, please report to the information desk."

Glutz let him finish. Then the attendant turned to the counter. "And, now, lieutenant, what can I do for you?"

"I'm Glutz," said Jerry, ready to spring over the counter. Anything to keep from hearing his name over the PA system again.

"Glutz," mused the attendant thoughtfully, and then, "oh-h-h-h," as the dawn struck, "you're the fellow I've been paging."

"That's right," said Glutz, straightening up a bit, rather proud, now, that his name had been heard over the PA.

"Some officer looking for you," the attendant went on, "said something about courier service."

Courier service, thought Glutz to himself. *I wonder what that is?* He had visions of being delayed in Tacoma again, and while he had mixed feelings about going to Alaska in the first place, the delay was getting him down. *If that's to be my destination for the next couple of years, the sooner I get there the sooner I'll get back.* Obviously, Glutz had forgotten the title of this book.

"You sit over there," the attendant said to Glutz, motioning to one of the benches near the information window," and I'll send the officer over to you if he comes around again."

"You going to page him on the PA?" wondered Glutz.

"Can't do that, don't know who he is," replied the attendant rather smartly, proud of his deductive thought processes. It wasn't long before Glutz heard the attendant's, "He's over there." Glutz looked over to see the attendant pointing in his direction to a company grade officer higher ranking than himself.

The captain came over.

"You Lieutenant Glutz?" he asked, somewhat indifferently.

"Yes, sir," said Glutz, snapping to his feet. At least for Glutz it was "snapping."

"We'd like to have you assume the duties of courier on this flight to Elfendwarf Air Force Base in Alaska."

Glutz got his usual kick out of the use of the first person plural pronoun with only one person standing there. He was more concerned, though, about making a favorable impression on his newfound senior officer acquaintance.

"Yes, sir, captain, I'll be happy to do it."

"Fine," said the captain. "An airman will meet you at the plane with the pouch and the prescribed small arm."

Pouch, courier, small arm—you don't suppose I'm going to be hauling a bunch of pigeons up to Alaska with responsibility to shoot them if they get away? Glutz smiled at the thought. Funniest of all was the thought of him using a small arm, or any arm for that matter, to shoot anything. It was a well established fact for all who knew him that Glutz couldn't hit a . . . no need to repeat the phrase, all of his friends knew it anyway.

Glutz had just nestled himself comfortably into one of the seats on the big MATS aircraft, when an airman came bursting breathlessly aboard.

"Lieutenant Glutz, A . . ."

"Here I am," said Glutz, frenzied at the thought of hearing that outburst once again.

"You the courier, sir?"

"That's right," said Glutz matter-of-factly, almost impressive enough to make one think that he knew what this assignment was all about. "Okay, here's your pouch," said the airman, handing over the mailbag with the word "classified" stenciled very prominently at least several times upon it.

"So, this is it." Glutz barely had time to think before the pouch was followed by a holstered .45 automatic.

"Here's your sidearm, sir."

"What do I need that for?" asked Glutz. "I probably couldn't fire that thing accurately if my life depended on it."

"Probably just as well," said a very serious airman. "I doubt that that weapon has ever been fired. The barrel is probably all rusted so that if you were to fire it, it would probably blow up in your hand." *What a deal,* thought Glutz. *Here we've got a pouch full of classified documents which are clearly classified for all to view and a weapon which can't be fired in the hands of an air force officer who couldn't fire it. Oh well,* thought Glutz, sliding down in his seat and dropping his service cap over his eyebrows, IT ALL COUNTS TOWARD TWENTY. He had remembered the title.

The plane droned on and in a couple of hours Alaska was too close to ignore any longer. The thought of two years up here did not really enter his conscious mind. He knew not what to expect but was not overly concerned. *Whatever turns up, I'll worry about it when the time comes,* he told himself. After all, there was no war on and he was going to be a public relations officer at Headquarters, Alaskan Air Force. That couldn't be too bad. The stewardesses aboard the MATS ship were something else. They offered nothing and from the looks of them that's just what they had to offer. They wore blouses (air force style) and long pants, had short hair, and wore low-heeled shoes. *They look more like airmen* (male enlisted men in the air force—for those who haven't been there) *than stewardesses,* thought Glutz. *Maybe that's what they are,* his subconscious fired back.

It seemed only a short time before the seat belt light flashed on indicating, in this instance, a preparatory procedure to landing. Unlike most commercial flights, where the passenger usually gets a "blow by blow" account, there was no further indication that landing was imminent; that is, other than the ground rushing up to meet them. The squeal of the tires meeting concrete and the reverse thrust of the four powerful engines told Glutz that he was on the ground once more. *That squeal always sounds the same,* he thought. *You'd think with modern engineering and chemistry what it is they'd be able to come up with a more appealing tire noise.* (Glutz intended no pun.) *When they do, the air force will get it last,* his subconscious told him. Glutz left the plane thinking that maybe something had already been invented.

Glutz looked all about him as he descended the portable stairway from the plane, hoping to see some sign of someone from the mail depot to whom he could unload his "precious" cargo. He had just completed his descent when his ever-alert subconscious made him look up to see a big smile on the face of the first colored officer he had ever seen. (Today, he would have thought Black, but in those days, it was still okay to think colored. People weren't so sensitive then. Maybe just as prejudiced but not so sensitive.)

The Negro officer flashed a broad smile at Glutz. "You the courier?" he shouted above the airfield noises.

"Guess so," Glutz responded. He was immediately taken by his new acquaintance. They hadn't exchanged a half-dozen words and yet Glutz already felt an attraction to him.

"Hop into the truck and we'll run over to the mail depot. There're some forms for you to sign." *I'd be surprised if there weren't,* Glutz thought to himself.

The trip to the mail depot was fun. The truck made a crusade out of every minor bump in the road, and the two lieutenants laughed over each of them. *This guy is no run-of-the-mill first lieutenant,* Glutz thought. *Wonder why he's so extra sharp?*

"Are you an ROTC grad?" Glutz asked the officer.

"Nope, never been on a college campus," the officer said proudly. "OCS" (that's officers' candidate school, for the uninitiated; its graduates are commonly known as "ninety-day wonders" even though commissioning sometimes takes up to six months). "Not much work available that amounted to anything when I got out of high school, so I figured to kill two birds with one stone, get a job and get my service obligation out of the way. Wasn't in two months before I decided that a career in the Air Force was the answer for me. Much better opportunity for a Black man in the military than 'outside.'" He said it so matter-of-factly. No rancor; no bitterness. *I wonder if I could be so objective in his position?* thought Glutz.

"You change what you can and keep working toward the rest," said the lieutenant, as if in answer to Glutz's thoughts. "Seems hard to believe that we should all be stereotyped by the color of our skin. Must have something to do with the carryover from the inferior nature of slavery. I know it ain't so and so does any White man who'll admit it. Oh well, someday it'll be over and we'll be accepted as the same. But that's not in my time; maybe for my kids . . . or their kids. Anyway, in the meantime, this is still the best country for us." And then, with just a moment's reflection, he went on, "Particularly in the air force."

"How did you get into OCS?" wondered Glutz. "You said you enlisted, didn't you?"

"Yeah, I enlisted all right, but like I said, after a few months I knew it'd be my career." He looked at Glutz. "Better an officer than an airman, you know," he said with that engaging smile.

"Sorry," said Glutz offering his hand. "I don't even know your name. Mine's Jerry Glutz."

"Smith, Jerry, Carter Smith from Enton, Oklahoma, but I won't shake your hand 'cause the way this truck handles . . . I take one hand off for two seconds and we'll both hear angels. Where you from?"

"Greyrock, New Mexico," said Glutz. "Ever heard of it?"

"Never heard of Greyrock," said Smith, "but there was a courier officer from somewhere down there, name of Bockbach."

"Wasn't Lenny Bockbach by any chance?"

"Yeah, that was it," said Smith, "Lenny was his name," sounding as if he was naming a song title.

"Lenny's from New Mexico, all right," said Glutz with some enthusiasm. "As a matter of fact he's from my hometown, Greyrock. Didn't know him very well. He went to a different school and was a few years older, but he's from the same town. Sure is a small world," reflected Glutz.

"Sure is," echoed Carter Smith.

The truck pulled up in front of a drab gray building with several overhead doors. "This is it," said the black lieutenant to his white brother. "Come on in and sign a few papers and you'll be on your way."

Glutz followed Lieutenant Smith into the mail depot and with utter (not udder) docility began to sign where Smith had marked the x's. Glutz paused in the middle of his first signature as Carter Smith's last comment recoiled into Glutz's conscious mind.

"On my way to where?" he asked thoughtfully, half of himself and half of Carter.

"Oh, I'll drop you off at the BOQ office on my way home," offered Smith. "It's hardly out of the way and won't be any trouble. I'm off duty here in a few minutes."

"Gee, that'd be great," said Jerry Glutz.

On the way over to the BOQ, the truck bounced some more though the roads seemed a bit better.

"Have you got a reservation?" asked Carter, eyes straight ahead on the terrain.

"Do I need one?" piped back Glutz, a nervous twitch and a bead of sweat accompanying his quick nervous reaction.

"Not really," added Carter, "but it's fun sometimes to compare the air force to civilian life. The comparison is often so ludicrous that it's usually good for a smile. Sort of like the incongruity of a young heiress at her coming out party, stepping lithely to the top of a banister in her beautiful evening gown and then tripping and falling unceremoniously down the stairs."

Just then the truck bounded past one of the major entrance signs at the air base; *Elfendwarf Air Base,* the sign read, *Headquarters, Alaskan Air Force.* Glutz could still hardly believe he was where he was. The truck screeched to a halt in front of the building that looked a lot like the mail depot or, for that matter, a lot like almost every other building on base. It had no overhead doors but it was obviously built of the same material and, most depressing of all, it was the same drab color.

"These places must have been designed and decorated by a sadist," Glutz muttered to himself as he sprang, less than enthusiastically, from the truck.

"No, believe it or not, there are some sadder looking buildings than this one around here," said Carter, having heard the last of Glutz's muttered words and answering what he thought to be a question. Inside there was a counter-like affair with a light on but no one behind it.

"Good to see you," said Smith to Glutz, offering his hand after having set down two of Jerry's bags near the door. "If you ever want to catch a flight out of here on leave, give me a call at the mail room and we might be able to work you in to your destination as a courier." Then a broad smile crossed his face and Carter added, "now that you're experienced, that is."

"Courier," Glutz mused, and his mind was cluttered with pigeons and statues again. "Thanks a lot," said Glutz over his shoulder, "I may take you up on it."

But Smith was out of earshot and had walked out of Glutz's life as quickly and as quietly as he had entered it just an hour or so before. Glutz gave it little thought because we are all used to these brushes with others, many of which appear promising but last not at all. An interested observer might have noted, however, how seemingly unfortunate it was that these two who seemed to be so positive, perhaps among the potentially best of two races, would never see each other again. Together they might have had a very favorable impact on their society. Perhaps alone each would anyway.

Presently, noises grew louder and an airman appeared behind the counter from the back room.

"Something I can do for you sir?" he asked without looking up apparently of Glutz since there was no one else in the room.

No, Glutz thought to himself, *I'm just on a luxury tour of the world and stopped in here on the recommendation of my travel bureau as one of the beauty spots of the area.* But, he thought better of it and merely responded, "Yeah, I'd like a room," and then with afterthought, "or an apartment or whatever you've got."

Glutz hadn't been in a BOQ before except as transient status at McCloud. *Never know for sure what lies behind these barren walls,* he thought to himself. *May as well speak up for whatever I can get.*

"We have two-room suites in the bonafide BOQ," said the airman. "Would you like to stay there?" still with the air of the temporary nature of a tour guide helping to plan a Caribbean cruise.

"What's a bonafide BOQ?" asked Glutz.

"There's only one," said the airman, "and it's the BOQ where the bachelor officers stay."

Since anyone in the air force knows that BOQ stands for bachelor officers' quarters, even if they've never been in one, Glutz wondered, mildly, what the airman was talking about.

"I thought that . . . ," Glutz started to say when he was briskly interrupted by the airman.

"Yeh, I know," said the airman. "BOQ stands for the same thing up here but the bonafide BOQ is where the *real* bachelors can live." For some strange reason, Glutz was still puzzled so the airman went on. "You see, there are a lot of married officers up here who leave their families back in the states to get a shorter tour. Then, there are Red Cross field workers, tech reps [technical representatives of aircraft and support systems supply companies, for those who are so fortunate as never to have known one], civilian employees of the air force and a host of others who live in the regular BOQs. The bonafide is for real honest-to-goodness air force bachelor officers. There's a dance floor over there in the basement, a bar, and the whole deal. It's really nice."

"Sounds like the answer all right," said Glutz enthusiastically. "Do you have any rooms?" *What a dumb question that was,* Glutz thought to himself, half embarrassed. *If he hadn't any rooms he wouldn't have . . .*

"No," said the airman, checking his roster as if to look for a vacancy. "There's never an open room over there. That place is really popular and those rooms fill up almost before they're vacated."

"B-l-u-u-l-p," Glutz sounded like a drowning man as he tried to start to say something but was interrupted by the airman's continuance.

"Would you like to be put on a waiting list?"

"G-r-r-u-m-p," sounded Glutz, trying to get out a response but again being stymied by the overzealous airman.

"I'll put you on the list right here. Only three ahead of you." Glutz looked up enthusiastically. "Shouldn't be longer that sixty to ninety days. Six months at the most," concluded the airman.

Glutz's heart sank. *What a stupid airman,* he thought. *Why did he have to give me the grandiose buildup and then let me down with a thump. I'll bet he couldn't make it on the outside!* That, by air force tradition, particularly of short-timers (those who don't have long to go before release from active duty, for those who've never had any time on active duty), is just about the nastiest thing that can be thought or said about an air force man.

The airman, seemingly undisturbed by Glutz's private thoughts, went rambling on. "Sign you up for the time being in BOQ number 235." *For the time being,* Glutz thought. *He calls six months, "for the time being."* Glutz had always been an optimistic soul and every day in the air force made him more that way.

"What's your name, lieutenant? asked the airman. "I need it for the record here."

"Glutz," said Jerry, unconsciously. "Lieutenant Jerome V., AO9" (the PA system at McCloud had made its imprint on his brain). The airman cut him off again.

"Oh, Lieutenant Glutz," he said, "you're supposed to call a Major Ralston at FR3-2780. There's a phone you can use right back here."

"What's the FR prefix stand for—Franklin?" asked Glutz of the airman as his fingers pressed into the hole before each, rotating the dial right, to the stop, for each letter and digit.

"No," said the airman, "frostbite."

Frump, it figures, thought Glutz as he continued to dial. Three rings, a click of the receiver, and then at the other end, a young voice said, "Hello."

CHAPTER V

Major Ralston was a rather tall, strapping man whose easy-going manner immediately appealed to Lieutenant Glutz. *So this is my new boss,* thought Glutz as the major was introducing himself. Maybe this last stint won't be so bad at that. The major was graying at the temples a bit and his physique showed the signs of rather pleasant living. It had obviously been a long time since he had seen an obstacle course. Nonetheless, he clearly had a good sense of humor, a keen wit and fine military bearing, even in his Sunday civilian clothes.

"Here, let's take your bags over to your BOQ before we head out to the house. Do you have your assignment?"

"Yes sir, I'm in BOQ number 235. The airman said there's no room in the bonafide BOQ, although I guess I can get in there later on."

Major Ralston responded with the unruffled smoothness befitting his field-grade rank. "Yeah, those dumb son-of-a-bitches never have got things straightened out right. They've got everything over there from squadron leaders in the Royal Air Force to rear admirals from the Yucatan Navy. It's no wonder you couldn't get in.

The visit to the Ralston household was most pleasant and relaxing. Housing up and down both sides of the street was the same. They were all the same size and shape and all painted the same drab color as the BOQ's and most other buildings on the base. But inside there was the zest and comeliness of family love and living that doesn't depend on frescoes and tapestries for its existence. Glutz met Mrs. Ralston, an attractive and charming woman in her middle thirties and was then ushered over to the living room divan on which he sank into his favorite position; sitting on his backside.

"What'll it be, Jerry?" asked Major Ralston, "martini, bourbon . . ."

"I'll have a martini, please," interrupted Glutz instantly. Glutz had never had a martini but he had never been in Alaska before, either, and that called for some bold action, for one reason or another. The pine scent of the martini was delightful and even the taste wasn't too bad after the first gulp (Glutz never did learn how to sip the ghastly things). About halfway through Glutz lit up a cigarette and from then on he was on his way.

Midway through the second martini, Major and Mrs. Corkerstrom came over from next door and joined in the cocktail hour or drinking bout or, well, whatever it was. The attractive Mrs. Corkerstrom easily engaged Glutz in conversation.

"Are you going to make a career of the air force, Lieutenant Glutz?" she queried.

Glutz gagged on the olive he had just inhaled which Mrs. Corkerstrom interpreted as a reply in the negative. While he turned from red to deep purple in the throes of apparent strangulation she continued her questioning.

"Well, why not? My husband is very happy in the service and so is Bud Ralston. We do a lot of traveling and meet lots of nice people. Then, just when we've seen enough of a place and enough of the people, we get to move on. Jim, Danny, and Jody, our three children, were each born in a different country. Sometimes we move to a new station and run into old friends whom we haven't seen for a long time, like we did with Bud and Alice here. We've had lots of fun reunions."

On the heels of Grace Corkerstrom's long monologue, Jerry Glutz had ample time to free the olive from his windpipe and send it, almost whole, down the esophagus.

"I'm sure the air force is a fine life," answered Glutz, "but I just don't like to move around so much and most of all, I can't make my fly skins anymore. Groundpounders [the explanation for that term must be obvious to anyone] are pretty much looked down on as second-rate in the air force."

"Oh, my husband Cliff isn't rated [that's qualified as a flier of one form or another—for those who haven't been any higher than a martini can send them], but he likes the air force a lot anyway." Glutz wished the olive had stayed in this throat.

"Well, we've got to get going," Major Cliff Corkerstrom said to his wife. Then he winked at Bud Ralston and added, "Return the favor soon. Remember, my name's Cliff so be sure to drop over sometime." Major Ralston's hearty laugh belied the fact that he had heard that "joke" from the same person too many times, before.

"Why don't you stay to have dinner with us," offered Mrs. Ralston, thoughtfully.

"Oh, no, we just couldn't do that," replied Grace Corkerstrom for both herself and her husband.

"No, we just couldn't," echoed Major Corkerstrom, making it difficult to tell whether he was making a legitimate refusal, saying what he thought should be said, or just mocking his wife.

"Yeah, why don't you stay," offered Bud Ralston, in such a manner as to make it difficult to determine whether he was making a legitimate offer, saying what he thought should be said, or just mocking his wife.

The Corkerstroms refused a second time and then from out of the background like a gust of wind storming through a mountain crevice (and similarly desirable) came Glutz's voice, "Sure, why don't you stay for dinner." Ordinarily, Glutz would have considered such a comment inappropriate, since he had just met the Ralston, himself, and had never been in their house before. But the two and a half martinis, which had never been in him before, colored his judgment enough to change his direction ever so slightly. The back of Major Ralston's neck showed just a dash of purple which, Glutz would come to learn, was a danger signal, but, other than that, there was little response to Glutz's generous invitation. Mrs. Corkerstrom did flash him a brief and sympathetic smile but that was about it.

The Corkerstroms left and Glutz plopped back into his concave position on the couch. Major Ralston mixed another martini and sat down beside him.

"Welcome officially to Alaska, Jerry," said the major, lifting his glass as if to propose a toast.

"Thank you, major," said Glutz appreciatively. "It's a pleasure to be here." He wouldn't really mean that tomorrow nor for most of the next two years, but he meant it today; that is, he and the martinis did.

"Well," said Ralston, "you're about to embark on your first assignment in the field of information services. How do you feel about it?"

"Information services," chorused Glutz almost despondently, "I thought I was going to be in public relations?!"

"Oh, you are," answered the major, "that's just what they call it in the air force."

"Oh," was all Glutz said, but he was thinking much more. Mostly, he was thinking that information services didn't sound anything at all like public relations and he didn't think any of the words meant the same thing, either. Public relations could be interpreted many ways but most of all, to Glutz, it had an image of Madison Avenue (not Main Street, Alaska), fancy dinners and exotic cocktails (not the slop chute, air force vernacular for—now get this—the officers field ration mess*), beautiful single women (Glutz hadn't even seen *a* single woman in this corner of the world so far), and smiles and handshakes with important people. How was he ever going to explain to his family and friends back home in Greyrock that he was an information services officer, when they all thought he was going to a far-off corner of the world to be in PR, to say nothing of trying to explain what information services *is*. His thoughts drifted back to the information booth at McCloud Air Force Base and the nattily attired civil service employee behind it. *Is that what they'll think?* he wondered. *Oh, no!!*

Major Ralston brought Glutz out of his reverie with a question.

"What did you major in, in college," asked the major, "journalism?"

"No," said Glutz. "I was going to major in one of the major language disciplines, but there were some major roadblocks involving a major in that area so I decided to major in economics because it provided the opportunity to take more major electives in more other major areas than any other major, major." Major Ralston was getting dizzy and so was Glutz, or was it goofy? Anyway, Glutz's problem was with the martinis. The major wisely decided not to pursue the major.

"What background do you have that qualifies you for work as an ISO?" asked Major Ralston. *An astute air force selection process,* thought Glutz, but even the martinis couldn't get him to say that.

"Just a keen desire to be of value to myself and to the air force, sir," was Glutz's prudent reply. One wonders what compartment of his brain the martinis opened up to extract that response.

---

*Only the last word is accurate to a description of many.

"That's the attitude we're looking for," winced the major.

"The good major was apparently able to rationalize the inexperienced warrior he had on his hands and went on to "talk shop.""

"Your first assignment's going to be a big one, Jerry," he warned. "Ned Solomon is coming up here to shoot a show for his weekly variety series, in a couple of weeks."

" 'That so," said Glutz. "It ought to be interesting."

"Yeah, it'll be that all right. Those TV personalities are fascinating people, but they're demanding as hell and unpredictable to boot." The major sounded like an authority but, peering into his probable background, Glutz wondered if he'd even met a stage personality.

Just then Mrs. Ralston poked her head in from the dining room. "Dinner will be ready in 15 minutes," she said.

"We've treated your arrival with regal anticipation," added the major, beginning to show a choice of words to unmask his occupation, had one not already known. "We've set aside a moose steak for you."

For some reason the thought of eating didn't do much for Glutz at that moment. Maybe it was the martinis, maybe the pack of cigarettes he had smoked along with them, or maybe both. In any event, the truth fell upon Glutz like a rock from a ledge. He was drunk! And he didn't fully realize how drunk he was until he got up to move to the table. The room began spinning as he moved toward the table, and a light revolving sensation gripped his stomach. To the experienced viewer of inebriates, Glutz's condition was obvious and Major Ralston was so experienced. Glutz, who had been garrulous and lingual throughout the afternoon, was now quiet as a tomb and the color of his face resembled the inhabitants of said edifice. Also, though this information was secret to himself, he was breaking out in a cold sweat. *Oh, to be anyplace but here,* he thought to himself. *Even that crummy cot in the transient BOQ would be better than this.* But, here he was and here he had to stay, at least for the next hour or so.

The Ralston family chatted pleasantly during the meal. Glutz tried to eat his moose steak (if that's what it was . . . he never really knew for his taste buds had deserted him entirely), but each bite was a deliberate effort. The lump in his throat seemed to challenge every swallow and now and again his stomach leaped to its new prey. More than once Glutz thought he'd see his meal back on the table before he could get outside. Somehow he got through it, though, and by the time the ordeal was over Major Ralston knew Glutz needed some fresh air—at least that.

"Lieutenant Glutz and I will take a walk around the block to settle that big meal," Major Ralston said kindly to his wife.

Jerry Glutz, on his tour around the block, was a sight to behold. With each step he lifted first one foot and then the other high in front of him, as if stepping over a parapet. He knew he was stepping strangely, but how better to control his movements, he had no idea.

"Beautiful Alaska evening," he said, in an effort to make conversation.

"Yes it is," answered Major Ralston, forcing back a chuckle and glad that the Alaskan darkness hid the grin on his face. Glutz was very conscious of his walking and his speech. Though the latter sounded all right to him, he knew that didn't mean a thing. Though still drunk, he was beginning to feel embarrassed about his inebriation. *Bad enough anytime,* he was thinking, and even his thoughts sounded slurred, *but unforgivable the first time I'm at my new boss's house on my first night in Alaska.* But, unforgivable it wasn't. Glutz would be this bad, and worse, again, and so would many of his future acquaintances. *I'll really regret this tomorrow; but I'll worry about that when the time comes,* his thoughts trailed off.

Speaking of time, the major must have been reading Glutz's mind.

"Let's cut back through this yard, Jerry. We'll have a cup of coffee and then get you home."

"Snow looks pretty deep in there," muttered Glutz.

Little should you worry, as high as you've been stepping on the sidewalk, thought the major. But, with a chuckle for his private thought, he said, "Naw, a good air force man can make it," instead.

Glutz's head was still buzzing over the cup of coffee and Mrs. Ralston's conversation, only half of which he could decipher. She wanted to know all about his background, where he was from and all that. Glutz just wanted to get "home." His head was going round and round and his stomach over and over. He knew if he spoke at the wrong time he'd barf right then and there.

On the way out, you guessed it, Glutz stepped in a snowbank. He didn't remember it though, and when back at the BOQ he was undressing for bed, he found himself with a wet shoe and sock.

Immediately, he checked his skivvies (undershorts, for those who haven't been in any branch of the service nor known anyone else who has) to make sure he hadn't wet his pants.

The next morning wasn't as bad as he expected. The sun shone brightly in his window and Glutz felt relatively refreshed.

"Don't hurry down to the office," the major had told him. "I'll expect you at work every morning at 0800 except tomorrow. Tomorrow you can sleep in and come in whenever you're well rested and get squared away" (get things straightened around, for those who seldom do).

Glutz was in no hurry to go anywhere this particular morning. He was simply grateful that he had nowhere to go. He rolled over and went back to sleep. Later, he woke with a start. 9:00 A.M. his watch read (it would have read 0900 hours had it been air force issue). Just twelve hours before he had "walked" out of the major's house, completely totaled out. *What an impression I must have made,* he thought; but it really didn't bother him as much as he thought it would.

Glutz sat on the edge of his bed and stretched and yawned. Slowly he moved into the washroom where he cleaned up his face and tuned in his electric shaver. After completing the rest of his morning "s" duties (that one you'll have to figure out for yourself), he slipped into his uniform and ambled across the street for breakfast at the "slop chute." Glutz entered the door aimlessly, little expecting to find anyone he knew. He was no less than startled when his eyes fell upon an old classmate.

"Paulie Plopp!" he shouted in disbelief.

Paulie looked up, a thin Hoosier smile spreading across his face as he did so. He was probably as pleased to see Glutz as Glutz was to see him, but Paulie never showed very much emotion. Glutz plopped into a chair across the table from Plopp.

"What're you doing here, Paulie?"

"On my way to Lapp AFB where it looks like I'll serve out the rest of my term." Sort of made it sound like a prison term. Maybe, at least subconsciously, that's how Paulie viewed his stint in the service. And, maybe it wasn't so subconscious.

"When are you going up there," Glutz wondered.

"Don't know for sure," replied Paulie. "I was supposed to go up there yesterday but as you can see, I didn't make it." Glutz could see that.

"Do you think you'll be here a week?" queried Glutz.

"No, I don't think it'll be that long."

"Oh, I s'pose you'll be gone in a day or two then."

"Hard to say," offered Paulie. "You know the air force. Could be here for a month or more."

Glutz knew the air force. Plopp might not get to Lapp AFB to serve out any of his remaining tour which had slightly more than a year to run. He didn't pursue the issue.

"What're you gonna be doing up there?" he questioned further.

"Dunno," said Paulie. "That's part of the problem. The job I was assigned to has been eliminated. The word was waiting for me when I got here."

"So was the word to stay here and await new orders, apparently," continued Glutz.

"Yep," answered Paulie, leaning back into his breakfast.

"How're you going to get paid if you aren't assigned to a unit?" Glutz asked.

"Don't know. Doesn't amount to enough to worry about, though," said Paulie between mouthfuls. He obviously wasn't very worried. And then he continued, "When my slot folded I was reassigned as special services officer, but it turned out that the slot is filled and the man who's in it has longer to go in the Air Force than I do."

"Didn't they know the position was filled when they assigned you to it?" asked Glutz.

"Guess not, somebody must have stepped on the guy's computer card with golf shoes on. Anyway, when they found out the slot was filled they were going to make me assistant special services officer."

"Why didn't they do that?" wondered Glutz.

"Because the special services officer is lower in rank and has been in the air force a shorter period of time than I." Glutz wondered what difference that made to the air force.

"Maybe they'll just forget about you and leave you here for the rest of your tour," offered Glutz.

"Maybe," said Plopp, wiping his napkin across his mouth to signify the completion of his morning meal, more than to wipe his lips clean.

"Maybe they won't even remember you when your tour's up."

Paulie Plopp's wiping motion jerked to a halt. *What if* . . . and then he remembered he had over a year to worry about that. He was not the one to be concerned with maybes beyond tomorrow.

"In any event," said Glutz . . .

"In any event," said Paulie, rocking his chair to its hind legs, having finished his breakfast and anxious to end speculation about his anticipated work at Lapp, "I'm here at least until tomorrow so let's plan on getting together tonight."

"Good idea," said Glutz.

"By the way, Jerry, we've been spending all this time talking about me; what're you doing up here?" Paulie leaned back toward the table. "Oh, I'm assistant information officer for the Alaskan air force."

"You're working on this base?"

"Sure."

"Then what kind of hours have you got? It's after 1000 hours."

"Oh today's my first day," said Glutz, "and my boss said I can come in anytime this morning."

Then he went on to recount the day and evening before at Major Ralston's house.

"Must be nice," said Paulie, rising from the table. "I've got to get a haircut now. Let's meet at the officers' club after work. Say around 1700 hours?" (subtract 12 to get P.M. time)

"OK," said Glutz.

"What time do you get off work?" Paulie wanted to know, figuring that maybe they could meet earlier or, perhaps, that Glutz couldn't make a 5:00 rendezvous.

"I don't know," Glutz responded, "I told you I haven't been to work yet, this is my first day. I told you that."

"Then how can you say you'll meet me?" *Oh, I'll get there when I can,* Plopp finished his thought privately.

The two lieutenants were ambling toward the door now.

"What did you come in here for, anyway?" Paulie wondered why Glutz had come into the field ration mess since he apparently had accomplished nothing.

"Why, to eat . . ." and then Glutz realized that he'd been in the mess almost an hour and hadn't eaten. "See you later." He waved a hurried good-bye to Paulie who was just going through the door and headed back for the chow* line. "I'll have two . . ."

---

*Editor's note: The term chow probably came from a comparison between army food and animal chows, before there was an air force. If so, the comparison is inaccurate. Sometimes air force food is good. Sometimes chows are too!

"Sorry, sir, we're closed. We closed just a few minutes after you came in here before."

"If you saw me come in why didn't you tell me?"

"Didn't know you wanted to eat, sir," said the airman, indifferently.

Glutz asked for a phone and made a call to Major Ralston. "Well, I thought you'd headed back to the states," was the major's cordial response from the other end of the line.

"No sir, just took you at your word and slept in this morning."

"OK, just so you don't make a habit of it," warned Major Ralston. "You on your way over now?"

"Yes, sir, I'll be over in a few minutes."

"Good, see you then."

"Oh major . . . MAJOR!!" But the phone clicked on the other end. Glutz dialed Major Ralston's office once again. "What building are you in and how do I get over there?"

The information services office was . . . well, it would be hard to describe. Steel desks, no pictures on the wall, tile floor. Perhaps the kindest thing to be said about it was that it wasn't too homey. But, the people made what would otherwise have been a bland atmosphere sparkle with personality.

There was the air force historian who looked to be between 50 and 150 years old. She had never been married and one look told the entire story. Rumor had it that all mirrors had to be removed from all but the men's rooms when she arrived. A high level conference had to be called before even those could be salvaged. She had become affectionately known via the glib tongues of the quick wits on base as the Alaskan air force's "hysterical biddy." Someone obviously had trouble with the term "historical."

Then there was smiling Ralph Moroney, the Irish Protestant whose quick wit and broad smile amply offset his lack of hair and charred lungs, resulting from smoking short cigarettes. Lyman Fengrew was a religious fanatic. He had so many "Jesus saves" and "Where will you spend eternity?" signs on his car that no one knew for sure what color it was. Once, in the future, he would refuse to buy cigarettes for Lieutenant Glutz because he was strongly against them. Not strong enough, however, to deny the same request when it came from the major.

And, finally, there was Gloria Inexcelsis. Glorie, as her close friends called her, was delightful, warm, and charming. There were only two problems. The first was that she was married and the second, that she was quite obviously second in command of the department. If Glutz ever had any question about that he needed only to compare paychecks. Hers was decidedly superior. On one occasion she would remind him, "Lieutenant Glutz, I'll thank you not to pick up the line on incoming calls until or unless I buzz you." Glutz would nod agreeably and then slink away like a bitten dog.

There was a photographer on the staff, too, and an airman-clerk. No special mention is given them, however, because the photographer was usually out of the office (rumor had it that he had his own business to take care of and could not spend a great deal of time with the air force) and the clerk was usually overlooked and seldom spoken to because he typed faster than the secretary.

Lieutenant Glutz spent most of the morning chatting with his new fellow employees and exchanging amenities. He shared an office with Major Ralston. However, his desk was in the corner, facing the wall with his back to the major. Ralston would come to think that he was positioned that way intentionally though the desk was that way when Glutz arrived. There were two doors into the Ralston-Glutz office. One opened onto the hall and the other into the general office. Keeping both paths opened cut the office in half and created even less space, even though it was seldom that anyone came in from the hall.

Glutz sat down at his desk and looked around the room. The walls were bare and so was the top, his desk. He opened first one drawer and then another. Dust, and a rubber band. He stretched it. Ouch! It cracked back against the knuckle of his forefinger as it snapped under the strain. *Synthetic,* Glutz thought. *World War II . . . this must really be an old desk.* Another drawer had a paper clip and in the big drawer on the bottom right-hand side, he spotted a couple of loose-leaf binders. One had old air force regs (regulations, for those who never knew they existed, whether in or outside the air force). Glutz threw them in the wastebasket and tucked the binder carefully back in the drawer. *Future records,* he thought. He would never use it again. The other binder had some personal notes in it, apparently by a Captain Sloughfoot who had preceded Glutz in the position. Rumor had it that he had gone off to mate. Alaska seemed a good place. *Wonder why he didn't take his notes with him,* Glutz muttered to himself. Then, he read a few passages and knew. *Incoherent ramblings of a . . .* Glutz's thought trailed off as he tore the papers in half. The binder got caught in the action so the whole thing was arched into the wastebasket. Clump!

The noise shattered the relative quiet of the office and turned the letter "d" the major had been writing into a diagonal line across the page. It had shocked him. The major scowled at Glutz's back and then went on about his business. Having finished his rearrangement task, Glutz turned in his chair and addressed the major.

"Major Ralston," he said, "it's 11:15. Have you any plans for lunch?"

"Usually go over to the club. They serve a good meal over there for about a buck." Then, as if anticipating a question from Glutz, he added, "My wife won't let me come home for lunch," and finished with a grin. Glutz didn't really believe that. In the first place, Bud Ralston didn't seem the type to have his wife telling him whether or not he could do anything. Second, if it had been true, he wouldn't have grinned about it. It was a small thing and not Glutz's business so he passed it off.

"Mind if I join you at the club?" he asked.

"Let's go," said Ralston.

Major Ralston and Lieutenant Glutz were beginning what would frequently be a very strange, if not strained relationship. Glutz was intelligent but he was immature, particularly in a military setting. Ralston was talented but he was getting stale. Frequently, the two would debate heatedly until noon and then walk out to a friendly lunch together. Glutz was to learn one thing he would never forget from Ralston. An effective superior could not afford the luxury of liking or disliking a subordinate on the job, except based on his performance. Ralston liked Glutz personally but the two would never jibe on the job. But, then, there were not two jobs in this office. There may not even have been one.

The fall day was brisk with signs of winter already on the horizon. So far as Glutz was concerned this was already winter enough. Coming from New Mexico it was a new experience. The two chatted amicably until the door of the club swung open to admit them. The officers' club, or open mess as it was formally called, was no big extravaganza. At one time, according to rumor, the base commander had put a sign on the door: "Officers leave your rank outside . . . wives have none." The general's wife saw it the first day. The next day the sign left the base and the next week the base commander did.

Inside it was dark, had what used to be carpeting on the floor, and the stale cigarette smoke from the night before still hung heavily around the light fixtures. However, one could immediately sense a feeling of informality and homogeneity. Sort of like a fraternity that doesn't have much of a physical plant. There had to be something to keep it going. Everyone seemed to care more, maybe because they couldn't care less?

To Glutz it was a big deal because it was exclusive. To him it had stature and gave him status. He had never belonged to a private club before and perhaps he never would again. Major Ralston had told him that there were plans in the making and that this club was temporary. Glutz didn't know about the plans, but he believed the "temporary" part. If someone didn't do something soon, it would come down by itself. Glutz went through the cafeteria line with Major Ralston and met a few fairly high ranking officers, none of whose names he remembered but he'd meet them all many times again. He was impressed with how nice they were to him.

On the way back to the office, Glutz was very inquisitive. He wanted to know something of what he was going to be doing in his new job. The good major was really quite vague. Glutz didn't know it then but it was because he, himself, didn't really know.

That afternoon Ralston took Glutz off base and downtown with him. He had some errands to run at one of the TV stations and figured it a good opportunity to have Glutz meet some of the personalities he'd be dealing with. Walking down the street, Glutz was a very docile, obedient servant to what he had learned in ROTC. Walk always one step to the rear of a senior officer, he remembered. However, to Major Ralston, who had never been in ROTC, it was all very confusing. Looking back over his shoulder to talk to Glutz as he walked was difficult enough, but every time they turned a corner or changed direction, Glutz was gone, having moved to the other side of the major.

"What the hell are you doing back there?" Ralston finally asked. "Get up here where I can see you; you're making me nervous."

"Yes sir!" said Glutz, and, then he told the major about his ROTC training. Ralston just shook his head. He knew he had a greenhorn on his hands, but this was turning out to be more than even he bargained for. From somewhere he remembered hearing or seeing the acclaim, "When better officers are made, ROTC will make them." *Into what?* he thought to himself.

Back at the base, it was just 3:00 P.M. and already getting dark. Glutz wasn't used to this, but he found it somewhat relaxing. *You can withdraw here, with the shadows,* he thought. At 5:10 P.M. he walked into the officers' club. Paulie Plopp was already there.

"Where ya been," Glutz heard before he saw Plopp's hairy form, sprawled out on a chair next to a table.

"Let's have a drink," said Glutz, ignoring Plopp's query.

"Can't," answered Plopp, "got to have a coat on in here after 5:00 P.M."

"Why?" asked Glutz, "is that the time they turn on the air conditioning?" His self-induced laughter at his own joke hardly let him finish it. Plopp didn't think it was so funny, though, or at least wouldn't admit it. His lips seemed to extend almost from ear to ear, up or down, to smile or frown, one at a time or together. Both up meant approval, both down meant disapproval, one up meant a reserved query. Right now, both were down.

"Let's get going," he said, leaning back in his chair and then whipping his torso forward to snap himself into a standing position without taking his hands from his pockets.

"Where to?" asked Glutz.

"To get dressed for dinner," Plopp responded. "Oh, you want to come back here to eat?"

"Hell no, the prices are too high in here and besides, you have to wear a coat after 5:00 P.M., remember?" Plopp snorted.

"Then, where are we gonna eat?" Glutz wondered again.

"At the slop chute, where else?" said Paulie, getting disturbed at Glutz's incessant questioning patter.

"You don't have to change clothes to eat there," demanded Glutz.

"I know that," answered Plopp, "but you do have to leave here to eat there. Besides that, I may want to change belts," and then anticipating Glutz's next question, he added, "to contemplate my navel [belly-button for sailors and others who can't spell] while sitting on the throne [commode for those not used to king's talk]. Who knows, I may even decide to defuzz it. That is if we have time, of course."

"Coats, belts, navels . . . this guy is really . . ."

"What?" asked Plopp, turning to face Glutz and at the same time opening the door into the face of one Captain Quaschwrinkle of whom we'll hear more later. "Sorry, sir," apologized Plopp, snapping to a tardy attention.

"M-m-m," heaved the captain as he stumbled by, looking nowhere but straight ahead.

"Is he drunk?" asked Glutz, of anyone or no one.

A young officer just entering the club saw and overheard. "Naw, he always looks that way. It's sort of a defense mechanism."

"What?"

"Yeah. An hour from now he will be drunk and he'll look the same way, so nobody will notice it until he gets up to walk. Then, he usually goes down on his knees."

"How does he get home?" wondered Glutz, evincing both interest and amazement.

"The jolt when his knees hit the deck seems to revive him enough to make it out. Whether he gets home or not I don't know, but I presume so 'cuz he's always at work on time."

"And he's a captain in our U.S. Air Force," mused Glutz, still too new to the blue to have tarnished his respect for both uniform and rank. "And there are lots more like that all over the air force," offered Glutz's new friend.

"Where do they come from?" Glutz wondered.

"Don't know for sure. Some say they came out from under rocks when the glaciers passed through here hundreds of thousands of years ago."

"Can't the air force get rid of them?"

"Oh sure, they do, but you see, like most parasites they multiply and so we get a new batch every spring with the thaw."

"Do any of them ever get promoted to major?" wondered Glutz.

"Don't think so. I've never seen one of 'em with oak leaf clusters on. Funny thing, too. Most bugs thrive on leaves." Glutz was too intense to get the small pun, but Paulie Plopp got it and his lips turned down.

The conversation ended and Plopp and Glutz ambled down the street toward the slop chute.

"Funny thing about bugs," offered Glutz, "they usually die off in the winter."

"Bugs don't have officers' clubs," was Plopp's only comment.

"Let's take a run into the BOQ," Glutz suggested as they approached the slop chute across the street.

"Go ahead, I'll wait for you there." Plopp had been the one who wanted to change clothes, but now it was Glutz who ran off to the BOQ to pick his nose, clean his toes, brush his teeth, read the "sheet," and grunt.

Meanwhile, Plopp had entered the mess hall (we must be more erudite with our terms) with every intention of holding out until Glutz arrived. However, the aroma soon melted his willpower and replaced his intentions with salivation and so by some stroke of magic Plopp found himself in line. He wished he had a better sense of smell so he would know what was being offered. "On the menu" didn't apply because there was none. Vision didn't help because, as usual, all delicacies were covered by an opaque sauce which showed only their form and this, Plopp had learned, meant nothing. Pork chops sometimes took on the appearance of chicken and chicken sometimes looked like meatballs, under cover. One always had to be wary of meatballs because rumor had it that they were vulcanized at the local tire shop and then heated by acetelyne torch before being brought on base. An attempt to swallow part of one could cause, the rumor went on, the addition of another string to one's vocal chords which would echo one's words before they escaped the larnyx casting them back into one's stomach. The net effect of this would be to render the victim mute except for a continuous rumbling in the stomach which would be deciphered only by putting one's ear to the abdomen. This, at best, would be inconvenient; for what air force officer would care to unbutton his shirt and rip his undershirt from the safe confines of his nattily pressed pants, just to shout, "Yes sir!" And then rely on the senior officer's ear being placed to the abdomen to hear it?

Anyway, Plopp didn't want to take a chance. He watched for any evidence of movement under the liquid cover and then carefully selected one "item" from each tray. If one turned out to be edible he could always come back for seconds. Plopp remembered being impressed, when he first came to the air force, with the thought of being able to go back for more food. Now he knew why more was available. Legend had it that no one had ever gone back for more, but Glutz would one day break that legend by eating seven steaks.

Plopp was into his dessert when Glutz finally walked into the hall. His mind had wandered while eating and he was surprised to look down and see his plate empty. He looked around for filchers but he was alone at the table. *Anyway, a person would have to be insane to steal any of this stuff,* he thought. He looked around the room and then realized it would be a possibility.

"How's the food?" was Glutz's first question.

"I dunno."

"What's to eat?" he said, again ignoring Plopp's first response.

"Dunno." Plopp repeated. And then it struck Glutz.

"You don't know how it tasted or even what you had?"

"The food's over there," apologized Plopp pointing to the steam table.

"I can see that," said Glutz. And then over his shoulder as he walked toward the chow, "Thanks for waiting for me."

"I will," responded Plopp.

Glutz stopped short, reflected, and then continued on. *It's not worth it,* he said to himself. *I'd probably never understand it anyway.*

Paulie Plopp was intent all the while Glutz ate. He stared at each morsel in anticipation as Glutz uncovered it from its camouflage. His reasoning was simple. He wanted to know what he had eaten. When Glutz was done, the two ambled out the front door into the Alaskan fresh air. Glutz filled his lungs with gusto and on the exhalation asked Plopp what he suggested for the evening's entertainment. Plopp, hands in pockets, rolled a toothpick from side to side of his wide mouth and said, in his unaffected Hoosier drawl, "Let's git it on" (you'll have to figure that one out for yourself; the author's moral code won't allow it).

"Get it on?" Glutz sputtered, choking on his own laughter. "Get it on here? With what . . . I mean, whom?"

"The guy in the room next to mine in the transient BOQ had it on with a fat WAF [women's air force] captain last night," said Plopp, apparently somewhat hurt by Glutz's chide.

"How do you know?" retorted Glutz in disbelief but with interest.

"Because the bed kept hitting the wall and I couldn't get to sleep."

"I mean how did you know she was a captain?" countered Glutz.

"Because he's a lieutenant and he kept calling her sir!"

"But how do you know she was fat?" Glutz persisted.

"I heard her hit the floor."

"Maybe it was her purse that hit the floor."

"Naw. Her purse hit the floor first," Plopp insisted.

"Maybe he hit the floor."

"Naw," said Plopp, equally persistent, "I saw him go into the room and he was a different size and shape than a purse."

"Let's go find her," suggested Glutz.

"I haven't been here that long," Plopp answered.

"And I never will be," added Glutz and then he paused to finish with, "I hope." Our two young debonair officers walked off to the base theater to see a movie.

Afterwards, they found their way to the officers' mess for a nightcap and by that time of night, it was. They sashayed up to the bar and sidled onto stools. Over in the corner Glutz spotted Captain Quaschwrinkle sitting by himself, staring off into space, a half empty glass in front of him and an overhead light outlining his features in a yellow pallor.

"Look," said Glutz, "he looks suitable for an ad for the local mortuary."

"Naw," said Plopp, "he's pale enough but too yellow, his eyes are half open, and he looks too stupid to be dead."

"I guess you're right, Paulie; maybe we could get the fat WAF captain for him," offered Glutz considerately.

"Look at him. What would he do with her?" disagreed Plopp.

"He wouldn't have to call her sir," said Glutz in defense of his original suggestion.

"Guess you've got a point there," admitted Plopp. Just at that moment, as had been foretold, the captain went to his knees.

As also predicted earlier in the evening, the sudden jar startled the good captain and he was soon seen pushing himself off one knee to his feet after having first placed one foot solidly on the floor. He looked for a moment, Glutz thought, like a player in the front row of a high school basketball picture. The ridiculous comparison made Glutz smile. Gradually, Captain Quaschwrinkle headed for the door; slowly, at first, and then with increasing confidence as he reached the exit.

Watching him passing under a light, Glutz exclaimed, "My God, Paulie, that guy was right. The captain doesn't look or walk any differently than he did on the way in and that was five hours ago."

Plopp looked but he wasn't impressed. He wasn't the student of humanity that Glutz was. The captain passed out the door (no pun intended) with effortless motion. He had obviously been there before. *I wonder if or how he does get home,* Glutz thought. The boys drank up and were logy. Not really drunk, they felt waterlogged from all the liquid and the smoke and flat air that contributed to their dissatisfied feeling.

"Let's go," offered Plopp.

"Go where?" wondered Glutz.

"I don't care, anywhere. To the BOQ if nothing else."

"Aw, there must be something better to do than that," Glutz pleaded.

"You name it," Plopp snapped back. Glutz thought for awhile and then finally conceded.

"OK. Back to the BOQ it is."

The next morning Paulie got his orders and inside of two hours he was off to Lapp Air Force Base. *I wonder what he'll do?* Glutz thought. *Who cares,* said the little voice from the back of his mind. *IT ALL COUNTS TOWARD TWENTY.*

Paulie Plopp hadn't even had a chance to see Jerry Glutz that last morning; or at least he hadn't taken the time to see him. He did call from the air terminal, though, and Glutz wished him Godspeed. Two years later they'd meet again, for a short time, under most interesting and unusual circumstances. As Glutz put the phone down and walked back to his desk he wondered why Plopp hadn't bothered to stop off at the office on the way to the terminal. After all, his plane wasn't scheduled to leave until 1100 hours. *Maybe he stayed up late with that WAF captain,* Glutz smiled to himself.

CHAPTER VI

"Sir . . . sir, the major said to be sure to read these in his absence."

Major Ralston had made a short trip to "the states" for a little "I and I" (that stands for rest and recuperation, and if you wonder why it isn't "R and R," you'll have to ask a former serviceman; the author's moral code won't allow its revelation), and there at the door of Lieutenant Glutz's office was Sgt. Al Lorein (the author chooses names so that readers can't be certain they are pronouncing them properly) chirping, as usual, like a squirrel. Al was a nice guy, one of the best typists on base, but Glutz had always felt that typing was for girls, not squirrels, even though he did some of it himself. Besides, Al has just won himself another stripe for re-upping (signing up for another four years) and so he held his arms akimbo most all of the time. In addition to wanting others to see his new stripe, he wanted to be able to see all four at the same time. Sometimes he changed his position, like now when his arms were full of papers. But for the most part he held fast. This position, with hands on hips and elbows out, made Al appear something like a bird. But, it gave the office some appeal and notoriety. Just think, an air force PR office with an airman who looked like a bird and talked like a squirrel. And, as if that weren't enough, he was the fastest typist on the base. Some said the department secretary was jealous but there was never any proof. It was true that she'd stick out her tongue, hiss, and spit at his shoes as he walked by but she always insisted that was simply the result of a post-nasal drip which became acute at certain times—like when Al passed her.

"Come in, come in," greeted Glutz tenderly. "What have we here?"

"I'm not sure, sir," chirped Sergeant Squirrel, er . . . Lorein.

"Didn't the major say?" continued Lieutenant Glutz.

"He wasn't sure either, sir, that's why he wanted you to look at them."

"Where did he get them?"

"I'm not sure, sir," the sergeant went on.

"Well, didn't he give you any indication?"

"He wasn't . . ."

"Yeah," Glutz interrupted, "I know, he wasn't sure, either."

"That's right, sir," Sergeant Lorein smiled. Having handed over the material, he snapped to attention, arms stiffly down, obviously proud that he had gotten his message across so clearly.

Lieutenant Glutz spread the papers out into several piles on his desk. He scanned them carefully for some clue as to their origin. Here was one, an invitation for the general to attend a ball in Sacramento, honoring the governor. *Boy, I'd better get that to him in a hurry.* He looked at the date and shrieked inwardly, *It's tomorrow!* And, then he looked at the year . . . *two years ago,* he deflated. Just then Glutz heard a soft noise as of someone clearing his throat. At first it attacked only his subconscious but then it came again, and the third time brought it to reality. Glutz looked up into the reddened face of Sgt. Al Lorein.

"Are you still there? What do you want, Lorein?" Glutz said, somewhat perplexed.

"I haven't been dismissed yet, sir," said the sergeant.

"You haven't been dismissed yet? Oh, you haven't been dismissed yet! Okay, you're dismissed," commanded Glutz somewhat jerkily. Sergeant Al, as he was referred to, turned on his heel and walked away.

Jeez, thought Glutz (if someone can think that), *I wonder where, his tree is. Sure hope everybody around here isn't like that. They surely aren't on the flight line.*

Continuing his preoccupation with the work at hand, Jerry Glutz soon came to the realization that what he had was a whole mess of stuff from Major Ralston's in basket, apparently removed periodically, without having been sorted to make room for more. There was an invitation to submit an application to the downtown queen contest for the previous summer. *How about our "hysterical biddy,"* I mean historian, Glutz thought. Oh well, it was too late now. There was other evidence of the past including letters of inquiry from several different newspapers in the Midwest. One correspondent had submitted a request to visit the

Yukon Air Force headquarters and his picture was beginning to curl up. *I don't blame you,* thought Glutz. *I'd curl up too after 18 months of being ignored. But it's hard to assume the fetal position or even suck one's thumb with only head and shoulders.* The rest of what Glutz saw before him was more of the same; outdated, obsolete. When Glutz had finally convinced himself that nothing was current, he cast the piles, one at a time, into his circular file. So far, that was the only file of his that had anything in it. Sometimes in the air force, it is referred to as "file thirteen." Major Ralston had another name for it.

Glutz had just dumped the last pile when a friendly voice penetrated the atmosphere.

"You catch on fast."

Glutz looked up. "Oh, hi Ralph." He was looking at the smiling face of Ralph Moroney, the senior sergeant on the ISO staff. Glutz had been told about sergeants from friends who had been in the army; particularly tech and master sergeants. They were the ones to know. They were con artists who could get anything anyone wanted, for a price, he had been told. Maybe so. Jerry Glutz never found out. Ralph Moroney was just a nice guy and a helluva fine writer. He was bald, short, stocky, smoked short, unfiltered cigarettes, and had a smile on his face and a chuckle in his voice most of the time.

"Want to go over to the fieldhouse for lunch, lieutenant?" Ralph said.

"To do what? Eat basketballs?" Glutz was a self-fashioned comedian, or so he thought. But, Sergeant Moroney ignored the jibe.

"It's a real nice facility they've got over there," Moroney went on. "We could shoot a few baskets and then hit the steam room."

"OK," said Glutz and the two sauntered off.

"Where're you two going?" Glutz turned around to stare into the blank face of the department secretary.

"What the . . . , we're going over to the fieldhouse, Glorie, be back in about an hour."

"What is it with her?" Glutz asked of Sergeant Moroney as the two turned the corner out of earshot.

"Oh, she's all right. Sort of a super sleuth. Wants to know where everyone is all the time. You'll get used to it."

"I suppose," answered Glutz, but he wondered about that.

At the fieldhouse, things were not busy. The buildings were immense and had absolutely every facility, but there were not many on hand. Glutz and Ralph climbed into their togs for a bit of basketball.

"Not many on hand today," offered Glutz.

"Most of the personnel on base probably don't know you're here yet," kidded Ralph.

Glutz laughed and the two hit the court. Neither was in much semblance of shape so the encounter didn't last long. The steam room and shower tasted good as did the cup of hot soup which followed. The walk back to the office was an enjoyable one and Glutz liked the opportunity to get to know Ralph better. He was an interesting guy, Sgt. Ralph Moroney. He had been in every branch of the service except the navy and, after hearing him talk, it made Glutz wonder if that would be next. At one time, Ralph had been a flier. Later, he served with the coast guard and was also a sergeant in the army. Unlike the legendary "heros" who reenter service life because they can't make it on the outside, Ralph frankly admitted that it would take a periodic few years away from the military to be able for him to appreciate it once again; and even then, he'd choose a different service. The fact that he had been able to hold and advance in rank served notice that he wasn't a flop.

"It's about time you guys are back," said Glorie cheerily.

Glutz's ears went red until he heard Sergeant Moroney say, "Thanks for being so concerned about us, deary."

There's something to learn from that man, Glutz thought to himself. Little did he realize how much.

That afternoon, Jerry Glutz got his first taste of boredom. There was nothing to do and he didn't know enough about the job yet to initiate anything of value. He hadn't learned that value was not a criterion of efficiency but initiation was. Time dragged on until 5:00 P.M. when he turned in his chair and marched properly from the office. Halfway down the hall he realized that all other officers were carrying bulky, zippered, leatherette pouches under an arm. He felt conspicuous and so turned on his heel, back to the office. Here he, too, had a pouch but alas, except for his swagger stick, it was empty. Quickly and efficiently, he scrounged around the area for something— anything—to fill it. On the desk he found the morning paper; from the magazine rack he took several magazines. *I'll return them tomorrow,* he thought, not realizing that they were already several months outdated. He had bulk now but he still needed unshaped shape.

"Oh," he exclaimed with satisfaction as he spotted Airman Fengrew's lunch bag in the wastebasket, his half eaten lunch still in it, "That'll do nicely."

Proudly, Glutz stalked into the hall, now the equal, in his mind, of any officer in the building. But alas, all other officers had departed and Glutz had the halls to himself.

"Rats," he muttered to himself. But no matter, tomorrow would be another day and he would be prepared, then. *Lyman's lunch will never make it, though. I'll have to work out something else. Oh well, I'll worry about that when the time comes.* He went back to the office once more, this time to drop his missile in the seat of his chair. Undismayed, our intrepid warrior sauntered off to the officers' club.

There wasn't much activity at the club. Glutz sidled onto a bar stool and hung there. The first scotch tasted good; cleared that Yukon dust out of his throat. The second was okay but then it struck. That afternoon Glutz had, for the first time, known boredom. Now, later the same day, he was lonely.

"I wonder if this is how Captain Quaschwrinkle got started," Glutz said, almost aloud.

The thought was timely for there, drifting across the floor in zombie-like fashion was old "Captain Quasch" himself. In a moment a drink was before him which Glutz hadn't even seen placed. *I wonder if . . .* but he dismissed the thought. Surely there were no clairvoyants here. Glutz thought it would be fun to see what made "Ol' Cap" tick, besides his heart, if that, so he ambled over to his table and stood beside him.

"I'm Jerry Glutz, new on the base. May I join you?"

"Mmrrp," said the captain in return, looking neither right nor left, up or down. Glutz took a chair.

"Been here long, captain?" he said.

"Frmrp," the captain responded.

"Me too," said Jerry, thinking that the captain may have made a statement. "The Yukon is sure an interesting place, isn't it? Just think, snow, rain, thousands of miles from anyplace and yet it's a civilization, cultivated almost entirely by air travel." Glutz was justifiably proud of his erudite statement. The captain just said, "grfrmp" (not even with a capital letter). Glutz went on. "I wonder what the mountains are like around here, under all that snow?"

The captain turned rigidly in his seat and glowered at Glutz, looking him fiercely in the eye. "Look kid, I'm not interested in all your idle prattle so pack up your ass and move it out of here."

Glutz was terrified. He was looking into a pair of yellow, bloodshot eyes, the depth of which seemed endless and empty. He felt a cold chill run up his spine and his skin crawl. Needing no elaboration, he did as the captain suggested and didn't stop 'til out on the street he inhaled a full measure of fresh air. Actually, Glutz would find out, the captain wasn't such a bad guy. He just didn't like being sober and he hadn't had time to get drunk yet and Glutz was wearing on his nerves—what there was left of them.

Jerry Glutz counted the change in his pocket and headed for the slop chute.

"It may not be the best but I can afford it, at least. And he was right. It wasn't the best and he could afford it. Glutz sat by himself in the mess hall. He eyed the people around him and noted they were a heterogeneous lot. Some civilians, some Red Cross workers, and a few air force officers. One was Chuck Mallbins, a captain who, it turned out, had been a bomber pilot during the war and, after being shot down and rescued, was unable to fly but had stayed on in an administrative role. Across from him was a rather handsome man of 45 or so, chatting cheerily with two fair maidens of slightly less vintage. They both looked like hat check girls from the Last Supper, but for this part of the Yukon that was decidedly above average.

The gent was Larry Witherspoon, a civilian employee of the air force who was a lieutenant colonel in the army reserve, except he wasn't. He had a son at West Point, except he didn't, and a daughter at an eastern school except there was none. In short, Larry was a chronic liar. Aside from that, the only thing he really was, was president of the local chapter of the ROA (reserve officers association), even though he had never risen above the rank of corporal and had been quickly discharged for an acute condition of gastric ulcers. He had a lieutenant colonel's uniform in his closet but never wore it. One day soon he would take his own life when things closed in on him regarding misappropriation of money and government property. But for now he looked harmless enough.

There were others around the room but in comparison to Witherspoon, they were unspectacular. Before passing over everyone though, one should make note of the base veterinarian. No one, least of all he, knew exactly what his job was. Someone said something about food inspection but that didn't seem to fit. Rumor had it that he had been on his way to help Santa care for his reindeer when he was accidently shot down over the air force base. Anyway, the only flying horse on base was at the filling station and that didn't look like it was going anywhere.

Glutz didn't know what fascinating backgrounds lay with the people in the room but someday he would know more. He rose to make his exit and arrived at the door simultaneously with Captain Mallbins.

"Excuse me, sir," Glutz apologized.

"No problem," Mallbins said and the two chatted amicably as they walked across the street. The captain invited Glutz to his room for some TV and talk. Glutz breathed a sigh of relief, for the thought of a night alone in his room was almost more than he could take, and he wasn't up to a potential confrontation with Captain Quashwrinkle at the club. Captain Mallbins was a nice guy and his TV a welcome diversion. He was quiet and unassuming, and he and Glutz became fast friends; they never fraternized on the social circuit because Chuck Malbins was married with a family in "the states" but they spent many a relaxing hour chatting during the next year or two.

Bed came early and sleep fast to Glutz that night, but it was no easier to get up in the morning and, for the first of a hundred or more times, Jerry Glutz came late to work. *How can I get up to go to no job,* he rationalized, and his weary mind bought it. The day turned out promising, however, when a wire came in that the brother of an air force general, affiliated with a national publication, would be arriving on the scene the next day and wanted to tour the Yukon. The ISO from command headquarters had gotten the message and belched it up to the Ralston-Glutz office. Ralph Moroney had seen the charge coming and, fearing a fatal scene for the inexperienced Jerry Glutz, had made the interception.

The command ISO looked less like an air force officer than Foo-Foo the sheep dog. He acted less like one, too. One wonders how he achieved his rank. Actually, he was normally harmless enough unless something needed doing. Fortunately, he had a most efficient senior master sergeant, a major in the reserve, who probably did most of the work.

Colonel Fliptop always had a bounteous array of fresh fruit which he would offer to anyone in sight when he got nervous.

Where the fruit came from in the Yukon, where they grew nothing but snow and ice, no one knew. But there it was. Later Glutz developed a facility to visit the colonel with a nervous look and harried inflection. This never failed to bring forth an apple or an orange or a banana which Glutz devoured appreciatively. Once, trouble arrived before Glutz and the colonel was seen offering a tangerine to the wall as Glutz arrived.

Moroney put the telgram on Glutz's desk.

"Looks like Fliptop has lost his grip again," he said.

"Why?" wondered Glutz.

"Look at his note in the corner of the telegram."

"I can't read it," Glutz exclaimed.

"That's what I mean," said Raph. "Each time there's a trauma, 'Shaky' panics. Then his writing looks like so many disassociated tracings on an electrocardiogram chart."

"Maybe I'd better go down to see him." Glutz sounded concerned.

"Naw, not now. Take a look at the TWX [telegram for those who can't spell or pronounce TWX] and then we'll call the message center to see if there's any more information. You can go down this afternoon after we find the solution to the problem. By that time his blood pressure will be back to normal and he'll be very receptive to whatever you have to tell him, providing he doesn't have to do anything."

For once Ralph Moroney was wrong. If Glutz had gone to see Colonel Fliptop then, he could have earned an apple, an orange, or banana; maybe even had his choice. Oh well, tomorrow was another day and, as it turned out, he'd get one then.

The message was very clear. Mr. Gilhooley would arrive the next morning at 0730 and wanted arrangements made for a tour of the Yukon via military aircraft. The problem started to formulate in Glutz's mind. *How do I pick him up? I don't have a car,* he thought. Sergeant Moroney must have heard his mind because he had the answer.

"Call the motor pool," he said.

"What should I call it?" Glutz grinned to himself, but then realized this was far too serious for sport.

"Yes sir," said the airman at the other end of the line. "We'll have a car at your BOQ at 0730 hours sharp."

"Good," Glutz retorted. "I'll be looking for it."

The phone was half to the receiver when Glutz noted that a noise was still coming through it from the other end. He returned the receiver to his ear just in time to hear it click. With a shake of the head he returned the instrument to its cradle and then began to walk off. Glutz had measured at least two paces until the phone started to ring again. He returned to the stand and once again raised the receiver. It was the airman from the motor pool.

"Will that pick-up be this evening or tomorrow morning?" he asked.

"I said 0730 hours," Glutz responded.

"Yes sir, I know, sir," said the airman in a nervous fast tense, "but tonight or tomorrow morning?" Glutz lifted the receiver and stared into the earphone, incredulous. He was no great master of air force terminology, but he knew that 0730 had been distinguished from 1930 so that one could clearly be identified as morning time and the other evening.

"What's your rank, airman?" Glutz said, more out of wonder than irritation.

"I'm a slick sleeve, sir," came back the voice from the other end of the line.

"A what?" Glutz asked again.

"I don't have any rank, sir."

"You don't have any rank? Everybody has rank in this air force." Glutz was building up steam and fast beginning to sound like the stereotyped authoritarian officer he had probably once imagined himself.

"No sir," the airman continued. "I'm just a basic airman."

"How long you been in the service, boy?" Now he found himself assuming the vocal role of a Kentucky colonel.

"Three years," the airman replied smartly.

"Oh-h-h-h," said Glutz, his air gone (demeanor, not lung capacity) and the wind gone out of his sails, (that's lung air) as well. An airman with three years who was still, or again, a slick sleeve. Glutz's steel trap mind had already picked up what that meant. *I wonder what the odds are that someone'll be over at 0730 to get me?*

That thought worried Glutz all evening. He went home to a light repast (tuna out of the can with crackers and water for a wash—don't knock it if you haven't tried it. You may not want to try it, either, but don't knock it) and went to bed early. Sleep didn't come readily so he rolled and tossed for a couple of hours and finally dropped off. He planned on setting his "automatic mental alarm" to 0700 but it didn't go off.

At 0715 a brisk knock came at the door. Glutz woke out of a deep sleep in which he had been involved for only a couple of hours. He lurched when his watch told him it was 7:15.

"Who is it?" he said sharply but with only inquisitive concern.

"Motor pool, sir, your car's ready," came the voice from the other side of the door.

"My car was due at 0730," Glutz reminded him.

"Yes sir, but that's the time the gentlemen gets in, so it wouldn't do to pick you up then."

"How did you . . ." but the airman interrupted, "I called the air terminal to check the flight time, sir. The manifest at the motor pool showed your destination and purpose so it was easy to check the times." Glutz didn't believe it. This couldn't be that slick sleeve.

"Come on in," Glutz shouted through the door. He wanted to see what he couldn't believe.

"No, sir. I'll wait in the car."

Glutz was already stuffing in his shirt. A couple of pats of water, brush teeth, a quick shave . . . er, sort of a shave, and he was off.

Once outside, Glutz began to lope around the car. Hardly before a step was taken, however, the airman methodically reached for the door behind him, swung it open, and braced it there. Glutz got the message and climbed in.

"How is it you're so efficient?" Glutz wondered sincerely.

"Just doing my job sir," replied the airman. Then glanced at the rear view mirror and said calmly, "You don't have a tie on, sir."

Glutz reached to his throat as a conditioned reflex and, sure enough, he didn't have a tie on. By this time they were at least three blocks from the BOQ and it was 7:28.

"My God, we've got to go back," Glutz muttered in horror. But the airman calmly reached for the glove compartment, dropped it open and pulled out a neatly folded tie.

"Here, this ought to do it, sir," the airman told Glutz. Glutz put the tie on quickly, asking no more questions, and hurried into the terminal as the plane carrying Mr. Gilhooley rolled to a stop on the other side of it. Glutz looked alert and as if he had been waiting there for at least an hour when Gilhooley emerged. The writer was a tall man with silver locks and a salt and pepper mustache. He looked a bit like what Glutz expected of a British diplomat, but there was an obvious sour look on his face and his expensive looking suit gave the appearance of having been slept in, which it probably had.

It was obvious to Glutz, from his appearance and apparent command of the situation, that this must be Gilhooley. Glutz rushed to his side and, moving somewhat against the tide of the traffic, began to introduce himself. "Mr. Gilhooley, I'm Lieutenant Glutz." Mr. Gilhooley looked at Glutz, appearing even as if he had just taken a fresh lime in his mouth and answered very politely and very British.

"Young man, I don't doubt that you are lieutenant whoever you are, but you must be equally certain that my name is Grimes, not Gilhooley, and I doubt very seriously that you are here to meet me as I am on my way to London, not Dublin, after having been imprisoned in the Orient for nearly thirty years."

Glutz did feel stupid but even more he felt perplexed. *If that guy is who he said he was, then where the hell is what's his name?* Glutz thought in very organized fashion. He looked around the terminal and didn't know what to do. Then like a flash from on high, he remembered the PA system at McCloud. "Lieutenant Glutz, AO999 . . ." He couldn't stand it. He must wash that from his mind forever. Nonetheless, he did want to know about a page so he stepped rather rapidly over to the information desk. It was manned by a civilian who, from the back, looked very much like the man at McCloud. Glutz could judge that only from the back because for a long time that's all he saw. Glutz shuffled his feet and cleared his throat but the stalwart inside paid no heed.

Finally Glutz said, "Excuse me!" Slowly the inhabitant turned toward the lieutenant.

"What'd ya do, fart?" To Glutz that wasn't very funny at the moment.

"I'd like to know," he said, "if you could page an incoming passenger for me."

"Could in a few minutes," said the gentleman "but by that time they'll all be gone except someone who's waiting around for somebody to come get him. Why don't you just stick around for a few minutes and see who's left.

"Thanks a lot," said Glutz sarcastically as he marched off.

"You're welcome," answered the clerk with no sign of affection nor enthusiasm.

"Glutz did get a clue, though, from Mr. Lazy. He looked around the terminal and saw that the crowd had pretty well thinned out. But there was no one who resembled a general's brother. The only man who seemed alone was wearing a pair of blue baggy pants, showing forth from beneath a newspaper. *It couldn't be,* said one of Glutz's silent mind elves. *It must be,* said another. *It might be,* suggested a third. *It's worth a try,* thought Glutz.

Over to the newspaper and legs he walked. Stopping just before them he looked at the shoes and pants. *It can't be,* he heard from within himself again. *Oh well, here goes.*

"Excuse me," Glutz said once again. The man moved the paper to one side, continuing to hold the other side high with his left hand. His face said "why?" but his lips didn't move.

"Are you Mr. Gilhooley?" Glutz offered apologetically.

"I sure as hell am and who might you be?"

"I'm Lieutenant Glutz, here to see you to your quarters and to help you accomplish your purpose in coming to the Yukon."

"Well, it's about time. I thought for awhile I was going to be stranded in this Godforsaken place. My brother's a general, you know."

"Yes sir, I've heard," said Glutz, and all of a sudden he didn't like being in the air force much anymore. But he swallowed hard and went on.

"My bags are over there, lieutenant. Why don't you pick them up and we'll be on our way."

Mr. Gilhooley sounded like he was leading the tour now and Glutz felt like continuing to let him do so. *Let him get outside by himself and he won't even find the car.* Glutz was wrong, though, because Gilhooley did march out of the terminal alone and when Glutz arrived on the scene with the bags, he was already seated in the back seat of the car. The airman, still looking out the front window, was carrying on a lively conversation with his new passenger in back. Glutz began to enter the back seat but was preempted by Mr. Gilhooley.

"You sit in the front seat with the driver, lieutenant. There's not enough room for both of us back here."

Glutz got out and went around to enter the front door which the airman had snapped unlocked for him. Glutz was so seething with animosity toward this newcomer that he could hardly speak. Finally he directed his voice to the airman, "To the BOQ."

His first sign of authority for the day made him feel better. Mr. Gilhooley said nothing.

By the time the "cab" arrived in front of the BOQ, Glutz had mellowed and was half out of the door after the bags in the trunk when the car stopped.

"I'll get the bags, lieutenant," said the airman, saving, yet losing, the day once again for Glutz. Inside the BOQ, Gilhooley knew his way around better than anyone except possibly the airman. While his room was being checked in, he turned to Glutz.

"You can take the day off, lieutenant. I've been enroute a long time and want to get cleaned up, catch some sleep, and put together some additional thoughts on my last stop. I'll see you back here for dinner at 5:00."

Glutz was stunned by this affront to his personal pride and then surprised to hear himself respond, weakly, "I don't get off until 5:00."

"Then make it 5:15."

"Yes sir, I'll see you then."

The two air force personnel exited the BOQ together.

"Oh, and thanks, lieutenant, and you too airman," Gilhooley shouted after them with perfect military protocol.

"Don't look so grim, lieutenant," said the airman. "He's not the worst of a generally bad lot. They've got a tough and tiring job. And, don't think they don't get the same thing and worse from their own editors."

"I suppose so," offered Glutz, cooled somewhat by Gilhooley's parting comment.

Jerry Glutz went back to the office and sat at his desk. The phone rang and on the third ring he finally came to his senses enough to answer. The secretary, Gloria Inexcelsis, was already on the phone. Glutz listened for a moment to be sure and then hung up. When her conversation was concluded, Gloria stomped into the office.

"Lieutenant," she said, "in the future I don't want you picking up the phone until I tell you."

With that, she turned on her heel equally abruptly and exited. Glutz stared after her, his mouth open wide enough for ten flies to enter simultaneously—except that it's too cold for flies in the Yukon. He was decidedly irritated, he could tell from several visceral reactions, but he didn't know what to do. A saying from his college days came to mind. "When in danger or in doubt, run in circles, scream and shout." He looked around and quickly induced that the area was not suited to such a release. His best and healthiest alternative was to rationalize. *After all, she is making more money than I am. It's up to the air force to pay me equitably; otherwise, why should I assume responsibility for my authority?*

There wasn't much to do so Glutz read magazines for awhile. He found that boring. He didn't like to read very much because he wasn't a good reader. Or was it that he wasn't a good reader because he didn't read very much? Anyway, he soon rose from his chair, grabbed at the seat of his pants to clear air circulation to his waist (he wore boxer shorts to facilitate this maneuver) and troddled (that's a new word you won't find in your dictionary—a cross between trotted and toddled; make your own mental picture) out of the office. Passing Gloria's desk he turned ninety degrees, bowed from the hip, glared eyeball to eyeball in a bug-eyed fashion and said, "I'm going to Sergeant Moroney's desk," a full fifteen feet away. He turned on his heel and sped off rapidly for fear that her return glare might penetrate his uniform and burn his bare back.

"Ralph, what do you say we step out for a cup of java (that's somebody's word for coffee, or at least it used to be; the editor's not sure whose).

Sgt. Ralph Moroney looked up in agreement. He had been busily at work on his typewriter, doing a story on the Yukon that he hoped to sell to *Outdoor Strife* magazine. This he could forgo for the moment to get out of the office for a stimulating cup of black coffee.

"Let's go down to command headquarters," he suggested to Glutz. "I'd like to have you meet a friend of mine, SMS [senior master sergeant] Sherman Nultz. Sherm's a major in the reserve who should probably be in charge of the Command ISO. He got out after the war and then tried to reenter but couldn't get his commission back."

"Must be a lot like that," suggested Glutz.

"Maybe in history," said Ralph, "but no personality like Sherm's."

Entering the senior master sergeant's lobby-office, the two witnessed Nultz poring over a wide loose leaf binder and taking notes on a pad of paper lying next to it. He looked up to greet Glutz and Moroney with a narrow but friendly smile. Quickly it left his face, and he returned to his present endeavor. Moroney introduced the SMS to Glutz and the former looked up again, shook hands, and returned to his pursuit. Moroney and Nultz conversed for a few moments, but careful observation would have made it immediately clear that Moroney was doing the talking. Nultz moved his gaze from loose leaf to pad and back, making notes as he went and clearly responding to Sergeant Moroney's comments, but with very little amplification. Glutz sat down looking on.

Finally, Ralph Moroney suggested a cup of coffee. Nultz looked up with furrowed brow.

"You two go on ahead," suggested Nultz. "I'll be along in a minute, just as soon as I wrap this up."

Moroney nodded his assent and turned on his heel to leave, followed by Glutz. To the observer, Glutz was now walking one step to the rear of Moroney. *Interesting,* the observer would have to think.

Glutz soon caught up with Ralph, though, and as soon as he did asked, "What's Senior Master Sergeant Nultz doing?"

"Probably nothing," Sergeant Moroney responded in an off-hand manner.

"What do you mean, 'probably nothing'?"

"Just that," continued Moroney, "probably nothing. One of the reasons I think so highly of Nultz is that he has the system beat to perfection. He always looks busy yet he never seems to produce anything tangible. Everybody thinks he's very busy and productive. Even he thinks he's very busy and productive, but he just doesn't ever come up with anything. I'm convinced, in my own mind, that he could do a whale of a job if he ever had one but I'm equally convinced that he's never had one."

"But, what's he taking notes for?" demanded Glutz.

"I'm not sure about that one," said Moroney. "But, I think that he feels reading and writing are part of the job and that's how he satisfies the latter requirement.

"What does he do with the notes?" Glutz was really interested and becoming more insistent.

"I looked into that once 'cuz I was curious, too," retorted Moroney. "He files them in his desk by a system known only to him and then when he goes on to a new assignment he destroys them."

"Doesn't he ever have bull-sessions with the other guys?" Glutz wondered.

"Oh sure, but I can't figure what he's driving at there, either."

Just then SMS Sherman Nultz showed up. "Hi, you guys, ready for coffee?" Seated on his folding chair backwards, Sergeant Ralph Moroney tilted it ahead.

"Sherm," he said intently, "what's with Fliptop?"

"What do you mean?" answered Senior Master Sergeant Nultz innocently.

"I mean how did he ever get to be a colonel and how does he hold his job?"

Nultz looked stunned. "Oh, Colonel Fliptop is a very competent staff man. The general thinks very highly of him."

"Then how come he gets so nervous and functionless whenever there's the least bit of pressure?" snarled Moroney out of the side of his mouth. Nultz came to the colonel's defense immediately.

"You've got to remember, Ralph, that he has a lot of responsibility in his job and is under considerable pressure." Moroney moderately ignored the defense.

"But what does he do?" the sergeant went on. The SMS looked incredulous.

"Why, he's the senior command ISO! You know that, Ralph!"

"Yeah, I know that," Ralph responded, rising to his feet and throwing the paper coffee cup he had just squashed into the basket. "Let's go, lieutenant. Time marches on," he said, quoting a World War II newsreel ending.

"What was all that about?" Glutz wanted to know on the way back to the office.

"I just wanted to know if he knew that Fliptop doesn't have a job, either."

"He doesn't, does he?" offered Glutz matter-of-factly.

"He sure doesn't," Sergeant Moroney agreed.

"Is that how you get to be a senior master sergeant?" asked Glutz, sounding like a little boy asking his father how to become a doctor.

"I don't know, lieutenant. All I know is that he is one."

"I wonder how Fliptop got to be colonel?" Glutz wondered again.

"So do I," said Moroney. "Maybe the general could tell us." The two entered the air command ISO office and drifted in separate directions to their "work" locations.

CHAPTER VII

At 4:55 P.M. (16:55) Lt. Jerome V. Glutz put on his service cap and goose-stepped toward the door. "Good night, lieutenant," Gloria Inexcelsis said as he marched past. Looking over his shoulder he saw her smile between western teeth (the kind with the wide open spaces for those who don't have them—or wish they didn't). He returned the smile and sped on.

"Maybe I should have told her where I'm going, leaving five minutes early and all," Glutz thought. "She might mark it down and tell the major when he comes back."

An airman sat in the car waiting for Glutz when he got to the exit of the command building. Glutz tried to get in the passenger side of the front seat, but the airman slid over to block him out.

"You drive, lieutenant," said the airman.

"And where might you be going?" said Glutz, irritated, melancholy, and apprehensive, all rolled into one.

"To the motor pool, sir," said the airman, with just a hint of a bit more respect for Glutz's rank than he had shown before. "The car's yours for the night. You can bring it back to the motor pool in the morning and get a ride to work from someone there, or you can leave it at your BOQ and we'll pick it up."

"What if Mr. Gilhooley wants it?" Glutz wondered.

"He can't have it," the airman told him. "He's a civilian and this is a government vehicle."

"But his brother's an air force general," Glutz argued.

"Then his brother can have it—but he can't." He noted Glutz's querulous look and continued, "I report to the sergeant at the motor pool, lieutenant, not to Mr. Gilhooley's brother." Glutz understood and the look was gone.

At the motor pool, the airman jumped out and Glutz was on his way again. He didn't relish picking up Gilhooley. The morning had been enough to last Glutz forever. The slop chute would have been a welcome relief tonight. However, as so often happens, the expected turns out to be the unexpected. Glutz pulled up in front of the visitors' BOQ and rolled out of the front seat of the car. He hadn't taken more than two steps when he heard a voice similar to but not the same as that of Vladimar Gilhooley. Glutz looked up to the second floor to see ol' Gilhooley perched on the window sill, leaning toward the ground, saying with the pose and gestures of an operatic soloist (female yet), "My deah, I thought you'd nevah arrahv." The man had a red tam on his head and a pair of loud speckled suspenders. Glutz was still sour over the thought of having to spend an evening with this creep but his viscera began to smile in spite of himself. "Come in, come in, lad," Gilhooley went on. "It's up to room 202 with ye." And then he leaped back into the room from whence he had come, with the agility of a leprechaun.

Glutz dragged himself to the top of the stairs and there was "the leprechaun" to greet him.

"Come in, come in, lieutenant," he said with warm enthusiasm as he ushered Glutz into his room. Gilhooley was lively and talkative, though he dressed in a hurry and was ready to go.

"Where to?" Glutz said, once in the car. He didn't know the base too well as he hadn't been around a whole lot more than Gilhooley, though the latter had arrived that very morning.

"Would you like to go to the officers' club? I can charge . . ."

"No-o-o, wouldn't think of it. This evening's on me, my young friend. Take a boy to camp sort of thing. We must go to the Mantel. I've heard so much about it from my brother."

"Where is that?" wondered Glutz.

"I don't know but we can ask someone," offered Gilhooley. "It's supposed to be reserved just for the top brass."

The Mantel wasn't hard to find. Not because it didn't look the same as every other building on base, because it did. Not because it had any more aesthetically toned surroundings, because it didn't. But because it had a big sign out in front which read "The Mantel." The sign wasn't any different than many of the others on base either, but it was bigger.

Glutz pulled up in the rear of the building and the two men exited from the car. Since there were no signs to indicate an entrance, they entered the first door they saw. An exhaust fan was churning loudly just over their heads and another door just to the left looked anything but posh. The odor of fresh raw potatoes permeated the air. Glutz took three steps up into what turned out to be the kitchen and saw a young man, presumably an airman, peeling potatoes with a paring knife. A quick glance told Glutz that at least half of each potato went into the can, still attached to the peel. The airman was jumpy, like a quail in season, and he looked up in response to Glutz's first footstep on the floor.

"How does one get into the Mantel?" Glutz asked of the airman.

"You're in it," said the airman. Obviously he didn't understand so Glutz searched his mind for another approach.

"Where's the front door?" Glutz asked.

The airman rested his hands on the edge of the tub used for waste, paring knife in one and a half peeled potato in the other. He looked at Glutz quizzically for a moment and then answered, "It's around the front of the building," pointing out the back door with his knife and then waving his arms in a sweeping motion to denote an encompassing of the building. Backing down the steps, Glutz thanked him with a hand motion and then turned to hide an embarrassed look and led Vlad Gilhooley to the front door.

Around the front, the entrance looked like the kitchen door from the outside but once in the door a vast difference was immediately apparent. The floor was carpeted as was the stairway leading directly upstairs. To the left was a bar and behind it and off to the far side a doorway, presumably leading into the dining room. No one, save our two guests, was in sight. Gilhooley stepped to the bar, put one foot on the rail indicating he'd been in a bar before, and tapped the bell. Nothing happened, and after a strained thirty seconds or so, his voice rang out from cupped hands, imitating a hillsman's call through vast expanses from a mountaintop.

"Hallo-o-o," he said mutedly. Then, almost immediately the potato peeler appeared, tying a behind-the-back string of a red bartender's jacket in completion of putting it on. "What'll it be, gentlemen?" he said, completely oblivious to the notion that he had seen them just a few moments before in an entirely different capacity.

They ordered and as he was mixing the drinks, Gilhooley asked with a falsely accented brogue, "Have you a twin young man?"

"Me? No, why?" said the airman.

"Because ye look just like the gent we saw peeling potatoes in the kitchen a few moments ago." The airman smiled although Gilhooley couldn't see it.

"We're a little shorthanded this early," he said. "You'll be seeing more of me before the night's over." With a second drink in hand, Glutz and Gilhooley walked toward the dining room at the latter's suggestion.

"Would you mind seating us, my friend," Gilhooley asked of the bartender, "or is there someone else to do that?"

"No, there's no one else to do that but there's no one else in the dining room either, so you can sit wherever you like." They took a seat near the window, even though the table wasn't stable, and rocked whenever either of them leaned on it. *Reminds me of the tables in the lunchroom at school,* Glutz thought. The tables and decor were consistent, though, he thought, with everything else on base; they all looked alike. *So this is for the big brass. I wonder what they've got for enlisted men.* In many ways he would find out that what they had for the enlisted men was better.

"Now, lieutenant," said Gilhooley, "I want to be sure to get to all parts of this theater. I understand that some of your installations can be reached only by air, so first thing tomorrow, I want you to arrange an itinerary and transportation by military aircraft." Glutz wasn't sure what Mr. Gilhooley meant by itinerary; he didn't know for certain what "this theater" was; and he hadn't the faintest idea how to go about setting up air force transportation or even whether Vladimar Gilhooley would be able or expected to pay for it. But somehow with a few scotches under his belt, those problems didn't seem paramount.

"Don't worry, Mr. Gilhooley," Glutz said confidently. "I'll take care of everything." *That is, Sergeant Moroney and I will take care of everything,* he thought. *Tomorrow is time enough to worry about that,* his thoughts went on. Tonight Glutz was a lieutenant in the air force and whee-e-e, it was fun.

Just then, the waiter came in with menus under his arm, buttoning his jacket, which looked like the kind of starched thing the boys wore behind the lunch counter at New Mexico State. His t-shirt showed at the top as had the bartender's and it looked unmistakably like that worn by the potato peeler. As a matter of fact . . . well you guessed the story by now.

"What'll it be, gentlemen," said the waiter with all the finesse and aplomb of a short order cook, while handing the menus to his only two guests.

"Why don't you get us another drink from the bar while we're making up our minds," Gilhooley suggested. Then he said to the waiter's back, "and you needn't change to your red jacket to mix the drinks."

During the dinner, Glutz made more overtures about how he would manage the affairs of Mr. Gilhooley during the latter's stay in Alaska and see that he got absolutely the finest treatment.

"A man of your stature deserves the best," said Glutz through a third and a fourth scotch and soda, "and, I'm here to see you get it. You know," he went on, "these career men have to watch out that they don't step on any toes but us short-timers don't have to be concerned and I'm not."

Vladimar Gilhooley was quite recessive in the face of this demonstration. *Don't tell me, show me,* he thought, but was too kind to say.

After dinner Glutz was bold and on the upswing, the scotch having paralyzed his cortex, temporarily releasing him from some of his usual inhibitions.

"What do you say we go to the movie at the base theatre or downtown, Mr. Gilhooley," he suggested.

"No, lieutenant, I've got to get a good night's sleep if I'm to be off around the Yukon tomorrow."

"How about a nightcap at the O'Club (officers' club for those who possess no imagination whatsoever) then," he said almost pleadingly. "I'll buy." Glutz had two dollars in his pocket which wouldn't keep him at any bar very long, he knew, but he figured Gilhooley was good for at least a drink or two. That was a disappointment because Gilhooley took him up on the payment offer and then begged leave to retire as soon as he finished. Glutz looked at his empty billfold and followed him out the door. One lousy drink. He felt more like drinking now than before and to top it off, he'd have to borrow lunch money for the rest of the week.

"Tell you what lieutenant. It looked to me like the staircase in the Mantel led right up to the second floor. I'll bet they've got rooms over there nicer than the BOQ and if so, I think I'll stay there. Let's check it out."

So now instead of drinking, which is what Glutz really wanted to do, he would get the chance to haul Gilhooley's suitcases across the base.

"Come over and have breakfast with me in the morning, lieutenant," Gilhooley said as he waved goodnight from the porch of the Mantel.

The hell with you, thought Glutz, jumping in the car and speeding away before Vladimar could name a time. It was almost midnight before a sweating and exhausted Jerry Glutz arrived at his room. He was so uncomfortable from the alcohol and subsequent work that he could hardly jerk off his pants. But do so he did, and cast them onto the bed beside him. The shower felt wonderful; so great in fact, that he stepped from it completely refreshed and not the least bit tired. Glutz turned out the light, jumped into bed, and tried to catch some sleep. But he couldn't do it. He wasn't tired now. Finally he realized it was no use and flipped on the light. *May as well read,* Glutz thought. He looked around the barren room. Even the wallpaper was too plain to stare at. Down in the day room he found a popular magazine which was only nine months old. One of the feature stories was about a girl home for the Christmas holidays and what she did during them. *Oh well,* Glutz thought, *the icy frescoes of Christmas in the North and thoughts of my own Christmas holidays while in college may help me to sleep.* That they did, but not until 2:30. *I wonder what time I'm supposed to call for Gilhooley in the morning,* Glutz thought as he drifted off to dreamland.

At 7:30 there came a sharp knock at the door.

"Lieutenant Glutz in there?" said the voice of the knocker.

"Here," said Glutz, waking from a sound sleep and sounding like a third grader in Miss Primm's class.

"Telephone for you," the voice continued.

Glutz jumped from the sack (that's what the air force calls a bed because it's more accurately descriptive) and hurried into the hall. Crouched like a gorilla about to leap he looked first left and then right.

"Where?" he said, but "the voice" was gone and along with it "the knocker." Glutz heard a buzzing sound and looked down to see a phone off the hook. He picked it up but all he heard was a dial tone. *That must have been Gilhooley,* he thought. *I'd better give him a call and see what he's up to.*

The phone rang twice before a voice from the other end gave an emphatic, "Hello!"

"I'd like to speak to a Mr. Vladimar Gilhooley," said Glutz.

"Is this Glutz? Goddammit, get over here. I expected you here for 7:30 breakfast."

Then why didn't you say so, you dolt, Glutz thought, remembering how he had hurried away to avoid, hearing a time. But he quickly thought better of it and said, "Sorry, Mr. Gilhooley, I didn't realize we had set a definite time."

"Yep, damm right we set a definite time," Gilhooley exploded, "and that time was 7:30. Now get over here or I'll see you get sent back to OCS" (officers' candidate school for those who haven't heard of a "ninety-day wonder").

I'm ROTC, thought Glutz haughtily. But he didn't pursue the issue. He set the phone down with a deliberate bang and immediately began to think of excuses he would use if Gilhooley chewed him out. Naturally, he would just have dropped the phone by accident and Gilhooley would probably believe it, based on what he thought of Glutz at the moment.

Glutz got ready in a hurry and jumped into "his" air force car for the short trip to the Mantel. Walking up the stairs, he was most apprehensive. When he saw Gilhooley sitting in the dining room all by himself, sipping on a tomato juice in a giant glass, it didn't ease the pangs. Glutz put his service cap snugly under his arm and marched over to face the music. Gilhooley looked up with a blank expression and then a smile crept over the ruddy complexion of his face.

"Ah, good morning, lieutenant," he said most pleasantly. "Do have a seat. Won't ya have one of these Bloody Marys with me?"

"That tomato juice?" Glutz asked, to be sure they were both talking about the same thing.

"It's not only tomato juice, me boy," said Vladimar, "but a shot of vodka and a dash of hot sauce with a slice of lemon, as well."

Drink for breakfast? Glutz said to himself silently, *I thought only alcoholics did that.* He glanced at Gilhooley's complexion and decided there was not necessarily a need to change his mind. *And vodka,* his thoughts went on, *no wonder his name is Vladimar,* as if Gilhooley got his name after he started imbibing vodka. Come to think of it, maybe he did. *Oh well,* Glutz's thoughts continued, *Guess I might as well. This day won't get any better and maybe a little vodka will bring the sun out.* And bring the sun out it did. So much so, in fact, that Glutz thought another, after the first, would be even more delightful. That early morning sip made him bold, too; so bold in fact that he didn't mind nudging Gilhooley a bit.

"Aren't you going to have another?" he asked of his correspondent friend.

"No, but you go ahead if you like," Gilhooley said in a rather apathetic tone. So go ahead Glutz did and he soon felt even a little bit better. So good, in fact, that when the ham, toast, and eggs he'd ordered came, he wasn't hungry enough to eat them. Or at least he didn't want to take the time away from his drink. But he had enough of his normal consciousness to know that he couldn't show up as an unschooled lush and so he did nibble away at his breakfast, chancing to take a sip whenever it seemed OK to do so.

Breakfast completed, Mr. Gilhooley threw several bills out from a crumpled handful he had retrieved from his pocket.

"Keep the change," he blustered to the waiter.

"Sorry, sir, we can't accept tips," the airman responded apologetically.

"Then send it to your mother," Gilhooley said without raising his eyes and set out for the exit.

Glutz had been so dazzled by Gilhooley's cordial nature when Glutz had first arrived that he began to think it must have been someone else on the phone earlier. Then, with the help of the bloody marys, he had forgotten the phone call entirely. Now, however, Gilhooley's true personality was coming back and along with it, Glutz's recollection of the phone call. But he had a pretty good buzz on and so he didn't mind Vladimar too much yet.

The air force officer climbed in behind the wheel of the car alongside Gilhooley, who was already slouched into position in the front seat passenger area.

"Where to?" said Glutz ebulliently.

"Where to?" roared Gilhooley. "Where to, indeed?"

Glutz turned his head toward Gilhooley and his lips began to move as if he were about to say something, but there was no chance.

"How the hell should I know where to? You're supposed to tell me where to! I came all the way from the east coast to get locked up with some greenhorn who asks me 'where to'!"

Where to, where to, where to echoed from ear to ear through Glutz's head, made hollow by the impact of the vodka. He burped the tomato juice from the excitement, let out the clutch (an air force car, you know; no air conditioning either) and jerked away. When he realized the next move was up to him, Glutz swallowed hard and recovered quite rapidly.

"Good, Mr. Gilhooley, I'll be happy to set up your tour. Just wanted to know if you had any preconceived idea of where you would like to go, having an air force brother, and all."

Gilhooley didn't answer. He just sat slouched in the car, looking at the tips of shoes between his parted knees and bending his folded hands backward to hear his knuckles crack.

At air command headquarters, Glutz marched into the office area ahead of Gilhooley and invited Vlad to have a seat. Then he hurried out of earshot to run over to Sergeant Moroney's cubicle.

"This guy wants to go on a tour of the whole command area, Ralph. What the hell do I do? I don't even know where the installations are, let alone how to get there."

"Yeah, I know. There's only one road around here and that leads into the sea," injected Ralph sarcastically. "Tell you what. You take him down to 'Shaky' Fliptop. Let the colonel feed him a couple of oranges and a banana. Meantime, I'll set up some sort of travel agenda and when you get back, we'll call the air terminal to see how we can get him around."

"OK," Glutz said over his shoulder, and he was off to retrieve his correspondent. Following a few words of explanation, the two were off in the direction of Lieutenant Fliptop's office.

"Where're you going, lieutenant?" Gloria Inexcelsis wanted to know.

"In your ear, baby" Glutz mumbled, but too softly for anybody to make it out. Gilhooley was close enough to hear something, though.

"What?" he wanted to know.

"I said I hope the colonel's in good cheer, maybe," Glutz answered.

That didn't make much sense to Gilhooley but he wasn't interested enough to care much. Down in Lieutenant Colonel Fliptop's outer office, Glutz deposited Gilhooley again and walked past SMS Sherman Nultz toward Fliptop's main office.

"The colonel in?"

"Yes sir," Nultz responded clearly, while continuing to take notes from a looseleaf binder on his desk. He didn't look up.

As Glutz entered Lieutenant Colonel Fliptop's office, the colonel stood with his back to Glutz, hands behind him, feet apart, in a position approximating "at ease." One hand clasped the other as he moved the latter in and out of the former rhythmically.

"Good morning, sir" Glutz said cheerily from some semblance of the position of attention. Fliptop spun quickly on his heel.

"Have an orange," he said in shock, gesturing with open hand to the bowl on his desk.

"A Mr. Vladimar Gilhooley, brother of the air force general of the same name, is here on a tour of the command," Glutz introduced. "He's a correspondent for an east coast publication."

"Give him an apple," said Fliptop jerkily.

"Major Ralston probably told you about him before he left."

"Left?" shouted Shaky. "Left? I thought you said he was here."

"Mr. Gilhooley is here, colonel," Glutz went on, ignoring Fliptop's fruit.

"Here? I thought you just said he left!" demanded Fliptop further.

"Gilhooley, I mean Major Ralston has left, sir. Mr. Gilhooley is outside," answered Glutz, himself getting a bit unnerved from the confusion.

"Oh. Well bring him in, bring him in, lieutenant. We can't let an honored guest sit out in the anteroom all day, now can we?"

"No sir, we can't," Glutz agreed, turning to go for Gilhooley. *I wonder what an anteroom is,* he thought on the way. *Sounds like a place to make bets for poker.*

Lieutenant Colonel Fliptop seemed quite calm as he pointed out sites of possible interest at various points in the command. Almost all were army or navy installations; only a very few were air force.

"How does one get out there, colonel?" Gilhooley wanted to know.

"That's Lieutenant Glutz's province," Fliptop answered, pointing toward Glutz as to his fruit, with an open handed, palm up gesture.

"I don't think military planes go into any of those places, other than the air force bases, except on a very infrequent and irregular basis, colonel," Glutz said.

"That may be, that may be," Fliptop shot back. "Nonetheless, they are important military places which I think Mr. Gilhooley should know about. Getting him there is your province," he repeated.

It was as apparent to Gilhooley as to Glutz that Fliptop would offer little and time spent with him was essentially time wasted. Fresh fruit was a plus in this part of the country, but one needed only so much vitamin C and once he relaxed, Lieutenant Colonel Fliptop was much less generous with his offerings. Gilhooley was the first to rise from his chair, thank the colonel, and invite the lieutenant to be on their way.

Back in his office, Glutz parked his correspondent once more and returned to Ralph Moroney.

"Here are three places you can send him for starters," Ralph offered, pointing to three different locations on a map laid out on the sergeant's desk. "I'm somewhat familiar with them be-cause I've written stories on the outdoors on all of them so I can brief him while you call the air terminal to see what flights are available."

This sounded great to Glutz, so he returned to Mr. Gilhooley with Sergeant Moroney at his side. Following the usual intro-duction amenities, Moroney and Gilhooley walked toward the sergeant's desk, leaving Glutz to call the air terminal and sched-ule flights.

"Sorry, sir, nothing going out that way for three days."

"Sorry, sir, a flight left for there at 0630 hours this morning. There won't be another scheduled this week, I'm sure."

"Yes, sir, there's one scheduled at 1430 this afternoon, but the weather's uncertain in that vector area so we won't know for cer-tain until later. The flight could be delayed."

It can't be, it just can't be, Glutz thought to himself. *I've just got to get him off somewhere before Major Ralston returns tomor-row.* Unfortunately, the major had given Glutz no orientation to these types of arrangements, but that wouldn't stop him from expecting something of Glutz if he (the major) got the "hot seat" for lack of cooperation. Glutz hurriedly made arrangements for Gilhooley to be included in the afternoon flight's manifest and then returned to Sergeant Moroney's cubicle where he and Gilhooley sat chatting, obviously both enjoying their association.

"There's a 1430 flight to one of our remote sites, and room for you if you'd like to go."

"Where is it?" asked Gilhooley. Glutz mentioned the name and Sergeant Moroney pointed to the map on his desk.

"This is it here, Vlad," said Moroney, having patently made more personal progress with Gilhooley in a few minutes than Glutz had in several hours.

"It's the one we've just been talking about."

"Sounds great," said Gilhooley, looking at his watch. The watch said "tick-tick." It also told Mr. Gilhooley that it was 11:45.

"Care for lunch before I take you to the terminal?" offered Glutz, sensing that he was on the outside looking in on the cur-sory friendship established between Gilhooley and Moroney.

"How about it, sergeant?" Gilhooley said to Moroney. "Care to have lunch on me?"

"I'd like to," Moroney said, backing off from a first name basis, "but, I've got to get over to the fieldhouse. If I had my blouse off, you could tell from a quick look at the waistline that I need a good workout, and I haven't been over there at all this week yet."

"Let's go to the officers' club then," Glutz offered, since Sergeant Moroney, who wouldn't be welcome there, wasn't going along.

"No, I think not lieutenant, I'd better get down to the terminal and make sure everything's in order before flight time. I can grab a sandwich down there."

Life's a strange thing, a sensitive onlooker might have thought. Moroney was not a person to take to people easily, but he charmed them all. He enjoyed Glutz's company but not Gilhooley's so much; and, Glutz, well, he's just a shavetail (brown bar—second lieutenant for those who thought that was a barbershop term).

Lieutenant Glutz experienced an inward sigh of relief when he drove off from the air terminal after escorting Gilhooley inside. Glutz stopped at the officers' club and sat down to lunch with Major Corkerstrom and a Lieutenant Colonel Sullivan. Both were most friendly and made him feel right at home. He easily forgot the subtle snub from Vladimar Gilhooley.

With Gilhooley out of the way, Glutz went back to the office to resume his normal routine of looking for things to do. He wasn't as good at it as Senior Master Sergeant Nultz, and he didn't have any outside writing commitments as did Sergeant Moroney. The secretary, Gloria Inexcelsis, was busy at the typewriter too. Glutz didn't find out until much later that she was a stellar correspondent, writing many personal letters to her friends in far-off places. As for Glutz himself, being no master at the art of make-believe, he was content to busy himself with the task of poring over weekly magazines and working crossword puzzles from the daily paper. He was shocked from his reverie by the general's voice emanating from a box hanging on the wall over Major Ralston's desk.

"Bud," the voice said.

Glutz wanted to answer, but this was his first experience with the intercom and he didn't know what to do. He had seen a few in the movies but they were all desk models, nothing like this. To an observer, Glutz would have appeared visibly upset. He thought to go and ask Ralph or Gloria, but his mind quickly discarded the idea. He must answer quickly, but to whom and how? He had the speaker in his hands now, feeling for some button to push to reverse the call.

"Bud?" the voice said again and Lieutenant Glutz nearly jumped out of his skin. He dropped the "thing" on Major Ralston's desk.

"Bud, what the hell's going on in there?" the general said again. Glutz was totally perplexed now and could only talk at the box.

"Major Ralston's out of town, sir," Lieutenant Glutz shouted into the box, though it was held only inches from his mouth.

"Well, who are you?" the general went on.

"I'm Lieutenant Glutz, sir." His mind added, *Jerome V. AO999,*, but he knew that wasn't necessary.

"Well turn that thing down, lieutenant, before you crack an ear drum . . . Mine!"

"Yes, sir," said Glutz, fumbling again to find a volume knob. He had turned the back of the speaker toward him.

"What?" said the general.

Glutz turned it back toward him, "Yes, sir," he said, his voice trailing off in momentary exhaustion from the anxiety.

"Ralston out of town," he heard the general mumble. "There's no way to get out of town . . . no place to go. That lieutenant . . ." and then he turned the speaker off. Glutz sat down at his desk, his face white, visibly shaken by the incident. Sergeant Moroney appeared at the door.

"What was that all about?" he said.

"Oh, just the general calling," Glutz said looking up but still pale. "I took care of it all right."

"I can see you did," said Moroney in a you-know-what tone of voice. Sergeant Moroney then adroitly changed the conversation. "What are you going to do with that correspondent, Gilhooley, when he gets back?"

"Sink him in 20,000 fathoms," answered Glutz despondently, his chin in his hands and his eyes staring nowhere.

"No, I mean really," Moroney went on. "I think I sort of cooled him down but he feels he's wasted a lot time up here so far and I don't think he's in a mood to waste any more."

"Oh, I don't know, I'll think of something," Glutz said, his thoughts obviously elsewhere. "Anyway, Major Ralston's coming back tomorrow. He can take care of him then. Come to think of it, though, I do think I'll call base ops (operations, for some reason or other) to see if he got off all right." Glutz looked at his watch to see it was 3:45, or 1545 hours.

"Gil, who?" said the voice at the other end of the line.

"That's right," misunderstood Glutz, "Vladimar Gilhooley. He was scheduled out on the flight at 1430."

"Oh, that one," the voice at the other end of the line volunteered.

"No, that hasn't taken off yet, but it should any minute."

"Well, is he around?" Glutz asked.

"Is who around?" the voice answered.

"Vladimar Gilhooley, a correspondent. He was to have been on your 1430 flight."

"Well I told you, the 1430 flight hasn't taken off. Oh, there is one civilian guy here, sitting over on a bench in the waiting room."

"What does he look like?" Glutz asked intently.

"Oh-h-h, I don't know, but he's sitting looking at the tips of shoes with knees spread and hands folded, cracking his knuckles."

"That's him," snorted Glutz into the phone speaker, but intended for Sergeant Moroney who stood at his shoulder.

"Do you want to talk to him?" the voice at the other end suggested.

"No, I sure don't," Glutz said, "Just call me when the plane takes off," and he hung up.

The airman at base ops looked puzzled as he first gazed into the silent receiver and then hung up.

"What's the matter with you?" asked the airman standing next to him. "Your wife going to leave you again?"

Airman Seegul ignored the sarcasm and breathed out slowly. "I've just had the strangest call. Some guy called to see if that guy out in the waiting room was here, and then he said he didn't want to talk to him."

"Who was it?" wondered Airman Guise.

"I don't know, but he asked me to call him when the plane takes off.

"You be sure and do that," said Guise, turning away and going back about his work.

Glutz waited for a call but nothing happened. At 5:00 P.M. the rest of the office cleared out but he sat at his desk, chin in hand. *What to do?* he thought. Surely he didn't want to go down to base ops and have to face Gilhooley and at the same time he didn't want to sit behind his desk all night, waiting for a call telling him Vladimar had found a way out, or worse yet, a call from Vladimar screaming that he hadn't. At 5:45 Glutz realized that no more flights would be going out to remote locations that day. He sat back and tensed up waiting for a call from Gilhooley: 6:00, 6:15, 6:30, it never came. Finally, Glutz could stand it no longer and cautiously, apprehensively, he dialed base ops.

"Gil who? To where? Just a moment lieutenant, and I'll check."

Glutz daydreamed during the pause, a welcome relief from the anxiety he had been experiencing. The airman's voice shocked him back to reality.

"Yes, sir, that plane left at 1545 and Mr. Gilhooley was on it." *1545,* Glutz thought, *that's a quarter to four and I've been sitting here since 5:00, for an hour and a half waiting and hoping for something that had already happened.*

Lieutenant Glutz rose from his chair and put his service cap on his head. He was weary but relieved; tired but hungry and thirsty. The thought of the bar at the officers' club brought on his thirst, and, temporarily at least, subdued the hunger.

The scotch was good and it was entertaining watching the hat check girls from the last supper, several of whom were on the scene as usual. They were up on the dance floor, waddling around to the latest tunes in some weird fashion, with almost any partner they could lay a hand on and sometimes without. The air command's hysterical biddy never became a member of this vaunted scene, however. Rumor had it that she hung her shingle at the NCO club but Glutz couldn't find it. One of the hat check girls was married to a captain who sometimes came over to the club to watch his wife dance from a distance, when he could get someone to relieve him of his babysitting duties with the kids, that is. Another was a fat WAF captain.

A couple of scotches and Glutz began to get hungry. The kitchen was closed, so he munched popcorn and thought alternately of how he would arrange magnificent flights around Alaska and of how he would tell off Gilhooley the next time they met. His popcorn finished, he checked the clock on his wrist to find it was 10:00 P.M., and a tired lieutenant went home to retire and prepare for his next day's encounter with Vladimar Gilhooley. The thought of a breakfast Bloody Mary was appealing while the essence of scotch flowed smoothly through his brain, but after he had showered and brushed his teeth, the sack had much more appeal.

Seven o'clock wasn't such a bad hour the next morning and Glutz rose to greet the day and Vladimar Gilhooley, pushing from his mind where he would send him and how he would get there.

He shaved relaxedly and comfortably. At 7:20 he tied the blue tie and draped it down over his sky blue shirt. He was still in reasonably good physical condition and filled the uniform out well, the mirror told him. He strode to the phone as he imagined a Patton, or MacArthur, or Herman Goehring would have done. Lifting the phone he dialed the Mantel.

"Vladimar Gilhooley, please," Glutz said confidently and in a tone several notes lower than his usual voice.

"One moment," said the voice on the other end. This morning the silence was measured by a confident Lt. Jerome V. Glutz, bolstered by the anticipation of the Bloody Marys he felt sure there'd be for breakfast.

"I'm sorry, sir, Mr. Gilhooley has checked out."

"Checked out!" Glutz shrieked, "checked out! I can't believe it. He was supposed to have been here at least three more days."

"I'm sorry, sir," said the disinterested voice at the other end of the line, "but he's gone."

Glutz studied the receiver as he hung up the phone. *That Bloody Mary, er, Gilhooley,* he thought, *just when I was getting groomed to really be doing something for him . . . like drinking Bloody Marys for breakfast with his money,* Glutz subconsciously injected.

Glutz walked over to his office, arriving there at about 0815 and feeling like the number before the 8. *Why did Gilhooley check out?* he wondered. *Maybe they made a mistake. Maybe he went to another BOQ.* Glutz called the visitor's BOQ and the Mantel again. He got a "no" at both places. He called the air terminal for a confirmation that Gilhooley had, indeed, left Alaska. He hung up the phone just in time to catch the greeting of Major Ralston coming in the door.

"Good morning, Jerry. How's it been in my absence? Have you minded the store well, I hope," Ralston spit out cheerily between his intermittent "dum-de-dum" humming of a tuneless melody. Glutz opened his mouth to answer, but Major Ralston was too fast.

"Where's Gilhooley? Out around the sites?"

"He's gone," Glutz answered quickly.

"Good. One day is enough of those guys, anyway."

"But he was supposed to have been here for three days," Glutz bleated.

"Oh, he probably got tired of it up here. You know how those big city boys are. Give them one night away from the bright lights and they go scurrying for shelter." And then, as an afterthought, he mused, almost to himself, "Some shelter . . . Who wants to find shelter in a jungle?"

But Glutz wouldn't give up. He was insistent on conveying his concern to the major.

"He was here only one day, and went to only one site, and was there for only two hours." Ralston's humming stopped. The back of his neck got red. He turned and glowered at Glutz, arms at his side, his jowl hanging in the "attack" position.

"Where did you send him?" he demanded. Just then Sergeant Moroney stepped in.

"I think we worked it out okay, major," said Moroney. "I gave him a briefing on the spot and he seemed pleased."

"Okay," mumbled Major Ralston, staring at the floor, the back of his neck returning to its normal color. And then he looked up again. "What'd Fliptop do?" Moroney gave the major a knowing look out of the corner of his eye. "Yeah, I thought so," Ralston said, answering his own questions.

Have a banana, Glutz thought to himself but he didn't utter a word. The major sat down at his desk and the office was off to another productive day.

Three days later, a letter found its way to Ralston's in basket. Attached to it was a buck slip from the general.

"Read it and weep," were the general's only comments. Ralston picked up the letter to read it. The back of his neck got pink, then bright red, then beet red, and then purple. He opened his mouth at Glutz who was diligently working on a crossword puzzle in the morning paper, at his desk across the small office. No sound escaped, however, and the major put his lips together again and continued reading.

Dear General: (the letter started)
    I had the pleasure of visiting your command a few days ago. I'm told by my brother, General Gilhooley, that it's an active, productive, and strategic operation. I have no reason to believe it's not. However, I regret that I didn't see enough of it to substantiate that observation first-hand. I can testify to the fact that the airman who works the afternoon shift at the visitors' BOQ has a good sense of humor; that at least one overnight in the Mantel is adequate though surely nothing pretentious; that the versatile young man who seems to run it

all by himself is industrious, if poorly clothed; that one of the dining room tables is unstable; that at least one of your aircraft is noisy and uncomfortable; that the food at at least one of your sites is outstanding; and that the young second lieutenant in your public relations office is very accommodating and also very green. Unfortunately, I'm not sure that my readers will be interested in that information and my editor is certain they won't.

So now I'm faced with the prospect of having spent several hundred dollars, several days and at least two nights with nothing to show for it. As a matter of fact, the only bright spot in the whole trip was a brief visit with one Lt. Col. Fliptop who gave me a delightful and thorough briefing of the entire command. Whatever story I do come up with will have to be based on the Lt. Col.'s comments, and whatever I can pick up from my brother (the air force general).

Thank you for the courtesies of your command. I'm sorry I don't have a more favorable story to report.

Sincerely,
Vladimar B. Gilhooley

"S-O-B," Ralston muttered half out loud.

"Who me?" Glutz asked querulously, not knowing for sure what had been said.

"Yes, you too," Ralston said without looking up.

CHAPTER VIII

Friday evening was tough for a young single guy relatively new to Alaska. Jerry Glutz went over to the slop chute for supper and sat down at one of the long tables next to a couple of uniformed Red Cross workers. At first they ignored him but he waited for an opening and then jumped in.

"Excuse me, fellas, but what's there to do up here on a Friday night?"

One of the Red Crossers looked at the table and remained silent. The other one looked at the first, across the table from him and answered, "Not much."

"Well what do you fellows do?" Glutz went on. Now the second looked at the table and the first looked at the second.

"Not much," he said. "Actually, we watch TV mostly," the second Red Cross worker volunteered (no pun intended, because actually the Red Cross workers weren't volunteers at all). "We were stationed at some pretty lively places in the past and now that we're here we just enjoy our leisure and the slow pace of things.

"Where were you stationed before?" Glutz asked.

"Guam," the first one said as he looked at the second and the second looked at the table. *And before that, Iceland, I'll bet,* thought Glutz. Glutz realized he wasn't in his element so he rose to his feet, having finished his dinner, and begged leave of the two Red Crossers.

"I hope we helped some," number two said looking at number one while one was looking at you-know-where.

Not much, thought Glutz, all the while feeling he had heard the term somewhere before.

"Fine," he said, and walked off.

Outside the door, Glutz made a half turn toward the officers' club and then thought better of it. He wasn't in the mood for a drink this night. Back at the BOQ he stopped off at the pool table. No one else was in the room. He picked up the eight ball and gazed into it as into a crystal ball. Then he set it down and moved on out of the room. In the TV room, there was one lone soldier slouched down in a soft chair holding one leg in the air with both hands folded at the knee. He made a frequent twitch of the hand and cleared his throat in a high pitched tone. He didn't recognize the entrance of Glutz into the room. Glutz passed over behind the fellow and noted he was watching a test pattern on the TV.

"Just turn it on?" Glutz supposed.

"What's that?" said the other guy, seemingly unstartled.

"Did you just turn it on?" Glutz repeated with more emphasis.

"Oh. You mean that test pattern. No. That was on when I came in here. Matter of fact, the knobs are busted and I don't think you can turn it off."

"How about pulling out the plug?" Glutz suggested.

"I suppose you could do that, but see there? The plug goes through that little hole in the wall, and must be plugged in, in the other room." Seeing that Glutz didn't get the complete picture he went on. "The door to the other room is locked. I've just been sitting here counting dots in the outer black circle of the test pattern."

"How many are there?" Glutz asked, just to be saying something.

"I don't know," said the other young officer. "I keep losing count. It's hard to maintain a point of reference because they all look the same and the circle is continuous."

"So it is," said Glutz disinterestedly. *Most of them are,* he thought to himself.

"I'm Jerry Glutz," said Glutz, offering his hand to his new acquaintance.

"So you are," said the other. "My name's Ned Day."

"Nice to know you, Ned. How long you been up here?"

"Oh not long, fifteen to twenty minutes, I guess," Ned said plainly.

"I mean in Alaska," Glutz clarified.

"Oh, I thought you meant . . ."

"Yeah, I know," said Glutz.

"Well, let's see now, I've been in Alaska, one, two, four, six, thirty, sixty, ninety, two, seven, . . . about two months." Glutz's first notion was to hightail it back to the Red Cross workers, but his second premonition told him that this might be more interesting.

"What do you do for excitement up here, Ned?" Glutz asked and then immediately wished he hadn't, remembering what Ned had been doing when he entered the room.

"Who, what, excitement? Where? Here? There's no excitement here." Glutz disagreed. He had just seen more excitement in his new friend than anywhere since he'd come to Alaska. "Well, what do you do when you're not watching TV test patterns?" Glutz pressed on.

"Oh, I'm a supply officer," said Ned. "Actually, that's one reason I'm here, because we issued this TV to the BOQ the other day and I wanted to see if it worked."

"What would you do if it didn't?" Glutz inquired.

"It doesn't," said Ned. "That test pattern is an internal phenomenon. It's supposed to be broadcasting reruns from a station downtown."

"Well, what are you going to do about it?" Glutz's questioning continued.

"Me?" said Ned, obviously amazed. "Why, nothing. It's not my responsibility. That TV belongs to the BOQ. We just issued it. It's not my responsibility to see that it works."

"But, surely, someone who works for you could get it fixed and then, since you live here, you could watch a TV that works."

"I'm sorry," said Ned in the manner of Pontius Pilate. "I'd like to help, but it's just not my responsibility."

I hope nothing ever is, Glutz thought to himself.

He walked out of the room leaving Lt. Ned Day still with his knee between folded hands and staring at the test pattern. Glutz walked up to his room, unlocked the door, and spread out on his bed. He stretched first his arms, then his legs, while he stared at the ceiling. *Friday night at Elfendwarf Air Force Base,* he thought. *What an exciting way to continue one's life.* His mind raced through some of the other Friday nights he'd spent elsewhere in his life, and tonight became even more dismal. And then, what to do to make something of this predicament. He really knew little of what was available. The officers' club? No, not again. The base movie? No, not the latest movie on the air force again. What about downtown?

"Maybe I should go downtown! There must be something there; even if it's only a different bar." Charged with enthusiasm for a new dimension and anticipating an evening comparable to some which just happened to come along in the past when nothing was expected, Glutz leaped from his bed and climbed into his best (and only) sport coat. Then he stopped. How would he get downtown? In the first place, he didn't have a car; he had sold it shortly after his arrival in Alaska after comparing its cost of operation to his paycheck. Most numbers in the comparison were about the same. And then he had an idea.

Ned Day had been around for a little while. Maybe he knew something. Glutz shuddered at the likelihood, but it was worth a try. He went back to the day room (not named after Lt. Ned) where Ned had been watching test patterns, but it was empty. *Boy, I wonder where he lives. There are a lot of rooms in this BOQ.* The thought of going door to door crossed his mind but failed the test when he realized that, unless he got lucky, the night would be over when and if he found Lieutenant Day. A take-off on the idea did click, however, and Glutz went up to the first floor. He knocked on three doors before he got an answer, but the occupant had never heard of Lt. Ned Day. He had probably heard *from* him, though, because it turned out that he lived in the adjoining suite.

Glutz then went up to the top floor and knocked at the first door. After a long pause it opened and there stood one of the Red Cross workers. Glutz was too surprised to say anything for a moment. The Red Cross worker wasn't surprised, but he didn't say anything either. Glutz could see his associate in the room watching "The Continuing Adventures of Three Black Sheep" on TV. Glutz remembered having seen the episode before coming to Alaska. Finally he spoke.

"Hi there, Mr. Red Cross," he said enthusiastically. "Do you happen to know a Ned Day?"

"Yes I do," said the now cordial Red Cross Worker. "He lives right over there," pointing to a room across the hall and a couple of doors down.

Glutz turned toward the appointed door and began to walk away.

"I believe he's a tech rep for the Flyco Aviation Corporation."

Glutz stopped and turned on his heel. "Not this guy. He's a lieutenant in the air force."

"Then, I don't know him," continued the Red Cross worker. Glutz muttered something under his breath, turned the other way and walked down the stairs.

More than a half hour had passed now since Glutz had begun his search for Ned Day and at least a suggestion for a way to get downtown. Alternative possibilities, such as seeking out information or assistance from someone else were subconsciously bypassed for the intrigue of tracking down the elusive Ned Day. Glutz took a step out the door into the crisp fresh evening. Then all of a sudden the situation was clear. He rushed to his room and picked up the phone to call the base locator.

"Let's see, Lieutenant Ned Day lives in 2017420."

"Yes, I know that," answered Glutz, "but, what's the room number?"

"Those rooms don't have numbers," said the airman from the other end.

"Yes, they do," said Glutz.

The airman continued as if to ignore him. "The names of the officers should be in the holders, for that purpose, on each door."

"No names, no holders," Glutz countered.

"Well just a minute," said the airman testily. Glutz could hear a conversation at the other end of the line. Then there was a pause, followed by some loud clanks as the airman returned to the phone and apparently beat it with a hammer. "He's in room 4," said the airman, and hung up. Glutz looked at the receiver and then did the same.

Several sharp raps on door 4 of building 2017420 brought no response except from the occupant next door who earlier said he didn't know Lieutenant Day. Now he stuck his head into the hall, thinking the knock was at his door. He looked at Glutz dreamily and then slammed his door (after pulling his head back in, of course). The slam of door 3 must have had its impact on the occupant of room 4 because, just as Glutz was turning to leave, he heard a switch click and saw light flood out from under the door. Soon Lt. Ned Day appeared from behind it, squinting in the bright light. His great toes thumped alternately on the floor as he struggled to bring his body back to life.

"Oh, it's you," he said to Glutz, peering at him through one half-shut eye. *So it is,* thought Glutz, *so it is..*

Seeing Lieutenant Day standing there squinting in his blue monogrammed pajamas with silver bias sewn onto the shoulders and great toes thumping on the floor temporarily caused Glutz to forget why he had come.

"Would you like to come in?" offered Ned Day, stepping back out of the way and gesturing toward his "living room" with outstretched hand and unfolded arm.

"Thanks," said Glutz, and he walked in. Glutz slumped into a chair and Ned Day walked past him. Opening his closet door he took out a lounging robe and put it on. *My grandmother used to have one like that,* Glutz couldn't keep from thinking. Ned then slipped into a pair of slippers and headed for the refrigerator, located at the foot of his bed. He took out mayonnaise, bread, bologna, lettuce, and milk. Having poured himself a glass of milk and made a sandwich he sat down in a chair and began to enjoy his evening snack. To this point, not a word had passed between the two since Glutz entered the room. *Maybe he likes an audience when he eats,* Glutz thought, and then dismissed the idea before Ned could see the smile which had formed briefly on his face.

"I thought I might go downtown tonight and was wondering how to get there," Glutz said finally. Ned Day kept eating. He swallowed and then cleared his throat.

"Mmhmm," he sounded in a high pitched tone. "It's kind of," he continued in the same pitch and then dropped an octave to finish, "late for that isn't it?"

Glutz looked at his watch and noted that it was 10:15 (2215 hours), but Glutz's watch couldn't tell time on a military basis (that's not the plural of base).

"What time do they close up the bars and restaurants?" he queried.

"I don't think they do," Ned told him. Obviously, the two were not on the same wavelength and Glutz was wondering what to do about it when Ned Day continued. "Mmhmm," he said again at the same pitch. "Don't know what you want to go down there for anyway. Nothing down there but bars and B girls."

"What's a B girl?" Glutz wanted to know.

"I don't know," Day said, taking another munch of his sandwich and washing it down with the milk.

"What d'ya mean, you don't know?" demanded Glutz. "How can you know they're there and not know what they are?"

"I mean," said Ned, "that I don't know what the B stands for. I know what they do. They sell companionship and champagne."

"What?"

"Well, I went down there one night when I first came here. This girl comes up and asks me if I'll buy her a drink. I looked around and didn't see anybody I knew so I said sure. Then she wanted another one so I bought another."

"What were you drinking?" asked Glutz.

"Ginger ale," answered Ned, taking another slug from his glass of milk.

"Gingerale and what?" continued Glutz.

"Ginger ale and ice," answered Ned.

"And, what was she drinking?" Glutz went on.

"I don't know. I didn't ask her."

"Maybe she was drinking gingerale and ice, too." Glutz suggested.

"Oh no, she couldn't have been," Ned protested. "Her drinks cost twice as much as mine."

"That's what I mean," concluded Glutz. Ned looked at Glutz as if he thought the latter insane. "Anyway, continue on with the story," Glutz insisted. Ned took a huge bite from the remainder of his sandwich and did as he was bid.

"Well, after the second drink, she suggested I buy a bottle of champagne and we'd go in the back room. 'What's in the back room?' I asked her. She told me we'd have a party. I didn't ask her how much the champagne cost, and then when we picked it up she said she needed twenty dollars. I didn't think much of it at the time because I knew champagne was expensive. Also, I figured any party they were going to have champagne at must be a pretty high class affair. Being new in Alaska I thought it'd be a good idea to meet some new people so I decided to go, even if it did cost twenty dollars. After all, I'd always been told that you get what you pay for.

"Anyway, she led me into a back room—it was pitch black in there. Over we went to what felt like a corner booth and sat down. At first I thought it must be a seance or something like that and that a light would come on soon. Then I felt my shirt move and reached down to tuck it back in. Here she was, trying to open my belt with one hand and pull my shirt from my trousers with the other. 'What's going on here?' I said. She told me she was starting the party. 'I'm sorry, but I don't allow those privileges; particularly with a strange girl,' I told her. Actually, I'd never even been asked for a dance by any girl before, but I didn't want her to know that. Then she took her hand from my belt and said, 'Let's go.' By this time I could see a little bit so I got up and followed her back into the main bar. I went to the bartender to demand my money back, but he said he couldn't refund money for an open bottle. I told him neither of us had touched the bottle so he took it and pulled the cork out. 'We open them when we sell them,' he said, taking a long draught from the bottle and handing it back to me. I wouldn't take it so it fell on the floor and shattered."

"What'd you do then?" Glutz asked with sincere interest.

"I walked right past that B girl and out the door, and I haven't been back since," Ned continued righteously. *An expensive but worthwhile lesson,* Glutz thought.

"It was an expensive, but very worthwhile lesson," said Lieutenant Day.

"Maybe the B in B girl stands for *bad,*" Glutz suggested.

"Maybe so," agreed Ned, finishing off the milk at the bottom of his glass, then rubbing his hands together to distribute the last crumbs from his consumed sandwich.

Glutz got up and slipped rather silently out of the room. Ned Day didn't appear to see him go. Back in his room he debated whether to go downtown to see for himself if what Day had said about the place could possibly be true. It was only 11:00 P.M. and Ned had said cabs ran on and off base past midnight. The big sign Glutz had seen on the street that day in town suddenly appeared in his mind. "All American City!" "No, it can't be," he said to himself. With that he disrobed and stepped into a cold shower. It was brisk and invigorating. After a super-quick toweling off ceremony, Glutz stepped into his pajamas, propped up two pillows and leaned back with a book from a meager supply of novels. *Reminiscences: Douglas MacArthur,* read the title on the autobiographical sketch. *Twenty dollars,* he thought. *Twenty dollars for a bottle of champagne.* He shook his head from side to side in disbelief and then again "All American City" came into his mind. Presently he opened the book's outer cover and pressed it back. *Maybe sometime I'll have to go down there and find out for myself.* He picked up the book and began to read: "The MacArthurs are of Scottish descent. A branch of . . ."

CHAPTER IX

After a weekend that dragged by with little or nothing to do, Glutz was eager at the 6:30 A.M. clamor of his "Big Ben" alarm bell. He could look back to a Saturday night of continuous "Westrons," as Dave Perry from Annapolis called them. To add spice to that evening, Glutz had been duped into a bet on how many bad guys would be eliminated during the total of the four evening westerns. Perry always won, as Glutz found out later. He said he figured the odds, but some suspected he had a friend back in "the states" who sent him the count after the original showings there two or three weeks previous.

Everything went as it should this particular morning and Glutz relished each task because he had time and was looking for something satisfying to accomplish, no matter how small. The shower felt good but was equalled or exceeded by the shave following. Even the shoe shine, badly needed, was not a chore today. Glutz grinned to himself as he sent the buffer back and forth over the jet black shoes. He remembered the words of his cadet squadron commander back in ROTC at an 8:00 drill one morning when he had risen too late to shine or shave. The captain of the football team had come over and clumsily relieved him with orders to report to the cadet squadron commander.

"Mr. Glutz," said cadet Lt. Col. Wilerams, "it would be nice if you would shine your shoes and shave before coming to drill so the basic cadets could look up to you and not down on you."

Glutz grinned again. *He'd be proud of me this morning*, he thought.

The aroma at the slop chute was absolutely delicious. Glutz was so taken by it he even tried to think up a new name for the place as he waited in line. The American fries were the best he could remember seeing and the scrambled eggs and bacon looked equivalent. Then all of a sudden he saw it. SOS—perhaps the most famous dish in the American military for decades; Glutz had heard a good deal about it since high school, but had never seen it before going on active duty in the air force. Actually, he couldn't abide the justification for its name. True, it was a rather gooey looking creamy mess with innumerable black specks scattered throughout. True also, it was served on toast which had long since changed its texture (if not its chemical composition) since coming from the toaster. Still, the taste and aroma, just now wafting past Glutz's nostrils once again, were enchanting. *It's just the sight of the stuff people can't take,* Glutz thought to himself. *I'll bet blind people would love it.* But, he had to agree on reflection that he hadn't seen too many blind people in the air force, except, perhaps, in terms of drunkenness or incompetence.

Glutz picked up his tray and walked over to a table where he sat by himself. Soon Capt. Charlie Mallbins joined him, a big smile on his face.

"What you doin' up so early, Jerry?" Charlie drawled, "the landlady kick you out of your room?"

"Nope," Glutz responded honestly, "I'm turning over a new leaf, Charlie. From now on it's early to bed and early to rise for me. No more late howlin'. It's not worth it in the morning." Charlie deepened his perpetual smile.

"Why?" he said, half in jest, but with a real note of seriousness.

Glutz looked up in shock, spilling a tidbit of SOS on his dark blue tie as he did so. Later, when it dried, it would look like a bird had flown over him on his way to work and scored with a tracing. Not an air force "bird," either.

"Why?" Glutz half asked and half demanded. I'll tell you why. Because it's more fun to get up feeling fresh in the morning and put in a good productive day than to go out and raise hell all night." Now, it was Capt. Mallbins' turn to choke on his breakfast.

"You really believe that?" he asked with an incredulous air. Glutz knew immediately that he didn't, but he had to defend himself as best he could.

"You'll see," Glutz said. And Capt. Mallbins did see. Glutz showed up for breakfast one more time during the year, and that was late one Saturday morning. Charlie and Glutz strode to the office together and then bade each other goodbye for the day.

Glutz continued to his office where he arrived fifteen minutes early only to see Airman Fengrew the only one in attendance.

"What's on the docket today, Fengrew?" Glutz asked the airman.

"Huh?" was the response received.

It shouldn't have been surprising. The question was stupid. Glutz only asked it as a means of showing his momentary command, being the only officer in the office. Actually, there was no continuity. Seldom did any one person know what another was doing. Maybe because seldom was anyone doing anything. The rest of the staff, including Major Ralston, arrived approximately on time.

"De, de de dum de dum," Glutz could hear the Major coming around the corner at 8:30 A.M. sharp. Glutz pulled out a tablet and began to write.

> TO: The Commander
> FROM: Lt. J. V. Glutz
> SUBJECT: Arriving on Time
> It has come to my attention that you have
> continually been reporting late for work
> mornings. Even though you are a general
> officer, I feel it is my responsibility as as-
> sistant ISO to inform you . . .

Ralston stopped at the door to the office and stared in disbelief. "Well, look who's here early, Jack the Ripper in a blue suit. What happened? Conscience get too painful for sleep?"

Glutz smiled.

"What are you writing?" Ralston asked half interested.

"Just a letter to the general telling him to get to work on time."

"Yeah, that's what you ought to do all right," the major retorted.

The day, like most days, was a dud. Nothing to do but make work and Glutz wasn't very good at that. The only highlight was a call from base housing telling Glutz there was room for him in the bonafide BOQ. *Great,* thought Glutz, *a party over there tonight, and I'll get a good chance to see what it's like.*

Glutz was relieved to see the day end. He felt flat from having done nothing all day. *Little incentive,* he thought, *for making an effort to get here on time in the morning.* The thought of the party that night perked him up a bit, though, and the two scotches he stopped for at the club on his way to the BOQ helped even more.

After a hurried dinner at the slop chute, Glutz was back in his room climbing into his civies (non-uniform clothes, for those who wear them often). His head was light and the blood in his veins felt like champagne as the thoughts of the party danced in his head. *Women, scotch, dancing, women, scotch, dancing,* his mind went round and round.

Some of the girls who were at the party he'd met, but most of them he hadn't. Glutz nodded to those he knew on his way to the bar for a bracer. Half-way through the second drink, high rhythm began to come on and he eyed the dollies for a dancing partner. Glutz was torn between approaching those he knew and those he didn't. It would be more relaxing talking to and dancing with acquaintances, but none of them turned him on much. A few of the "new" babes looked pretty inviting, but opening conversations was usually stilted and awkward.

Glutz continued his visual survey of the room until his eyes fell upon one blonde curvaceous creature whose features blended in well with her overall physical attraction. *Oh, the hell with it,* Glutz thought as he approached her. *Nothing ventured, nothing gained,* said a rather quiet voice from somewhere in his head. *Novel,* said Glutz to himself in response, *novel.* He smiled down at the pretty young thing and she smiled back.

"Care to dance?" Glutz asked casually and comfortably, quickly becoming the suave male he featured himself tonight; he and the scotch.

"I'm not a very good dancer," she answered with a sweet look and an unusual but pretty little voice which exactly became her. Glutz began to melt as she let her hand ride softly into his.

"Don't worry about that," he assured her, "neither am I and neither are most of the rest of these people here. I have a remedy, though. It's called scotch and soda and it's the best dance instructor you can possibly imagine. Two glasses of instruction, with ice, of course, and I become a model ballroom dancer. Come on, I'll show you, lovely lady, but first you must have a lesson yourself."

She was on her feet now and the two were crossing back over the dance floor to the bar.

"I'm not a very good drinker, either," she said, looking up timidly and admiringly into Glutz's bigger and perhaps bluer eyes.

"You don't have to be a good drinker to be a good dancer," continued Glutz "just a *big* drinker." His companion just smiled again.

"I'm Peggy Santone," she said, holding out her pretty, petite, well-manicured hand.

"And, I'm Jerry Glutz," he said.

"Hi," uttered each, almost simultaneously.

Glen Elling, one of the longtime inhabitants of the BOQ came over and engaged the two in conversation.

"Hi," he said, looking from Glutz and quickly to Peggy, a much more impressive view.

"Hi," Glutz responded. Peggy just looked up and smiled with her beautiful powder blue eyes. "Peggy, meet Glen Elling," Glutz continued.

"Hi," Peggy offered. Her voice sounded exquisite and Glutz got a chill thrill from its tone and whisper. He could feel the goose bumps on his arms from excitement.

"Okay if I have a dance with your lovely companion, Glutz?" Glen Elling asked.

"She's the one to ask," Glutz said tactfully and proudly at the thought of Peggy being considered his date.

"Sure," said Peggy, wrinkling her nose like a bunny and, again, with her cute little smile.

Glutz watched the two for a moment and was a bit distraught to see that she seemed to be paying the same kind of attention to Glen that she had been to him. But the scotch had built him up so high it couldn't let him down far. He reached for the ice tongs and gingerly put another cube of ice in his glass. Then he walked casually across the room and nested in one of the easy chairs. He slid down a bit, stretched his legs out straight and let them fall apart. Then he reached in his pocket for a cigarette, lit it, waved the match out like a magic wand and dropped it in a nearby ash tray. He took a long puff on the cigarette, leaned his head back against the chair and exhaled heavily.

This is the life, Glutz thought to himself. *I'd love to take Peggy home tonight. I'd love to . . . but, I really don't care if I do or not.* He wasn't thinking even to the end of the party. He didn't care if tomorrow ever came, and wasn't worrying about what shape he'd be in if and when it did. He took another long inhalation from his cigarette and flicked the ash into the tray for that purpose.

"Hi," said a familiar voice next to him. He looked up to see Peggy sitting on the arm of his chair, one leg folded under her.

"Hi, Peggy," Glutz answered most enthusiastically, "dance over already?"

"Three of them," Peggy said. "You mean you weren't even watching me?" she added and smiled.

"Where's your drink?" Glutz asked, pretending to look around for it.

"It's gone," Peggy answered.

"You mean you inhaled the glass and all?" Glutz chided in an attempt at humor.

"No, that's over there somewhere," Peggy said, pointing in the direction of the bar. Actually, Peggy had come to Glutz not because of him but because of his bottle. He, perhaps, could have figured that out, but he chose to think otherwise.

"Well, you can't stand on one leg," Glutz told her. "Let's go see if we can't fix you another." Peggy was immediately agreeable so Glutz took her hand and the two walked over to the bar. Glutz was becoming much more suave now, he and the scotch. He calmly fixed the scotch and suspended two ice cubes in the amber glass. He kissed the glass lightly and said, "One for you," looking deeply into the drink. Then he handed it to Peggy, bent over for a peck on her cheek "and, one for me," he told her. Peggy smiled back at him, holding the glass in both hands, and Glutz walked back to his chair and sat down. Such coy suaveness she had surely never seen, Glutz told himself . . . and the scotch. He exchanged a few pleasantries with a couple next to him whom he hadn't met, and then, his glass being empty, went back to the bar for a refill. He had hardly returned to his perch when Peggy was at his side once again. This time it was obvious that the scotch was taking hold. Peggy was much more garrulous and gregarious.

"Empty again?" Glutz was looking over at her and following his query with a peck at her lips, which were only a few inches from his own.

"Yup," she said straightening up.

"You stay here," Glutz told her, "and I'll be right back." He returned shortly with an amber glass looking exactly like its predecessors except perhaps a bit more amber. Peggy was still perched on the arm of his chair, watching him. Glutz sat down and grinned up at her. "This one'll cost you," he said pulling her chin down to his lips. The kiss was long and it tasted good.

Glutz felt Peggy's elbow on his shoulder and it warmed him. Suddenly the room around him became nonexistent and he was aware of only Peggy and himself. He noticed she was saying nothing. *Maybe she's got the same feeling I have,* he thought, and felt a pressure soar within him. Glutz felt he was the lord and master of the situation, he and the scotch. He rose to his feet and turned partly toward Peggy.

"Come with me," he ordered and Peggy rose to obey. Glutz led her out of the room and up the first flight of stairs. He took a key from his pocket and turned it in the lock. Twisting the handle, he removed the key and pushed the door half open. He turned to Peggy.

"Come in," he invited in a tone of semi-authority.

"Oh no, you don't," she said. "I'm not going into any bachelor's . . ." Glutz put his hand in the small of her back, moving her into the room and closing the door behind her, in one motion.

"We'll stay just for one drink," he assured her.

"Okay, but we're not going to do anything," she half told and half asked.

"Of course not," Jerry assured her. He went to the refrigerator in his shower room and drew out a bottle of scotch.

"Scotch and water okay?" he hollered into the next room.

"Okay," she said. He looked back into the refrigerator and noted it was empty except for a tray of ice cubes. Glutz took out the ice cubes and slammed the door. He set two glasses on the edge of the bathtub and began to work the ice cubes free of the tray in which they lay captive, fastened solidly to the sides and the bottom.

"Nice party," Glutz shouted into the next room.

"M-hm," Peggy answered expressionlessly. Glutz carried the drinks into the next room. A stout scotch on the rocks for him and an equally stout scotch on the rocks for Peggy. She sat in a chair, legs folded under her, ostensibly reading from a magazine. Presumably even she didn't notice it was a three-month-old issue of *Outdoor Snarf.* Glutz handed her the drink and she looked up into his eyes, her lips red and slightly moist. A shrill of passion surged through him again, but he was still cool. Turning around he walked over to the davenport and sat down. Holding his drink in both hands and leaning forward to rest both forearms on his femurs, he addressed Peggy again.

"Nice party."

"M-hm," she answered without looking up.

Glutz's body became anxious and he could wait no longer. "Come here," he said, his arms outstretched from shoulder to fingertips as he sat rigidly on the edge of the couch.

"Hm-m," she answered, again without looking up, turning a page in her outdated magazine.

Glutz got up and walked over to where Peg sat. She continued her ruse, pretending not to notice his closeness as he looked down on her. He hadn't seen her top profile before, and it was nice. Her forehead, eyelashes, her nose made just the right protrusion to compliment her lips and they, too, were formed almost perfectly. His hunger for her grew more intense and though a lion surged inside him, he reached down gingerly to lift her stabilizing hand from the back of the magazine she stared at.

"Just a minute," she said pulling her hand away. Then she closed the magazine, set it on the side table and rose, putting her arm around Glutz's waist and following his first step toward the couch. "I don't know what I'm doing here," she muttered to herself. Glutz attempted to angle toward the bedroom, but she stopped him short. "Oh no, you don't, buster," she said unequivocally, so Glutz settled for the couch.

Peggy sat down first and looked straight ahead. Glutz eased her shoulders back until their angle pulled the rest of her torso to the couch. He then lifted her legs and slid alongside her. This was a moment of passion Jerry Glutz had not known before. As a king of beasts he moved instinctively toward the conquest of his prey. She lay on her side, pressed firmly against him. Every contour of her body he could feel against him. Those of her countenance he was free to explore; first her nose, her high cheekbones, her chin, and then the culmination of her soft, textured lips. One hand slipped slowly yet conclusively under her sweater onto her bare back and then under her bra strap. The other moved simultaneously and almost surreptitiously under her panties and onto her bare buttocks. Peggy pulled herself closer as if clinging to the neck of her conqueror. She raised her top leg sharply and then suddenly drew back.

"What's the matter, honey?" asked Glutz, his soft voice filled with affection and kindness.

Peggy moaned ever so lightly and jerking her head up— BLATT!!—she vomited over his shoulder and onto the floor.

Someone once said, and it has been oft repeated since, "Candy is dandy but liquor is quicker." The author might have added "but too much of either will make a person vomit."

Glutz was stupified. In a fraction of a second she had gone, in his eyes, from the most tantalizing and erotic morsel of feminine pulchritude imaginable to a despicable sick drunk. He wasn't totally an all or nothing guy, though, so, perhaps by conditioned reflex, he decided to make the best of a bad scene. Glutz pulled off his barf-laden sweater and threw it in the washroom sink he then filled with water. The next morning he would dry it and see the sleeves go as far as his elbows when he tried to put it on.

Through all this, Peggy was leaning, chin in hands, elbows on knees, still on the couch.

"I'm such a bad girl," she muttered to herself and/or to Glutz.

"No you're not, Peggy. That could happen to anyone," Glutz rationalized for her and himself. "You shouldn't feel embarrassed. Just slip into the washroom and hand me out your slacks and sweater. I'll take them down to the laundry and spot them out."

All of a sudden Glutz was the modern day counterpart of Sir Walter Raleigh. Strange what a difference there can be between helping an old lady across the street and "being on the prowl."

When he came back from the laundry he found Peggy sitting on the commode; lid down, chin in hands, elbows on knees. Her apparel consisted of panties, bra and socks. An hour ago Glutz would have gone into orbit at the sight. Now he didn't even see it. Peggy didn't look up. Glutz closed the door part way and then reached one arm through the orifice, Peggy's slacks and sweater dangling at the end of a slightly damp hand.

"Here they are," he said, "laundry for Miss Santone." Nobody thought it was very funny. Nobody laughed. Could he have seen through the door, Glutz would have observed her stare up blankly and then take the clothes from his hand.

"Thanks," she offered weakly.

Glutz paced the floor for what seemed like forever until finally Peggy emerged. She looked quite the same as when he had first seen her that evening, but somehow the flower had wilted. Peggy looked only at the floor.

"Could I brush my teeth?" she asked.

"There's only my toothbrush," Glutz answered sheepishly.

"That'd be fine," she said, still looking down. Glutz retrieved his toothbrush and toothpowder.

"Hope you don't mind toothpowder," he said.

"Toothpowder's fine," Peggy responded, still looking for quarters.

Glutz helped Peggy on with her coat. Neither needed to say so; both knew that it was time to go. Out in the fresh air Peggy revived a bit and began to talk. Mostly she talked about trivia, but Glutz wasn't listening closely so he wouldn't have known. It was a cool night and when they got into the car, Peggy slid her arm inside his, snuggled up and leaned her head on his shoulder.

"I hope you'll take me out again, Jerry," she hinted, raising her head from his shoulder to look at him. Glutz stared straight ahead toward the road.

"Sure I will," he assured her. They drove on silently for a time. "There's a special buffet at the officers open mess on the army post on Sunday," he said, leaving her head on his shoulder this time. "Would you like to go?" The question was rudimentary and he asked it almost without thinking.

"Oh, Jerry, I'd love to," she said, kissing him on the cheek.

Then, I hope you can find someone to take you, the imp in his mind said, but he couldn't bring his conscience into repeating it.

"Sounds like fun," he said instead.

"What time?"

"I think they serve from 6:00 'til 8:00 P.M., "but, I know if we get there by 7:30 we'll be safe. I'll be by for you around sevenish, okay?"

"Okay," she said.

The car pulled up in front of Peggy's apartment at that point. She waited for him to open her door and when he saw that she was waiting he went around and did so. At the door, he felt a peck on the lips was expected so he offered it. Peggy kissed him back hungrily.

"See you Sunday night," said Glutz, pulling away.

"About 7:00 P.M.," she reminded him in response. Glutz waved an affirmative as he got into his car to drive off.

He drove around in a circle for awhile and then headed downtown. Last chance, read the alternately flashing white lights of the sign in front of "the place."

"Maybe it is," mused Glutz, as he pulled up to the curb and took the keys from the ignition. Inside there was a din, like a Chinese funeral procession, but Glutz didn't really notice. It's difficult to describe the way he felt. Even he would have had a hard time. He really didn't want to be here, but he wasn't tired. The scotch from earlier in the evening wasn't doing much anymore, but its residue left him with a dull headache over the eyes. Glutz peered through the dark, smoky room toward the place where all the noise appeared to be coming from. The smoke drifted in layers around the light from the next room. Glutz walked in and sat down.

In self defense he lit a cigarette, something he rarely did, and began to sip from a drink which somehow had found its way to his hand while in the bar room. Looking up, he saw the reason for the hoop-la. Out on the dance floor a stripper was grinding down to the last portion of her costume. She slithered up to Glutz, perched near the floor's edge, and began winking a rather small, mostly bare, breast at him with an intermittent snap of the shoulder. Glutz was becommg a bit giddy, perhaps from the hypnotic result of being in an oxygenless room. He reached out to press firmly on the little mound of flesh, easing the tasseled cap from its tip as he did so and then pressing it to his forehead.

"Do I look like a Shriner?" he asked of le femme, but his voice was muffled by the noise and inaudible, even to himself. The dancer kicked Glutz soundly in the shins, but he only smiled and leaned back in his chair, the tassel from the pasty dangling at the side of his nose. Seeing the effect, she came over to his chair and leaned a wet kiss on his lips. Removing the pasty from his fore head, "You're a real tiger," she said, fastening it back in place over the nipple of her small breast. She leaned over for another kiss, but Glutz stopped her with his forearm, pushing her back as he rose. Grabbing her elbow, he swung her around and laid a firm hand, slap! on her fanny.

"I sure am," he said, "and you ought to be home with your mother." With that, he turned and walked toward the door.

"You shit!" she hollered after him. *Guess she must have heard Major Ralston talking about me,* Glutz thought to himself as he made his exit.

Back at the base, Glutz was dead tired. He couldn't wait to get out of his clothes and into the bed. The sheets felt like clouds from heaven. *Got to set the alarm,* Glutz said to himself. *Late once more and the major said he'd hold up my promotion.* Glutz looked at his watch. 0200 hours. Or, as they say in the air force, the little hand is on the two and the big hand is . . . *Wow!* he thought. *Gotta get up in five hours and with all that sauce in me that'll be like sleeping an hour.* He rolled over and the Z machine went on instantaneously . . . z-z-z-z.

CHAPTER X

"I can't understand where he is."

"I don't know where he is now, but he'll be in the soup when he gets back here," was the response.

The first voice was that of Sgt. Ralph Moroney as he set down the phone after hearing it ring at least fifteen times. Glorie Inexcelsis, secretary, was the respondent and she went on.

"The major's neck is red as a lobster's shell."

"Heard anything from that goddamn kid yet?" Major Ralston barked over at Moroney.

"No sir, not yet," the sergeant replied.

"Can't understand it," the major continued, pacing back and forth, fists knotted behind his back. "I told him once more and he's through and that was only last week and here it is, the little hand's on nine and the big hand . . ."

"Yes sir," Sergeant Moroney injected, "It's 9 o'clock." Moroney had been civilian once and he learned to tell time then.

Back at the BOQ, Glutz slept on blissfully until 9:45 A.M. Then he woke with a burst and somehow knew it was well past 7:00 A.M. A glance at the radio-alarm confirmed his fears. The alarm had been turned off, apparently by Glutz in his sleep. He jumped from the sack and made haste for the phone.

"Major Ralston, please."

"He's fit to be tied, Jerry," said Glorie.

"Hi ho Silver," said Glutz, "let him out of the pen and put him on."

"I'm already on, lieutenant," snarled the major who had picked up another receiver.

"Yes sir," said Glutz. "I'm very sorry, but I overslept."

"So you did, lieutenant. Well, get your clothes on and get down here," the major continued rather warmly.

"Yes sir," said Glutz, but the phone on the other end had already been cradled. He looked into the instrument for a moment and then set it down. *No sense making a mad dash now,* he said to himself. *Fifteen minutes more or less won't make hell any worse.* Still, the apprehension put on some pressure, so Glutz decided to skip the shower and let it go with an electric shave. He looked through the mirror with bleary eyes, hardly recognizing the face in there he was shaving. Socks and shoes went on in a jiffy as did his other blues, and soon he was trudging on down toward the headquarters of the Alaskan Air Force. When he arrived on the scene, Major Gluefingers was in Ralston's office, but he knew the circumstances and left immediately.

"Lieutenant Glutz," Major Ralston began. Glutz sank back in his chair to prepare for the onslaught. Suddenly the major paused and came over to Glutz's desk. He bent over to whisper in his ear. He said it ever so softly. "Before we begin this admonishment, please go wash the lipstick from your face. An officer should have good military bearing when he is being reprimanded." Major Ralston grinned and Glutz walked out of the room. In the restroom he still saw a rather unclear countenance in the mirror, but he was able to zero in on the red smudge and eliminate it.

He walked back to the office, half expecting the major to be over his "mad." He wasn't!

"Lieutenant," the major began again, "You'll recall that I told you I'd tolerate no more absences." Glutz nodded. "I'm sorry, but my only recourse is to discipline you." Glutz nodded again without looking up.

Discipline, he thought. *I wonder what that means. Maybe he'll confine me to the base or to quarters for the weekend. No,* he answered himself. *I don't think he could do that. I've seen it or heard about it somewhere, though. Maybe in the movies.*

Major Ralston rambled on, but Glutz wasn't listening. He was too busy trying to speculate on his fate. *Maybe I'll get demoted,* but he answered himself again. *No, there isn't anything lower than a brown bar* (second lieutenant, for those haven't known one). " . . . and so," the major concluded, "I'm directing you to report to squadron headquarters tomorrow morning when the little hand is on the eight and"

"At 0800 hours, sir?" concluded Glutz.

"That's right," the major retorted emphatically.

"But, tomorrow is . . ." Glutz began to plead.

"I don't care what you've got planned for tomorrow, Jerry," (the major was more affectionate now) "you'll just have to get someone else." Glutz contemplated his new fate. He didn't think the squadron headquarters would be open on Saturday. He had tried to tell Major Ralston that, but the good major didn't seem to want to listen.

At the end of the day Glutz stopped at the club for a drink and then went to the slop chute for supper. Afterwards he retired to his BOQ room and relaxed in front of the TV. He dozed off there and drifted back into a state of consciousness at about 10:00 P.M. Not knowing what the next day would hold at squadron headquarters and feeling kind of groggy, Glutz brushed his teeth and climbed into the pad.

At 6:45 A.M. he felt much more gingery than most mornings at that time. He usually didn't get so good a sleep. As he showered and shaved, Glutz wondered what the squadron had in store for him. He had dispelled the thought that no one would be there, because surely the major wouldn't send him on a wild goose chase. Glutz knew they couldn't give him any manual labor because he was an officer. What else they might have for him he couldn't imagine.

He took his walk to the squadron at a leisurely pace because it was a fresh, crisp morning and he had plenty of time. The urgency of the hour was upon him, however, and he had no intention of being late this day. At 0755 he arrived at the squadron headquarters. No one was there, but, perhaps because he was five minutes early. He waited 15 minutes more, but still no one showed. A bit frustrated and irritated and at the same time relieved, he tracked his way back to the BOQ after trying all the doors and looking in all the windows. One door was open, to the day room, but no one was there.

Glutz picked up the phone and dialed Major Ralston's number.

"Hello," a young voice answered.

"Is your dad there?" asked Glutz.

"Is dad here?" the voice seemed to ask someone. "No he's not."

"When do you expect him back?" Glutz wanted to know.

"When's he coming back, Mom?" Glutz had enough. "Let me speak to your mom, please, young man."

"My name is Kathy," said the voice on the other end, vexedly.

"Mrs. Ralston, this is Lieutenant Glutz. Would you ask the major to call when he returns, please? Thanks very much."

Glutz laid down on the bed and began paging through a magazine. It was even less interesting than a dead head trip to the squadron headquarters.

Twenty minutes went by and then the phone rang.

"Glutz, this is Major Ralston."

"Yes, sir," said Glutz. "I just called to tell you that I went over to squadron headquarters this morning and there was no one there."

"What did you go over for?" the major asked rather irritably.

"Because you told me to go over there at 8:00 this morning to report for extra duty," Glutz answered.

The major seemed incredulous. "Didn't you know that the squadron is closed on Saturdays?"

"I thought it was and so yesterday I tried to tell you."

"Oh, never mind," the major interrupted again.

"Should I go over there on Monday?" Glutz wanted to know.

"No, just show up for work on time," the major paused and then added, "That's when the big hand is on . . ."

"Yes, sir," Glutz broke in, "I know, 0800 hours."

On Saturday night Glutz went up to Capt. Karl Luke's quarters. It was sort of like going to the toilet. You usually knew what to expect. Karl was always there on Saturday nights. At 6:00 P.M. he had dinner at the officers' club. At 7:30 P.M. he took a shower, and then afterwards he shined his shoes and wrote a letter to his mother. Someone once said that he had graduated from the Naval Academy. Knowing Karl, that seemed a little far-fetched, so the rumor gradually changed to say that Captain Karl had attended the Military Academy. Some said that he had just wanted to go to the Air Force Academy. In any event, he had the most highly polished shoes anyone could remember seeing. That was not like the Academy graduates at all. No one really hung around with "Karly" too much, as Glutz affectionately called him. But, everybody sort of liked him. He was refreshingly and naively honest and straightforward; a hard commodity to come by in or out of the service. He was also always good for a can of cold tuna, some crackers, and a bottle of Zip cola.

Glutz knocked twice at the door before it opened. There stood Captain Karl in his after-shower regalia.

"Hi Jerry," he said cheerily. "Come on in. How about a can of tuna, some crackers, and a bottle of Zip cola?"

I thought you'd never ask, Glutz thought to himself.

"Thanks," he said, "I will."

Captain Luke went immediately about preparing (opening the can of) tuna. He brought it on a tray where Glutz sat actually submerged in a chair which had lost its springs. He would obviously not be able to get out by himself.

Almost no verbiage was exchanged between Captain Karl and Lieutenant Glutz. Karly went about shining his shoes and then writing the letter to his mother. Glutz slumped silently in his "chair," wolfing down the canned tuna, munching on the crisp crackers, and intermittently taking belts from his bottle of Zip cola. At the same time, he was staring at an old TV set at an even older movie. Presently, the tuna, crackers and Zip cola were all gone. Glutz brushed the crackers from his hands, simultaneously leaning into the back of the chair. But, the chair wasn't a true ninety degrees, so the angle of his torso was still somewhat forward.

"Delicious, Karly," said Glutz complimentarily.

"M-m-m," answered Captain Luke, putting a pencil to his tongue while pondering the next thought to be set down in his letter to his mother.

Glutz watched TV a bit longer and then, tired and bored, he rose to leave. Karl didn't look up. Without a word, Glutz made his exit. "Sometime we'll get together for a movie," he was going to say, but then he didn't. Karly was a nice, if a bit unusual, guy. Glutz liked him a great deal, but still felt uneasy around him because he was so quiet.

Back in his own room Glutz felt ready for bed, but when he got there, he found he wasn't. He tossed and turned. First one thought and then another flashed through his mind. Some made him uneasy, others spread a grin across his face, even in the dark, and still others passed through his consciousness with no discernable impact. *I wonder, what Ralston will have in store for me on Monday?* he thought first. The apprehension made his stomach turn a bit and then he forced the thought from his mind by replacing it with another. *Good thing the mind can entertain only one concept at a time,* he thought in between. The mental image of Karl Luke in his honeymoon bed with some faceless wife brought a grin to his face. He was reminded of several jokes he'd heard about just such a situation and the smile grew broader, almost into a laugh.

Then, suddenly he remembered the next night was Sunday and he had a date with Peggy. Once again apprehension, though this time a different kind, and distaste crept into his being. *I have no desire to see her again,* he thought. *I'll call her in the morning and beg off. No, I can't do that. There's nothing wrong with her. If anyone's at fault, I am. I've got to go through with it and then, that's all.* He stared into the darkness for what seemed an eternity, until finally sleep came.

As is always the case, the late hour of his slumber didn't enhance his alertness early next morning. It was a struggle to rise at 11:00, without breakfast, to make the last service. The chapel on base was interdenominational and Glutz arrived just as the Catholic Mass was letting out. He passed Jim Gross, a buddy from headquarters, coming out of the chapel as he went in. Looking straight ahead, Gross cupped his hand to his mouth and angled its corner toward the passing Jerry Glutz.

"Hiss-s-s!! All Protestants are going to hell," he whispered, poker faced and never slowing down. He had already passed when Glutz turned around to holler after him, in subdued normal tones, "Catholics are already there!"

Then, he turned with a smile and took a half step into an oncoming Franciscan priest who had probably had the Mass just completed. "Oh, excuse me, Padre," Glutz said flushing.

The priest smiled, nodded his head, and walked on humming a tune, the words to which begin, "Won't you come along with me . . ." Obviously he had overheard at least Glutz's part of the conversation with Airman Jim Gross.

Glutz sat down in a pew and, though they were wood and straight and hard, he was comfortable. Glutz didn't go to church regularly, but was always comfortable there. He thought about his childhood, the trips each Sunday to church with his folks, his confirmation and wondered why he didn't come more often. Grand church or simple chapel, he always found the spirit of peace here, equivalent to nowhere else.

Through most of the service, Glutz's thoughts wandered, as usual. He didn't catch a great deal of the sermon, at least not consciously, but it was a good experience anyway. He thought again about Peggy and his date coming up that evening. Still not very excited about it, in this atmosphere it at least seemed palatable.

Relations between Protestants and Catholics crossed his mind. Glutz remembered the wild stories that used to go around and the bitterness that sometimes existed. He noted that there was little or none of it in him nor among his contemporaries. But, racial bias still existed. Perhaps, less in the service than elsewhere, but the undertones were here, too. He reflected on the inconsistency between the precepts of Christianity and racially segregated churches. *And, the same people,* he thought. *How can that be?* Even he, he admitted, was not untainted. *Maybe someday,* he thought, and then found himself rising with the rest of the congregation to sing the recessional hymm.

Sunday afternoon he bowled a few lines, and then went back to the BOQ to get ready for his date. He still wasn't very excited, but poured a scotch to drink between "chores" and eventually saw the roses begin to bud. At 6:30 P.M., as he got into his car, Glutz felt good and clean and comfortable. The apprehension returned when he arrived at Peggy's house. *Maybe she's not here,* he hoped.

Inside, Peggy was hoping the same thing until she saw his car drive up. Her palms became sweaty while his sphincter contracted as he approached the outer door. Of course, neither knew of the other's dilemma.

Glutz knocked briskly at the door. *Here goes nothing,* he thought. Peggy hesitated, leaning on the inside of the door. When she could wait no longer she opened it.

"Hi Peggy," said Glutz huskily, feigning enthusiasm. "Ready to go?"

"Hi," Peggy responded weakly.

In the car, there was no conversation. Glutz broke through the chill with the first words. He had pondered long on what to say.

"Have a nice weekend, Peggy?"

"Yes, it was fine," she said. Silence again.

"Peggy . . ."

"About the other night," Peggy broke in. "I mean you really didn't have to take me out again. It wasn't right of me to ask you."

"You didn't ask me, Peggy. I asked you," Glutz assured her. "Remember? And, I asked because I wanted to," he lied. "Okay?"

"Okay," she said. "It's just that . . ."

"It's just that nothing," he injected. "Now, let's have a good time, like we would have had the other night if . . ."

"If I hadn't vomited on you!" she interrupted sobbing. "Oh Jerry, I'm so ashamed. I don't see how I can ever really look at you again. You should have thrown me in the gutter."

"No, but I thought of the trash can for some of my clothes," he answered, smiling. Peggy began to sob again or was it . . . yes, it was laughter. The two burst out laughing together, and the tension was eased considerably.

Once at the club, Glutz had hopes of a drink to relax them but it didn't work. Peggy was still rather stiff and he could feel the artificial air in himself. They danced once clumsily and even with the candlelight, the dinner and wine left something stilted and undone. At nine o'clock Glutz suggested they leave and Peggy was ready. He thought that they might stop at his place. In the back of his mind he had an idea of continuing where they had left off previously, but knew that really wasn't possible; and actually, he didn't want it anyway.

"No," Peggy said emphatically, "I don't need a reinstatement of that memory and besides, I've got to set my hair for work tomorrow." That reminded Glutz of a joke, too, but he decided to dismiss it.

At Peggy's apartment, Glutz leaned over to compress her lips. She met him warmly, but moved away rapidly.

"Thanks Jerry, you're a nice guy. Good bye!" She said rather sharply.

Glutz walked from the house compelled by a subconscious desire to lick his lips to see if he could taste anything. He didn't think so, but there seemed to be a strange odor in the air. *Wonder why she said good bye instead of good night,* he thought as he drove off.

CHAPTER XI

On Monday morning Glutz reported for work as usual, about ten minutes late. He hurried down the hall somewhat breathlessly in some sort of a twisted hope that Major Ralston would be late, even though he knew the major was always on time. He turned the corner into the main part of the office and headed intently for the smaller room he shared with the major.

"Good morning, lieutenant, good morning, Lieu, good morning, good . . ." the staff greeted him, cheerily, as he sped by.

"Good morning!" Glutz puffed in return. He spotted his office and couldn't believe his eyes. He'd done it! Major Ralston was not in his office! He'd actually beaten the major to work! Glutz pulled his coat off hurriedly and hung it up. He set his service cap in its usual place at the edge of the desk. Quickly, he began looking through his drawers for something to make it look like he was busy. All he could lay his hands on was a copy of *Alaskan Air Force Regulations Manual* which would one day earn him the unofficial title of "Ronald Regulation," the most learned man in that subject on the base."

Soon he became engrossed in one of the regulations governing time off, a favorite subject of his, and he didn't note the passage of time. Gradually, it dawned on him that he had now been in the office for some time, and he had not heard Major Ralston come in. Could the major have come in without his knowledge? Obviously not. Glutz immediately dismissed that thought from his mind. Could he be somewhere else in the building? Not likely for this long a time. His coffee period wasn't here yet, but it was rapidly approaching and the major always did his best work first thing in the morning. Glutz waited a few moments longer until the apprehension was gnawing at his innards, and he had to find out.

"Glorie, where's the major this morning?" he said haughtily, as if to be "one up" on his superior officer once again. Glorie looked up somewhat surprised.

"He's out at King Caribou hunting today. He'll be back tonight. Didn't you know?"

"No," Glutz responded, "I guess he expected that I'd be over at squadron headquarters today so he didn't bother to tell me."

Glorie went back to whatever she was cutting. "Why aren't you?" she asked without looking up.

"It's a long story," Glutz drawled.

"I'll bet it is," she said. Glutz was thinking about last Saturday's trip to the squadron HQ (headquarters, for those who don't recognize the symbols for water too well). He went back to reading his regulations.

Shortly before noon, Sgt. Moroney came into the office, appearing to be somewhat more intent than usual.

"The governor just died after an operation," Moroney said. "The general will want to send personal telegrams of condolence, I'm sure. You write one to the people of Alaska, and I'll write the one for his wife."

"Whose wife?" Glutz asked, bewildered.

"What do you care? You're not writing it," snapped Moroney.

That's right, Glutz thought to himself, *I'm not,* and he turned to address himself to the task at hand. In a moment he turned back. "Write a telegram . . ." his voice trailed off when he saw that Moroney was out of sight, "to the people of Alaska," he continued his mutterings to himself. "I hardly know any of them. I don't even know the general very well."

Nonetheles, he gamely took out his pad and pencil. *Dear People of Alaska* he started. That was his purpose all right, but it didn't make sense, even to himself. He started again. *Today, the blue field of Alaska's state flag has turned red with the spent blood of its expired governor.*

Oh gad, Glutz thought, *this is an impossible task.* He rose to his feet and took a couple of steps before he was reminded that he had his "Indian" pants on. They had *crept up behind.* Two stiff-legged steps like a wooden soldier, a grasp of the seat of his pants, one jerk, and his pace was once again free. Relatively certain that his "ballet" had passed unnoticed, he continued on his journey to Sergeant Moroney's office.

"I can't write this thing, Ralph," he said. "I . . ."

"Never mind," Moroney responded, continuing to type. "I'm almost finished with the second one."

"Gee, thanks, sergeant," Glutz apologized. "I just haven't . . ."

"Yeah, I know," Sgt. Moroney interrupted. "Here," he said, ripping the sheet of paper from the typewriter and adding another from his desk, "take these and call them to the news media just as soon as you've verified the governor's death."

"Hello? Courier? This is Lieutenant Glutz, Jerome V. A-09 . . ." *Oh, what am I doing,* he thought to himself.

"What?" the voice on the other end interrupted, apparently having heard only garble from what Glutz had started to say.

"This is Lieutenant Glutz at the air force base," Jerry began again.

"Yes, Lieutenant Glutz, what is it? came the staccatoed voice from the other end of the line.

"Is the governor dead yet?" Glutz continued, somewhat confused.

"The governor!" rasped the voice at *The Courier,* "What's wrong with the Governor?"

"He had an operation," Glutz half told, half asked. *At least I think he did,* he thought to himself. He wasn't sure of anything after finding out that *The Courier* didn't seem to know anything about it. "Well, don't take my word for it," Glutz continued excitedly, "but we heard here that the governor had a serious operation and either died or is on the verge of it."

"Hold on," said the *Courier* voice apathetically. Glutz could hear him (or her, if she smoked a lot) talking to a third party.

"Some lieutenant on the phone says the Governor had an operation and is near death."

"Yeah, I guess he had an operation, but I haven't heard there is any problem," the third party said.

The voice from *The Courier* began to repeat the story to Glutz.

"Never mind, I heard it," Glutz interrupted.

"Well, anyway, that's all we know," said the voice from *The Courier.*

"Will you know more later?" Glutz wondered eagerly.

"Dunno," said the voice at the other end. "You've got all the news we've heard so far."

Glutz was incredulous. "Well, don't you have communication with the Capitol?" He was perplexed.

"You've got the airplanes, we don't," answered Mr. Apathy. "If you learn any more you can call us," he invited.

"Well, just don't quote me," Glutz admonished.

"On what?" said the voice. "You haven't said anything yet."

He hung up and Glutz took a moment or two to follow his favorite pastime of looking into the receiver, as if it would provide some clue to the appearance and raspy voice of the strange person to whom he had been talking.

Glutz set the phone down and sat back in his chair. Now that it was all over he felt hyperventilated and exotic from the near encounter with fate. Just think, he had been called upon to write a sympathy note to the people of Alaska on the death of the governor, over the general's name. This was truly a red letter day. He had already forgotten that he couldn't have written it.

Sgt. Moroney walked into Glutz's office at that point. Glutz leaned back in his chair and, resting the back of his head in his folded hands, he said, with a superior air, "Well, Ralph, what does it look like?"

"What does what look like?" Sgt. Moroney muttered. Glutz leaned forward now, the base of his metal chair clanking against the bottom of the seat as the latter was returned to its normal position.

"I mean, what's the situation with governor?"

"Oh, that," Moroney continued, without looking up. "Seems there's been a little misunderstanding."

"What do you mean, a little misunderstanding?" Glutz pressed on.

"Look, lieutenant," the sergeant said irritably, "quit pushing. I'll explain it to you, but give me a chance."

"Sorry," apologized Glutz.

"Forget it," Moroney said, and walked away.

Glutz was dying to know more, but he wasn't anxious to get into any verbal fisticuffs with the verbally experienced Sgt. Moroney. Withdrawing his mind from the crisis, he put his feet on the desk and continued with the regulations he had started earlier. Presently, Moroney returned to the scene.

"Sorry I hollered at you like that before, lieutenant." Jerry Glutz looked up and smiled. He admired the sergeant a great deal, and now, the two were buddies again. That made him very happy.

"Forget it, sergeant," he said, feigning the use of his authority.

"I guess I lost my head for a minute because the whole thing's a little embarrassing."

"What do you mean?" Glutz wondered, his brow furrowed.

Sergeant Moroney went on, seemingly ignoring the Lieutenant's injection. "I overhead the general's driver talking about a dead or dying governor this morning and I assumed it was the governor of our state. He did have an operation, you know," Moroney was quick to include.

So I've heard, Glutz thought to himself.

"Anyway," the sergeant went on, "it turns out that the governor was on the general's car to keep it from going over thirty miles per hour on the base. The thing wasn't working right, so the security police stopped the car for speeding. Well, needless to say, the general wasn't pleased so his driver 'operated' on it on the spot and said he was 'near death' all the way over here, worrying that it wouldn't work and he'd accidently speed again. You know, the general doesn't like to drive too slowly, either."

"No, I didn't know that," Glutz said, half in jest.

"Goes to show you, lieutenant, always be sure of your facts before using them."

"I'll remember that, sergeant," said Glutz. *My write-ups were better than yours,* Glutz was tempted to say, remembering now that he hadn't written a thing, but it would have been too cruel a thrust. Besides, he wanted Sergeant Moroney to like him. Glutz looked at his watch.

"Lunch time, Ralph," he said to Sergeant Moroney. "Care to join me?"

"Where're you going?" queried the sergeant, his thoughts obviously elsewhere.

"To the NCO (for noncommissioned officers, for those who have been there) club, if you go with me," Glutz said. Glutz knew that officers could only go to the NCO club when invited by a noncommissioned officer, and 'noncom's' couldn't go to the officers' club, even on invitation.

"No, you go ahead," Moroney rejoined. "Maybe I'll join you later."

"But, I can't go there without you, sarge, you know that."

"Tell 'em I sent you," Moroney mumbled, looking at the floor, his thoughts still afar.

"Ralph, I can't . . ."

"Then, go someplace else, lieutenant," Moroney shot back, staring at Glutz coldly. "I'm not your keeper." On that note the sergeant turned and stomped off toward his desk.

"Someplace else is a joint downtown," Glutz mumbled after him. Moroney heard it and turned on his heel. A wry grin turned up one corner of his mouth, bringing the dimple out on his cheek.

"Lieutenant, you are something else, you really are. C'mon, let's go," the sarge said, motioning Glutz toward him. Glutz picked up his service cap and trod after Moroney.

"We'll be at the NCO club," he told Glorie Inexcelsis, as he whisked by.

OK, Sonny, she thought to herself.

Even though Major Ralston wasn't "home" today, Lieutenant Glutz and Sergeant Moroney returned from lunch on time, because Moroney was a creature of habit of being on time, and in spite of Glutz being a creature of habit of coming late. Glutz went to his desk and pulled open the drawers. There wasn't much there. Only the book on air force regulations. "No more of that today," Glutz thought. He rose from his chair to see what magazines administrative services might have to pass the time, and ran into Sgt. Moroney on the way.

"Lieutenant," Moroney started, "since it's kind of quiet this afternoon [he meant, since the major's not here], I think I'll go home early. The wife has a doctor's appointment and I'd like to take her, OK?"

"OK," agreed Glutz, puffing out his chest to think that he should be asked. It never occurred to him to think what might happen if he were to say "no." It never occurred to Sgt. Moroney that he might, either.

So Moroney left and Glutz went on to administrative services. The trip was fruitful in that he found several magazines with several promising articles and, more important, each had a crossword puzzle or similar game. Lieutenant Glutz returned to his desk and settled down to business. At about 1415 (that's really 2:15 P.M., but it seems more progressive to think in air force terms—small pun) the phone rang and Mrs. Inexcelsis picked it up.

"Just a moment," she said calmly, "let me refer you to Lieutenant Glutz." Cupping her hand over the mouthpiece, she told Glutz, "It's Colonel Overland."

"Who?" Glutz whispered, as if the colonel could overhear him.

"Colonel Overland," she repeated, "OSI." (That's sort of like the air force's FBI for those who've not been in the air force or were too straight to know.)

"My God," Glutz blurted out in terrified tones. "What have I done to deserve a call from him?"

"I don't know," Glorie said softly, yet impatiently, "but, please take the phone. He's been waiting almost a minute."

Glutz picked up the hard plastic phone nervously from its cradle and promptly dropped it on the floor. He picked it back up just as promptly and put it to his ear.

"Excuse me, sir, I had an accident." He had probably defecated in his drawers over the excitement at the moment, but that's not what he meant. The colonel didn't acknowledge the apology.

"Lieutenant," he said, "there's been a suicide over in barracks 4220."

"A suicide!" Glutz shrieked, not knowing what to say next. "Ah yes, a suicide."

There was a pause and then Glutz added, "Is he dead?"

"He's dead, all right," the colonel answered. "Shot in the temple."

Shot in the temple, Glutz thought confusedly. *Must have been Jewish.*

"And, he wasn't even Jewish," the colonel laughed from the other end of the line.

"Yes, well, who did it?" Glutz blurted out, still not knowing what to do, how to act or what to say.

"It was a *suicide,* lieutenant," the colonel responded dryly.

"Yes, but who . . . oh yes, a suicide," Glutz answered himself. There was a pause again until Glutz picked up the conversation. "Well, what do you want me to do, sir?"

"You'd better get over there right away," the colonel told him.

"Who was it, colonel, do I know him?" That was a stupid question because Glutz didn't even know the colonel. The colonel thoughtfully ignored that fact, however, and answered Glutz.

"I don't know whether you did or not, lieutenant," he said. "His name was Larry Witherspoon, the president of the local ROA chapter." (ROA stands for Reserve Officers Association and includes some who were or are on active duty on a somewhat temporary basis. Some say, about those who have left active duty, that they still want to sing the hymn, but don't want to carry the pack any longer.)

Larry Witherspoon, Glutz thought. *He's the guy who has . . . had,* he corrected himself, *the reputation for spinning wild tales to the bad looking dollies in the chow hall.* One night Glutz overheard him telling of a son at West Point and a daughter in some eastern girls' school.

"Why did he do it, colonel?" Glutz asked rather inanely.

"I don't know, lieutenant," said the colonel. "I haven't had the chance to ask him. You can do that yourself when you get over there. I'd be interested in what he has to say!"

"I thought you said he was dead, colonel," asked Glutz quizzically.

"He is," said the colonel. A long pause again before Glutz picked the conversation back up.

"Colonel, is there anything I should take along?"

"Yeah," Colonel Overland muttered under his breath, "take your mess kit along and gobble up some brains. It sounds as if you could use them."

"What was that?" Glutz asked.

"Just get yourself over there fast," remonstrated the colonel. "The news media will probably be asking questions soon and you've got to have some answers."

Me! thought Glutz, his eyes bulging. He wasn't even sure what media meant.

Glutz called the base motor pool for a car. It was now almost 2:35 P.M. (we switch back to civilian time because 1435 isn't as promising as 1415). The motor pool said they could have a car for him at 4:45.

"What day?" Glutz asked sarcastically, and hung up.

Nervously, he circled the small office, partly in search of his hat, but more so to see if he couldn't find something of value to take along. He mustn't get over there and be the rank amateur, he knew, but he also knew there was little chance of avoiding it. Finally, he picked up a large pad of paper and a pencil and swirled out the back door of the office.

"Where are you going?" Mrs. Inexcelsis hollered after him.

"Who knows?" he answered, too late and not loud enough for her to hear.

BOQ 4220 was about a mile from air command headquarters. It took Glutz twenty minutes to get there. He had hurried the first few blocks, but then slowed down the rest of the way, partly because he was too tired to move faster and partly because he hoped the gory part would be gone when he arrived. Fortunately, it was. The coroner, Col. Overland, and the vice president of the ROA were huddled together. The body was gone and the cleaning lady had been there. Lieutenant Webfoot, the ROA VP, had come up through the enlisted ranks and so he was older than most lieutenants in the Alaskan air force. He may have been older than most captains, too. He was even older than some majors and lieutenant colonels, and they were old. He seemed to be a weapons fancier and was explaining to Overland and the coroner some of the characteristics of the revolver which had apparently "done the job."

Colonel Overland saw Glutz and invited him into the conversation.

"You must be Lieutenant Glutz," said the colonel, extending his hand. "These are the coroner, Mr. O'Dell, and Lieutenant Webfoot, vice president of the Reserve Officers Association."

A natty army uniform with the rank insignia of a lieutenant colonel hung in the closet of the deceased. Overland could see Glutz staring at it. "I was just apprising these men of some of the facts we've already put together, lieutenant. Maybe you'd like to hear them."

"Yes, I would," said Glutz, sniffing about the room now, a la Sherlock Holmes.

"As you may know," the colonel began, "Mr. Witherspoon was employed by the air force in a civilian capacity here on the base."

"He was also president of the ROA, nominated by me," Webfoot added.

The colonel glanced his disapproval at Lieutenant Webfoot, whether for the interruption or the nomination is unknown, and concluded, "Except he was no officer. It turns out that the furthest he ever got in the army was to the rank of corporal, and then he was discharged for ulcers."

"He certainly wouldn't kill himself over that," Glutz injected insightfully.

"Maybe his son flunked out of West Point," quipped Lieutenant Webfoot ruefully. Colonel Overland scowled and the smile shrank from Webfoot's countenance.

The colonel continued: "No, the ROA didn't catch up to him, but his own machinations did."

"That sounds fatal, all right," cracked Lieutenant Webfoot. The smile quickly drained from his face once again as the colonel scowled.

"It seems," the colonel went on, "that he had somehow devised a scheme to misappropriate government funds, but now the investigators have closed in on him, and that's how we were able to get to the core of the matter this fast."

"Some sour apple, he was," Lieutenant Webfoot included, looking around for some indication of reinforcement and approval for his pun. Glutz smiled and Webfoot gobbled it up.

The colonel went on, "It's hard to figure. Witherspoon was divorced, no children, apparently came up here to get away from alimony payments; money shouldn't have been a problem, yet he got himself into a spiraling jackpot."

"And, today the big payoff," puffed Lieutenant Webfoot with haughty affectation.

"Today the big payoff," concluded Colonel Overland.

Refusing rides from Colonel Overland and Lieutenant Webfoot, to show his vanity for manliness and fearful of a trip with the coroner, Glutz walked the three blocks back to the BOQ since it was approaching 5:00 P.M. and the "shop" would be ready to close by the time he returned there—the real reason for rejecting the rides. On the way to the BOQ, Glutz wasn't exactly sure what to do with the information he had. As a matter of fact, he had no idea what to do with it.

Back home in his suite, Glutz plopped on his bed and stared blankly at the ceiling. What to do? Should he call some kind of notice of the death into the radio station? TV? The newspapers? He picked up the phone to dial Sergeant Moroney, hoping he might be home by now. Surely he would know. Lieutenant Glutz put the phone to his ear, but there was no dial tone.

"Hello!" he said instinctively.

"Hello," came a voice from the other end. It was Colonel Overland. "Hello, Lieutenant Glutz?"

"Yes sir," Glutz responded.

"This is Colonel Overland, Glutz. Have you called the story in to the media yet?"

"Not yet, colonel," Glutz responded.

"Well, you'd better do so," the colonel continued. "Otherwise the rumor mill will get started and we could get all kinds of bad and erroneous publicity from that."

It'll be bad whether or not it's erroneous, Glutz thought to himself.

"Who should I call, colonel?" Glutz thought the colonel might know, at least more than he himself did.

"That's your department, lad," the colonel told him. "You're ISO and we're OSI, remember?" Overland said, chuckling out loud. "Be a man of letters, boy. Don't get mixed up."

Glutz missed the colonel's humor in his frenzy. "OK, colonel, I'll take care of it," he said, more to get the colonel off the line than anything.

After Colonel Overland hung up, Glutz got his dial tone and called Sergeant Moroney. "Hi, Maxine," he said, recognizing the sergeant's wife's voice when she answered. "This is Jerry Glutz. Is Ralph in?"

"This is the babysitter," the voice on the other end told him. "Technical Sergeant and Mrs. Ralph Moroney are out at the moment. May I give them a message on their return?"

Glutz waited, half expecting to hear, "This has been a recorded announcement." When that message didn't come, he said, "No, that's all right. Thanks anyway," and hung up the receiver.

Within moments Glutz's phone rang. Not having moved far, he picked it up on the first ring. The woman at the other end was giggling. Hardly able to stop, she said between chuckles, "I'm sorry, Lieutenant Glutz, that was a mean trick to play, but when the phone rang Ralph said he wished we had a maid, so I decided to give him one. Seems he had a bad day at the office today." Half day, Glutz reminded her mentally, but decided not to say it aloud. "Just a moment," Maxine Moroney said, still giggling, "I'll put him on." Lieutenant Glutz could hear Sergeant Moroney pick up the phone.

"What is it, lieutenant?" Moroney said less than enthusiastically. Glutz told him about the suicide and about Colonel Overland's directing him to call the data to the news media.

"What should I do?" Glutz repeated his question of Colonel Overland to Moroney.

"Call the news media," the sergeant responded dryly.

"But, what shall I tell them?" Glutz went on, unaffected by Moroney's sarcastic response.

"Don't ask me, lieutenant. It seems my judgement's not the most in demand today." Sergeant Moroney was obviously depressed over the governor episode.

There was a pause to which neither responded and then Glutz heard a click in his receiver. He stared at it a moment before setting it back down. Sergeant Moroney had lost his composure. The picture was clear to him. Of all the people at command HQ, he was the last Glutz would have expected. The prospect didn't bolster his confidence in what he had to do. Yet, in a way it did. Moroney had just shown he was no superman.

Maybe he, Lt. Glutz, was just as capable, if he'd just give himself the chance. Glutz sat down to pen the message.

News Release

This afternoon at Elfendwarf Air Force Base, Larry Witherspoon, civil service employee, apparently took his life by his own hand.

Glutz was using some words he had heard or read before, but they lacked the right sound as he read them. He set the paper down again and continued on.

Mr. Witherspoon, 42, had been working on the base since last August. No motive for the apparent suicide has been given. There are no known survivors.

Glutz remembered the use of the term apparent from news releases he had heard in the past. He liked it and used it freely. Probably helps to keep out of lawsuits, he thought.

He called the short news release in to the TV stations, radio stations and newspapers. Then he sat back and waited. Glutz was very apprehensive. He had never done anything like this before. In college, when he wrote a paper, if the instructor didn't like it, he'd get a low grade. Here, Glutz didn't know what could happen, but he was sure it would be something bad. Besides, each of the media had asked for his name when he called the story in.

Lieutenant Glutz turned on the radio and his mind wandered away. Bizarre thoughts followed one another through his mind. *What's the worst that could happen?* he said to himself. And then the possibilities suggested themselves. Stern reprimand, court martial, dismissal from the service. The last wouldn't be bad, Glutz thought, except under the circumstances. A couple of news periods went past and Glutz didn't hear his story on the radio. He couldn't be sure it wasn't on, though, because his mind had been wandering. Still, he thought he would have heard, had it been on.

At 8:00 P.M., the acid still chewing at his stomach walls, Glutz decided to call Major Ralston, figuring he'd be home by now.

"Major? This is Jerry Glutz. Sorry to bother you, but there was a suicide on base today, and I had to phone a news release in to the media. I'd like to read it to you."

"Shoot!" Ralston barked back at him.

Oh, that word, Glutz thought, and the mental image of a court martial returned to him, but he quickly dismissed it. The major probably wondered why Lt. Glutz wanted him to know the content of the news release now, after it had been sent in. But, maybe he had been through the same thing himself, in an earlier day of his career, and knew Glutz would like to sleep that night. Anyway, the major assured Glutz that the wording was fine and hung up. The Lieutenant had probably never enjoyed a scotch and cigarette so much as the one that followed.

Next morning, Glutz was late for work again, but he was almost relaxed as he entered the headquarters building. Major Ralston had told Glutz over the phone the night before that he'd be in about noon since he had arrived home rather late from his trip. Besides, the lieutenant had finally done something to earn his keep and, next to the nothingness of the previous month's efforts, it stood out in his mind as almost worthy of a commendation. As a result of all this, he arrived on the scene smiling and whistling, greeted the office staff, and then only at the last second spotted Major Ralston. He had come in on time after all. Glutz's heart sank and the trepidation of previous mornings returned.

"Good morning, sir," he tried to say cheerily and confidently, as he walked past the major.

"Good afternoon," responded the major cordially, but without looking up. The major's back-of-the-neck thermometer showed the likelihood of an impending storm, however, even though the surface signs were ostensibly calm. The beet red meant "warmer weather ahead." Glutz knew the sign and what it meant, so he kept his mouth shut.

Shortly, Sergeant Moroney leaned on the door frame to the entrance of the two offices. "The lieutenant turned in his first news release last night, and a pretty good one at that, major. Did you happen to pick it up at ten o'clock on the TV?"

"No, I didn't," Major Ralston responded coldly and without looking up. "But, I got a firsthand shot over the telephone."

Glutz winced again at the major's use of the term shot, feeling once more that he wasn't completely out of danger. Sergeant Moroney looked at Glutz quizzically for a moment, but then the wonder was gone.

"Well, anyway, lieutenant, it was a good news release."

"Thanks," said Glutz, looking to the major for a hint of approval. But Major Ralston gave none. He continued to write at his desk and when Glutz looked up, Sergeant Moroney was gone. Glutz turned in his chair and dug for his book on air force regulations, wanting to avoid a confrontation with the major at the moment. Glutz had hardly turned around to face his desk when Ralston got up and stretched widely, arms bent, elbows out and fists clenched near his ears.

"Lieutenant," he said in the middle of his yawn. To Glutz, who didn't see him, it sounded like a growl and he almost wet his pants in the shock.

"Yes sir!" he said sharply, spinning about abruptly in his chair.

"I'm going over to the base exchange," (that's the base department store for those who haven't been trampled on there) the major said, concluding his yawn and finishing his sentence. "If anyone asks for me, tell him I'll be back shortly."

"Yes sir," Glutz answered more normally but smartly, still.

Glutz went back to his book on air force regulations and stared at it without seeing. He was toying with the idea of going down to see Senior Master Sergeant Nultz, Lieutenant Colonel Fliptop's leaning post, when a voice boomed into the room.

"Bud?" It was for Major Ralston and it was coming from the intercom just above his desk. Glutz was panicky. He remembered it immediately because beads of perspiration began to form between the folds of his lower back. Springing from his chair, he hurried to the box and began a frantic inspection to find a button he knew must be there to depress and return his voice to the caller. In the search, his face moved to within barely an inch of the box and just as it did, the voice boomed again.

"Bud!" it said more loudly this time. Glutz recoiled from the shock, like a spring in reverse, tripping over the major's chair as he flew backward and landed in it, one leg hanging from the knee over the left arm of the chair.

"Who is it?" asked Glutz of the box, not knowing what else to say.

"This is General Sullivan from Lapp Air Force Base."

Glutz recognized this immediately as some sort of joke, probably being played with the knowledge of Ralston, to embarrass Glutz, and perhaps, even by the major himself. No way could General Sullivan from Lapp, if there was such a person there, be on the other end of the squawk box.

"I am the general," he heard the voice say from the other end, and with equal confidence he answered, "And, I am the Statue of Liberty."

"Who is this?" barked the voice at the other end. Obviously Glutz's voice was getting through without a button on the box. He could not be sure, now, of this conversationalist, so he became more cautious.

"This is Lieutenant Glutz, sir," he answered.

"What's going on over there, lieutenant, and where is Major Ralston? Are you having a party?"

"No sir, I just didn't understand how the intercom worked," Glutz sputtered, "and the major is at the base exchange, but he'll be back shortly."

"Well, have him see me when he does come back." Lieutenant Glutz didn't have to ask who he was talking to. It really was the general.

"Yes sir," he said sharply. "I'll do that."

Glutz was bewildered. He half expected to get court martialed, but on brief reflection, thought that might be as good a way as any to dispense his military obligation. Glorie Inexcelsis was roaring with laughter over the episode, but one thing Glutz did not see in it was humor. He walked out of the office and slumped into the empty chair of the air command historian.

"You think it's funny, Glorie. How'd you like to tell the general from Lapp that you're the Statue of Liberty?"

"I think you're funny, lieutenant," she said, and went on laughing.

Just then a paper airplane wafted onto the desk where Glutz sat. Glutz looked hurriedly about to see if anyone saw the action. He knew Sergeant Moroney was the aggressor and half wished the major would have walked in and caught him. Slouching in his chair, Glutz opened the plane leisurely to find nothing more than the usual message.

"What's going on over there?" it read.

Glutz responded with a digital symbol familiar to at least all members of the American male population and, refolding the plane along its original lines, sent it on course over the partitions, back to its originator. Just as it left his guiding hand, Major Ralston's voice became audible to all.

"If there's nothing more to do in this office, perhaps we could get by with a few less people," he said sarcastically.

Glutz saw the back of the major's neck as he passed and noted that the barometer was working well. *When the barometer is red, warmer weather's ahead,* Glutz thought to himself. Glutz followed Major Ralston into their office to tell him that General Sullivan had been looking for him, but the phone rang first and the major answered it. Glutz was about to leave, but Ralston motioned him back.

"No, let me look into it, Penny. He's still single and if your daughter looks anything like you, I know he'd be happy to take her out. I'm sure we can work out something. Let me look into it and I'll call you back." Ralston hung up the phone and began to say something, but Glutz started first.

"General Sullivan is apparently sitting in for General Stockton. He called over that thing while you were gone," Glutz said, pointing to the intercom box, "and said he'd like to see you right away when you got back." Ralston got up and began to move around his desk toward the exit of the office.

"Don't go away," he told Glutz. "I'll be back shortly and I want to talk to you," he warned. Halfway through the door he stopped sharply and turned partly toward Glutz. "What did you tell him when he called to see me?" the major wanted to know.

"I told him you were at the BX," said Glutz.

"Thanks," said Major Ralston coldly, stomping off in the direction of the general's office.

When he returned, Glutz was back at his fond pastime, studying air force regulations. He looked up briefly, but not long enough to catch the major's eye. He didn't want to do that, because he thought there might be fire in it. If he saw the fire, it might singe him. But apparently there wasn't any fire. The major looked calm enough and didn't cast toward him that brief look of disgust Glutz knew so well. Glutz almost generated enough courage to ask Major Ralston what the general wanted, but something inside the dark recesses of his mind cautioned him and he thought better of it.

Just then Major Glueshoe, a close personal friend of Ralston's, walked into the office and Glutz was soon happy that he had remained silent.

"What's up, Bud?" Major Glueshoe asked in standard salutation form, smiling first at Glutz and then looking toward Ralston.

"Not too much," said Ralston, "except I just stepped over to the BX for a few moments and the kid here was nice enough to tell General Sullivan about it when he called in on the squawk box." Ralston's neck was red, but Glueshoe didn't see it, or perhaps he didn't know what it meant. In any event, his response was sprightly.

"Too bad Sullivan didn't know in advance you were going," Glueshoe suggested. "Maybe you could have picked up something for him."

Nice going, Glueshoe, Glutz thought to himself. *Why don't you go see the general. Maybe he could get something from you; like the bubonic plague.* Fortunately for Glutz, most of his gems were thought but never uttered. As a result, the silence in the room was deafening. Major Glueshoe had some hair over his ears which ran around to the back of his head where it met to form sort of a halo, but no hair on top. He, too, began to feel the tense mood, now, and lo and behold, it was manifested on the top of his head. It became the same color as Ralston's neck. It was much more functional because of its placement. Up there, one could use it perhaps to fry an egg or melt some butter; the back of the neck—that would just run down into his shorts.

Glueshoe wanted out when he recognized what he was in, so he rose quickly, made some muttered verbal gesture toward Ralston, glanced momentarily at Glutz, and then departed. What a look, Glutz thought. Almost like he was trying to drive a screw into his sinuses with his tongue. In tense and unsettling situations, all people adopt some compensatory measures. Some turn to drinking, others to smoking, others to eating, and still others to sleeping. Glutz went to his security blanket, the book on air force regulations, and resumed reading. Major Ralston was different. He continued writing in longhand on his yellow lined tablet. To the casual observer this would have appeared a legitimate business endeavor, except that most of what he wrote got only as far as the wastebasket.

The scene was now an office of ostensible tranquility when suddenly the major stopped writing. Leaning back in his chair, he toyed with his pencil, obviously searching for or considering some sort of plan. Finally he spoke, his face flushing a bit as he did.

"Jerry," he said, with all of the amicability he could muster, "the holidays are coming upon us and it must be sort of lonely being a bachelor this time of year."

"That's what I've been thinking myself," Glutz answered. "Wish I could get out of here and go home." *I'd probably stay there and not come back,* his thoughts continued in secret. *I wonder what he's got up his vertebrae this time,* Glutz thought. Really, he couldn't imagine. *Maybe the major's getting the spirit of the season and will give me leave to go home. No, he already said he wouldn't do that. Maybe he's going to invite me over for Christmas dinner. That would be nice and very much like him, but I wouldn't ruin a nice family day like that.* Glutz finally realized that the best way to find out what Major Ralston was after was to keep both his mind and mouth quiet and listen, an almost insurmountable task for the impetuous young lieutenant. But, this time he was so curious that he did it.

Major Ralston flushed at Glutz's last comment; first his neck, then his face and ears, but he continued smiling.

"You know," he went on, "Colonel and Mrs. Silver have a daughter coming home for the holidays and I hear she's a knockout. Maybe you'd like to take her out."

Now Glutz remembered the phone call. "He's still single, and, if your daughter looks anything like you, I know he'd be happy to take her out." *So that's it,* Glutz thought. He decided to make the major sweat a little. The opportunity might never arise again.

"I don't know, major," Glutz said rather cautiously. "I've been pretty busy and the thought of a blind date doesn't particularly appeal to me."

If you've been busy, it's been elsewhere than around here, Major Ralston thought. But, he quickly dispelled it. He must be positive now. *Look upon Glutz as a handsome young lieutenant in shining blue, just perfectly suited to Colonel Silver's daughter.* At least, so he told himself. "Well, of course, it's up to you, Jerry," the major continued, "but, I'm sure she'd be a fine date, and besides, there are lots of private parties coming up and I'm sure you'd be invited to all of them."

"Don't suppose I'd be invited to any without her," Glutz said dreamily.

"Some you would, some you might not be," returned Major Ralston, riding the fence like a native cowpoke or an experienced politician. The imp in Glutz's mind was running away with him so he decided to run the string out for awhile. Colonel Silver was a great guy and he expected his daughter would be too. But, the Glutz-Ralston tables were momentarily turned and Glutz liked it that way. The situation would be reversed again soon enough.

"But, how do I know that she'd like me?" Glutz went on, baiting the major with every word.

"Why wouldn't she?" said Major Ralston earnestly. "You're a nice looking young man with an engaging personality and a good wit." *And I fly paper airplanes,* Glutz added to himself.

"I hope that will be reflected in my next evaluation," smiled Glutz, taking a line from the mouth of his superior. The major smiled too, but briefly

"OK," Glutz said, "you've convinced me with your usual smooth manner, Major Ralston. I'll do it."

CHAPTER XII

It was Friday evening and Lieutenant Glutz, Jerome V., AO9999999, was on his way to Colonel Silver's house. He was driving the car, heading in that direction, getting closer by the minute, but he didn't want to go. He didn't like blind dates and he was afraid of colonels. Glutz stopped his car in front of the house and turned out the lights. He hated the apprehension, too, of being watched by the whole family while he drove forward and then crept back, looking for the right address. Maybe no one was watching him, but it was as if they all were and that was just as bad. Well, anxiety wasn't disappearing by staying in the car so he pulled the keys from the ignition and got out. Someone was putting up Christmas lights in front of the house, probably Mrs. Silver. As Glutz walked toward the house she turned to greet him.

"Hello," she said cheerily. "You must be Lieutenant Glutz. I'm Mrs. Silver."

"Yes," said Glutz, "I thought you might be. It's a pleasure to meet you, ma'am," he added in his best military courtesy.

"C'mon along inside," Mrs. Silver continued. "I'm sure Cindy is ready."

Glutz walked in the door just as Colonel Silver was descending the last few stairs from the second floor. "Evenin' lieutenant," the colonel said with sort of a Southern drawl. "Ah'm Colonel Silver."

"Yes sir, I know," Glutz said, clicking his heels together and commencing a salute before he caught himself and reached out for a handshake instead.

"C'mon in the livin' room boy, and we'll sit for a minute. Cindy will be down shortly."

"Thank you," said Glutz, starting to click his heels again and then almost tripping himself when correcting his error and continuing to walk toward the living room. Glutz sat down comfortably on the couch across from the colonel. There was an awkward momentary silence before the colonel spoke.

"Well lieutenant," he said, "how do you like the air force?" Just then Mrs. Silver made her timely entrance into the room.

"Oh Sterling," she reprimanded. "Lieutenant Glutz didn't come here to talk about the air force."

"Please call me Jerry," Glutz said looking first at one, then the other of them.

"It makes me feel much more at home," he added with amazing candor, for him, in his new environment.

"Sure 'nuf, boy," the colonel assured him. "We'll do just that."

Then a shuffle of crinoline, or something that sounded like it, drew the attention of all three to the other side of the room. A young, attractive girl, obviously Cindy, had just entered the room. Glutz did a quick study of her figure and features before reverting to being the person he thought he ought to be in this situation. Cindy was very attractive. She was tall and, though still in her teens, moved with almost majestic grace. But, one very obvious trait stood out which Glutz thought to be quite unusual. She looked very much like her father; not at all like her mother. The boys, on the other hand, whom he had seen in the yard and, briefly, running through the house, looked a great deal like their mother and nothing like the colonel. *Luckily the colonel is a handsome man,* Glutz pondered, shrugging his shoulders of mental imagery. He thought of his own appearance and shuddered at the countenance of a girl who might look like him.

Dream time over, though it passed in a flash, Glutz rose to his feet to meet his blind date. Mrs. Silver did the honors.

"Dear, this is Lieutenant Jerry Glutz; Lieutenant Glutz, our daughter, Cindy."

"How do you do," Cindy said with a gracious smile, displaying her attractive personality.

"Hi Cindy," Glutz responded with considerably less class.

There was an awkward moment, again, and then Cindy took the initiative. Her mother was tactfully allowing her to run her own show.

"Would you care to sit for a while before we leave, Jerry?" she offered a bit clumsily. "I don't know what our schedule for the evening is," she added then with considerably more poise.

Glutz was more at ease now. He could at least talk without gulping air which would only turn to gas, he knew, and perhaps prove embarrassing to all in the event of a forced emission of one sort or another.

"Perhaps we'd better leave now, Cindy," he suggested. "There's no special schedule, but I think most of the guests will be arriving shortly."

"My, sounds like a fancy affair," Mrs. Silver inquired with considerable interest.

"No, it's only at the BOQ ma'am," Glutz assured her. "The adjoining rooms have a common door so we've decorated a few of them and will leave the doors open to give us more room."

Colonel Silver gulped at the thought of his daughter going to a party in a bachelor officers' quarters. Mrs. Silver was concerned too, but was comforted by thoughts of her own single days. *There's safety in numbers,* she consoled herself.

Once outside Glutz took a deep breath of fresh air and relaxed a bit more. He had a very attractive date and was happy with that, but he was dismayed and somewhat surprised that he could not look on her as such. He felt like an escort at the Miss America pageant. Closing the door when she had been seated in the car he said to himself, *This is going to be a real lost evening if I can't regard her as Cindy Silver rather than Colonel Silver's daughter.*

The four blocks to the BOQ were short, but the conversation was stilted and filled with small talk. Glutz was ambivalent toward the arrival and thought perhaps Cindy was too. On the one hand he was glad the trip was over and at the same time didn't relish the first moments of the party . It was an impromptu thing and Cindy was probably overdressed. That was his fault, of course, because he hadn't told her. But after a few moments in the present environment coupled with the apprehension of dating a colonel's daughter, it was a marvel that he remembered where the party was. Then too, many of the attendees would probably be temporary cast offs from other elements of normal society, like Glutz himself. Some of the girls, it was rumored, had come to this country to hunt bear and had become such, instead. Others, of course, were attractive. Most of the guys would rather have been someplace else, but such was life in the republic. Anyway, they were here and the time was now.

Cindy walked elegantly across the slate corridors of the BOQ to the place where the party was being held. It reminded Glutz of Miss New Mexico inspecting the animal entries in the pavilion at the state fair. Presently they came upon the party and the introductions began.

"This is Colonel Silver's daughter, Cindy," Glutz boasted each time.

Ken Glenn, the "little napoleon" of the BOQ, looked upon him with disdain but said nothing. Cindy showed poise during the awkward introductions, made so by Glutz's interminable salutations. When it was finally over, Cindy asked to be excused and, accompanied by one of the other girls, headed for what had been turned into a ladies' room for the evening.

Once out of earshot, Glutz said to his pal and confidant, Lt. Joe Willy, "Gee, Joe, I sure wish I could be more comfortable with Cindy."

"You might start by stopping your reference to her as 'Colonel Silver's daughter'," Willy countered rapidly. He turned, with some impatience, and walked away. Glutz knew he was right, but to stop saying it was one thing; to stop thinking it, quite another. Anyway, he would try.

Cindy returned and Glutz invited her to dance to a blaring portable stereo owned by one of the occupants of the room, Stan Wonderweld. Glutz spotted the well known glass of milk and scotch next to the stereo, telling him that Stan had been there and left.

"Where's Stan?" he asked the first passerby, partly to make conversation and partly to impress Cindy with the fact that he was no stranger here.

"Probably in the other room vomiting blood," someone hollered above the music. "He should be back shortly." Wonderweld had an ulcer and so he drank milk with his scotch, or, scotch with his milk, depending on what his stomach felt like. This salved his mind if not always his stomach. Usually it healed itself eventually, however. But not always!

Glutz and Cindy finished the dance and went over to sit down, but there were no seats available.

"Let's try the other room, Cindy," Glutz suggested. "Maybe there's a place to sit down in there." At least the bar was in the other room Glutz knew. Maybe a drink was what he needed. Entering the adjoining room, Glutz narrowly escaped a kick in the head. This room had a makeshift chandelier, and Ken Glenn was swinging from it. The room had been chosen for the bar because of its chandelier. As a matter of fact, Glutz remembered now, Glenn was the one who chose it. Cindy came alive at the sight.

"Oh look at him, Jerry," she giggled. "With those short hairy arms and legs angled up like that, he looks like a gibbon."

Glutz wasn't sure what a gibbon looked like, but had to admit that Lieutenant Glenn probably resembled one. Glutz managed a toothy smile without looking Cindy's way. The tension was eased a bit and a scotch would help more, he thought.

"Care for a drink, Cindy?" he asked quite comfortably.

"Please," she smiled.

"I'll get it," he added quickly, not wanting to embarrass her by asking what kind, in view of her age and probably lack of experienced variety in drinking. *She won't go for a scotch,* he thought, knowing one usually must develop a taste for that. *A 13 should be safe,* Glutz thought (that was local jargon for 7 & 7's, which usually didn't come up to standard at a BOQ party). He had just handed it over when Ken Glenn, back on his chandelier, one handed this time, came swinging by again and, without looking, kicked it all over her dress.

"Why you! . . ."

"It's all right, Jerry," she said. "It'll come out."

"Not standing here it won't," he assured her. Without another word he left her side and returned momentarily with their coats.

"Here," he said, helping her in. "Let's get you home for a change of clothes." There was a word of protest on her lips, but it was never uttered.

"Okay," she said.

Sure of his destination, Glutz pulled up in front of the Silver house with confidence this time. The December weather was nippy; not bitterly cold but the car hadn't warmed up on the short trip.

"You must be chilled through, Cindy," Glutz said, looking over to her as the car came to a halt.

"No," she said, "the spilled drink didn't get through to the bare skin."

I'd like to, he thought.

"A hot cup of something would taste good, though. Won't you come in for one?"

Glutz started to decline but then he thought of the party he was supposed to go back to; Glenn swinging from the chandelier, the gorillas attired like girls, the blaring stereo.

"I thought you'd never ask," he said instead.

The house seemed to be deserted but for a dying fire in the fireplace. "Sure is quiet in here," Jerry uttered softly.

"Mom and daddy have probably gone to bed. Think I'll have a hot chocolate, Jerry, what would you like?"

"That would be fine" he said, and then became relaxed enough to be himself. "On second thought," he corrected, "have you got anything stronger?"

"I'm sure daddy does," she assured him. "What do you have in mind?"

"Well," he said, "a hot toddy would taste just delicious right now."

"I've heard of it," Cindy told him, "but that's all."

"Well," Glutz said again, "first we'll need some bourbon or blended whiskey."

"That should be right he-r-e," she said, reaching for a high cupboard and extending to her tip toes. "There!" she gasped, having pulled out a half-full bottle of Sour Crow. She handed it to Glutz who held it at arm's length admiringly.

"You know, Cindy," he said, "an optimist would say this bottle is half full, and a pessimist that it's half empty."

"And what do you say?" she asked him.

"I'd say," he said, "that in a few moments it won't be either," pulling out the cork and taking a straight swig. The expression of distaste on his face was exceeded only by that on Cindy's.

"Oh Jerry," she said, "that must be awful."

"To tell the truth," he responded, "it's not too good. Let's get the rest of the fixin's and improve it."

"What else?" she asked.

"Well, we'll need sugar and water and cinnamon."

"Yuck!" Cindy gagged. "That sounds awful."

"It is," agreed Glutz, "but when you add lemon and whiskey, it's not too bad."

So Glutz added lemon and whiskey and passed Cindy's cup to her. She took a sip and made a face.

"O-o-o," she sallowed her cheeks as if to try to blow the sip back out. "Are you sure something isn't missing?"

Glutz took a taste from his hot cup. "Hm-m-m," he responded, sounding like the mad scientist pondering a new concoction which showed no sign of a catalytic action. "Cinnamon stick!" he exclaimed.

"Cinnamon stick?" she asked.

"Yeah, cinnamon stick!" he assured her. "It has no cinnamon."

"I know that," Cindy told him, "but, is it supposed to?"

"Of course, of course," he rasped, feigning impatience and rubbing his hands gleefully over his "brew."

"We don't have any cinnamon sticks, Jerry," she told him over her shoulder, a hand on the handle of each of two cabinet doors. "Will cinnamon from a shaker do?"

"Yes, yes, anything," he exhorted her gasping, "Only please, hurry." Cindy Silver produced a small shaker of cinnamon which had obviously been in the cabinet for a long time. He blew the cinnamon dust from it covertly as he turned the shaker upside down and shook it vigorously. Nothing emerged. Putting the plugged holes near his eye and again feigning the scientist, he immediately spotted the problem.

"Aha!!" he exclaimed gleefully. "I see! I see! Quick nurse, a toothpick," he shouted, extending his arm fully, first with the palm down and then ceremoniously turning the palm up in anticipation of the toothpick delivery.

Having emptied the clogged pores of the shaker, Jerry Glutz, still dramatically ceremonious, shook the cinnamon twice over his cup, as if in measurement, and then raised the cup to his lips to taste.

"Nectar!" he purred. "Nectar of the gods."

"Let me taste it," Cindy demanded, reaching for the container.

"No, no, my fair maiden," he hushed, "let the master brew it. Unless the herbs and spices are mixed perfectly, grave danger can result to one so sweet as you." Cindy giggled. "Now," he continued, "taste and know the treasure of the perfect . . ." he was silent for a moment, searching for the word to conclude his mood of fiction . . . "concoction," he said finally, obviously disappointed with his inability to come up, spontaneously, with a better word. Cindy sipped the drink and Glutz drew himself back from her with one sweeping step. "What think ye maiden?" he queried. "Is it not the fairest of the fair for the fairest?" Cindy giggled again.

"It's okay," she said, leading into the other room.

He followed meekly and watched her sit down near the fireplace, leaning against a floor pillow, legs extended before the flame. She stared fixedly at the flame shadow, dancing up and down her leg. Glutz sat down Indian style, directly in front of the fire, chin in his hands, and stared into the fire. Cindy moved suddenly, knocking Glutz's glass over with her knee.

"That reminds me," she said without remorse for having spilled the drink. "I should change this dress. Don't imagine the spot looks too good," she continued, looking down at the now-dry stain from the kicked drink at the party, compliments of the chandelier swinging gibbon, Lieutenant Glenn. "Excuse me for a moment," she said to Glutz, rising to her feet.

"Certainly," he assured, rising to his feet also, out of conditioned respect for the fairer sex. "Tell me where to get a towel to wipe this up and I will make myself productive while you're gone."

"There are several right under the sink. Suit yourself," she told him, flying up the stairs. Glutz got a towel and dried the floor. It looked like the stain would mark the carpet permanently. However, the only light in the room came from the now-dying fire. "Well, at least it won't show at night, unless someone turns on the lights," Glutz consoled himself. He went into the kitchen and reached for a handful of ice to build himself another drink. Returning to the living room, he threw another log on the fire and sat once again in the Indian position, staring at the flame. The new log brought the fire back to life and the spot reappeared. It looked like a shadow, though, so Glutz didn't notice it.

Looking deeply into the flame, Glutz could see episodes of his past life. More particularly, there were people, girls he had gone with. He saw their faces in a long line. Shirley Ranfrants in high school. In college Rita Burke. There were Helen Clarin, Peggy Santone, and now Cindy Silver. All marched right on through and out of the fire, but Cindy's face remained in the center, full blown and smiling at him.

"Hi tiger," she said.

"Hi," he responded, talking to the face in the fire.

"Is this my drink?" she continued. Glutz spun around.

"Oh hi, Cindy," he repeated.

"You said that once," she reminded him, plopping down next to him and copying his style of sitting. She reached over for the floor pillow and propped it up behind her. Taking a rather large sip from her drink, she lit a cigarette and took a deep drag. Exhaling, she began to speak.

"Christmas time," she said generally, "all fall I've waited for it and now it's finally here. I wish the time would slow down."

Glutz thought of his own life, his air force tour, and how he wished it were over. Like a garment in process, a life was expanded, day by day. And now, at least for this moment, at least for this night, the fabric of their two lives, his and Cindy's, had been woven together. Someday, he thought, the garment of his life would weave into that of another and for many years they would work together, as threads of fabric, to strengthen the fiber of each and to produce and develop other fiber, offspring, so as to leave the world just a bit better when their interwoven lives should end, at death. He thought of the girls whose life fabric had been interwoven with his in the past. Some for months, some for weeks and some, like Helen and Peggy, just for a few days. Then their fabric had parted, to continue their separate weave in separate directions. Would it be the same with Cindy or, this time, would it be different? He had no way of knowing, but tonight was tonight and it was here to be enjoyed.

Cindy smelled delicious and looked lovely.

"You smell delicious and look lovely," he told her, half embarrassed for fear of repetition since he couldn't remember if he had said it or just thought it the first time. She had put something on when changing into the brown slacks and powder blue fluffy sweater she now wore. Glutz couldn't pin it down, but this aroma had gifted his nostrils before. On Cindy it was even better. Glutz put his arm around her and drew her closer.

"Just a minute," she said, taking one last draw from her cigarette and snuffing it out in the ashtray. Then she turned to him, cupped his jaws in her parted fingers and kissed him. He embraced her heavily as they inched, together, to the floor. His pointed tongue pierced her lips and her teeth parted, like the mouth of a dumbwaiter, before it. The tips of their tongues met and danced before each other as serpents. Had his dental caries been truly alive they would have interpreted the dance as a response to the pulse beat in the tooth pulp. But, to Glutz, it was an erotic experience. He slid one hand down over her buttocks and drew her toward a stiff proposition.

"Thanks a lot," she said disgustedly, snapping to a sitting position and brushing her hair back past the sides of her head.

"For what?" Glutz asked innocently.

"For ruining what started out to be a wonderful evening and a promising vacation. I don't know why, and I had no reason to, but somehow I had hoped you'd be different."

"But I am," Glutz assured her, convincing himself that he had made the pass more or less as the thing to do.

"You sure are," she said gustily. "You even use the same words as the rest of them."

"The rest of whom?" he demanded, just a hint of irritation in his voice.

"The rest of the guys I've been out with," she answered more meekly.

"Well, apparently you're not very selective about whom you date," Glutz said.

"Apparently not," she agreed with obvious emphasis toward him. "It seems that I'm simply a poor judge of character."

"And, you think that I have none," Glutz concluded, the hint of an impish smile on his face. Cindy smiled too and raised herself to a seat on the davenport. Glutz reached over and clasped her hand in his. They squeezed simultaneously and then both loosened their grip as abruptly as it had been tightened.

"Don't be too hard on me, Cindy," he said softly. "We're made of the same stuff, you know; those other guys and I."

"Oh, I know," she said, throwing her head to one side. "I expect too much. It's just that I'm waiting for that knight in shining armor to come along and sweep me off my feet."

"You have to deserve that, Cindy," Glutz told her maturely.

"What do you mean?" she demanded, pulling away and turning her head fully toward him.

"What I mean," he said, "is that the unwritten rules in this society tell us that any guy is going to go as far as he can with any girl and will keep trying so long as there's any chance he's going to be successful."

"And they also say," she continued, "that if the girl really likes the guy he's eventually going to score, don't they?"

"And, that after he does, he'll eventually get tired of her and drop her," he concluded.

"Oh, Jerry," she slumped onto the couch, dropping her chin onto her chest, "why do things have to be so complicated?"

"I don't know," he said staring off into space. "I don't make the rules, I just live by them. And, I can tell you one more thing, too. When a guy and a gal do 'get it on' as a friend of mine would say, it's exciting at first, but when they finally break off, he's just as sick of himself as he is of her."

"I don't know about that," Cindy said pensively, "and I guess I don't want to find out, but, sometimes I think I do."

"You don't," Glutz told her, "believe me, you don't!"

Just then the door opened and Cindy jumped up.

"Who's there?"

"It's just your mommy and me," Colonel Silver's voice curled around the entry into the living room. *And a couple makes three,* Glutz thought.

"What've you two been doin' in here? Spoonin'?" the colonel chided, making his physical presence fully felt, now.

"Why, daddy," Cindy feigned shock, "you know me better than that. Anyway, I thought you and momma were in bed."

"We were, but that was last night," the colonel went on with his kidding. "Actually your momma and I got kinda bored just sittin' around with all the Christmas spirit outside, so we decided to go for a walk."

"For two hours?" Cindy asked in disbelief.

"Is that how long you two have been here? Musta got here just after we left. Actually, General and Mrs. Stockton invited us in for a little Christmas cheer," Mrs. Silver told them, sitting down next to the colonel and poking him in the arm with her forefinger.

"We had a little of that right here," Cindy told them rather proudly.

"Ya' did?" the colonel acted startled. "What'd ya' have?" he went on, winking toward Glutz.

Glutz blushed but the room was still rather dark so the blush was hard to see, like the spot on the carpet. And the colonel's wink was impossible to make out.

"What'd we have, Jerry?" Cindy said, looking toward him, having forgotten what it was they had tasted.

"A modified hot toddy," Glutz said, trying to smile but remembering that Cindy might be considered too young to drink by her parents, or at least her father.

"A hot toddy," Colonel Silver said jubilantly. "Those are g-o-o-o-d. What say we all have one. C'mon, lieutenant, let's you 'n' me get out in the kitchen 'n' fix one up for each of us." Mrs. Silver and Cindy looked at one another and shrugged their shoulders while Lieutenant Glutz obediently followed Colonel Silver into the kitchen.

"Now boy, what d'ya' put into one of these things?" the colonel asked Glutz, while looking at his watch. *You don't find the recipe there,* Glutz thought to himself, but of course didn't say that.

"Well, let's see," Glutz started out as he had before, "you take . . ."

"I see all these bottles settin' out here boy," the colonel interrupted. "I'll get the glasses out and you figure what to put into them."

"Yes, sir," Glutz responded but not attempting to click his heels this time.

The drinks made, Glutz offered what he thought might be the best one to the colonel. The colonel sipped and smacked his lips. "M-m-m-m," he sounded rather loudly, "that is good, boy. Where'd you get that recipe?"

"I got it from an old sea captain," Glutz told him, smiling, knowing that he was the man in control for the moment. Glutz carried two of the drinks to the other room for the ladies and then returned for his own. The colonel waited for Jerry to return to his seat and then raised his glass for a toast.

"Here's to the young folks, Mom," he said. "Wouldn't it be fun to be there again?" Mrs. Silver just smiled her warm tender smile to both of the young folks. A light had been turned on in the room and it was brighter now. Glutz could see the smile plainly, and it warmed him more than the drink. But, the drink had relaxed him and brought forth his next comment.

"You know, colonel," he said, "I don't know if you meant it or not, but I was thinking earlier this evening how nice it must be to be at your stage and position in life."

"I don't know about position, lieutenant, but sometimes I feel like I'd like to be on the next stage, the one leaving for Palmer, or Seward, or Washington, or somewhere." That was funny and the colonel had humor in his voice as he said it. Glutz had heard it somewhere, but where he couldn't remember. He smiled as if he hadn't. "I s'pose the cow always looks plumper on the other side of the fence, though," he continued.

"I think you mean the grass is always greener, Dear," his wife injected.

"There ain't no grass where I come from, Honey, you know that," he said with his eyes sparkling. It became apparent to Glutz that Mrs. Silver had "made" this man with her comments and manner. Whether she knew it and did it on purpose, or just fit into the pattern naturally, he, of course, couldn't know. But it would be interesting, to learn, Glutz thought.

Colonel Silver changed the subject.

"Musta' been some kinda' party you two attended to be home as early as you were," he said teasingly, but probably a bit curious.

"I . . . we . . . you . . ." both Cindy and Glutz started out in unison. They looked at each other.

"You go ahead, Cindy, your dad asked the question," Glutz teased, winking toward the colonel.

"But, it was your party, Jerry," charged Cindy, smiling at her dad.

"Will somebody please tell us?" pleaded Mrs. Silver. "I'm dying of curiosity, too."

"Too? Who else is?" kidded the colonel. His wife looked at him with a measure of artificial disgust and then her attention went back to the kids.

Glutz finally took the initiative. "It was some kind of party, all right. This one clown, believe it or not, was swinging from the chandelier."

"He looked just like a monkey or gorilla," Cindy broke in giggling.

"That sounds like some kinda' party all right," the colonel said, copying Glutz's words with a deep laugh. "But, I can't see why it'd drive you out. It would make me want to stay."

"It did," said Glutz in a bit of a lie, "until he clumsily kicked Cindy's glass out of her hand in one of his throwback undulations."

"It went all over my dress," she continued, "so Jerry thought we'd better get home to let it dry off." Glutz anticipated the next question.

"We didn't go back because the party wasn't really that great. The BOQ is kinda crummy, the music too loud and the whole thing was more or less a din." Cindy looked at Glutz approvingly.

Mrs. Silver picked up the conversation after a slight pause.

"You know, Dear," she said to her husband, "wouldn't it be nice to have Lieutenant Glutz at our anniversary party next week?"

"Yes, it would," said the colonel, looking to his daughter for approval. She was noncommital, but the offer had already been made.

"It's next Tuesday evening," she went on, "at 6:30 at The Mantel." Glutz was excited at the thought.

"That would be wonderful," he said.

"Well, we'll be glad to have you," the Colonel went on, "but right now it's going on midnight, and I have a staff meeting in the morning, so we'd better call it a night."

Glutz was embarrassed that he hadn't watched the time himself. He rose to his feet quickly.

"Yes, I've got to be going too," he said, as if of his own volition. Pretending to steal a glance at his watch, he added, "The sun will be up before we know it."

"The sun doesn't come up until 10:00 A.M. this time of year," Cindy reminded him.

"And, 10:00 A.M. will be here before we know it," said Glutz, recovering nicely.

"Well, it won't be here before I know it," yawned the colonel, stretching his arms. "I'll be up four hours by that time."

Glutz didn't need any more hints. He moved swiftly out the door, stopping only long enough to turn and say good night to all. His face was still flushed a bit from the embarrassment, and he did look a bit like good ol' St. Nick, particularly at this time of night. *Merry Christmas to all and to all a good night,* Cingy thought.

It was a cold night and Glutz drove home with dispatch. The bed felt good, and the covers felt better. It was with very little effort that Lt. Jerome Glutz sped off into the land o' nod.

On Monday morning he was at the office early, not because of a newly developed interest in his job, but because he couldn't wait to tell Major Ralston of his invitation to the Silver wedding anniversary.

The Major marched in at 8:05 A.M. and Glutz sat there beaming. Ralston's neck got red at the sight of Glutz's pumpkin grin as his knuckles got white. He thought Glutz was gloating because he had arrived on time and the major had just marshalled in five minutes late.

"Good morning sir," chirped Glutz in almost a fawning manner.

"Morning, lieutenant," rumbled the major as he squeaked into the chair.

"You'll never guess what happened to me over the weekend, major, that is, Friday night to be exact." Ralston stopped his pen in the middle of a word and lifted both it and his head up.

"That was the night of your BOQ party, wasn't it?"

"Yes sir," said Glutz, as giddily as a temptress coaxing her prey into a deadly entrapment. Ralston dropped his head and pen and continued his writing.

"You got raped by an ape in the hay," he rasped disinterestedly.

"No sir!" And then a pause. "Be serious, major. I got an invitation from Colonel and Mrs. Silver to attend their twenty-fifth wedding anniversary dinner tomorrow night." Ralston almost drove his ballpoint pen through both paper and desk pad. He retrieved it rapidly, however, and went on writing.

"What are you writing, major?" Glutz changed the subject.

"I'm writing an invitation to you to quit bothering me, lieutenant. Now get to work."

Doing what? Glutz thought. *I've done every crossword puzzle around here, to the extent I could figure them out, that is.* "Aren't you even interested in the party, Major?" Glutz insisted.

"I'll be interested in the party next Wednesday after you've been there," the major said without looking up. "Not today when you don't know anymore about it than I do. Now get to work and quit bothering me."

"Yes, sir," Glutz obeyed, turning in his chair to stare at an empty desk. Presently he opened a drawer to retrieve his air force regulation book, blew off the dust and resumed his perusal.

CHAPTER XIII

On Tuesday evening after work, Glutz was invigorated. There was no tomorrow. He was looking forward to tonight, The Mantel and all that "brass" and their wives. Even the shower and menthol shave couldn't perk him up, he was so "on top of it." And then he got scared.

My God, he thought. *How am I going to act?* Glutz knew most of them but did they know him? *That's easy, dummy,* he said to himself. *You simply go up to each of them and introduce yourself. Good evening colonel or general so-and-so, and Mrs. so-and-so, I'm Lieutenant Glutz.* That voice that sometimes showed up to twang his confidence was back. *"What's 'a matter, ol' buddy, don't you have even enough confidence to think of yourself in capital letters?* Glutz did have to admit he was thinking small. But, he ignored the mental voice.

Seven-fifty was the magic hour (that's 1950 for air force buffs). At 1700 hours (5:00 P.M.—oh, it's so confusing) Lt. Jerome Glutz was ready. 1950 seemed like it was light years away. He felt like a freshly corked bottle of champagne, ready to bubble over at the pop of his cork. His legs and arms felt effervescent and his head was clear and alert. As the time approached, however, his spontaneous enthusiasm began to wane. As imagery shifted to reality, much of his "caged tiger" desire to get going dissipated. At 7:40 he had to rush to get into his car to arrive at the appointed time. It was only a five or seven minute drive, though, and when Glutz arrived in front of The Mantel, he hesitated. Shutting down the ignition and switching off the lights, he leaned back hard in the driver's seat. Glancing at his watch, he took a deep breath, fully inflating his cheeks, and exhaled as rapidly. Then, his mind having gone completely blank for the moment from conflicts of thought, he lifted the latch to his car and got out in his usual "lean-to-the-road" fashion.

Walking up to the door, he had not a thought for Cindy Silver who, at least for the record, was this evening's date. *Really,* he thought, *it's Mrs. Silver who invited me here. Maybe to get you better acquainted with her daughter,* the inner voice told him, but he paid no heed. *Most of the women here,* he thought, *I don't even know. And most of the gentlemen,* his inner voice reminded, *don't know you.* Troublesome meddler, this subconscious talker of Glutz's. Usually he paid no mind to it, but sometimes, when it came in large doses, "he" was difficult to suppress. *I sure hope I can think of something to do or say when I get inside.*

Glutz had hardly stepped inside, however, before he saw Mrs. Silver busily engaged in a conversation with two other ladies. Her back was to him. Over at the bar was General Eagles, commander of the theater command, army, navy and air force. No one stood near him and the entire bar room was surprisingly neat, quiet, and orderly. Hardly a chair was asymmetrically placed and there seemed to be very few people around. Glutz sidestepped past Mrs. Silver and her conversants offering a "Good evening, ladies" as he passed. Mrs. Silver recognized his voice and looked up immediately.

"Good evening, Lieutenant Glutz," she said with impressive expression. She very properly introduced him to her friends. "Cindy's not here yet," she told him, "but she'll be along in a minute with her dad. Do step up to the bar for one of your favorite drinks," she urged, with all of her southern graciousness and hospitality. Glutz nodded politely, acknowledged his pleasure at meeting the two ladies and seeing Mrs. Silver, offered his compliments on her anniversary, and then "bellied up to the bar."

He found himself standing right next to General Eagles who was still facing the same way, foot on the bar rail, elbow on the bar. Glutz was uncomfortable. He could feel that his neck and ears were hot. *And it's not from the room temperature, either,* he thought.

"Good evening, General," Glutz offered, casting a sideways glance at the senior general officer in "these here parts."

"Evenin' Lieutenant," the General responded cordially. That southern voice, Glutz thought, sounds just like Colonel Silver. "Well, ya' heard one southerner ya' heard 'em all, boy," he could almost hear the colonel saying. Immediately Glutz's thoughts drifted to a story he had heard of the general's entrance into the air force.

Being a general officer, Glutz assumed that General Eagles had graduated from a military academy as had Colonel Silver and General Stockton, the Air Command Commander.

"Not that boy," Major Ralston had told him. "He's from a small but highly regarded college in the South." Major Ralston thought it was Crimson Tech.

"Did he get an ROTC commission on graduation?" Glutz wondered.

"Don't think so," Ralston said. "As I recall hearing it, the Dean asked him to leave before graduation."

"What for, Major Ralston? Do you know?" Glutz was getting more curious.

"Well, I'm told," said Major Ralston, obviously enjoying the bone account of a skeleton in someone else's closet, "that the Dean was upset because his daughter was pregnant."

"Well, why in hell should he take it . . ." Glutz began adamantly, and then his voice tailed off. Ralston turned his back from Glutz to hide a coy smile. "Did he do it, Major?" Glutz asked with childlike enthusiasm. "Don't know, Lieutenant. He's not of my age group. I was playing with trains and building sand castles at the time, not air castles. Besides, I was in a different part of the country." Major Ralston was thoroughly enamored of the subject and particularly liked Glutz's boyish detective-like curiosity.

Glutz's thoughts drifted hazily for a moment before he realized that he was being called back to reality by the General's emphatic voice.

"The bartender is here to take your drink order, Lieutenant," he was saying.

"Drink? Oh yes, drink," blurted Glutz, recovering. "A-a-a scotch and water," he finished.

"Yes sir," answered the bartender. "Any particular kind?"

"Kind? Oh, I don't know. What are you drinking, General?" asked Glutz, with still semi-dazed courage.

"Medieval Times," the General answered casually.

"Okay, then," said Glutz getting more comfortable by the moment, "I'll have Medieval Times and water."

"Medieval Times is a whiskey," the bartender told him, "and, only the General drinks it."

"That's okay," Glutz said agreeably, "I can handle . . ."

"I *said* only the General drinks it, Sir," the bartender emphasized to Glutz.

"Oh, okay." Glutz got the message. "I don't care then, any kind of scotch is fine." The bartender nodded and left.

"Ya' really oughta' choose a brand, Lieutenant," said the General. "Gives a person an air of distinction. Something to be selective about."

"Yes Sir. That's a good idea, Sir. I'm going to have to develop a program for that." Lieutenant Glutz wondered if the former Dean at Crimson Tech drank Medieval Times.

Glutz looked over his shoulder and saw Cindy standing near her mother. He wandered over and stood next to her. She looked at him and smiled coolly. Then she looked back to the ladies. Glutz's blood was chilled by the atmosphere. He didn't know how to act in this situation, so unusual to him, but he knew he had to do something. He chose quickly to do the only thing he knew how to do, talk.

"Hi, Cindy," he said cheerily. "Can I get you a drink?"

"That'd be fine," she answered, smiling briefly and coolly once more.

Glutz was glad to walk away toward the bar. *Wow,* he thought, *wonder what's dulling her blade?* (that's "cooling her off," for those who haven't enjoyed the helicopter service, unless, of course, they may have experienced some culinary success). Glutz got to the bar and realized he didn't know what drink Cindy wanted. He looked toward her, but she didn't appear to be noticing him. *Oh the hell with her,* he thought. *If that's the way she's going to be, I'll get her anything.* That thought scared him, though, so he remembered what she drank.

Back with the four ladies, Glutz felt as conspicuous as a great toe sticking out of a holey sock. He moved away from the gathering and wasn't even missed. Glutz began to mill around, but he didn't really know anyone. It seemed everyone else was a colonel except for two or three generals. *Wouldn't Ralston love to be here?* Glutz gloated. Then he immediately returned to the uncomfortableness of the situation. The scotches weren't doing their job tonight. They didn't seem to be able to resolve the conflict between wanting to relax and realizing the potential need to "be on his toes" at any moment. Glutz knew most of the senior officers present, at least who they were. But he doubted that very many knew him. At least none of them showed any great interest in talking to him. He nodded a rather shy "hello" to those few whom he thought would know him, but that did little to calm him. Looking around for some friendly face, Glutz glanced to the bar and noted that General Eagles had gone. He was nowhere to be seen, either. *Apparently, he flew the coop,* Glutz thought to himself. He looked at his watch and was startled to see it was 9:15 already. *Maybe I can make an exit pretty soon myself,* he thought. Then Cindy entered his mind. *Wonder where she is?* But he didn't even look around, recognizing that the atmosphere was uncomfortable enough without being near her.

Just then a robust voice penetrated the hum of conversation that had permeated the room.

"Ya' know Sterling," the gruff voice was saying, "I betcha' I could lick anyone in this whole goddam command in arm wrestling."

Not only is that voice gruff, but it's also a little drunk, Glutz was thinking. Unknowingly, he was also warming up to the atmosphere, rapidly becoming aware something interesting was obviously brewing. Glutz looked to the bar, from whence the voice came, and immediately recognized it as coming from the mouth of General Stockton. He was addressing Colonel Silver, who sat beside him on a barstool (not the same stool, though, of course). By the time Glutz caught sight of the event, the action had already begun. General Stockton and Colonel Silver had been teammates on the football team at The Academy where the latter had been captain, though a year junior to the general (not an air force captain, a team captain, for those who know there's a difference). The general had a muscular build, but was considerably shorter in stature and, of course, arm length, than the colonel, also well proportioned and put together. *Boy,* thought Glutz, *The General must really be bombed to take on Colonel Silver in arm wrestling in front of all these other colonels. He doesn't have a chance with the difference in arm length.*

The match began and the competition seemed intense. The arms bent grudgingly, first in one direction, then the other. Arteries showed prominently in both throats. The crowd of colonels gathered close, while, though Glutz didn't realize it at the time, the ladies were inconspicuous by their absence. Suddenly, the back of a hand went down on the bar. It was over. Colonel Silver had . . . had lost!

Glutz couldn't believe it. The two officers held a rematch at the general's insistence; and then another. Each time the match seemed tense, but each time the general emerged victorious. Glutz was thinking, *I wonder if . . .*

"Silver'll get his star yet if he keeps that up," he heard someone say. Glutz didn't recognize the voice and he didn't want to turn to see who it was.

Victorious now, the general's voice was back in action even more ebullient, and maybe a little drunker, than before.

"Ya' know, Sterling," he was saying, "I bet I can lick any son of a bitch in this command in leg wrestling." Maybe Glutz just imagined that he saw the colonel wince. In any event, his response was inaudible but apparently positive. The general looked around and focused on one of his staff.

"Don," he said harshly, but not particularly loudly, "get some of your boys and move the dining room tables over to the walls. Sterling thinks he can take me in a stellar leg wrestle. We'll show 'em," the general added, winking at Colonel Gephardt, chief of air material for the command. Gephardt's mouth dropped open as he stared at the general in disbelief. "Better close your mouth before you start drooling and get the carpet wet," General Stockton told him, hacking out a laugh with a slap on Gephardt's shoulder. Don Gephardt did as he was bade and an "arena" was soon cleared in the center of the dining room.

The two gladiators entered, taking their positions on their backs, the head of each opposite from the other's feet. The match here was even more ludicrous. If Colonel Silver's arms were longer than Stockton's, his legs were even more longer. *With that leverage,* Glutz thought, *Stumpy couldn't flip Sterling Silver, even with a fork.* Glutz's mind was sometimes humorous, too, but it was also wrong.

"You can count for us, Don," demanded the general, pressing Colonel Gephardt into action once more. And so they began.

"To your marks," Colonel Gephardt said, and two legs rose straight into the air. *What a skyline,* Glutz mused, *it looks like the Empire State Building next to a spire from St. Patrick's Cathedral.* Two pant legs fell from the ankles they covered, exposing the superstructure of both towers as rather hairy.

"One, two, three," Colonel Gephardt shouted as the legs rose and lowered; "Contact." Ankles locked in battle, but the first shot was a dud as the general's leg slipped down the inside of the colonel's, the heel of his shoe coming to rest in Colonel Silver's armpit. *Foul!* Glutz thought, but somehow the word never formed in his mouth.

"One, two, three, contact," Gephardt shouted again and this time the legs locked in battle. General Stockton started to go over backwards, but then suddenly the impetus was reversed and Colonel Silver ended up in the backward sommersault. Two more engagements brought the same result until the general's appetite for a conflict seemed satiated. Rising to his feet, Stockton's face was flushed from the encounter.

Colonel Silver was tightlipped and looked in neither direction as they returned to the bar. General Stockton had his hand on the colonel's nearest shoulder.

"Ya' know Sterling, you're quite a fighter, I'll bet you could lick anyone in the command, but me."

"Yeah, I'll bet he could," Glutz thought.

The rest of the evening was anticlimactic. Glutz approached Cindy Silver at the end of the evening.

"May I give you a lift home?" he asked her.

"No thanks, I'll be going home with Daddy and Mother," she told him; again with the same cool smile.

Glutz thanked Mrs. Silver for the evening. The colonel was still engaged by the general at the bar. Mrs. Silver was very gracious once again; and, if the evening hadn't worked out to her satisfaction for Cindy, it didn't show.

"Do stop over to the house for a cup of coffee on your way home, Lieutenant."

"I sure do appreciate your offer, Ma'am," said Glutz, "but I am awfully tired and Major Ralston said if I show up late for work once more he's going to send me to Alaska." Mrs. Silver smiled kindly as he let go of her hand to turn to leave. Glutz didn't realize how tired he was until he got home, disrobed, and folded into his "sack" (that's bed for those who've been only in the feed business). He went off to dreamland post haste.

CHAPTER XIV

The next few days were quite uneventful, as it was the Christmas season. And then the day before New Year's Eve, Major Ralston came in with the good news.

"You're being transferred, Lieutenant Glutz." Glutz couldn't believe his ears. *Transferred,* he thought glowingly. Visions of palm trees, bright sun, sandy beaches, and hula girls danced through his head.

"Transferred?" Glutz said, surprised. "Where to?"

"To the Division," Major Ralston told him.

"The Division," Glutz repeated in disbelief. "Where's that?"

"Over there," Ralston said, pointing out the window to a building about two blocks away, even less imposing and more penal appearing than the one he was pointing from.

"What am I going to do down there?" Glutz queried, seriously interested and puzzled now.

"The same thing you've been doing here," Major Ralston told him.

"Nothing?" Glutz shuddered to himself, but the major interrupted.

"You're going to be Assistant Public Information Officer."

"Reporting to Captain McBooboo?" Glutz finished Ralston's sentence.

"Reporting to McBooboo," Ralston assured him.

Glutz pondered his pending situation. Captain McBooboo was sort of a nervous cat. His voice was raspy and high-pitched and was interrupted only by that of a senior officer, a sip from his ever-present coffee cup, or a bite at his cuticles. If you haven't already guessed it, he did have an ulcer which didn't help his disposition and was not salved by his chain smoking and constant coffee. On the other hand, he might be better to report to than

Ralston, because there might be something to do. Also, Ralston had once told McBooboo he'd never get the job done, when he first accepted the assignment. This McBooboo hadn't forgotten and it might help him and Glutz to learn to "breathe through the same straw," Glutz was thinking. Furthermore, McBooboo wore enlisted men's uniforms with his rank on them and Li'l Abner boots. Glutz thought he could compete with this sartorially.

New Year's Eve was a gas at the BOQ, and Glutz enjoyed his scotch. Peggy was there and there were lots of other girls, but Glutz was more intent on his new job. *I really wonder what I'll be doing there,* he thought. Subsequent to the announcement, Glutz had been told that he would be transferred because a ranking captain was being transferred in and had "bumped" him (that's taken over his position, for those who don't know the air force union). He also knew that in his new position, he wasn't replacing anyone; but, that didn't necessarily mean that there wouldn't be anything to do, because in his present position he *had* replaced somebody, and there was nothing to do. After several scotches, that statement confused Glutz, but there seemed to be some logic in it.

On January 15 the big day came, and Lt. Jerome V. Glutz AO9999999 reported to the office of Capt. Ralph McBooboo promptly at 0800 hours. Snapping to attention, he clicked his heels and saluted smartly.

"At ease, Lieutenant, you aren't in the Luftwaffe," McBooboo told him, chuckling at his own humor. Then he stood up and reached out his hand to Glutz. "Welcome to the 17th Air Division," he said encouragingly. Glutz looked up at the placard to the left of McBooboo's desk. The captain's head turned and his eyes drifted to the same place. "Oh yeah," he continued, "15th Division, but numbers aren't important anyway," he rationalized. "Allus get this place mixed up with the one I used to be at." Glutz doubted that there was a 17th Division in any command, but it didn't make any real difference.

McBooboo nestled back in his chair, holding a lit cigarette between the first brown fingers of his hand, his right leg thrown over the arm of his chair and his left hand on a styrofoam coffee cup.

"You're taking on a mighty important assignment down here, Glutz. I suppose you know that," McBooboo told Glutz with an air of sophistication and superiority.

"Yes sir," Glutz returned, thinking, *I suppose that's why it hasn't been filled before.* Just then the captain leaned back in his chair and the unbalanced piece of archaic furniture leaped ahead of him. Lurching forward to keep from going over backwards, his coffee cup rocked in his hand, pouring the steaming java over it and some onto his pant leg.

"Ow!!" he ejaculated, among some other choice terms. Quickly he pulled his wrinkled and used handkerchief from his hip pocket, and began to rub the liquid from his wet pants over his scalded leg. More phrases came forth, the type of which, until recently, had seldom been heard in places of honor.

Glutz spun about in an effort to contain himself.

"You don't have to laugh, Lieutenant. It's not a bit funny." Glutz didn't say anything because he was biting his lip, trying to keep from laughing.

The time it was taking McBooboo to scrub the lint out of his pants gave Glutz a chance to look around the captain's office. *This place is big enough for a couple of good size trucks,* he thought to himself, *or maybe three or four Jeeps.* It was furnished sort of like a garage, too, except there seemed to be no grease on the floor. The floor was poured cement and the walls were cement block, painted a color less promising than the original cement gray. It was empty except for the semblance of a steel desk behind which McBooboo was just finishing the scrub job on his pants from the facsimile of a chair, previously mentioned.

Yes sir, Glutz continued to himself, *this'd make a real fine garage for the motor pool. Except it's three stories up,* he continued to himself, looking out the window. *Besides, the stairs are far too narrow to drive a truck on and,* he concluded, looking at the floor, *there's no drain for the grease pit.*

The humor of the situation was diffused by Glutz's random thoughts, so he was able to turn back to Captain McBooboo, who seemed to have fully recovered from his coffee ordeal.

"Yes sir, young man, this is a mighty important responsibility you're getting into," he reiterated, this time leaning forward with his forearms on the desk to avoid any recurrence of the balancing problem. The coffee cup was still held firmly by his left hand and another cigarette between the two brown fingers on his right. "You know," he went on, "Major Ralston said I wouldn't be able to handle this job when he sent me down here, but I've shown him how wrong a man can be. Bud thinks he's the only ISO officer around. Well, he knows differently now."

Lt. Glutz wasn't very interested in all of the captain's self aggrandizement and so his eyes continued, with his mind, to wander around the room. McBooboo noticed the lieutenant's lack of attention and so he skirted to another subject.

"I want to take you around the office this morning, Lieutenant. Get you acquainted with the staff. You'll be reporting to the editor of the base paper."

"Why?" Glutz blurted out in amazement.

"Because your job's going to be writing stories for the base paper."

"I don't know how to write," said Glutz blankly.

"Then how the hell did you get into the air force?" thundered McBooboo, in the first of many outbursts to which Glutz was to become accustomed.

I didn't think it was a requirement, Glutz thought to himself, but knew better than to repeat it aloud.

"Who is the editor of the paper?" Glutz asked.

"His name's Sergeant Berry," McBooboo answered, rising from his chair and coming around the desk to lead Glutz from the room.

"*Sergeant* Berry?" Glutz repeated querulously.

"That's what I said, Lieutenant, Sergeant Barry Berry."

Well, that's a new one, thought Glutz. *A lieutenant reporting to a sergeant.* He thought it best, though, to say nothing. "Oh well," he mumbled, "IT ALL COUNTS TOWARD TWENTY . . . or three, or two or whatever."

"What?" McBooboo barked.

"Oh nothing, Captain," Glutz told him. "I'm just thinking out loud."

Captain McBooboo sensed the incongruity of the situation, however, and that the unorthodox reporting structure called for an explanation. "Actually, you'll be reporting to me, but Sergeant Berry is the editor of the paper so you'll take your work direction from him."

Glutz found himself strangely not upset by this turn of events. Apparently, he was beginning to be able to rationalize almost anything. *You can lead a horse to water, but you can't make him think,* he thought, and then was bothered by the fact that he couldn't figure how that statement related to the situation at hand, and besides, it didn't ring right.

Sergeant Berry was virtually lying in his chair, feet up on the desk, ostensibly reading the most recent issue of the base paper, the *Elfendwarf Megaphone*. When he heard the two officers enter, he peered around the paper and put his feet on the floor. Glutz noticed that this office looked like a garage, too. But it would only have room for about one jeep and maybe a motorcycle without a sidecar, if the door would be widened. He noticed one other thing, too. Sergeant Berry had Li'l Abner boots on and an enlisted man's uniform. Only the rank and insignia differed from McBooboo. *I wonder if I've got a pair of those boots,* Glutz thought. *And, maybe Berry would like to swap one of his EM* (that's enlisted man for those who haven't been in the air force long) *uniforms for one of my officer's threads, now that he has an officer reporting to him.*

"Sergeant Berry, stand up and meet Lieutenant Glutz."

"Lieutenant what's?" Berry asked, rising to his feet.

"Glutz," Glutz repeated.

"That's what I thought you said," Berry chuckled, slapping his knee as he rocked in laughter from the pseudo-alliterative sound of his word and the lieutenant's last name.

Captain McBooboo, apparently failing to see the humor, went on. "Lieutenant Glutz will be working with you on the base paper, Barry," he said.

The sergeant had a thing about being called by his first name, and found it very frustrating because he never knew whether he was, or not. Nonetheless, he kept on.

"Great," he exploded, grabbing for Glutz's hand, but reaching only his fingers to the second joint. *I wonder if he wants to kiss it,* Glutz thought. Berry squeezed heartily and then let go. "What's your background, Lieutenant, linotype operator?" He slapped his knee again and roared with gusto.

McBooboo and Glutz both looked at him blankly, and the captain turned to leave, followed closely by Glutz.

"So long, Lieutenant, I'll look forward to working with you."

"Me too," Glutz breathed softly into the back of the captain's neck. Next the two of them visited M/Sgt. Willy Bills.

"What do you do here?" Glutz asked him boldly.

"I write for the base paper."

Do you ever get an answer? Glutz thought, but once again he knew it best left unsaid. Sharing the office was Tech Sgt. Happy Daze.

"I write for the base paper, too," he offered in his pleasant Southern drawl before Glutz had a chance to ask. Finally, Lt. Glutz was ushered into an office with two more sergeants and a civilian girl. At least he assumed she was a civilian because she wasn't wearing a uniform, not even a birthday suit. But on reflection he knew that didn't necessarily mean much. He also assumed she was a girl because she had pink booties on—size 10. Captain McBooboo was still outside the office when Glutz entered.

"You all write for the base paper, too?" he queried, not expecting to be surprised.

"Yes sir," two of them shouted in chorus.

"Not me," said the other. If you were thinking it was the girl who didn't write for the base paper, you're right. She typed for the base paper. She was also the secretary for Captain McBooboo, the two sergeants in her office, Technical Sergeant Daze, Master Sergeant Bills, Sergeant Berry, and now Lieutenant Glutz. Her name was Laura Lunsmann.

"Do you have much to do, Laura?" Glutz asked sort of sardonically after they had been introduced.

"Not too bad," she said, "they mostly do their own work, except for the captain."

"Can't he type?" Glutz went on.

"I don't know," Laura said, "I've never seen him."

"There's a typewriter in his office," Glutz reminded her.

"But, there's no ribbon in it," she added coyly.

Six writers, Glutz thought to himself, *on a weekly paper that's probably six pages. That's pretty expensive copy time.* Glutz sat down in his chair and looked out the window. Laura picked up the phone, called someone, and began jabbering. The two sergeants in the room went back to doing whatever they had been doing. It was difficult to tell from looking at them: five non-coms (that's non-commissioned officers for those who don't remember from earlier in this book) and an officer reporting to another non-com who's the lowest in rank of all. There had to be something here deeper than meets the eye. Glutz was soon to find out.

Sgt. Barry Berry burst into the room loudly and enthusiastically. "Lieutenant," he said, "How'd you like to be sports editor?"

"Sports editor?" Glutz recoiled, "Do you have a sports page?"

"We're going to," Berry told him, "as soon as we get a sports editor and that man could be you! Do you know anything about sports, Lieutenant?"

"A little," Glutz answered humbly.

"That's good, Lieutenant, that's real good. A little knowledge is a good thing. Too much knowledge is dangerous. If you think you know everything you make judgments too fast, don't listen and watch to learn what's really going on. A little knowledge. That's good, Lieutenant, that's real good." Sergeant Berry walked out of the room with a pleased smile on his face.

So now I'm the sports editor of The Megaphone, Glutz thought. *What do I do now?*

The next day he found out. At 0900 hours he found himself on the way to the fieldhouse. He was going to interview the base golf pro, and perhaps the top softball pitcher, even though neither season would start for another several months.

When Glutz arrived at the fieldhouse he went to his pockets for the slip of paper with the golf pro's name on it. Needless to say, it wasn't where he thought he had put it and while searching himself over, his mind wandered, as usual. *I suppose this guy's a sergeant,* he was thinking. *Everyone else I meet seems to be.* Captain McBooboo loomed as one notable exception. *Oh, here it is, Sgt. Ray Bawls. Sure enough.* Glutz entered the main door and stared at the trophy case. There were figures of all sizes, as in most such cases. But Glutz didn't see them. *If I'm going to do a story on this guy, I should have a picture of him for the paper. Where to get a camera, and, what to do with it when I find one.*

He got to a nearby phone and called the ISO office. Laura answered on the second ring.

"A photographer? Just a minute, I'll put Captain McBooboo on."

"I don't want to talk to that damn kid about a picture," Glutz heard McBooboo bellow in the background. "Have Sergeant Bills talk to him."

"Master Sergeant Willy Bills, here," was the next thing Glutz heard over the phone.

"Do you take pictures?" Glutz asked him point-blank.

"Pictures? What kind of pictures? Movies, stills, or what?"

"No movies, I mean snaps with a 4 by 4." Glutz had heard someone in the office use that terminology, even though he hadn't figured out what it meant. Presumably, it referred to the size, in inches, of the camera used for taking pictures for the base paper.

"Oh yes, sir," Master Sergeant Bills assured him. "I sure do."

"Well, then, how about coming over to the fieldhouse to take a picture of Sergeant Bawls for a story I want to do in the base paper?"

"Ray Bawls?"

"That's it, sergeant. You know him?"

Master Sergeant Bills ignored the question and went on, "What do you want to take a picture of him for? He's got a kisser that'd stop a clock."

"I don't think there'll be many clocks reading the paper," said Glutz disgustedly. For once he had the courage to say what he was thinking. "Besides, I need a picture of him to accompany my story."

"Why do you want to do a story on him?" said Bills, puzzled. Jerry Glutz's patience had run out.

"Sergeant, we're not getting the job done. Will you or won't you come over here to take a picture for me?"

"Of you or for you?"

"Sergeant!"

"No I won't sir. That is, I can't."

"What do you mean, you can't?" Glutz was becoming hostile.

"Well sir, the base photo lab takes all the pictures."

"The base photo lab?" Glutz resounded violently. "Where the hell's the base photo lab?"

"I'm not sure, sir," Bills responded rather weakly. "I've never been there."

"Then, give me the phone number," the lieutenant thundered. *Boy, these non-coms,* Glutz thought. *You really have to draw them a picture. For anyone else I wouldn't have had to specify* phone number. *But for him, if I hadn't, he may have given me the serial number off his desk.* Bills had left the phone, apparently to get a number for Glutz. The next voice was that of Sgt. Barry Berry.

"Hello?"

"Look," said Glutz weakly, for he was fast becoming exhausted from the encounter, "I'm just trying to get a number for the photo lab so I can get a picture taken of Sergeant Ray Bawls, the alleged base golf pro, to accompany a story you asked me to do on him for the base paper."

"The base photo lab?" queried Sergeant Berry.

"That's it," said Glutz.

"Phone number?" asked the sergeant.

"You've got it," Glutz said.

"Picture for the story in our paper?"

"Right on," said Glutz, perking up.

"Great idea, great idea!" Sergeant Berry rejoined enthusiastically, and then he hung up the phone. Turning to leave, Berry mumbled half to himself and half to Laura Lunsmann. "Picture for the story. Good idea! Good thinking! That Lieutenant's going to be all right," and then pensively he added, massaging his chin with his fingers and thumb, "wonder why he thought he had to call me for permission?"

Glutz stared into the dead receiver as he had done several times before. Then he hung it up slowly. His first instinct was to get angry, but his mind quickly flashed to so many similar experiences from the past. "Oh well," he murmured to himself, "IT ALL COUNTS TOWARD TWENTY."

He looked in the base telephone directory and finally found the number he sought under "B" for base photo lab. *Oh well,* he thought again, as he dialed the number, *It could have been filed under "T" for* the *base photo lab.* Just then someone picked up the phone at the other end of the line.

"Base photo lab," he heard a male voice say, "Sergeant Bulb."

"Now I know why it was listed under 'B,' " Glutz mumbled.

"What?"

"Oh nothing," Glutz continued, "I was just talking to myself."

"Listen, buddy," Glutz surprisingly heard Sergeant Bulb say, "we're busy over here so if you have nothing better to do than talk to yourself, do it on your time, not mine," and he slammed down the phone.

"Just what the hell's going on around here?" Glutz shouted into the phone. Then he gave a nasty jerk and the cord separated from the phone box.

"Now you can take it home for a souvenir," said the man behind him. He was a sergeant, too, but Glutz wasn't listening. Absentmindedly, he stuck the phone in his pocket and walked off in search of another. Finally he made the connection and Airman Tripshutter was on his way. They met outside Sergeant Bawls' office.

"Lieutenant Glutz," said the airman.

"Yes sir, I mean, yes!" answered Glutz. Reporting to a sergeant had confused him a little.

"I'm Airman Tripshutter," he said, hitting himself weakly in the forehead with his flashgun as he tried to salute. "Ouch! But my friends call me Bug." Lieutenant Glutz was about to ask him why until he realized that he looked like one. He couldn't quite decide what species, though.

"Pleased to meet you, Bug," Glutz said, reaching out his left hand to avoid a bout with the camera the airman now held in his right. Seeing Glutz's left hand, Airman Tripshutter acted instinctively, giving Glutz the boy scout handshake. *Oh boy!* Glutz thought. *I wonder if he wants to whisper a secret saying in my ear.*

They entered Sergeant Bawls' doorless office to see him sitting behind his desk, feet up, tossing a golf ball in the air. *Sgt. Ray Bawls* read the placard on his desk.

"You Sergeant Ray Bawls?" asked the airman. Bawls nodded, bringing his feet to the floor and reaching out his right hand as he rose. Tripshutter put the flash attachment in it. "Here," he said beseechingly, "hold this a minute while I put a film pack in the camera." Bawls obliged.

"Let me know when you're ready, airman," Glutz instructed, officiously. After a few clicks along with the insertion of the film in the camera and relieving Sergeant Bawls of the flash attachment, Tripshutter told Glutz he was ready to go. "OK," Glutz said, "you stand over here, sergeant, and hold this trophy that I brought along from the trophy case. Big smile now," he encouraged. Bawls smiled broadly, exposing his broad yellow teeth. *Good thing this isn't in color,* Glutz thought.

Airman Tripshutter took a number of pictures and then announced he was satisfied.

"Good," Glutz said, and then to Sergeant Bawls, "I'll take the trophy back to the trophy case."

The sergeant handed over the trophy and Glutz and the airman turned to leave. *Guess I'll call him later for the story,* Glutz thought, looking at the late hour on his watch. Then it dawned on him that Sergeant Bawls hadn't said a word all the time they were there. *Wonder why?* Jerry pondered.

"Th-th-thanks, f-f-f-fellas," Bawls blurted out. *Oh no!* Glutz thought.

"Y-y-y-you're welcome," he answered nervously, not meaning to stutter at all. Anxiously, he took a piece of paper from his vest pocket and spread it out on the desk with shaking fingers. "Here," he said, "please write down some of the key highlights of your life, particularly your golfing achievements, and drop it off to me in the mail. If I get it by Monday noon, that'll be plenty of time for next week's paper." Ray Bawls smiled knowingly, took the paper, and put it in his top drawer.

"Thanks again, sergeant," said Glutz, putting out his hand. "It was a pleasure. Maybe you can give me a few tips on the game sometime." Glutz hated golf but couldn't think of anything else to say. Sergeant Bawls took Glutz's hand, smiling again, and nodded.

Then, as Glutz walked through the door, Bawls couldn't contain himself any longer.

"S-s-say Lieutenant," he said, "h-h-h-how come y-y-y-you've got that f-f-phone receiver in your p-p-p-pocket?"

Glutz looked down at the protruding end and the cord hanging from it, dragging on the ground. You could have fried an egg on his cheek as he grinned sheepishly.

"Oh, that's just to ground me," he answered over his shoulder, and kept right on going. Sergeant Bawls looked puzzled.

"G-g-g-ground him," he echoed. He thought of coffee, electricity, and flying, then just shook his head. He didn't understand. But that's because he didn't understand, or know, Lieutenant Glutz.

Outside the building, Glutz looked at Airman Bug Tripshutter.

"Good job, Bug," he encouraged.

"Thanks, Lieutenant," Bug smiled. Glutz looked at his watch again. It was past quitting time.

"Say, Bug," he said, "do you have a car here?" Tripshutter nodded in the affirmative, pointing to a blue car with ALASKAN AIR FORCE painted on it.

"Good," Glutz said, "how about a lift to the parking lot to pick up my car?"

"Sure, Lieutenant, glad to," the photographer said. Glutz got in and they drove the two blocks to division headquarters where Glutz had parked his car.

"Where is it?" the Airman queried.

"I'm not sure," Glutz told him. "Maybe you'd better just drive up and down the rows until we find it."

The lot was a big one, about the equivalent length of two blocks and six double rows deep. They made the tour once, then twice, now three times. No sign of Glutz's car.

"Somebody must have stolen it," said Glutz disinterestedly. "Oh well, can you give me a ride to the BOQ? I'll call the Security Police from there."

"Which one?" Bug asked.

"The big one," Glutz told him. The airman nodded his assent.

No one said a word for a block or so. Then Tripshutter took his eyes from the road to look at Glutz and say, wonderingly, "Boy, that Sergeant Bawls sure stutters. Did you notice that, Lieutenant?"

"No, I didn't notice," said Glutz dryly. Tripshutter looked back at the road shaking his head from side to side.

"Don't know how you could have missed it," he muttered under his breath.

Pulling up at the BOQ, Jerry noticed a car below his window. *That looks just like my car,* he thought in the flash of a second. Even before he could finish the thought, he realized that it was.

"I sure hope you find your car, Lieutenant," Airman Tripshutter interrupted.

"I'm sure I will," Glutz consoled him. "Don't worry about it."

"What does it look like?" Tripshutter asked.

"Just like that one over there," Glutz said, pointing to his car.

"That's just the trouble," the airman complained. "So many cars look just alike."

"Ain't that the truth," Glutz muttered getting out of the car. "Thanks for the ride." *Guess I didn't even take the car to work this morning,* Glutz whispered to himself, patting his metal friend on the rear door as he passed.

On Monday morning, Glutz was late for work. That wasn't unusual, but the reason was. The night before Glutz had stayed up to watch an old late movie. It was so boring and he was so un-tired that he pulled his companion out of the refrigerator. It read scotch on the front. He proceeded to drink most of it and when he finally went to bed, it was late. As a result, aside from being tired in the morning, he also had a few cobwebs between the ears. Entering the Division headquarters, he passed Squadron Leader Albert X. Merry of the British Royal Air Force.

"I say there, Leftenant," said the squadron leader, "Is it now fashionable for Alaskan Air Force officers not to wear ties?"

Glutz looked down. Sure enough, he had no tie on. He smiled, did an abrupt about face and turned tail back to the BOQ. *I wonder where the squadron is that he's supposed to be leading,* he thought on the way. Squadron Leader Merry was an exchange officer of the British Royal Air Force. Having made his contribution, he left the scene as quickly as he arrived. Perhaps his squadron was waiting for him.

Back at the BOQ, Glutz put on his tie. He noticed his Li'l Abner boots in the closet next to his survival gear so he put them on too. *Captain McBooboo will like that,* he thought. When Glutz finally did arrive at the office, Captain McBooboo was waiting for him.

"There's going to be a world-wide weapons meet in Florida and we're in it," he told Glutz enthusiastically between sips of coffee and drags on his cigarette.

Glutz thought of the 45-caliber pistol, issued to him when he had arrived in Alaska. *I wonder where it is,* he said to himself. If he had looked closely, he would have noticed it next to his survival gear in the closet, when he put his Li'l Abner boots on less than an hour before. Glutz also remembered that he had never fired the 45, and that the only time he had fired a weapon, at summer camp in ROTC, he did little more than kick up sand on the side of the hill.

"What kind of weapons are we going to fire, Captain?" Glutz asked with half interest.

"*We're* not going to fire anything, Glutz," said the captain condescendingly. "It's a weapons meet for the fighter pilots and they're going to fire rockets at drones."

Glutz was still confused. The only drone he knew about was the male honeybee and, while he had seen the air force do some pretty strange things, he couldn't imagine them going quite that far. *I do remember throwing firecrackers at mosquitoes as a kid, but rockets at honeybees . . . hm-m-m,* he mused.

Captain McBooboo shocked him back into reality.

"Lieutenant, are you listening to me?" he demanded.

"What? Oh yes, Captain, I surely am."

"Good. Sergeant Daze will accompany the team to the meet and you will write the stories for the base paper from his telephone reports. What you'll do is take the information on a daily basis and then put it all together for the weekly edition. Got that?"

Glutz wasn't tracking McBooboo's directions.

"Captain?" queried Glutz.

"What is it?" responded the captain, rising from behind his desk and placing his cont cap squarely on his head.

"What's a drone?"

"A drone is what the fighter pilots are going to shoot rockets at," roared the captain, lighting a cigarette as he burst through the door.

Glutz had to go to the toilet so he decided on "the bay." The bay was a long narrow room with about sixteen open toilets and half as many urinals. Sometimes a childish airman would come in to use a urinal while Glutz was seated on a nearby stool. He could spot them in an instant. They were the ones who would go directly onto the drain at the bottom of the urinal, because they liked to hear the gurgling noises. This particular day there was a long line of airmen sitting along the wall as Glutz entered the bay. He wondered what they were doing there. He also wondered if they knew or even if they cared what they were doing there. *After all,* he thought, *IT ALL COUNTS TOWARD TWENTY.*

Glutz picked up the morning paper, entered, and sat down on "the throne." Shortly, a young lady opened the door to the bay, apparently thinking she was somewhere else. When she saw Glutz, pants at his ankles, poring through the paper, she froze. Her face turned scarlet. Glutz looked up unalarmed.

"Which would you like," he asked, "the sports page or the comics?"

That unglued her so she was able to turn and leave. The airmen in the hall let out a huge guffaw. When Glutz had finished his chores, he buckled his belt and left. The airmen laughed again.

"That's OK fellas," he told them, "She didn't know where she was going! Do you?"

It was Wednesday evening and Lieutenant Glutz sat in his chair at the office waiting for the final results of the weapons meet. Finally, the phone rang. It was Sergeant Daze.

"We lost, Lieutenant."

What the hell does that mean? Glutz thought. He was getting precious little information, so he began to ask questions.

"How many teams were there?"

"Six," Sergeant Daze told him.

"Where did we finish?"

"Third."

"Who was first?"

"The Fighting 32nd."

"OK, give me the rankings, Sergeant."

Glutz took the list and began to write the story. *Who-What-Where-When-Why,* he could hear McBooboo's voice yet. *Those are the questions you always address first when writing an article for a paper. You are the eyes and ears of the public.* Glutz remembered thinking that sounded at least appropriate, if not original. *Always tell the story in the first paragraph so that little is lost if subsequent ones need to be deleted.* Glutz remembered that, but he decided to do it differently this day. *What the heck,* he thought, *those guys deserve a better shake than me just reporting they finished third.* So he decided to give them one.

Plagued by bad weather, he began, *our intrepid fliers of the Blazing 15th finished better than half the field in Florida.*

When he finished the article, he put it on Sergeant Berry's desk and drove over to the officers' club for dinner. He had hardly gotten into his second scotch when the paging system sent his name over it. *Lt. Jerome Glutz, please call the operator. It's probably Captain McBooboo,* Glutz thought, *calling to send me on some errand he doesn't want to do. I don't need that tonight.* He took another sip of his scotch and didn't answer the page.

Next morning when he got to the office, McBooboo was waiting for him.

"Watch out for him today," Laura Lunsmann told Glutz. "He's really hot under the collar. Sergeant Berry already got a taste of his venom."

"What's the problem?" Glutz asked her. She didn't have time to answer.

"Glutz, come in here," he heard the captain's voice booming from the other room.

"Yes sir, what is it?" Glutz asked meekly, reporting at attention in front of the captain's desk.

"What is it, indeed!" shouted the captain. "Look at this!" he bellowed, giving Glutz a copy of the base paper which had just come off the press. McBooboo was so visibly upset that his hands were shaking; so much so that Glutz couldn't read the paper.

"You're shaking so much I can't read the paper, Captain," Glutz said.

"Here," roared the captain, throwing the paper at Glutz.

Then, Glutz saw it.

"The headline of the weapons meet is wrong," he said to himself, but out loud.

"Yes, the headline of the weapons meet is wrong," mimicked the captain, "and I consider it to be your fault, Lieutenant," he roared.

"My fault?" retorted Glutz in amazement. "Just how do you figure that?"

The captain told him in a hurry. "You wrote such a lousy lead that by the time Sergeant Berry finished rewriting it, he got confused and made the heading wrong."

The heading read "74th WINS WEAPONS MEET: 15th IS THIRD." It was true that the 15th was third, but the 32nd had won the thing. The 74th had finished last.

Captain McBooboo was beside himself, Glutz thought the accusation was incredible. The captain went on, "My four-year-old son could have written a better story than that," he threatened.

Glutz lost his cool. "Then maybe next time you ought to have him write it," he told the captain.

"What!!" McBooboo screamed. "Don't you know I could have you thrown in jail for insubordination?" *Sometimes I think that's where I am,* Glutz thought to himself.

"I'm sorry, Captain," he said to McBooboo, "I didn't mean anything by that."

"You'd better be sorry," McBooboo told him.

He then proceeded to rave on as to how much of an incompetent Glutz was, how ungrateful he was for all McBooboo had done for him and on and on. Finally, he stopped to catch his breath. Thinking the captain had finished, Glutz turned to leave.

"Come back here, young man. Where do you think you're going? I'll tell you when you can leave!"

Glutz came back to listen to another barrage and then finally he was dismissed. Captain McBooboo got up from his desk and stormed out of the room toward the bay. Once there he stepped hastily up to the urinal and, still being overweight, he opened his vest, took out his tie and went in his pants. Hurriedly, he rushed to his car and went home to change. He had a terrible time trying to get his pants off over his Li'l Abner boots.

On the way back to his office, the captain pondered what to do about the gigantic error in the paper. It should be delivered right now, but somehow that error had to be corrected. Finally, the thought came to him.

"That's it," he shouted happily. "We'll print up five thousand '32nds' and I'll put that stupid Lieutenant Glutz in charge of a detail to paste them over the '74s'."

"Five thousand?" Glutz queried when hearing of it. "That's the most stupid thing I've ever heard of," he muttered under his breath. Then aloud he said, "Why don't you just include a retraction in next week's paper, if anything? The body of the story's right, and it's not an error relative to our division, anyway."

"That sounds like something you'd say, Lieutenant. We'll paste those 5,000 stickers on even if it means that the paper doesn't get out until tomorrow. You're in charge and Sergeant Berry will help you."

"Why don't we all pitch in, Captain? We could do it a lot faster," Glutz offered.

"Because we didn't all make the mistake, Lieutenant. You did!"

So the rest of the office staff cooled their heels until McBooboo left and then proceeded to pitch in and get the job done. It was 9:00 P.M. when the last '32nd' was pasted over a '74th.' Glutz screwed the top back onto the jar of rubber cement and heaved a giant sigh of relief. Then he turned 33⅓ degrees in his chair to face M/Sgt. Willy Bills.

"Do you realize it's 9 o'clock, Billy?" he said. Glutz never could remember whether Sergeant Bills' first name was Billy or Willy and his last name Wills or Bills. The Master Sergeant didn't seem to notice.

"2100 hours on the military clock," Bills reminded him. Glutz was just too tired to think in terms of military time this late.

"Do you realize that the paper's already more than six hours late, and not one call has come in wondering why? Really makes me wonder if anybody reads the thing."

"Oh, somebody reads it all right, Lieutenant, you can be sure of that."

"Who—Captain McBooboo?"

"Yeah, him and also Sgt. Barry Berry."

"I'm not so sure about Berry," Glutz complained. "If he had read it this week, we wouldn't be here. If he doesn't read the body any better than he reads the headlines, he doesn't know much about it, that's for sure." M/Sgt. Willy Bills didn't answer. Instead he put on his cap and headed for the door.

"Can I give you a lift somewhere, Lieutenant?" he obliged.

"I don't know," Glutz responded with a frown on his face.

"What do you mean you don't know?" queried the Master Sergeant. "Don't tell me you're going to stay here and do some more work!"

"Are you for real?" Glutz said incredulously. "I'm leaving all right, it's just that I can't remember whether or not I drove my car over today. Let me call the BOQ and find out."

It was Thursday night at the BOQ and nobody answered the phone. Thursday night had that in common with every other night of the week. No one ever answered the phone. Glutz thought about that while he was listening for the rings and then, *That's not true,* he thought further, *I sometimes answer the phone at the BOQ when I'm there.* Then he realized that he wasn't there this night and hung up.

"I'll take that ride home now," he told Master Sergeant Bills.

"Left your car at home today, did you?" Bills asked.

"I don't know," Glutz told him. Bills lifted the back of his hat and scratched his head, but he didn't say a word.

On the way to the BOQ, Master Sergeant Bills had a thought.

"You, know, Lieutenant," he said. "It just might be that more people read the base rag this week than any other time." Glutz looked at him quizzically.

"Why do you say that?"

"Well, because it's going to be pretty obvious to anyone looking at the paper that the '32nd' has been pasted over something. Wouldn't you pick it off to see what was printed underneath?"

"I guess you've got a point," Glutz agreed. "If you call that reading the paper, then I guess there will be more."

The next morning Captain McBooboo was in the finest of moods. He was stooped over the edge of his desk when he saw Glutz walk past.

"Hey, Jerry, c'mon in here for a minute," he hollered cordially. Giving the raised eyebrow *What now?* look to Sgt. Happy Daze who had just returned from Florida, he turned on his heel and entered the captain's office.

"Ya' know what?" said McBooboo, taking a drag from his cigarette and a sip from his coffee cup, almost simultaneously. He didn't wait for Glutz's response. "I just came back from Colonel Stamfranz's office. I asked him what he thought of the way we corrected the headline error in the paper, or if he even noticed it. Know what he said?" Again he didn't wait for Glutz's reply. "He said the first thing he did was to pick it off and see what was underneath. Har! Har! Har! Isn't that a stemwinder? Pick it off to see what was underneath."

Glutz didn't see the humor. *You could have saved him the trouble by not pasting the correction on in the first place,* he thought to himself, but of course didn't say.

"Maybe Sergeant Bills was right about more readership this week."

"What's that, Lieutenant?" queried the captain.

"Oh nothing sir," Glutz said.

"OK," the captain accepted it. "Say Jerry," McBooboo went on. "I think it's about time we start giving you a little responsibility consistent with your rank. After all, you did do a nice job of pasting those 5,000 stickers on the base paper. Har! Har! Har!"

Glutz still didn't laugh. When he saw the irritated look on Glutz's face, Captain McBooboo didn't laugh anymore, either. Just then Airman Bug Tripshutter came in from the base photo lab.

"Here it is, Captain," he said, handing McBooboo a picture of Master Sergeant Bills holding a copy of the base paper while Lieutenant Glutz pasted a '32nd' over a '74th.'

"Good," said the captain, "What say we put that picture in the paper this week? Sort of a laugh on ourselves."

"If you put that picture in the paper," Glutz injected, "I'll be the laughing stock of the whole base. Already my friends think there's more to this caper than meets the eye. They can't believe that I'd be put on that kind of a detail for what I purportedly did."

McBooboo frowned.

"Leave the picture here," he told Airman Tripshutter, and then with one final grin and a sideways nod of the head, he put the picture in the middle drawer of his desk. Glutz destroyed it and the negative that afternoon.

The captain looked up once again.

"Back to that assignment I was beginning to tell you about, Lieutenant," he said. "It'll mean sparing you from the paper for a week or so, but I think I can talk Sergeant Berry into that." Captain McBooboo seemed to be serious. "Here's the deal," he went on. "Next week's safety week throughout the Alaskan Air Force, and because we're the biggest base, I think it would be a great touch if we had a really worthwhile, impressive display. Let me tell you about what I saw in a safety magazine just the other day."

Glutz listened as the captain went on.

"It was at this fabulous shopping center near some big city in Nevada. There had been quite a few car accidents on the premises; you know, fender benders, but they were getting to be quite a nuisance. One of the location managers came up with the idea that a few pictures and statistics put together in a display in the center court of the building might help reduce the accidents in the parking lot."

"Did it work?" Glutz asked.

"I don't know whether it did or not," the captain responded, a bit on the irritated side. "The point is that it gave me this idea. We could stage a simulated accident just off the side of the road at the entrance and exit to the base. We could 'unveil' it in the morning of the first day of safety week, just before cars started arriving on base and every one of them would have to drive right by it. I think it would be great for creating an awareness and best of all, Colonel Stamfranz comes by there every morning. He'd really be impressed. So that's your assignment, Lieutenant. Go to it."

Glutz looked less than totally enthusiastic. "Don't we have to get somebody's permission?" he wondered.

"Don't worry about getting somebody's permission, you've got mine," the captain chuckled. And then, reflecting a moment, he went on. "How the hell should I know whether you need somebody's permission or not. Check into it. And be sure to make the display as realistic as possible."

Glutz was thinking of a true-to-life display. "What if I have to spend some money?" he asked the captain.

"Well, don't spend very much, Jerry. You know you don't make much. Har! Har! Har!" McBooboo truly loved his own humor.

Glutz had to admit he was pretty bored with his job most of the time. About the only time he wasn't was when the good captain was screaming at him, and then he was too irritated to be bored. Here was a chance for him to use some imagination. He didn't have much time, but he didn't have much else to do either, so he set out to do the job right. First, he went over to the base motor pool to see if there were any vehicles there which had recently been in accidents. He didn't find any, but the NCOIC (that's non-commissioned officer in charge, for those who haven't been in the service or the military for a long time or for very long at a time) told him that the way some of the airmen drove, there'd probably be one in by the end of the day. Glutz didn't know whether the good NCOIC was kidding or not. Besides, he needed two wrecked cars. So, he decided to try another means. Like jobs have their contacts, so he took "a shot in the dark" and asked the NCOIC if he knew any junk dealers downtown who might be able to help him out. Glutz told the sergeant his plan. Maury Zenderhockle roared with laughter. It would seem that never before had the motor pool NCOIC heard anything quite so hilarious.

"Set up a fake accident at the gate to the base," he bellowed. "Haw! Haw! Haw! Sure I'll help you out, Lieutenant," he assured Glutz, after regaining some of his composure, and then he burst into laughter again, slapping his Southern knee several times in the process.

Lt. Jerry Glutz drove down the main street of Cannondaze, looking for the establishment of one Sam Leveschevitz. Turning off a main road, he followed the gravel for several hundred yards; and, after taking the bounce of three or four muck holes filled with water, his car arrived at a tall green fence. A dog barked savagely from behind the fence somewhere. Sergeant Zenderhockle had told Glutz about the dog so to him it was a good omen, a sign that he had arrived. Walking somewhat apprehensively over to the gate, which was open, Glutz noticed another sign. "Sam's Auto Parts," it read, "Used, Misused and Abused . . . None Unused." Glutz ran the humor through his mind, but his task today was far too serious to think about it in frivolous terms. The dog was still barking, but Glutz couldn't see him and there seemed to be no one else about.

Between barks Glutz hollered, "Is anyone here?" Nobody answered, except for the dog's continuing bark.

"Is anybody here?!" Glutz hollered again. All at once there was an overpowering odor which almost dropped Glutz to his knees. He caught it in his throat and nostrils just as he was deeply inhaling to let out another call with gusto.

"Wow," he coughed under what breath he had left. "I sure couldn't take a steady diet of this stench." It was loud enough for someone close by to overhear.

"You get used to it after awhile," a voice responded, breathing directly down Glutz's neck. Glutz turned around to find himself staring into a face, full of soot and sweat, of what appeared to be a transient hobo. Glutz gulped a deep breath and gagged once again. Half scared and half choking, he was finally able to gather presence of mind and lung.

"I'm looking for Sam Leveschevitz," Glutz gasped.

"I'm the only one around here, with or without that name," Glutz's new acquaintance told him. *His breath smells like ape shit,* Glutz thought to himself, *I wonder if he thinks he's Tarzan.* He decided not to ask.

"I'm a lieutenant from the air force," was all Glutz could think of to say.

"I could tell by your uniform," Sam said dryly, and then added, "what can I do for you?"

"I'm looking for two or three wrecked cars," Glutz told him. "Can you help me out?"

"You're in luck," Sam answered without the hint of a smile. "I just happen to have a couple in stock. They're real bargains, too," he went on.

"I hope so," said Glutz, "because I don't have any money."

"You don't what?!" Sam shrieked, turning back to face Glutz and blowing his fart breath down Glutz's throat. Glutz was truly shaken.

"We-l-l-l," he stammered, "you know we don't get very high pay in the air force."

"So I've heard," said Mr. Leveschevitz, turning around again and leading Glutz somewhere toward the other end of the junk-yard. "They ought to take you up for a flight when they pay you," he went on, "that would make it . . ."

"Seem higher," Glutz interrupted.

"Say, you air force officers are sharper than I thought," Sam said.

Just then they arrived in front of three junked cars, stacked atop one another.

"Would any of these do?" Sam asked.

"No, they've got to look like they've just been in an accident." Sam scratched his head.

"Well, I wouldn't say these look as if they've come off the assembly line recently."

"No," Glutz corrected, "they've got to look like they've been in an accident with each other. You see," he said pointing to the top of the pile, "that top one would be all right, but it doesn't have the dents in the right place, compared to the ones below it." Leveschevitz turned around and made a grand bow, sweeping his cap from one side of his person to the other.

"I am sorry, your highness," he admonished himself. "May I show you something just a bit more elegant." Then, straightening up, he put his cap back on his head. "Just what the hell is it that you're after, Lieutenant?" he demanded of Glutz.

"Well, you see," Glutz began humbly, "we want to stage this accident in front of the main gate at the airbase as a reminder, during safety week, for all drivers to be careful."

Sam scratched his chin, whether pensively or to kill a cootie, he didn't say. "Why didn't you say so?" he did say, "I've got four cars over here that were in two different accidents in front of the very gate you're talking about. They weren't smashed up all that badly, but the adjuster totaled them out, anyway, because, as you'll see, they aren't too new."

When Sam Leveschevitz pointed to the cars, Glutz knew what he meant about age. Calculating quickly, he found that the four of them totaled (no pun intended) an age which exceeded his. Almost half of this combined total, however, was accounted for by one of the cars.

"I'll take the other three," Glutz told the dealer. "How much do you want for them?" Sam ran his fingers through the stubble on his chin once more. "Seein' as you're from the air force," he told Glutz, "I'll give you the three of them for $125."

"One hundred twenty-five dollars?" Glutz was incredulous. "Those junkers weren't worth that before they were hit."

"Sometimes they're worth more on a heap than as a heap," Mr. Leveschevitz chuckled with a straight face. "OK," he went on, "make it $75."

That was still too much for Jerry to swallow, so he entertained another idea. "How about those two," he asked, pointing to the oldest two of the three, "and that one," pointing to the fourth, which he had spurned earlier.

Sam wanted to get rid of the oldest one. "I'll give you the three of those for $62.50," Sam agreed, as if the deal were taking money out of his pocket. It was still too much money for Jerry to spend, and he was virtually certain he couldn't count on McBooboo.

"I guess not," he said to Sam, turning toward his own car which was at the exit to the salvage yard. *That is, if they haven't hauled it in here yet,* Jerry thought in horror. Nervously, he looked around at the piles in the yard. His car didn't look that much different from some of them in here, but he didn't spot it. He ran for the exit just to make sure. It was still there. Only after he saw it safe did he hear Sam hollering behind him.

"Just a minute, Lieutenant," Sam was calling to him, waving his arms and running toward Glutz. "Don't feel you have to run off just because we had a little disagreement on price. I've decided I can come down five dollars more."

"No," Glutz muttered dejectedly. "I was thinking of getting something for about $25, but even I can see now that the thought was ridiculous."

"I can't sell my cars for that, Lieutenant," Sam said, appearing to share Glutz's melancholy, "I'd go out of business." Glutz got into his car and drove off.

His mind was buzzing, but nothing made any sense. Then it hit him.

"Why not?" he hollered out loud.

He drove directly to the BOQ and ran up the stairs to the door of Capt. Lucifer Loopholes, the base prosecuting attorney.

Captain Loopholes, one of Glutz's best friends, had a car that was only a few years old, but looked like it had been through several accidents. All it needed was a few dents to make the effect real. Most surely it had never seen the inside of a garage and, after several years out in the elements, the paint was badly faded and there were even a few rust spots. Loopholes was not intrigued with the idea.

"I admit it's not the best looking car on base," he told Glutz. "but then neither is yours. You've got some dents in your car, too."

"That's just the point," Glutz told him. "We stage the accident with two cars, yours and mine."

"Nothing doing!" Loopholes was adamant. "I'm not banging up my car for the sake of one of Captain McBooboo's crazy schemes."

"You won't have to," Jerry assured him. "I'm sure that Sergeant Zenderhockle at the base motor pool can figure out a way to make your car look like it's been in an accident, without it actually having to be in one."

"How's he going to do that?" Luci Loopholes asked, unconvinced.

"How the hell should I know!" Glutz charged, somewhat irritated that his good friend should prove to be the stumbling block to his brilliant scheme. Loopholes didn't want to antagonize Glutz by rejecting his idea summarily (as he might have said in court). He'd offer Glutz some hope, remote as it was, and tomorrow Glutz would have the screwy idea out of his head.

"Tell you what, Jerry," he said, "you go over to see this sergeant, whatever his name is, and if he can figure out a way to make my car look like it's been in an accident, without having to be in one, you can use it for your display . . . or, whatever you call it."

Glutz was aglow with new hope (no pun intended for the few of those who will read this and live there).

"Now that that's settled," Loopholes said, turning the cork out of the top of his bottle of scotch, "let's have one with soda." Glutz agreed. He leaned back against the top of the couch in Luci's quarters (that's "suite" for those who haven't spent much time in a BOQ. Those who have know that it isn't very "sweet"). Swirling the drink around in his hand, he thought of the display he would put together at the gate to the base.

"Captain McBooboo will really be impressed," he said, after finishing the first scotch. "So will the base commander," he whispered, after finishing the second. "Maybe, it will even make the wire services and get national coverage," he muttered, downing the last sip of his third scotch and soda. He leaned over and, putting his glass on the floor and his head on the end of the couch, he fell asleep. Captain Loopholes just shook his head as he put on his pajamas and climbed between the sheets. Tomorrow would be another hard day of prosecuting. He wondered what it would bring for his friend, Jerry Glutz.

CHAPTER XV

When Glutz woke up the next morning, Luci Loopholes was gone. Glutz looked at his watch to find that it was 0755. *I'll never in the world make it to the office in five minutes,* he thought. *I'd better call Captain McBooboo and tell him I'm on my way directly to the motor pool.*

The door to Captain Loopholes' room locked behind Glutz. When he got to his own room, he found that his door was also locked. He reached in his pocket for the key. It wasn't there. *Now where could I have left that damned key?* And then he remembered.

Running out to the car, he saw it, still in the ignition. *Now, how to get it out of there,* he thought. Just at that precise moment, out of the BOQ, strolled Squadron Leader Albert X. Merry of the British Royal Air Force. Glutz wondered again where his squadron was. Squadron Leader Merry squinted up at the sky and then cast a furtive glance at what appeared to be a watch on his wrist. *I wonder if he uses a sun dial,* Glutz thought.

"Oh, Mr. Terry," he smiled broadly, waving to and getting the attention of the RAF officer. Not wanting to take the time to call him "squadron leader," he didn't know what to say. Terry gave him a "What the devil is the matter with you now" Lord Plushbottom look. "It seems that I've left my keys in the car," Glutz said. Noting Merry's frown he went on to add, "that is, I've locked them in the car." He tried to talk as British as possible without attempting to copy the accent for fear that would sound too phony. Merry seemed unimpressed.

"And, just what would you like to have me do about it, young man?" he said to Glutz. Glutz really didn't know. Momentarily, he thought of something.

"I thought I might use your phone to call into the office and tell Captain McBooboo that I'll be late. Then, maybe I could have one of the hangers in your closet to get inside the window of my car and snap the lock up."

"I'll give you the hanger, Lieutenant, and I'll tell the Captain that you'll be in presently, but I don't care to have you use the phone as it would mean leaving the door unlocked." If Glutz had thought quickly, he would have realized that he could probably have made the phone call while Merry was getting the hanger; but, at least on this morning, he wasn't thinking that quickly.

"OK," he agreed. "Please tell the Captain that I'll be going directly to the base motor pool, and will be in later in the morning." Merry agreed, got the hanger, and was off.

Glutz twisted, turned, and bent the coat hanger until finally he heard the door click open. Grabbing the keys, he slammed the door and headed for his room. Before he could get the door unlocked, the phone started ringing. Frantically, he turned at the lock as the phone rang merrily (no pun intended) inside. Finally, on the seventh ring, he picked up the receiver.

"That you, Lieutenant?" came the voice from the other end of the connection.

Who the hell do you think it is, thought Glutz, gasping for the breath he had lost while making the mad scramble for the phone. He recognized the voice of one Squadron Leader Albert X. Merry.

"Yes, this is Lieutenant Glutz," he answered.

"Squadron Leader Albert X. Merry, here," said the voice on the other end. "What was it that you wanted me to tell the captain?"

"That I'll be going directly to the base motor pool, rather than coming into headquarters first," Glutz responded.

"You'll be doing nothing of the kind!" Glutz could almost feel McBooboo's hot breath from the other end of the line. "You report in here first, and right now."

"I'm going over to the base motor pool to work out the details on the safety week display," Glutz pleaded. "What have you got for me at the office?"

"Never mind what I've got for you, just get in here. You're already over thirty minutes late."

Glutz looked at his watch. It reminded him of the interservice joke. "For those of you in the army, the time is 1500 hours; for those of you at home, it is 3:00 P.M.; and for those of you in the air force, the big hand is on the twelve, and the little hand is on the three."

That's what his watch showed, all right. The big hand was on the twelve (12), and the little hand on the three (3), but he didn't know whether it stood for 0300 or 1500 hours. *I guess it's a moot point* (as Loopholes would say), thought Jerry, *since the watch is stopped, and it's really a bit after 0830 hours.*

"OK, Captain," Glutz agreed, "I'll be right over."

"Make it snappy," the captain bellowed, and hung up. Glutz showered quickly, cut himself with his electric razor, as was his daily custom, put on a change of shorts, a clean shirt, and headed out the door. At division headquarters, he went directly to McBooboo's office. The captain had quieted down.

"Come in, Lieutenant," he said cordially. Glutz was stunned, and it made him nervous that the captain should have changed moods so quickly, so he came in and said nothing. The captain went on, "I just want to see what progress you've made in setting up the safety display for the main gate for safety week." Glutz was still astonished.

"Oh, that's coming along just fine, Captain, just fine," he said defensively. "I should have all the plans made by the end of the day, and I'll report to you just as soon as I do." Like the coward on the playground, Glutz was happy to have made friends, once again, with the bully, even though he might expect another explosion at any time, he knew. "I'm about ready to go over to the base motor pool to talk to Sergeant Zenderhockle about getting some help from him."

"You go right ahead, Glutz," McBooboo said, almost affectionately, "don't let me stop you. Just let me know what's going on." Glutz assured the captain that he would and left.

Over at the motor pool, Zenderhockle remembered Glutz. "Yes sir," he greeted the lieutenant. "What can we do for you this morning?" Glutz told the sergeant the story. It was clear that Maury was in a good but impish mood this morning. "I've got a hell of an idea, Lieutenant," he said. "If Captain Loopholes' car is in the shape you say it is, what he really needs is a paint job. As long as it doesn't involve any out-of-pocket expense, and is of benefit to the air force, we can do just about anything we're equipped to handle. Now, of course, we couldn't just bring it in here to paint it, but if . . ."

"Yes," Glutz encouraged him, "go on."

"If," the sergeant continued, "it were to be busted up in the service of the government, then we'd have to fix it up in at least the condition it was in before the accident. Now, if we had to pound any dents out of it, we surely couldn't put it back in the shape it's in now without painting it, could we? And, we couldn't paint one or two fenders without painting the whole thing." Glutz was beginning to get the picture, but he wanted to be sure.

"Go ahead," he said to Zenderhockle, indicating him to continue.

"Gee, thanks, Lieutenant," Zenderhockle said. "We'll do a good job for you."

"No," Glutz admonished, "I mean go ahead and tell me more about your plan."

"Well," said the sergeant, "it's really very simple. What we do is smash the hell out of Captain Loopholes' car for your display, and then bring it in here, knock the dents out of it, and then re-paint it. We'll even take off the rust spots for him. It'll look as good as new, and won't cost the Captain a cent."

"Sounds great," agreed Glutz, "but just what's in it for you and your men? Why do you want to go to all this trouble for me?"

"Well actually, sir, we wouldn't be doing it just for you. You see, it gets pretty boring around here. Mostly what the guys do is change oil, wash cars and trucks, and clean up the floor. Some of them are darn good body men, but they don't get much of a chance to do any of it." Glutz felt there was more. Zenderhockle surveyed the lieutenant momentarily to see if he thought he could be trusted with the whole truth. Apparently, his conclusion was in the affirmative, so he went on. "There's one other thing too, Lieutenant. The guys get pretty antsy here doing the same thing day after day. You might say they get sort of aggressive from the boredom. Lately, they've been hollering at one another quite a bit. I'd like for them to have something to take out their aggressions on. If they could smash the hell out of somebody's car, I think it'd do the trick. An officer's car would be even better, and a captain, particularly the "Legal Eagle," that'd be just perfect. The only thing better'n that would be the motor pool officer's car, and that's out of the question."

A thin smile crept across Glutz's face. "I think I can work it out, but I'll have to get Captain Loopholes' permission, first."

"That'll be just fine, sir, but the men won't have to know that you got his permission, will they?"

Glutz felt like a hero. The sergeant was almost pleading. "No, the men won't have to know," he assured Sergeant Zenderhockle, confidently. He turned to leave, but as he got to the door, he had another thought. This was Jerry Glutz's day for great ideas. "What about my car?" he asked the sergeant.

Zenderhockle shook his head disapprovingly. "Sorry Sir, I'd like to, but you just don't rank high enough."

"Absolutely not," Luci Loopholes said emphatically at the suggestion that his car be partially demolished to accommodate Lieutenant Glutz's hair-brained scheme. Loopholes paced about the room rectangularly as an apprehensive tiger, sensing a snare nearby and certain he would not avoid it.

"But, Luci," Glutz implored, "you'd have a brand new car. Just think of it, Luci, it would look just as it did the day you drove it off the assembly line at Detroit."

Captain Loopholes stopped for a moment to glare at Glutz. "I didn't drive that car off the assembly line in Detroit, you idiot. I bought it in California."

"Well anyway," Glutz went on, "it was new once, and you can remember what it looked like."

"Yes, it was new once," Loopholes reflected, "and I remember what it looked like. But you give it to those monkeys down at the motor pool, and I'll never ever recognize it again."

"Oh, sure you will," Glutz coaxed him. "They'll fix it up as good as new."

Loopholes, still pacing with his hands behind his back, went over to the window and looked out. It was so dirty he could scarcely see his car out at the curb. "They'll fix it up all right; and, God only knows when."

"I'm glad you brought that up, Luci," Glutz encouraged him. "We'll have to make sure that we get a definite date from Sergeant Zenderhockle as to when the car will be repaired."

"Not me, you!" demanded Loopholes, pointing a shaking finger at Glutz. "You'll make sure that it's back here; and within three days of the end of safety week."

"Then, it's OK to use your car?" "I didn't say that," Loopholes muttered in response, but Glutz didn't hear it.

"Gee, that's just great, Luci. You're quite a guy. I'd better call Sergeant Zenderhockle at home to make sure he and his boys can get it set up in time."

"Hey, wait a minute!" Luci hollered, but Glutz was already out the door. It was no use. Lucifer Loopholes, captain, air force base prosecutor, had been had again. *Good thing there's no penalty for figurative sodomy,* he said to himself.

The next morning, Glutz was up early for a change. He rapped enthusiastically at Captain Loopholes' door.

"Come on in," he heard the response from inside. Loopholes was shaving.

"Hurry up, Luci," Glutz said, throwing the captain his shirt. "We've got to get over to the motor pool to drop your car off, give the airmen instructions on where to put the dents, and then get you over to your office."

"What about breakfast?" said Loopholes out of the side of his mouth, while stretching a facial gesture on the other side to make his cheek taut for shaving. Loopholes never missed breakfast.

"Sorry Luci," Glutz told him, picking his pants up off the couch to hand to him. "We won't have time for breakfast this morning."

"We," said Loopholes stretching the other side of his face. "Who's we?" Jerry Glutz had been to breakfast just once since he had come on base and that was a Saturday morning when he hadn't bothered to go to bed all night.

Captain Loopholes was still shaking his head when he finally deposited himself in his car. Deposit was a fairly accurate description, as the good captain was rather broad abeam amidships. Then he remembered something he had forgotten and hurriedly rolled his window down as Glutz backed away from the curb. Glutz didn't see him so he honked his horn. Glutz reached over and rolled down the window on the passenger side of his car.

"Where the hell's the base motor pool?" Luci asked disgustedly.

"Follow me," said the lieutenant to the captain.

Captain Loopholes was not totally intrepid as they approached the motor pool. Partially, he was concerned what some of his fellow officers would think when they heard that he had driven his automobile to its destruction before going to work. He was particularly concerned with what his CO would think (that's commanding officer, for those who haven't been in the service of country or spouse—if male—for very long). He had a mental image of it showing up in his efficiency rating. "On one occasion, Captain Loopholes did, willingly and without fear or duress, drive his private vehicle to the base motor pool for the purpose of having it smashed beyond recognition by the airmen and NCO stationed at that facility." A cold chill ran up his spine . . . or, was it down . . . he couldn't tell for sure. *Oh no,* he said to himself, *how do I allow myself to get into these messes?* With that they arrived at the base motor pool.

Glutz jumped from his car as if in fear that Loopholes would get away, and motioned the latter toward the large overhanging door. He pushed a button as if he'd been here before, and the big double door began to rise over his head. An airman came running over.

"Say, just what the hell are you . . . Oh, sorry Lieutenant, but you can't be running that door. I'm the only one authorized to raise it, and Airman Zipwing is authorized to lower it."

"Well," said Glutz with an air of authority, "You just tell Sergeant Zenderhockle that Lieutenant Glutz and Captain Loopholes are here with the latter's car and he'll understand."

"I'll have to get Airman Zipwing to put the door down first, Lieutenant." Glutz was irritated.

"Get going," he said firmly, between his teeth.

"Yes, sir," the airman said, and waltzed away with a quick half-salute.

Sergeant Zenderhockle was shortly on the scene with a big broad grin. He gave a snappy salute to Glutz, and then motioned Captain Loopholes in through the big door. Mostly, he looked at the car.

"Very nice," he muttered to himself. "Oh yes, that'll do very nicely." Loopholes looked like he had the world's most bitter pill in his mouth. He was greeted by a big salute and a bigger smile as he stepped from his car. Luci thought it was more scorn than smile that he detected on Sergeant Zenderhockle's face.

"Thanks for bringing the car over, Captain," the Sergeant told him. "You can be sure we'll take good care of it, and you'll have it back good as new within just a few days after safety week."

"What does he mean by a few days," Luci snarled at Glutz, as if Glutz was the interpreter.

"Oh, two, three, a week at the most, Captain," Zenderhockle answered. Glutz was happy to see that Luci was somewhat relieved by the encouragement from the motor pool sergeant.

"Captain Loopholes must be quite a guy," Zenderhockle said to Glutz. "It takes quite a man to give up his car for a whole week or two for a cause like this. You can be sure we'll get it back in tip-top shape for him, too." He said all this as if speaking to Glutz, but loud enough, so that Loopholes could hear. Luci was actually smiling as he and Glutz walked to Glutz's car.

"You know," he said to Glutz "it really makes me feel good to contribute to the safety of motorists on this base. It really does. And, I'll tell you what else, that Sergeant Zenderhockle is nobody's fool. No, sir. He sure isn't." Glutz knew that Zenderhockle was no fool. He wondered, though, if he and/or Captain Loopholes was.

Over the weekend, Glutz worked feverishly to get the display ready for the "grand opening" on Monday morning. Loopholes helped as did a number of "slick sleeve" (that's those without any rank at all, for those who didn't read the earlier part of the book or have a short memory) airmen. They went to the base hospital to get mannequins which the medics were most helpful in making look really messy. Then they took Glutz's car over to the designated location after having picked up Captain Loopholes' car from the base motor pool on the way. Loopholes' car was drivable, but you'd never have known it from looking at it. All three fenders were smashed (the fourth one was missing), the windshield glass was busted, one of the headlights was out of its socket and hanging over the ground by just one wire, the hood was caved in, and one hub cap was gone. When Loopholes saw the mess, he turned red and then pale.

"Those sons a bitches," he muttered to himself, and then he turned squarely toward Glutz. "They'll never get that car back to normal." Glutz agreed, but he didn't dare say so.

"Oh sure, they will," he encouraged. "You'll be amazed at what they can do these days with a few hammers and a little equipment."

"I've seen what they've already done with a few hammers and a little equipment," declared an exasperated Loopholes.

Glutz didn't respond. Instead, he loaded the two mannequins in the front seat of Loopholes' car, and told him they'd meet at the main gate where the display was to be set up.

"How am I s'posed to get there?" the captain blurted.

"Drive your car," Glutz told him. "It just looks like it's totaled out, but it really isn't," he said.

Loopholes shook his head, but did as Glutz bade him. Sure enough, the car started right up, and a somewhat surprised Luci Loopholes followed Glutz down the street toward the main gate. Little did he know what a sight he presented. A car driving down the street under its own power, even though it looked completely totaled, with three "people" in the front seat, two of whom, though sitting erect, appeared to be mortally wounded. Being a quiet time of a quiet day on a quiet road, Captain Loopholes passed only one car on the way to the main gate. That was almost more than enough, however. The driver and sole occupant of that car, formerly being of sound mind and body, jerked his neck quickly at the sight of Loopholes' car and his two fellow occupants. Simultaneously, he jerked the steering wheel in another direction, stepped down the boulevard between a parked car and a giant oak tree, missing both by inches. This action behind him, Loopholes never even noticed it had happened as he waltzed his car merrily on toward what appeared to be its last destination.

Glutz pulled in behind the main gate and jumped out of his car. He motioned Loopholes to swing his vehicle around and where to park it. Then, just to put on the capping touch, he got back into his own car, backed up and floored the accelerator, shooting about ten paces into Loopholes' one remaining headlight. Loopholes, unsuspecting, quickly braced himself against the steering wheel. His two "friends" lurched forward against the dash. Glutz roared with laughter until Loopholes crawled out of his car holding the back of his neck.

"Whiplash," he moaned. Forgetting that he had hit Luci from the front, not the rear, Glutz rushed to his aid. Luci waited until he was close enough, and then let him have a sock in the gut.

"Why you . . ." Glutz started.

"I should have hit you in the head," Loopholes told him motioning in that direction. Glutz thought it best to go on to another subject.

"C'mon, let's get started." Now the two cars were already neatly together in what ended up as a real accident, so only the positioning of the mannequins remained.

"Where should we put the dummies?" Luci asked Glutz, reaching through the shattered windshield to fish them out.

"You're just fine, right where you are," Glutz told him, grinning.

"That's more fact than fiction," Loopholes muttered, thinking of what had happened to his car.

"Leave that one right there," Glutz told Luci, referring to the "blood-covered" mannequin that Loopholes had dragged through the windshield, up to its waist. The other mannequin was propped out of the driver's window of Glutz's car, staring up at the sky. The slick sleeves then put some painter's canvas over the collage and they all withdrew.

Glutz and Loopholes had the truck driver drop them off at the Officers' Club, where a cool beer tasted good after their ordeal. "Boy," dreamed Glutz, "just wait 'til the Base Commander gets a look at our handiwork. Won't he be surprised!"

"Yes," agreed Loopholes. "He sure will be." But he wondered in what way.

On Monday morning Glutz hurried over to the display to pull the canvas off his genius idea before any cars from off base arrived. Then he walked jauntily toward the division headquarters, whistling happily as he went along. When he arrived, he heard Captain McBooboo speaking apologetically on the phone in low tones.

"Yes, I know, sir. Well, I'm sorry, sir. I really didn't know anything about it, sir. Yes, I realize that, sir. Yes, I surely will, sir."

Glutz heard the phone click as McBooboo hung it up. Then he heard the captain walk out of his office muttering to himself. As he walked past Glutz's door, he caught sight of the lieutenant. He walked past the door before he realized it, and then came back.

"Glutz!" he screamed at the top of his voice.

Glutz's clothes stayed where they were, but he jumped an inch inside them.

"Yes, sir!" he shouted on conditioned reflex.

"Glutz," the captain repeated, a bit more softly. "Just what the hell have you gone and done now?"

"Done now?" Glutz echoed.

"Yes, done now," McBooboo said again.

"I don't know what you mean, Captain."

"You don't know what I mean?" the captain said softly. "You don't know what I mean?" he said a little louder. "You don't know what I mean!" he shouted. "That damned display you set up out at the front gate has already caused nine accidents, and the base commander wants it out of there, right now. Right now, Glutz. Do you hear me? RIGHT NOW!"

"Right now," Glutz agreed, and he raced off to go somewhere. Just where he was going, he wasn't sure.

Once outside, he decided that the best thing to do would be to head for the base motor pool. There his friend, Sergeant Zenderhockle, would help him out. But this day Sergeant Zenderhockle wasn't as helpful as he'd been in the past.

"I'm sorry, Lieutenant. There's nothing I can do right now. I haven't got a truck or anything to go over there. I can't even spare a man to help you drive one of the cars back. They're all down at the main gate helping tow wrecked cars out of the thoroughfare so that others can drive on base. They say traffic is backed up for almost a mile. What happened anyway? Must have been a real scene."

Glutz's heart sank, but he didn't know what to say. "Yeah, it's a real scene, all right," he managed. Then, he just shook his head and walked off. Finally, Glutz made his way to the main gate, got into his car, pulled the mannequin in beside him, backed the car out of the accident, and drove off. The security police just stood there with mouths open and tongues hanging out.

Back at the BOQ, Glutz called Loopholes' office to tell of his predicament and to get his assistance in taking Luci's car over to the motor pool to have it repaired.

"I'm sorry," said the friendly voice at the other end. "Captain Loopholes is in court and won't be out for the remainder of the day." At this point, Glutz remembered that he hadn't even noticed a traffic back-up at the main gate. *Maybe it was just a ruse,* he thought. Captain McBooboo probably just got things bent all out of proportion again, and doesn't understand the situation. Absentmindedly, Glutz turned on the radio while he was thinking.

"And the news from Elfendwarf Air Base this morning is filled with irony. On the first day of the air force's safety week, the air police at the main gate report the worst chain of accidents on record. Traffic is reportedly backed up for three and one-half miles, almost into town, and civilian and air force personnel are unable to get onto the base to go to work. The Base Information Officer, Captain McBooboo, is reportedly unavailable for comment."

Glutz just shook his head again, put down the receiver which he was still holding, and ambled out the door in the direction of the main gate. Without looking up, he opened the door to Loopholes' car, got behind the wheel, and started up the engine. This time, he didn't even bother to pull the mannequin inside the car. The airmen didn't stare as he drove away, either. But there was something causing a dull scraping sound which virtually brought the car to a stop each time Glutz took his foot from the accelerator. When he got to the motor pool, Glutz got out to see what the scraping was. It was one of the wrecked fenders scraping against the tire, the one Glutz had banged in his last-minute accident with his own car. The sharp edge of the fender had now peeled the rubber on the tire down to the cord. Loopholes would be happy to hear that, he knew. Glutz went to look for Sgt. Maury Zenderhockle.

"I'm sorry, Lieutenant," Zenderhockle was saying, "I just don't have any place to put the Captain's car right now, to say nothing of fixing it." Lt. Jerome V. Glutz AO 9999999 was normally a very patient person. Now, his patience was running low.

"Listen, Sergeant," he told Zenderhockle, pointing an accusing finger at him. "You get that car in the garage and you get it fixed in a week like you said you would, or, you'll wish you had."

The sergeant was willing to compromise in the face of these threats from the usually placid lieutenant.

"OK, Lieutenant," he agreed. "I'll keep the car here, but there's no way that I'm going to get it fixed in a week. We just don't have the parts."

"What about your promise?" Glutz reminded him.

"Well," Maury said quickly, "that was when I thought you were going to have it out on display all week. I didn't know you were going to bring it in today." Actually, he had no plan for fixing the car next week either, and both he and Glutz knew it.

"OK," Glutz told him, "you've got 'til next week to get the car repaired." Then, he turned on his heel and walked off.

That evening Captain Loopholes was waiting in Glutz's room when the lieutenant returned from his harrowing experiences. He immediately noticed Glutz's downcast mood.

"What's the matter with you?" Loopholes asked him. "You look like you just saw an accident at the main gate," and then he burst into raucous laughter.

"It's not all that funny, Luci," Glutz said in dull tones. "Didn't you hear the radio?"

Luci shook his head; he'd been in court all day. Glutz went on to tell the prosecutor what had happened.

"Oh, that's not so bad," Luci said cheerfully. "You did the best you could, and now I'll get my car back a week sooner."

"Oh no you won't," Glutz said spitefully.

"What d'ya mean, 'oh no I won't,'" demanded Loopholes, imitating Glutz.

Glutz told him what Zenderhockle had said. Now, it was Loopholes' turn to become incensed.

"C'mon," he motioned Glutz, pulling his tie off the chair and heading out the door.

"Where are we going?" Glutz asked, following him out.

"To have a talk with your friend, the Sergeant at the motor pool."

Glutz stopped in his tracks.

"He's not there anymore, Luci. He's surely gone home for the day by now."

"What time does he leave?" Luci asked, looking at his watch for one reason or another.

"I don't know," Glutz told him, "but it's after 1730 hours, and no NCO on this base works that late."

"What the hell time is 1730 hours?" demanded Loopholes, looking at his watch again with a frown in his brow.

Glutz began to tell him, "That's when the big hand is on the six and the little hand . . ."

"Oh, shut up, you smart ass," Luci said, "and, just come along."

"Where are we going now?" Glutz wanted to know.

"We're going to find Sergeant Zinklehooper or whatever the hell his name is, so I can get my car fixed."

Glutz started again, "I just finished telling you . . ."

But Loopholes was adamant, "I don't care what you just finished telling me," he said. "Sankledooper has to be somewhere and we're going to find him."

"His name is Zenderhockle," reminded Glutz, following along.

"Your changing his name won't help hide him," muttered the captain and prosecutor.

Over at the motor pool, only an airman remained, and he was apparently washing vehicles, although the water from the hose seemed to be just running down the drain. *Maybe, he's washing out the drain,* Glutz thought to himself. Captain Loopholes had no time for such frivolous thinking.

"Where's the NCOIC around here?" Captain Loopholes demanded, not wanting to take another stab at the name.

"There is no NCO in charge around here," the airman said without looking up. "I'm the only one here."

So that's what the IC stands for, Loopholes thought to himself, *I wonder what the NCO means?* But, he had no time to continue with that train of thought, either.

"Listen, young man," said the captain in an irate tone, "I'm looking for the Sergeant, and I don't have much time. Where is he?"

The airman knew that Captain Loopholes was serious, so he toyed with him no longer.

"He's probably over at the NCO club," the airman told him. "Either there or at home." Luci stomped out with Glutz following close behind.

"Where the hell's the NCO club?" he wanted to know.

"Follow me," Glutz said with authority, and took the lead for a change. It was a walk of several blocks, and when they reached their destination, Luci was in the lead once more. He stomped into the club and immediately spotted Zenderhockle sitting on a stool at the bar.

"Sergeant," Captain Loopholes shouted, and immediately everyone in the room looked up. That made Luci pretty uncomfortable, but diverted his attention for only a moment. He tapped Zenderhockle on the shoulder. "Sergeant," he said again without really thinking of the consequences, "when will you have my car fixed up, as you put it, 'good as new?'"

Zenderhockle was visibly irritated. He wasn't accustomed to having officers address him in such a manner. He liked even less the fact that he was the center of somewhat dubious attention here in the temporary home of all those closest to him.

"Captain," he said in a surly tone, "I'll tell you what I told the Lieutenant here this morning. I'll take your car in, because I agreed to do it, but I can't guarantee that it'll be fixed up in a week. Now, that's simply the best I can do." With that, he turned back disgustedly to his beer on the bar. Captain Loopholes was not accustomed to being addressed like that by anyone and the increasing tenor of the situation was beginning to make him boil.

"Now, let me tell you something," he said, purposely omitting the term 'sergeant' this time, because of the attention it drew. "You told me when I brought it in that you'd have my car fixed up within a week after the safety display was over, and I expect that you'll do just that."

Sergeant Zenderhockle turned around again, this time having cooled off just a trifle. "So I did, Captain," he agreed, "but, that was before I found out that the display was going to last less than half a day. Some of the vehicles in that dent procession at the main gate belong to the government, and they take first priority." Zenderhockle was good at finding 'ways out' and he thought that statement would be a real stopper. How could Captain Loopholes put the arm on him (that means exert pressure, for those who live in a vacuum) to do his own private car, when there were air force cars that needed attention first? Surely Loopholes couldn't go anywhere else to complain, particularly since his car was 'approximate cause,' to use the prosecutor's own terminology, of the damage to the government vehicles. But, Zenderhockle had underestimated the good captain.

"Well, I'll tell you something, Zimperhoople." Loopholes was so irritated that he didn't care whether he called the man by the right name or not. Anything was better than 'sergeant' in this place. "The fact that you may have government vehicles to repair is your problem. The fact that you have my vehicle to repair is also your problem. It is also my problem. I expect that you'll have my car repaired, good as new, no later than one week from today."

"And, if I don't?" the sergeant began.

"And, if you don't," Loopholes continued bending down to whisper the remainder of his threat in Maury Zenderhockle's ear.

"On what charge?" Zenderhockle shouted as Captain Loopholes turned to leave this uncomfortable setting.

"Rape," he said softly over his shoulder as he walked through the door.

Glutz had been quiet through the entire interchange, a rather remarkable feat in itself. Now he spoke.

"Seems to me you were kind of tough on him, Luci."

"Seems to me he'd better get that car fixed up for me in a week, or I'll be rather tough on him," Luci snarled.

"Would you really charge him if he doesn't get it fixed?" Glutz wondered.

"I'd charge him physically, if not legally," Loopholes said with the hint of a grin on his face. "But, as for you," Luci went on, "that's the end of my cooperation with any of your harebrained schemes."

Glutz was all defensiveness. "How could I help it?" he excused himself. "It was a good idea that just didn't work out."

"So was the Bay of Pigs invasion," Captain Loopholes muttered.

"Well, that's over with," Glutz breathed with a heavy sigh. "Let's go over to the club and have a couple of drinks and dinner."

"Sounds like what I need," answered Loopholes.

On the following morning, Glutz sat at his desk contemplating his navel. He was rather tired this morning, because he had had to get up extra early so that Luci Loopholes could eat breakfast and get to his office on time. Glutz normally didn't eat breakfast, and he didn't normally get to work on time, either. But, with Loopholes' car out of commission, Glutz did feel the responsibility for seeing that he got where he had to go; particularly after the good captain reminded him of it several times, and pounded on his door this very morning until the lieutenant finally got up.

It was a dreamy morning, anyway. Not much happened on Tuesdays and Captain McBooboo was in a pretty good mood because the base commander was able to joke about the incident on the afternoon of the previous day. Not only that, but the story had made the national wire services and the command and air command commanders had had several phone calls from around the nation kidding them about it. While the display didn't exactly come off as planned, it did bring to the attention of everyone that Elfendwarf was concerned about motor vehicle safety, and it told the whole nation that the air force was. The base commander couldn't be too unhappy about that. However, the fact still remained that Glutz had gone ahead without Captain McBooboo's final and formal approval, and so the lieutenant couldn't be exonerated. Therefore, the captain felt it appropriate to take to himself whatever accolades were forthcoming over the incident. This didn't bother Glutz too much, though. It did mean that McBooboo was in a good mood and, after all, IT ALL COUNTS TOWARD TWENTY . . . *except for me,* Glutz thought. He opened his desk drawer to count off the number of days until his release from active duty . . . 381 days.

Just then the phone rang.

"Would you be interested in leaving the air force?" the caller asked.

Glutz's mind flashed back and forth. His first thought was that it was one of his so-called friends at the BOQ. They were always looking for angles to get out, but never found any. But he didn't recognize the voice. Then a terrible thought crossed his mind. Could it be that Zenderhockle was so influential in the air force that he was having Glutz thrown out for his part in the embarrassing moments in the NCO club the night before? Glutz managed to erase that immediately. He knew sergeants were powerful, but that was ridiculous. *Maybe I'm getting kicked out over that display at the main gate,* he thought. Maybe Captain McBooboo's mood this morning was only a facade, or maybe he was happy because Glutz was getting kicked out. All these thoughts flashed instantaneously.

Then Glutz said, "What do you mean?" and held his breath.

"This is Sergeant Kermer of the personnel office," the voice said. "The air force has been authorized a reduction in force and, since you are one of the several thousand lieutenants who is scheduled to leave within the next year or so, you are offered the option of leaving in ninety days or extending your tour of duty."

Glutz was dumbfounded. He had looked forward to this day for a long time, but now that it could be upon him, he didn't know.

"Can I call you back?" he asked his caller.

"Sure can, Lieutenant. Just as long as you do it sometime this week." Glutz hung up the phone and pondered. Then he got up and walked into Captain McBooboo's office. McBooboo was sitting behind his desk, Li'l Abner boots on the desk (McBooboo's feet were in them), reading a paper. He didn't hear Glutz enter. Glutz walked right up to the head of the captain's desk and stood at some semblance of attention.

"Captain McBooboo," he said, in a normal tone. There was no response. "Captain McBooboo," Glutz said again a bit louder. Still no answer. Glutz leaned forward, placing his knuckles on the flat surface of the captain's desk and perching his head just behind the paper the captain was reading. "Captain McBooboo," he said again, quite softly with just a hint of emergency.

McBooboo caught sight of the crown of Glutz's head peering over the top of his paper. The paper flew up in the air as the good captain went backwards in his chair. In the split second of movement, it was apparent to his steel trap mind that he was headed on a quick trip to the floor. He grasped desperately for anything to hold him up, but the only item within reach was his half-filled coffee cup. He took it along with him as he sprang over backwards to the floor. But, the coffee did not stay in its cup. It distributed itself generously over the front of his blouse (that's air force terminology meaning jacket).

"Oweee!" the good captain ejaculated as the heat of the coffee embraced the nerve endings just beneath his chest. Glutz turned away from the scene to hide his uncontainable laughter. He was laughing so hard, though silently, that he lost most of his vision from the tears that welled up in his eyes. McBooboo picked himself up and attempted to brush himself off, but the ample wetness stayed.

"Lieutenant Glutz," he mumbled, continuing to brush, "sometimes I think you are the most lightheaded person ever to wear an officer's uniform." Encouraged by Glutz's lack of response to his unkind words, McBooboo's temper began to flare. "As a matter of fact," he continued, "if you're representative of what ROTC turns out these days, I pity the people dependent on the air force for their security."

Glutz, just beginning to control his laughter, sought desperately for something humorous to say, to excuse the smile that was still all over his face. "When better officers are made, ROTC will make them," he offered, paraphrasing a saying he'd heard somewhere. McBooboo just shook his head in disgust, which Glutz took as his cue to leave.

When he got as far as the door, Glutz remembered why he had come. He turned around to find the captain close on his heel, headed toward the door to get another cup of coffee. So close was he, in fact, that McBooboo had to ascend to his tiptoes to stop his momentum and avoid running into Glutz. He lifted his empty coffee cup skyward as he ascended.

"Glutz," said he, once back on solid ground, "will you please get out of here? You are going to drive me to the point of hysteria, though I have never been there before." That was a laugh, Glutz thought, but he ignored it.

"The reason I came in to see you," Glutz plunged in, "is to ask you if you think it would be a good idea for me to leave the air force."

Captain McBooboo heard every word of it, but didn't believe a syllable.

"I think it would be an excellent idea for you to leave the air force," he said sarcastically. "But, since I don't have the authority to make that happen at the moment, I'll settle for you just getting out of my way so I can get another cup of coffee."

Glutz stepped to one side as the captain huffed past. Glutz followed the captain down the hall like a puppy does, just as fast as his little legs could carry him.

"But it's true, Captain," he remonstrated. "Sergeant Kermer from personnel called me just a little bit ago, and told me that the air force had authorized a reduction in force and I can leave in ninety days."

McBooboo stopped in his tracks.

"No shit!" was the first utterance that came to his lips. "There were days when I almost despaired of ever getting rid of you. As a matter of fact . . ." but then, he realized what he was doing. After all, Glutz was leaving. This was a time for jubilation! The thorn in his side was being removed. This called for a toast of sweet wine, not a verbiage of sour grapes! McBooboo moved on down the hall to the coffee machine and said, as he put his coin in the slot, with a look of all seriousness. "You know, Lieutenant, this is not a decision to be considered lightly." And, then he stopped. A scowl ran over his forehead. "They aren't kicking you out, are they?" McBooboo knew that wasn't likely, but if they knew what he knew about Glutz . . . well, he'd let Glutz answer for himself.

"No, they aren't kicking me out," Glutz assured him. "It's just that I have the option of getting out if I want to."

McBooboo assumed his serious composure once again. "As I was starting to say, Lieutenant," he continued, "leaving the armed forces is not a decision to be taken lightly. Although no circumstance is perfect, there are many others which might be a whole lot less desirable. I suggest you take the rest of the day off and think about it."

"Thanks, Cap'n," Glutz hollered over his shoulder as he had already turned around and was moving away. Without knowing it, Captain McBooboo had sealed the door on Glutz's decision. What little doubt there had been was now dispelled.

"Where's Sergeant Kermer?" Glutz asked of an orderly who seemed to be loitering under a sign that read "PERSONNEL."

"Dunno," said the orderly. "Who's Sergeant Kermer?"

Glutz swept by him and went into the big room where he asked again.

"You're lookin' at him," was the response this time. "What can I do for you, Lieutenant?" The sergeant had looked up only briefly, and now he was working at his papers once again.

"I'm Lieutenant Glutz," Glutz told him.

"Jerome V., AO9999999," the sergeant answered in a monotone.

Glutz was impressed. "That's right," he said.

Sergeant Kermer looked up as if to say, *Of course that's right.* But, what he did say was, "What can I do for you, Lieutenant?"

"I've decided to leave the air force," Glutz told him. Kermer kept working at his papers. "I have just one question," Glutz went on. The sergeant still gave no evidence of having heard. "Can I waive the ninety days and leave now?"

Sergeant Kermer looked up as if stunned. His jaw dropped to the depth of its leverage reach. "I don't know," he said finally. It had been a long time since he'd had to say that and he was obviously shocked to have his ears hear what his mouth had just uttered. He continued to stare in amazement.

"Well, can you find out for me?" Glutz asked. Sergeant Kermer continued to stare into space. "I say, can you . . ." The sergeant was finally shocked back into reality. He snapped his head as if trying to wake up. Then he blinked his eyes and squinted.

"I suppose I can," he said rather quietly, half to Glutz and half to himself. Finally, he regained his composure. "Yes, I'll look into it, Lieutenant," he told Glutz authoritatively. "Call me tomorrow and I'll let you know."

Glutz went home and poured himself a big scotch. He pulled his tie loose, sat down in one of two big old easy chairs which adorned his "suite," and took a big pull from the glass. He was simply delighted. *Just wait until Loopholes gets hold of this,* he thought. Then, he looked at his watch. *Holy smoke!* It wasn't even noon yet and here he was, having a drink. Absentmindedly, he got up and threw the drink in the toilet, glass and all. *Now, that was a brilliant thing to do,* he said to himself, realizing what he had done. Rolling up his sleeve, he retrieved it. Not having the appliances to ensure its cleanliness, he now threw it in the wastebasket. Then he stepped on it to make sure the maid wouldn't think it got there by mistake and retrieve it. Glutz's mood suddenly went from one of exhilaration to one of melancholy indecision. *What the hell can I do now?* he thought. *It's too early to start drinking. I surely don't want to go back to the office and spar with McBooboo. I'm not tired enough to go to sleep. I'm not hungry enough to eat; besides, I don't want to go to the officers' club. McBooboo might see me there, and then he'd expect me back at the office this afternoon.*

Glutz slumped back into the chair. What a quandary to be in. Then the light bulb went on in his head. *That's it,* he told himself. *I'll go over to the motor pool and see how Captain Loopholes' car is coming.* This he did and to his surprise, they were actually working on it. *Will miracles never cease,* he thought to himself. Not only were they working on it, but it appeared that they weren't too far away from having the thing restored. Sergeant Zenderhockle was over near a floor drain, listening to the gurgling noises as he poured a large can of what appeared to be drain oil, into it. Glutz snuck up on him, in his normal surreptitious manner, without malice or forethought, and found himself beside the motor pool NCO without the latter's awareness of his presence.

"How did you get so far on Captain Loopholes' car in half a day?" Glutz asked Sgt. Maury Zenderhockle innocently. Maury's hands rose in the air simultaneously, leaving the half-empty drain oil container to fend for itself in midair. It stayed there just an instant until gravity drew it unceremoniously to Zenderhockle's left great toe. The can tipped to the right, covering most of the front of is right shoe with drain oil and distributing more of it inside the shoe where it was eagerly greeted by his sock. So happy to receive the oil was the sock that it rolled in it lavishly, thoroughly displeasing Zenderhockle's foot, which sent a message to his brain telling him so. In the meantime, Zenderhockle pranced around in ever decreasing concentric circles, dragging the stinging toe as he went, pulling and pumping the leg behind him, until it looked as if the sergeant might fly up his own fundamental orifice, or so Glutz thought. *Well, I've done it again,* Glutz said to himself. *That makes twice in one day that I've startled the bejeezus out of someone. Lucky nothing more serious has happened.*

Zenderhockle came back with fire in his eye. He literally bit his tongue to keep from saying what he was thinking.

"How does your toe feel?" Glutz was asking him, with feigned concern, but not much empathy.

Maury bit his lip again. The tongue still hurt from the first time. "Oh, it feels just fine, Lieutenant. I'm so glad you happened along," he said sarcastically. With that he walked right by the lieutenant and limped over to a small bench upon which he rested wearily, leaning heavily with the palm of his hand on his right knee for balance as he sat down.

Glutz was anxious to get back to the subject of the car. "How did you get so far so fast?" he said once again, pointing to Captain Loopholes' car. Zenderhockle breathed a heavy sigh as he pressed against his left knee this time, as if to relieve the hurt from his thumping toe.

Then he answered. "I came down here myself yesterday. My gout was bothering me, and I got into a hell of a hassle with the wife. So, I decided the best thing to do to get it off my mind was something with my hands."

Glutz's medical curiosity changed his priorities for the moment.

"Gout!" he shouted. "You've got gout at your age? I thought only czars and wealthy royalty got gout!"

"Yea, well there aren't any of them guys around here, so it had to go somewhere."

"Gee, I sure am sorry to hear that," Glutz sympathized, shaking his head.

"Yeah, well I haven't noticed it for the past few minutes," the sergeant said, rubbing his left shoe. "Maybe the drain oil has helped lubricate the joints and ease the inflammation." He went on, "I came down here yesterday and started working on the Captain's car. Some of the other guys called me at home, and when they heard that I was down here, they came on down too. Once we got going, it seemed like it'd be fun to see how good a job we could do and how fast we could get finished. 'Course we had trouble getting started 'cuz it was Sunday and none of us is authorized to use any of the tools and equipment on the Sabbath, but we managed to get around that." Zenderhockle smiled wryly at his humor and Glutz didn't know whether he was 'stroking' him or not.

"When do you think they'll have her done, Sergeant?" Lieutenant Glutz asked him.

"Take a look," he told Glutz, waving his hand across what would have been the expanse of the car. "Looks to me like they've got just a few hours' work left. Unless some emergency comes up, it should be finished by the end of the day for sure."

Glutz wanted a better indication. "What would you consider an emergency?" he wanted to know. "Like if the General's car came in to be worked on or something?"

"No," responded Sergeant Zenderhockle, "I was thinking more of a world war or something like that. You know, if we got bombed and got put out of commission or something like that." He grinned and so did Glutz. It was obvious that the two had an attraction for each other.

"You know what," Glutz suggested, "if I could drive Luci's car over to pick him up tonight, he'd drop his drawers. I'm s'posed to pick him up with my car, you know."

Sergeant Zenderhockle didn't know and he really didn't care, but he did like the idea of pleasing Captain Loopholes. He didn't like the threat of being threatened by such a threatening personage as the base legal officer. He'd like to erase any reason for that from the docket.

"I don't see any reason why we couldn't accomplish that, Lieutenant. Just come on back about oh-h-h," he looked at his watch. It had Steamboat Willie on it, in air force uniform. "I'd say about 1630 hours."

Glutz thought hurriedly, "Ten from sixteen, that's . . . 6:30! I can't come back here at 6:30, I've got to pick Captain Loopholes up at 4:45 at the latest."

"I said 1630 hours, Lieutenant," Zenderhockle reminded Glutz, "not 6:30 P.M." And, then to make sure he had made his point, added, "1630 is 4:30 P.M."

Glutz's memory jogged him. "Oh yeah, the little hand is on the four and the big hand is on the . . . that's 16 minus 12, not 10."

Zenderhockle interrupted the lieutenant's deep thought processes. "Sorry, sir," he said. "I can't make out what you're saying."

"It's OK, sergeant," Glutz was telling him. "I've got it all squared away now. I'll be back here at 1430 . . . I mean 4:30, promptly, for the car."

Glutz strode off whistling a tune no one had ever heard before, while Sergeant Zenderhockle, temporarily forgetting the oil can, gout, and drain oil, just shook his head.

CHAPTER XVI

Lieutenant Glutz sat admiringly in Captain Loopholes' car outside the base legal office, waiting for the captain to emerge. Presently he did. With an obvious look of irritation, he checked his watch, and then looked up and down the street. Several times he looked past his car with Glutz in it, not for a moment even thinking that it might be his. Glutz was enjoying his candid view, and so decided to prolong it. Finally, Loopholes looked at his watch for the Nth time and then stomped down the stairs. Glutz honked the horn. Captain looked at the car for a brief instant and then looked away again. He had caught Glutz's image through the windshield, but it took a moment to register in his mind. When it finally did, his head shot around once again, as if propelled by a bullet. He looked at Glutz, then he looked at the car; then he looked at Glutz, and then the car. Then he took a step closer and repeated the process. He approached it gingerly, the car, that is, as if it might devour him or disappear, or both. Finally, he leaned over and touched it ever so lightly on the fender.

"My God!" he exclaimed, "It's real." And then he ran to the window and stuck his head inside, peering around. "Whose car is this? Is . . . Is it? . . ." He was almost afraid to ask, but then with courage he blurted it out. "Is it mine?"

Glutz nodded.

"It is mine!" he shouted, waving his hat in the air and then twirling it on the end of his finger as he spun around. A middle-aged lady passed, pushing an infant in a baby buggy. He kissed them both. Then he ran around to the driver's side and opened the door. Glutz slid over in the seat. Loopholes noted that the inside was much the same. There was still a dab of "blood" on the seat from the mannequin on "safety day," but otherwise the

213

interior was in good shape. Luci leaned into the front seat and looked at the odometer. It read 69,437.6 miles. He got back out of the car and slammed the door. Gingerly he circled the vehicle, stepping back every once in awhile, as an artist would, to survey the work.

"My God, man," he finally shrieked, "those guys at the motor pool did themselves one hell of a job!" And, then he paused. "But, how the hell did they get it done so fast?" Glutz told him the story.

Captain Loopholes was completely taken by surprise. "Wow!" he said over and over again. "Wow!" He got into the passenger's side of the car and propped his head against the seat.

"Don't you want to drive your 'new' car?" Glutz asked him.

"No," Luci said dreamily, "you just drive it, and I'll lie here soaking up the pleasure of it all." Glutz drove away from the curb. In a moment, Loopholes sat bolt upright. "You know what?" he said. "I was just thinking. Anyone can have a shiny new car. That doesn't take any talent or pride. But, to have an old timer like this one, that looks like new . . . well, that's something else again. That's something else," he repeated. Reaching out the open window, he patted the door as if it were alive and ran his fingers over the paint job. "Wow!" he said again, and slumped back into his 'dreaming' position, once again.

A long interval of silence ensued until finally Glutz turned to Luci. The captain's eyes were closed, but a smile lingered on his face. Glutz knew he was awake.

"Where do you want to go tonight in your new chariot?"

"How about to the moon!" came the response from his passenger.

"Seriously, Luci, do you want to go right to the club, back to the BOQ, or what?" Glutz wanted to know.

"Oh, let's go back to the BOQ," Luci suggested. "We can have a drink or two and then go over to the club for dinner." Glutz headed in the direction of the BOQ and another long pause followed.

Back at the BOQ, Glutz went his way and Captain Loopholes to his own "suite," as the base billeting loosely referred to it. Luci, stationed on the second floor, always was ready first and came by to get Glutz.

"Make us a scotch," Glutz told him. "I'll be out of the shower and ready in a minute." Luci did as was suggested. Putting Glutz's drink on top of his dresser, he sat down in a chair with his own.

"So what's new in your world?" he asked Glutz.

Glutz was toweling himself off after a shower. "Oh, not much of any . . ." and then he remembered. "Oh my gosh!" he said sort of to himself. In all the excitement about Captain Loopholes' car, he had forgotten that he was about to leave the military. This was too good to wait until later to tell, so Lt. Jerry Glutz, clad in skin-tight uniform, marched unceremoniously into his 'living room', reached for his scotch and soda, turned abruptly toward his good friend, and with one elbow leaning on top of his bureau, announced with a sway of his head.

"You'll never guess what happened to me today, Luci. You'll never guess in a millennium." Loopholes just stared at the naked lieutenant. "Come on, Luci, guess." Glutz challenged, not noticing the captain's stare. Loopholes still said nothing, but continued to gawk. "Come on Luci, what do you think?" Glutz pleaded.

"I think," Loopholes finally responded, his gaze still fixed on Glutz's "family jewels" or "tool kit" as it is alternately called in unprofessional circles, "I think," he repeated, "that if you'd part your hair in the middle, your nose wouldn't look so long!" Then he jumped up and burst out laughing. Glutz looked down at himself to see what Loopholes was talking about, and then walked back toward the shower room.

"The hell with you," he told Loopholes over his shoulder. "I've got some interesting news to tell you and you sit there making fun of my proboscis. OK for you, buddy. You can just go to your grave without knowing."

"I'm sorry, Jerry, I really am, but I just couldn't get over how human he looked, hanging down and leaning on those two duffle bags." And, with that, Loopholes burst into laughter once more.

Glutz was in the other room, now, getting into a shirt, tie, and sport coat for dinner at the officers' club.

"I'm getting out of the air force," he hollered in to Captain Loopholes. "Then see who you can find to make fun of," he added sarcastically.

"Oh, I'm sorry, Jerry. I didn't mean to say anything to offend you. If I had known that it would cause you to leave the air force . . . well, I thought that at least you would stay until your tour of duty was up."

"That's just it, wise guy," Glutz said, his head peering around the corner, "my tour *is* up. I got the word today that I can leave in ninety days . . . sooner, if I can get a waiver."

Lucifer Loopholes was suddenly silent. He knew that what Glutz was saying was not in jest. He knew, too, that he'd miss the lieutenant. They had grown close over the past months. For a moment nostalgia crept over him, and then, he realized that relationships are never permanent. He knew that was especially true of a career officer in the air force.

"Sit down and tell me about it," he said, quaffing a long draw on his scotch and soda.

Glutz filled him in on the details to date with Luci simply nodding as he went along.

"I don't know whether to envy you or not," he said when Glutz had finished. "A change is always exciting, but the uncertainty of it is sorta' scary, too."

Glutz nodded. He'd thought about that earlier in the day and he was thinking about it again, now.

"But," Captain Loopholes added, setting down his empty glass and rising to his feet, "the only thing we know for sure is that we never know for sure."

Glutz turned around with pursed lips and a forced frown. "Say," he said mockingly, "that sounds pretty profound."

Loopholes slapped him on the back, saying, "Let's go have some supper." The two walked through the door with arms of friendship wrapped around one another.

Next morning, Glutz went to see Sergeant Kermer first thing.

"I've been waiting for your call," he said. "I've got some bad news for you, Lieutenant," the sergeant warned. Glutz's heart sank. *Nuts,* he thought, *the whole thing has fallen through.* Now that he had made up his mind and conditioned himself to his decision, it was a bitter pill to swallow.

The sergeant went on, "We can't let you waive the ninety days, because we can't get your car shipped back for you that fast."

Glutz's heart jumped to his throat in excitement. "Get my car sent back?" he was saying half to himself and half to Sergeant Kermer. "Sergeant, have you ever seen my car? "

"No, but it doesn't make any difference. Even if it's a compact, we couldn't ship it back any faster."

"Sergeant, what I'm trying to say is that you can have my car, if it means getting back ninety days sooner," Glutz tried to explain.

Sergeant Kermer was busy shuffling papers. He didn't look up. "That's out of the question, Lieutenant. I couldn't possibly take the responsibility for your car. You'd have to dispose of it yourself . . . ," Kermer told him. "You'll have to sell the car first,"

Kermer hollered after Glutz. "Until then, I can't do a thing. My hands are tied." Glutz just shook his head and kept going.

Downtown, Glutz got an offer of $275 for his car. He had paid $600 and put in a new transmission. He turned down the offer and drove around the block. He thought of the ninety days. He went back to the used car jockey and said yes to the $275. Kermer began processing the papers.

In two weeks and two days, Glutz was on his way home. As he flew out over the ocean, he reflected back on a lot of people and a lot of memories. Captain Loopholes, Sergeant Zenderhockle, Captain McBooboo, Major Ralston, to name a few. He enjoyed the experience, but didn't think he'd miss any of them. He leaned back and went to sleep. Hours later, the screech of the big aircraft wheels touching down woke him. He sat up in his seat as the big air force plane drew to a stop at the terminal. The lights went on and Glutz felt a one-fingered drum beat on his shoulder. Irritatedly, for he had just awakened from a sound sleep, he turned around.

"Let's git it on," said the smiling face behind him, rolling a toothpick from one side of his broad mouth to the other.

"Paulie Plopp!" shouted Glutz excitedly. "What the hell are you doing here?"

"Probably the same thing as you," he answered, "I'm gittin' out."

"This calls for a drink," Glutz said, rising from his seat and clouting his head on the overhead rack. He didn't even notice.

"Or maybe two or three," Paulie continued.

Jerry Glutz had just been thinking about missing people a few hours before. He couldn't say he had missed Paulie in the months since he'd seen him, but it was good to be together again. It sure was!

The two soon-to-be erstwhile lieutenants hurried to the transient BOQ (that means temporary, for those who haven't been in the air force). They parted for a shower and shave after being assigned rooms with a promise to pick one or the other up, whoever was finished first. Minutes later, Paulie knocked at Glutz's door.

"Let's git it on," he hollered through the wood. Glutz smiled and let him in.

"Shit!" exclaimed Glutz, rummaging through his suitcase.

"What's the matter?" asked Plopp, sprawled out on Glutz's bed.

"I can't find my belt. Guess I must have left it an Elfendwarf." Paulie had an extra and the two were off to the club.

As they started to walk into the bar room, Glutz said to Paulie without turning, "I wonder if . . ." and there he was. There at the bar was one Warren Huenerloth. Glutz was happy to see him, too. "Hi!" Glutz greeted him. Huenerloth made no overt gesture of recognition. "Don't you remember me?" Glutz asked.

"Yeah," Warren said coldly, "I remember you. I don't remember your name, though."

Glutz introduced himself again and he introduced Lieutenant Plopp, too. Huenerloth seemed unimpressed. Then Glutz remembered the feigned indifference in Huenerloth he had to break through the last time. He also remembered that Huenerloth was scheduled to get off active duty a few months after Glutz went to Elfendwarf.

"What happened?" Glutz asked with sincere curiosity. Huenerloth knew immediately what Jerry was talking about.

"I decided to stay in a little longer," he answered curtly and then quickly changed the subject. Glutz didn't press the issue. Huenerloth seemed relieved.

"C'mon," said Glutz, taking his short-term-friend-of-two-years-ago by the arm and pulling him toward a table. "I'll buy us all a drink." Paulie followed the procession and sat down with the two of them.

"Now fill me in and tell me how you've been, Warren," Glutz demanded, after both were on their third scotch; Paulie drank beer. Huenerloth's memory seemed to be returning, and he began to become much more amicable. The coolness he had exhibited at the bar was washed away with the scotch.

"Oh, I've been just fine, Jerry," he offered enthusiastically, as if the two had been together just the day before. "I guess you've figured that I decided to stay in for awhile. Just a few days after you left, I got a letter from my brother telling me that there were no jobs outside the service. He said it's 'really cold out there.' So I decided to stay in for a few more years. I've probably got about one more to go and then I'll be getting out."

IT ALL COUNTS TOWARD TWENTY, Glutz thought to himself.

There was a brief pause in the conversation, no discernible noise except the TV in the background and Paulie's periodic slurp as he lapped up his beer.

"Say, Jerry," Warren started, as he came increasingly back to life with the help of periodic swigs of his scotch. "Do you remember that attractive girl you dated just before you went north?"

Glutz mused for just a moment. "Yes-s-s," he said. "I surely do. Helen Clarin. What in the world ever happened to her?"

"Well, I dated her for awhile," Warren said, looking sheepishly away from Glutz's surprised face.

"What happened?" Glutz wondered, when he recovered from trying not to show his shock.

"Not a lot," responded Warren, crystal ball gazing into the ice cubes in his scotch glass. Then he looked between Glutz and Paulie. "We just seemed to drift apart."

I'll bet you never drifted very close together, Glutz thought, but was too kind to utter. Glutz's mind went immediately to Helen. *I wonder what she's doing right now,* he thought, but Huenerloth's continuance interrupted him.

"She hasn't been here at the officer's club for months. The last time I took her out was before Christmas."

Glutz didn't comment. His thoughts were of Helen. Strangely, the time in Alaska had never happened. It was as if they had all been there at the club, just last night. He, Warren, Gayle, even Paulie Plopp sipping his beer with his arms wrapped around it.

Warren went on talking, but Glutz wasn't listening. Across town, as if through mental telepathy, Helen stared into the mirror. It was seven years since she'd been married. Kirby was in the third grade with no father. Why did it have to happen to her? Helen did a mental scan of the faces of the men whom she'd met since then. She had known none of them intimately. Nothing more than a casual kiss. She opened one button at the top of her blouse to expose the tops of her breasts. If not as firm as they once were, they were still full. Her face was still very attractive and, as she turned from side to side, her hair had as beautiful a sheen and dazzle as ever. She looked slowly over the course of her whole and entire body.

"Why me?" she asked herself again, feeling sorry for Helen. Her mind went back to faces of men. Many of them she had known only very casually, at the club or at the office. Most names she didn't remember. Her mind's eye focused on Jerry Glutz and passed to Warren Huenerloth, whom she sped past quickly, and there was Jerry's face again. She had really been out with him only once. She didn't remember his name. But, she liked what little she did remember. For a moment, she imagined his blond hair against the black sheen of her own. *What was his name,* she kept asking herself, pressing hard her memory for its return. The ringing phone brought her quickly from her trance.

"Jerry Glutz," she heard herself saying and then, "that's it!"

"That's what?" Glutz asked quizzically from the other end of the line.

"That's your name!" she told him exuberantly.

"Seems to me I had that piece of information before I called," he said in a rather weak and wondering tone of voice.

"Oh, Jerry, forgive me. It's just that it's so nice to hear your voice."

Glutz was completely taken aback. Before he could really put his thoughts together he blurted out, "Are you kidding me, Helen? It's nice for me to hear your voice, too, but I haven't seen you for a year." *And then it was only a couple of times,* he added to himself.

Helen bubbled over the phone. "Oh forgive me, Jerry. I must sound like an idiot," she apologized.

"A very attractive idiot," Glutz offered, regaining his composure.

"Oh Jerry, don't be silly," she said, opening another button of her blouse and looking at herself in the mirror. "You can't even see me."

Glutz was naturally encouraged by her receptiveness.

"Oh, yes, I can. I can see you as clearly as the last time I really saw you," he said. "I can still see you dodging as I tried to press your lovely lips the night before I left for Alaska." Helen wondered why she had done that, but passed it from her mind and ignored the jibe.

"How long you going to be in town, Jer?" she asked.

"Day after tomorrow," he told her. "Then, I'm home and out." Helen was sorry to hear that the time was so short, but wouldn't let it affect her mood or conversation.

"Come over," she invited him.

"When?" Glutz asked, shaking his head in wonderment. There was just too much happening here for him to handle.

"Right now," she retorted.

"Boy, that's some switch," he said for himself, but it came out loud. "I called you up to ask you out for dinner tomorrow evening, hoping you'd remember me, and you ask me over tonight."

"Oh, I accept for tomorrow night, too," she said with a giggle.

"I'll be right over," Glutz concluded, and hung up the phone before the bubble might burst. He went back to the table where

Paulie sat by himself. Huenerloth had left. Glutz didn't think or care enough to ask where he had gone.

"Mind if I leave you here?" he asked his friend Paulie. Paulie looked up through his drooping St. Bernard eyes.

"Where you going?" he wondered.

"The girl we talked about, Helen—she invited me over to her house."

"Go ahead," Paulie assured him with a wave of his hand which could have served well in chasing a fly. Glutz was more than half way to the door when he turned his head and shot over his shoulder, "I'll get you a date for tomorrow night."

What the hell's he talking about? Paulie thought to himself. *He's going over to a girl's house to get me a date for tomorrow night. I don't get it. Doesn't make sense.* Then he paused for minute. *Maybe she had a friend.* That figured, so he went back to his beer, finished it and returned to the BOQ.

Glutz stopped at the officers' club package store on his way out. He put his hand first on a cool six pack of beer, but then removed it and went over to the shelf where the scotch bottles stood proudly at attention. Glutz felt great. He coddled a bottle of "5-Star" to the check out. Then he remembered he didn't remember where Helen's house was. He didn't want to call her again, so he looked her address up in the phone book and then got directions from the check-out clerk. Hopping into a cab, he was there in no time. As he jumped from the cab and stuck his head in the front window to get his change, he thought of the movies he'd seen where the hero did the same thing. The difference was that, in the movies, the hero had a dozen roses in his hand, not a bottle of scotch. Glutz wished he had the roses, too, but he was glad for the bottle of scotch.

At the door, Helen stood beaming. She raised her head toward him and as he kissed her lips, she slid her fingers and palms under the lapels of his coat. This was unreal! He had met this girl once, over a year ago; had seen her twice; hadn't thought of her more than a few times since, and now . . . now he felt as though he had been in love with her forever.

Helen stepped back as Glutz slid his open hands under her arms, down her sides and rested them on her hips.

"It's good to see you, Jerry," she said, and she meant it.

"You look lovely," he said, and she did. Then Helen assumed a more sprightly mood. She grabbed him by the hand and pulled him towards the living room.

"C'mon in," she urged. She looked for a moment like a schoolgirl who was about to skip across the playground with her boyfriend behind her, holding on and trying to figure out what was coming next.

"Let me take your coat," she said, extending both hands, palms upward.

"First, you can have my hat," Glutz responded, putting his service cap on her head. It covered most of her face. Then he put his coat and jacket into her arms and she marched, dutifully, to the closet, where she hung them both up. "Mind if I take off my tie?" Glutz queried academically, as he already had it half removed and his collar button open.

"No, go . . ." she started, turning, and then seeing that it was already done, she smiled.

Glutz went to the kitchen, got some ice, and fixed them each a drink. He remembered where things were, once he saw the room, and also how Helen took her scotch. Returning to the living room, he handed her glass to her and then sat down against the corner of the couch. She took a small sip, set her glass on the lamp table near him and sat herself down beside him. Glutz was leaning back against the couch. Helen turned toward him. Her knee and part of her lower thigh exposed itself as she turned. Glutz saw it and felt a sensation just below and to either side of his abdomen. Meaning to show savoir faire, he regained his composure instantly and pretended not to notice.

Helen put his free hand in hers and wondered, "Now tell me all about what you've done since last we were together."

Since last we were together, Glutz thought to himself. *How wonderful that sounds.* He relaxed now and felt giddy as he remembered some of the things that had happened in Alaska and recounted them, one by one. Together, they laughed and laughed. He told her about Captain McBooboo and the rest at Elfendwarf. She liked the stories about Squadron Leader Albert X. Merry of the British Royal Air Force. But, most of all, she laughed at Captain Loopholes' car and the safety week display. Her laughter caused Glutz to double up, and they continued until tears were running from both their eyes (all four eyes, that is. Each had the standard number of two.).

Presently Glutz went to the kitchen to fetch himself another scotch. Helen lifted her glass, which had hardly been touched, and asked for him to refresh it. When he came back, things were quiet again.

They looked at each other for a moment and then she said, "Jerry, I've missed you. I didn't know that it was you for whom I've been lonely. I just knew I've been lonely and then tonight . . ." she paused for a moment, trying to decide whether to tell him the whole story. She decided not to, and so continued ". . . tonight, just when you called, I was thinking of you."

"Have you thought of me often?" he wondered.

"No, not often. But tonight, when you called, I was thinking of you."

Glutz felt better. He hadn't thought of her often, either, and for a moment he had felt guilty, thinking she might have.

"It's just as though we're supposed to be together," she said, moving closer to him. Glutz agreed that it was.

Glutz set his glass down on the table behind him without turning around. Gently, he lifted the glass from her hand and set it next to his. Then he turned out the light and drew her to him. She purred softly as he pressed her lips to his. Jerry Glutz had never been so happy, so excited, so much in love in his whole life.

"Not here," she said, as she drew her lips away. Taking his hand in hers, she led him up the stairs. "Sh-h-h," she warned, "Kirby's sound asleep."

Glutz woke up to rays of bright light shining into his eyes from between the shade and window frame. He rolled over to find that Helen was gone. He heard the water from the shower stop, and moments later Helen walked into the room in a handsome black housecoat with red lace trim.

"Good morning," she said cheerily, brushing her long black satin hair to the back of her head and shaking it off her shoulders.

"Good morning, beautiful," Glutz answered with a smile. He wanted to hide his glum feeling. Glutz didn't like himself this morning. What had seemed such a wonderful feeling of euphoria the night before, that he was sure it would last forever and ever, was gone. In its place was a dull feeling in his head and the taste of "zacklies" in his mouth (that is, his mouth tasted and probably smelled "zackly" like the other end of him). This was not characteristic of Jerry Glutz and he didn't like it. He wanted to get out, but he didn't know how.

"Sorry, I don't have time to make you breakfast," Helen was saying. "Will you be here when I get home from work this evening?"

Glutz was stunned into silence, and it seemed an eternity before he was finally able to choke out, "Oh . . . oh, no, Helen. I've got lots of things to do today at the separation center. I don't know how long that will take."

"Then, what time will you be by for me this evening?" she asked.

Glutz remembered! He had invited Helen to dinner before all of this got started, last evening. "Oh, yeah," he said haltingly, before finally regaining his composure. Then, with much firmer resolve, "What time would be best for you, Helen?" She noticed a difference in his voice from the evening before.

"Is there anything wrong?" she asked with some hesitation in her voice.

"No, there's nothing wrong, Helen," Glutz answered quickly. "Why do you ask?"

"No matter," she said, shrugging it off. "I'll be home around 5:00 P.M., so any time after 5:30 will be fine."

"OK," he said. "I don't know what time I'll finish, but I'm sure I can be here by 7:00."

Helen knew it was over, but she said no more. Coolly, she dressed for work. Glutz watched without emotion. When she had finished, she came over to the bed, kissed her right forefinger, and touched it to the middle of his forehead.

"Bye, dear," she said, and, with a wave, was out the door. Folding his hands behind his head, Glutz lay back hard against the pillow. He stared at the ceiling for awhile and then tried to fall back to sleep. There was no one in the house. Apparently, Kirby had gone to school earlier. After awhile, Glutz decided it was no use. He got up, dressed, and left the house. Not until he had locked the door did he realize that he had no car and had not called a cab. Down on the corner, Glutz ran into a young lad who looked to be about 12 years old. He had school books under his arm.

"You live around here?" Jerry asked him. "Yeah," was the kid's response.

"Then do me a favor," Glutz directed him, flipping the young lad a dime, "call me a cab."

"You're a cab," the kid said, and then ran off down the street, clutching the coin in his hand.

Glutz was too numb to be furious. His thoughts channeled most easily to Helen and the night before. But, he didn't want to think about that and so he repressed it. Instead, he forced himself to think of a way to get back to the base. He really didn't remember for sure which direction it was. Finally, he worked that out and decided the best way would be to "ride his thumb" back to the base. He was just reflecting on how unkempt he must look, and that he probably wouldn't pick himself up, were he driving, when a teenager with a "raked rod" and "duals" pulled up.

"Man, you look like you've lost it," he told Glutz. "Maybe I can help you find it, dad." Glutz had only a vague idea what the fella' was talking about, but he was happy to have the chance to sit down. "Where you headed, daddy?" the "Rod Rider" queried as he dug away from the curb. "Man that's in the tunnel," said Rod Rider, "that's where I'm going too. You must be in the 'space race', too. This here's space for nomads, man. What are you, comin' or goin'?"

Glutz took a deep breath and tried to think of a reply. He was only half listening and, even then, only half understanding what he heard. "I'm being released from active duty," he answered, absentmindedly. It was a plain, simple, basic statement, but somehow it sounded like the Queen's English, in contrast to what he was hearing from his riding companion.

"That's cool, man," Rod Rider went on. "You're gonna put the ditch on uncle. We call that the blue flu flew, man. That's cool."

Glutz didn't respond. He'd needed another deep breath and the last one just about put him away. Rod had a set of underarms that smelled like the south end of a bull, going north. Fortunately, they had arrived at the main gate.

"I'll get off here," Glutz instructed the driver.

"No man, I'll take you to your stack, man. I ain't never been on no blue flu, before."

"Oh, that's not necessary," Glutz assured him. "Besides, I can't get you on the base in this car because it doesn't have a sticker." Rod was about to protest that he knew better, but Glutz was already out of the car. "Thanks a lot for the ride," he offered, and waved as he walked onto the base. Rod lifted his arm to wave back, and Glutz was very glad that he wasn't any closer.

Glutz got to the BOQ and there was Paulie Plopp, just coming out the door. He looked Glutz over from head to toe.

"You just getting home?" he asked. "That's the same suit you had on last night."

"So it is," said Glutz, looking down at himself, as if he expected to see something else. Then he changed the subject. "Where you headed?" he asked Paulie.

"Going to get some chow. Time to put on the feedbag."

"You coming back here after?" Glutz wondered. "Yeah. I'll be back," Paulie told him. "My stuff's still in the room."

"Good," Glutz responded. "Stop by for me and we can walk over to the center together."

"OK," Paulie agreed. He put his hands in his pockets, hopefully playing with his change, and walked off.

Glutz went in and flopped on his bed. He dropped immediately off to sleep, for what seemed like minutes before he was abruptly awakened by a harsh knock on the door.

"Hey, Glutz," Paulie Plopp's voice demanded, "open up, it's PP."

"You do it on my floor and you'll have to clean it up yourself," Glutz mumbled inaudibly.

"Drop your cocks and grab your socks," Paulie sounded out louder. That's standard jargon of a barracks sergeant, used to announce the arrival of a new day to basic trainees. It didn't fit here, though, for, while Jerry Glutz did have more than one sock, he did not have, but one of the other items with which that rhymed. And, that one item was so small that even Glutz, himself, had trouble finding it from time to time; even if he didn't have his pants on backward. Two hundred twenty pounds of dynamite with a half-inch fuse, he affectionately referred to himself. As a matter of fact, on one occasion, early in his air force career, a fat WAC captain had told Glutz that his "barracks door" was open. When he finally figured out what she meant, he asked what she had seen, hoping for some response such as "One big soldier standing tall." Instead, she had assured him that she had seen only a small disabled veteran, leaning on two duffle bags.

Presently, Glutz regained consciousness and let Plopp plop in. "Give me a minute to shave and put on a clean uniform, Paul," Glutz asked of his visitor.

"No hurry," Paulie assured him. "We've got all day. No matter when we get there, it'll be a question of 'hurry up and wait'. They'll just tell us to 'pick a spot and mill around.'" Paulie knew that he was soon to be out of the air force and he was taking this opportunity to demonstrate all the quaint phraseology he had learned and would probably never be able to use again. But, he was right.

Over at the separation center, it was "hurry up and wait," and "pick a spot and mill around." Glutz didn't care. He lounged comfortably on his back just as he had done less than two years ago in the terminal at this same air force base, waiting to go to

Alaska. A cold chill ran down his spine as he remembered what had happened. That time he couldn't get out, because he had to drive his car down to the dock. This time he didn't have a car, having sold it in Alaska. *I wonder what could happen to me to screw things up this time?* he was thinking. Just then Lt. Paul Plopp's name was called.

"Hey, did you hear those sweet words," he said for Glutz's benefit, but directed them off into space as he rose to his feet and headed toward the counter. Forty-five minutes later he passed by Glutz again.

"Look at me," he challenged Glutz, moving around in his version of a fashion model. "I'm all done. Transportation and all. I'll be out of here by 3:00 tomorrow afternoon." (That's 1500 hours for those who aren't going to be in the air force much longer.)

"Good for you," registered Glutz. "I'll see you over at the slop chute for lunch, if I get out of here in time. Otherwise, meet me at my room at 5:00 and we'll go over to the club, together, if . . ." and then he remembered. He had a date with Helen, which he didn't want. He didn't want, really, to see Helen again. He was embarrassed about the previous evening, didn't have feelings for her, though she was a nice girl. All those things just added up to a confused feeling that he didn't want to see her again. He guessed it was really because, after last night, he could hardly appear casual with her. He thought she wanted more of a commitment and he was leaving tomorrow for good. What he had been thinking of the night before, who knows. Helen was beautiful, she was a nice girl, she was soft, and she was loving. He was elated at being back from his tour in Alaska and being on the verge of getting out of the service . . . and there was the scotch. Anyway, it was gone now. He thought of calling Helen and calling it off. He couldn't do that. He thought of just staying in his room; not showing up and not answering the phone, but he couldn't do that either. He'd go through with it, but it would be easier if Paulie were along, with or without a date.

Paulie broke the silence. "What's the matter with you, man?"

Glutz looked up at him blankly. "Oh, nothing. Why?"

"You looked like you were spaced out. I thought for a moment you were on a trip, and not by any known means of natural conveyance."

"No, I was just wondering if you'd like a date for tonight, and, if so, how we could arrange it," Glutz rationalized.

"Sure, let's git it on," Paulie agreed through his wide mouth.

"OK, Paulie, meet me at my room at 5:00. We'll have a drink and then go pick up Helen. She'll be able to line someone up for you."

"Line someone up," Paulie objected to the terminology. "I don't want somebody to shoot at, I want somebody to 'git it on' with."

"You'll be pleased with my selection process," Glutz assured him, with a mock haughty air.

Paulie knew that Glutz probably wouldn't know and certainly wouldn't see the girl before he did. No matter. How else better to spend an evening, the last in the active air force, than with a date.

He agreed, "Five o'clock, then," and was off.

That done, Glutz became uneasy about his name not being called. Just before noon, he ambled up to the counter.

"My name's Glutz," he started to say. "AO9 . . ."

"Sorry, sir," he was interrupted, "but your records haven't come through." Glutz frowned.

"How do you know they haven't come through?" he asked the airman incredulously, "I just stepped up here to the counter."

"Sorry, sir," the airman repeated. "It happens every day. People come up just before 1200 hours and it's always the same. They haven't been called and their records haven't come through. They'll probably be here tomorrow."

"Well, would you look anyway?" Glutz pleaded. "Maybe just this once they've been mislaid."

"Oh, they've been mislaid all right, but that's up at Elfendwarf. We don't make mistakes like that here. If they'd been mislaid here, I'd know about it and I'd have picked them up." Glutz was going to plead further, but after that last comment, he realized that there was no point in it. Then it dawned on him—this was the very same airman whom he'd had a run-in with about his car, on the way to Alaska. But this time the airman had one stripe on this sleeve instead of none.

"I see you've been promoted," Glutz noted with some sarcasm in his voice.

The airman third class looked proudly at his left sleeve and beamed. "Yes, sir. I sure was. Three times now. Just can't seem to make it past the weekend, though. Two beers, one fight, back in the 'pokey' and there goes my stripe. Actually, I'm getting pretty good at sewing them on."

Glutz smiled absentmindedly. "What do I do about getting out of here, now," he mumbled.

"Right over there," the airman pointed to the farthest door, in earnest. "That door will take you right to the officers' field ration mess where you can get lunch."

"I'm not talking about getting out of this building, dunce," Glutz slurred, dropping the last word to an inaudible volume. "I'm talking about getting out of the air force."

"Oh, you'll have to wait until your papers come to do that," the airman assured him. "Like I told you, they'll probably be here tomorrow. I'll call you when they come in."

"I won't hold my breath," Glutz muttered as he wandered, dejectedly, out the door. He was tired. He went back to the BOQ and went to bed.

It was 4:30 when Jerry Glutz woke up. He wasn't refreshed, but knew he would be after a long drink of scotch and a comfortable shower. He was right. Paulie was right on time at 5:00. Glutz and he walked over to the club and sat at the bar. Glutz felt better, but Paulie was on top of the world.

"Just think," he said, over and over again to his glass of beer, "I'm all finished."

Glutz looked over at him. "We've got more pressing concerns at the moment, Paulie. We've got to be over at Helen's house by 6:00, and we don't have any wheels" (that means no car for those who don't have one)."

"Oh yes we do," said Paulie. "I forgot to tell you. Just today I ran into a college running mate who's just going to where we've come from." Paulie didn't want to mention the word for fear he might have to go back. "He gave me his keys and said we can use his car for the night. He's going somewhere with someone else."

"That's super," Glutz agreed, "Let's go." He finished off his drink and stood up. The soon-to-be erstwhile Lt. Paulie Plopp followed him out the door.

"You know the way to this girl's house?" Paulie queried.

"Yeah, I think so," Glutz assured him. He did, and they arrived at Helen's house at about 5:55. Kirby answered the door.

"Hello there, young man. Is your mother home?" Kirby Callanan called and his mother came to the door. If she was surprised to see Paulie, she didn't show it. Instead, she showed herself bright and witty.

"Which one of you is Jerry Glutz?"

Before Glutz could say a word, Paulie put out his big "meat hook."

"I'm Paul Plopp," he said, shaking hands. "I feel like a real intruder, but Jerry said it was all right to come along."

"Yeah, I'm sorry, Helen. I should have called. But, I thought with knowing so many girls, you might be able to find Paul a date, so we could double."

"Well, I can if you want, Jerry, but it is quite late. Unless Paul really wants a date, why don't just the three of us go?" Glutz could feel gooseflesh. She'd said it all in just that one sentence. It wasn't going to be like last night. Glutz's reaction was ambivalent. He was glad there would be no need for explanation, but sad, in a way, that it was over . . . over, before it started. But then he got jealous. Was she going to make a "pitch" for Paulie, just to show Glutz up? His cheeks flushed. He was angered at the thought. No matter, she was behaving very professionally. He could be mature, too.

But, that wasn't it at all. Helen was a scintillating conversationalist to both of them. She danced as often with Paul as she did with Glutz. It was a strange evening for Glutz. He was relaxed and reflective. After tonight, he'd probably never see either of them again. He said a silent prayer for Helen's happiness. Now, perhaps more sober than last night, and at least more objective, he understood his thoughts for her. He didn't love her, although he probably could. But time was too short and it just wasn't in the cards.

When they walked to her door, he kissed her affectionately. And she kissed him back.

"I love you," she whispered. He held both her hands and withdrew a step.

"Thanks, Helen," he said. "Thanks for everything." They kissed again and then he turned and left. Helen watched them drive off and her eyes misted a little.

"What have I done?" she asked herself. "Why can't I be happy, too?"

CHAPTER XVII

Next morning, Glutz was back at the separation center once more. This time, they had his records. The airman spotted Glutz when he came in.

"Good morning, Lieutenant," the airman said cheerily. "Everything's ready for you." Glutz could hardly believe what he was hearing. The airman went on. "Your orders have been cut, pay voucher's all filled out, all you have to do is sign here . . . and here . . . and here . . . and here . . ." Glutz signed his name blindly. He didn't care. He'd done it before, but this was the last time. He was done! And it was only 10:30 in the morning. Not 1030 hours. He was beginning to think like a civilian again. He could still catch the train to Greyrock, and be there tomorrow.

Back at the BOQ, Glutz changed out of his uniform and into civilian clothes. Wouldn't you know it? He had no belt. He surely couldn't use the webbed air force belt. Once again, Paulie came to the rescue.

"Here ya' are, Jerry," Plopp said affably. "Send it to me when you get home." Jerry Glutz assured him that he would. That afternoon, as a last gesture of friendship, Paulie took Glutz to catch the train in his friend's car. Shaking hands to say good-bye, Glutz walked first to the ticket window and then took a window seat in his train car. He looked out the window to see Paulie drive away. Glutz was excited. He was also happy, relaxed, and tired. He took out his orders and read them. It was all over. He reflected on his time in Alaska. There were no bad memories. Every once in awhile he'd smile, remembering a particular incident. Finally, he thought of Helen. Maybe, he thought, at a different time, in a different place, it might have worked out. Then a depressing thought occurred to him. "What if she's pregnant?" That wasn't likely, he rationalized. Still, it was possible. He tried to shake his concern and, gradually, it ebbed and went away. Over the next few days, the thought of the possibility came back several times. But, each time he was convinced it was less likely. He sat back, closed his eyes, and went to sleep.

He would never see Helen Clarin again. But, there was something he would never know, and she was yet to find out . . . she *was* pregnant! The thought had occurred to her, too, but not until the day after the night before. Maybe she'd even thought of the possibility that night, but, if she had, she dispelled it. As the first month rolled by, she became more concerned.

It's just that I'm worrying too much, she rationalized. *That's what's throwing my cycle off.* Finally, she went to a doctor, one she hadn't seen before. The doctor told her it was too soon to be sure. When another month went by, she made plans to move. How would she explain it to Kirby? Helen went to the one friend in whom she could confide, Gayle Sterum. Gayle listened sympathetically.

"Why not leave Kirby with me. You can come back after the baby's born. Put it up for adoption, if you want, or bring the baby back. Tell Kirby what you want. He'll understand over the years." Tears welled up in Helen's eyes as she thought of leaving Kirby for six or seven months. But it was the only thing to do and she knew it.

The next week she moved to Lakeside City, California. She got a secretarial job working for a friend of Gayle's uncle. Her name became Mrs. Helen Clarin though she didn't wear a ring. When the time came, she drove herself to Mercy Hospital. She had been to the prenatal courses at the hospital and had preregistered for delivery. She also had learned to "read" contractions and, since she was alone, she made sure to get to the hospital in plenty of time.

In the labor room, the nurse told her that her doctor had been called and was on his way. She said an intern would be in to see her shortly. The intern arrived wearing a surgical mask. He explained to Helen, without really looking at her face, that he was wearing the surgical mask because of a cold. His voice was partially muffled by the mask, but it had an unmistakably familiar ring to it. The interning doctor was about to pick up the chart at the foot of Helen's bed to read her name, when his name was called over the loudspeaker.

"Dr. Callanan," the voice said, "please come to the desk." Helen's doctor was there and wanted to see him. He didn't know that the intern hadn't seen Helen yet. When Dr. Callanan told Helen's doctor he was just beginning to look at her chart, the two went to the labor room together. At first, the name Mrs. Clarin drew no response from the interning doctor. Then, when he stood back, observing Helen's doctor examining her, he recognized who she was. A lump formed in his throat.

Helen's doctor turned to the intern and said, "Please see to Mrs. Clarin. I have some other visits to make in the hospital. Call me when she's ready to deliver."

Dr. Callanan couldn't speak. He simply nodded. When Helen's doctor left, Dr. Callanan didn't know what to do. He stepped forward and listened to her heart; and then to the baby's heart. Then, as was so typical of his direct manner, he said, "You're going to have a fine baby, Helen." He stepped back a few feet and took off his mask.

"Darrell!!!" she shrieked, and then a contraction sent her pressing back onto the bed.

"Don't get excited, Helen." He assured her, "Yes, it's me." And, then he smiled, "But, don't worry, I'm really quite competent."

Helen had a baby girl. Dr. Darrell Callanan assisted Helen's doctor with the delivery. Later, he went to her room.

"What are you doing here?" she asked with a frown. "And, a doctor. Why, when we . . . you had only gone through . . ."

"Yes, I know, Helen," he helped. "When we were married, I had only a high school education. But, when the marriage didn't work out, I knew you were right. I needed to make something of myself, so I started out in college. First I started out to be a chemist, but I did so well in anatomy and physiology, that my advisor suggested medicine. I just finished my degree two months ago and am now interning here for two years."

Then he looked more serious. "Helen," he began. "Your name. Mrs. Helen Clarin. Are you . . . were you . . . married again?" Helen put the pillow against her face to wipe off the tears. Then, she looked back at him, resigned to tell the truth.

"No, Darrell," she said. "I'm not."

His face lit up like a Christmas tree. "That's great!" he said. "Just great!"

She looked at him quizzically. "What's so great about it? I just had a baby out of wedlock."

Darrell ignored her comment. "You know, Helen, I've thought about you so often. If it hadn't been for you, I'd never have made it this far. Sometimes, when I just couldn't study any more, I'd lie back on my bed and look at the ceiling in my room and dream about coming back to you. I figured you'd probably remarried, but I'd think about it anyway. It's what kept me going. After I'd finished this internship, I was going to come back to tell you all about it . . . and to see our baby. Married or not, I wanted you and our baby, too, to be proud of me."

"Oh Darrell," she said lovingly, wrapping his neck in her arms and pulling him towards her.

"Doctor Callanan. Dr. Callanan. To the desk, please," the PA was saying.

"I've got to go now," he told Helen, releasing himself from her grasp. "I'll be back later." And, then he stood up and smiled to himself. "Just think," he said self-assuredly, "two children and a wife in the same day. Not bad, if I do say so myself." He walked to the door.

"But, Darrell," Helen said half apologetically, "Ann isn't your daughter. She's . . ." Darrell looked back, from the door. "She is, if you want her to be," he said with a wink; and then walked out the door.

Helen was so happy she could burst. *He's the man I've always wanted,* she thought to herself. *And, he says I've done something for him. Well from now on I'm going to . . . I'm going to spend the rest of my life making him as happy as I am right now.* And she did.